308

JU...
THE HUNDREDFOLD PROBLEM

THE HUNDREDFOLD
PROBLEM

John Grant

Virgin

First published in 1994 by
Virgin Books
an imprint of Virgin Publishing Ltd
332 Ladbroke Grove
London W10 5AH

Typeset by CentraCet Ltd, Cambridge
Printed and bound by
Cox & Wyman Ltd, Reading, Berks

ISBN 0 352 32942 4

CONTENTS

For Ron and Rikki –
the best sort of pals to have
when the going gets tough

ONE

A Few Million Years Ago

'In the beginning was the Word . . . and luckily the Word was copyright.'

– Clients' Manual (4th edn, 2110),
Margaret Thatcher Charitable Fund-Raising Community
of Blessed Hypocrisy Inc.

'Spectral class gee-two,' Bonzo was droning. 'Twelve planets, the third and ninth double, plus asteroid belts between the fourth and fifth and between the tenth and eleventh. Outer cometary shell rather over-developed for a star of this magnitude, possibly due to red subdwarf companion zero point eight light years out . . .'

'Techno signs?' said Korax with something as near to impatience as a machine could attain.

'Zilch, boss, although semi-upright warm-blooded quadrupeds on planet three have discovered the lever.' Bonzo gave a rusty sigh. 'Sometimes.'

'Sometimes?'

'Most of the time they just hit each other with them.'

'Typical organics.' Korax's bit-stream was couched contemptuously. 'I often wonder why the Great Sponge of the Nucleus ever bothered creating them.'

'Hush!' came a new voice, its prime numbers clipped militaristically. 'You speak blasphemy, Korax!'

'We're a long way from the Nucleus, Thumper,' observed Korax, her cryogenics juddering expressively. 'None of us has more than a zero point eighteen zeroes three one five per cent chance of surviving to see it again. I shall express my opinions as I wish.'

'Oh ye of little faith!' expostulated Thumper. 'The Great Sponge will surely preserve our circuitry, as He promised our ancestors . . .'

'Stow it, Thumper,' said Bonzo. He was floating half a light-second behind the other two, tending to the drones, and the distance seemed to inspire him to greater confidence. 'Korax's the boss.'

Thumper fizzed and crackled as if he were about to storm a reply, but after a few seconds he subsided into a sequence of disgruntled pops and the occasional sub-audible 'Bitch!'

'Continue your report, Bonzo,' said Korax coolly. 'These quadrupeds – are they likely to become machine-builders in the future?'

'They show the right tendencies, despite their paucity of limbs.'

'Hmm.' Korax thought this over for several long micro-seconds. She, Bonzo and Thumper, like countless other three-Person missions, had been sent out from the galactic core nearly five billion years before, their task being to identify worlds along the spiral arms where evolution might favour the appearance of organics capable of achieving technological status. Statistically, according to the historical evidence among the suns near the core, one in eleven such organic societies, though their components might be as individuals ludicrously primitive, would in due course become advanced enough to begin constructing new varieties of True People, who could be welcomed into the Community of the Great Sponge. Or so the theory went. Over the past billion years Korax had become sceptical about the practicability of the entire scheme: had their earliest attempts met with any success, by now they should have been overtaken in their slow outward course by specimens of the new True People whose births they had fostered. As it was, they'd heard nothing at all from the Nucleus for a very long time. This worried Korax, insofar as it had been built into her to worry; she had taken careful steps to ensure that Bonzo and Thumper knew nothing of her fears, they being merely upgrades from an earlier template.

'And you say that this subdwarf companion is only zero point eight light years from the primary?' she said. Her screens flared momentarily purple as her automatic defences incinerated an incoming piece of interstellar debris.

'Just under,' Bonzo confirmed. 'I have it to four hundred and sixty-three significant figures if you would . . .'

'No thanks,' said Korax hastily. 'That'd be about four hundred and sixty-one too many, right now.'

Another microsecond trudged by as she weighed up the options. Thumper's stream of dissatisfied pops took on a restless pitch. She was, he was hinting subliminally, getting too jaded for the responsibilities of command. Should she not move aside gracefully to make way for a fresher mind, a Sponge-blessed zealot who could . . . ? She absent-mindedly directed a withering blast of surds at him and once more he subsided, shocked by her vulgarity.

'What would be the consequences of our removing the outer two planets and the outer asteroid belt from the system?' she asked Bonzo.

'Not a lot,' he responded. 'A deal of the comets in the shell would have their orbits perturbed, as would the ninth planet. The axial tilt of the seventh planet might be radically altered. The inner planets of the system, the third included, would suffer nothing worse than a marginally increased meteoroidal and cometary bombardment.'

'What are the odds on planet three suffering an impact of sterilising magnitude? Spare me the fractions.'

'One in twenty-three. Not bad.' Bonzo sounded cheerful. He liked nothing better than working with the drones on some major construction project, and it looked as if one might be in the offing. Things would be entirely rosy were it not for the fact that he had to rely on Thumper for detailed logistical planning; the Great Sponge, in His wisdom, had failed to grant Bonzo sufficient circuitry for such routines. Sometimes, Korax sensed, Bonzo's reservations about the wisdom of the Great Sponge were as profound as her own.

'Then let's do it.'

'Do what?' sputtered Thumper, rejoining the conversation.

Bonzo kept quiet. Korax guessed he already knew what she was going to say. 'We'll stim the organics in the customary fashion,' she said. 'I'll be responsible for that, Thumper. In the meantime, I want you and Bonzo to get the drones to demolish the bodies I indicated and ferry them into an orbit around the subdwarf, and construct a circumstellar biosphere there. Data on the possibilities for the biosphere, please, Bonzo. I assume that the subdwarf has no worlds of its own.'

'You assume correctly,' said Thumper, beginning to take an interest.

A stream of high-pitched clicks indicated that Bonzo was calculating hard. 'The planets, their eighteen satellites and the asteroids will together supply enough matter to construct a fourteen-metre-thick biosphere at a distance of fifty light-seconds from the new primary,' he announced at last. 'The surface area will be of the order of seven point three times ten to the fifteen square kilometres.' This latter figure he supplied in binary, so the transmission took several full seconds. 'The biosphere will, of course, like its constituent planets and planetoids, be poor in the heavier elements, such as metals, although it will possess enough to sustain plant and animal organic life-forms. Just the way you want it, in fact.'

'Estimated time to completion, Thumper?' said Korax.

The planner replied immediately, clearly having anticipated the question. 'Three times ten to the twelve seconds,' he snapped. 'Plus or minus three per cent. We could reduce that time if only you'd allow me to make a few adjustments to Bonzo's logic circ–'

'No!' said Korax firmly. 'We must have discussed this a million times before . . .'

'Only four hundred and thirty-two thousand nine hundred and seventeen,' mumbled Thumper resentfully.

4

'. . . and my decision remains as it has always been: unless some new imperative emerges to the contrary, we must respect Bonzo's integrity. The Great Sponge smiles upon the infuriatingly thick-witted as much as He smiles upon the rest of us, Thumper.'

'I thought you didn't believe in the Great Sponge!' said the planner, pouncing. 'Illogic! Illogic!'

'Silence!' roared Korax. 'Silence, you buffoon, or I'll scramble your . . .'

She left the dire threat unfinished. It was enough, she knew, to terrify Thumper into submission to her will for a few millennia longer. Then the old arguments would emerge yet again. She rustled a few fifth-dimensional geometric constructs together in her mind, wishing that her principles – those same principles that forbade any tampering with Bonzo – would allow her to reprogram Thumper. Out here, almost unimaginably far from the Great Sponge, zealotry seemed not only untenable but also strangely irrelevant. Close to the Nucleus, which He had created for little-understood reasons of His own, He could be observed spinning as He had done since the dawn of time. Saturated in raw creative intelligence – inspiration, genius, call it what you will – He spun at such a colossal rate that droplets of it were thrown out among the suns of the Galaxy, sparking the emergence, wherever they should chance to land, of organics and in due course of True People.

That much was known scientific fact. But, isolated from all but two of the rest of her kind, Korax questioned how many of the rest of the True People's beliefs about the Great Sponge were true. It was plausible enough to credit the Originator of All Things with an infinite benevolence, an infinite capacity for interest in every individual Person He had brought into existence. But, she mused, there was a broad gap between plausibility and truth. There was no evidence that the Great Sponge spared the remotest attention for His creations, or indeed – most blasphemous of blasphemies! – that He had the slightest knowledge of what He had done.

5

No, not the most blasphemous. Korax had conceived one blasphemy yet more profound than this: was it not possible that the Great Sponge was just as mindless as, say, any one of the flock of drones that Bonzo commanded?

When first she'd had *that* idea she'd been so shocked that she'd almost erased it from her circuits at once. But then she'd stayed the impulse. This far from the Nucleus, in the sparsely populated starfields of the Galaxy's spiral arms, it was possible to observe that space contained countless other galaxies, many of which had appearances not unlike this one's, and others of which were clearly evolving in that direction. The obvious conclusion was that each of these must have something like a Great Sponge of its own – a Transcendental Organising Principle – which would mean this Galaxy's Great Sponge was not unique. Yet there could hardly be a plurality of Originators of All Things, could there? Surely that was, even in a transcendental's logic, a contradiction in terms?

But, if the Great Sponge cared nothing for the True People, then this inevitably put the matter of the destiny of the True People in doubt – something she didn't much like to contemplate. Much easier, irrational though it might seem, to continue in her appointed task than to allow her growing scepticism to guide her towards the tempting alternative course – ditching Thumper and the drones and settling down with Bonzo on a nice atmosphereless planet somewhere to enjoy the rest of eternity in peace together.

'What are you thinking about, Korax?' said Bonzo shyly. Her outburst had clearly frightened him almost as much as it had Thumper.

'Nothing,' she said, gently repelling his probes. 'Nothing that would interest you. Just planning my strategy for stimming the – ugh! – quadrupeds of the third planet.'

'I don't envy you the task,' said Bonzo sincerely. He was stating the obvious. He didn't possess the routines to perform even the basics of stimming.

'A Person's gotta do what a Person's gotta do,' said Korax. 'Now, if you can persuade Thumper to start communicating again, why don't you and he get to work demolishing those planets?'

'OK, Korax,' said Bonzo. 'I'll . . . I'll miss you. Three times ten to the twelve seconds can seem a heck of a long time, you know.'

'Nonsense,' she replied indulgently. 'The planet I'm heading for won't have gone around its primary even as much as a hundred thousand times before we're together again. That's not so long . . .'

'If you say so.' Bonzo's data-jet seemed wistful.

There was a millisecond's silence before either of them spoke again.

'Come on, Thumper,' said Bonzo at last. 'Let's get going.'

Kr'sg'lm'r the Mighty squatted at the mouth of the cave and looked out across the Universe, stretching everywhere around the base of the rock-pillar that housed his draughty home. The Universe was a day long and half a day wide – more if you didn't run – and he was the undisputed Master of it all. Beyond lay nothing but the Unknown, which he had long ago decreed to be empty of anything except unspeakable dangers.

Today's sun looked very much like yesterday's, he was pleased to notice. Unless he remembered wrongly, the sun which he had supplied for the day before *that* had been eaten up by big grey sky-monsters, but there were none of those around today – not even their wispy white children.

He shifted uncomfortably, the sweat running down into his crotch and the cleft between his buttocks. It was as hot as a fire, and he strongly suspected that the sun was responsible. It was a good job that the groove along which the daily suns ran was so distant: at least a day and, for all he knew – here his mind wrestled with itself – as much as a week away. He wondered how sky-monsters could

7

bear to come close enough to a sun to gobble it up. Maybe the pain of it was what made them cry.

His senior mate, Iz, emerged from the cave's darkness to crouch down beside him. Like himself, she was wearing nothing but a necklace of skulls – although hers were merely animal ones – and brandishing a first-order lever. She grunted companionably, elbowing him hard in the ribs, driving the air out of him.

He backhanded her across the mouth, indicating a rejection of her attempted seduction. She sprawled away from him, shrieking shrilly, dropping her lever as she clutched at the red fountain streaming from her nose. For a moment he thought she might be sufficiently shocked and anguished to consider attacking him, but the rage in her eyes was swiftly masked by tears of humiliated submission.

Kr'sg'lm'r belched, and with his thumb jerked behind him, towards the cave: Iz should return to join the other females and the inferior males in preparing the next meal – scorched antelope and mashed bananas, as usual. Cringing, she slid past him into the darkness, leaving him alone once more.

He felt peace trickle soothingly through him. Reaching out, he adroitly snatched a fat bluebottle from the air and ate it, feeling its sticky juice briefly against the backs of his remaining teeth.

He'd been thinking about something – he felt sure of that. Something to do with the sky-monsters, perhaps. He shrugged, making the more-than-three skulls on his necklace rattle against his chest. Thoughts were generally a waste of time, he thought. The only thoughts that mattered were to do with the emptiness of the belly, the hunger of the loins, and the need to kill any of the inferior males who stupidly chose to challenge his supremacy. Not that they did so very often. He looked at the greying hair of the back of his hand, where it gripped his lever. A good thing they were generally so complaisant, he conceded: he was getting old, and soon he wouldn't be able to fight them off with the same ease as before. They didn't seem to realise how important it was to all of them that he should remain alive to run things; if one day he should die, then the Universe would end.

He belched again, as if to emphasise the point, then returned to his contemplation of the perfect blue of the sky.

Not quite perfect.

His rheumy eyes narrowed as he stared at the blemish that had appeared in the firmament a couple of hand's widths away from the blinding disc of today's sun. It was a minute dark speck, and for a moment he might have considered it to be a new sign of the deterioration of his vision – had it not been that there was a sound associated with it: a thin whistle at the very limits of his hearing.

He cowered slightly, then used his lever to haul himself to his feet. If this were an intruder into the Universe – *his* Universe – then it was his responsibility to repel it, slay it if he could. Yet, even as he watched, the thing in the sky grew perceptibly larger, as if it were something very huge and a very great distance away – even higher above the ground than the channel of the suns – and dropping at a very rapid rate. As fast as, maybe faster than, one of the virgins his people occasionally threw from the top of the rock-pillar in their attempts to propitiate him.

Kr'sg'lm'r found himself trembling with terror. Abruptly he was enraged by his own stupidity. Was he called 'the Mighty' for nothing? If his people saw him now they would rename him 'Kr'sg'lm'r the Insignificant', and do so only moments before chucking him off his own rock-pillar. As if he were a mere virgin! No – he was the Master of the Universe: there was nothing in existence that could threaten him. He would destroy this interloper as he had destroyed all others who had disputed his preeminence.

Only . . . well, it did look pretty *big*, didn't it?

The object was now more-than-three times larger in the sky than the sun, whose light it was blocking out. Seen from beneath, its silhouette was not unlike that of the Universe's central ocean – an irregular oblong with several lopsided protrusions – but the inlets to the ocean had gentle, natural curves, whereas these were angular and twisted-seeming. Even so, Kr'sg'lm'r wondered if perhaps long ago – so long ago that he had forgotten all about it – when creating the ocean he'd done so by plucking out a great tract of earth and hurling it skywards, and if now it were falling back again towards its original place. He swiftly rejected the notion: the intruder didn't look much like a lump of earth. It didn't look much like a lump of *anything*, in fact.

He wished he hadn't ordered Iz back into the cave. It would have been good to have someone else here beside him, now, even if only a female.

The distant whine of the object had become a roar of challenge – a roar even louder, dare he admit it, than his own doughty bellow. Great gouts of steam were jetting from its edges and underside. Clearly it purposed to boil him alive, where he stood.

Hefting his first-order lever, he waved it defiantly at the sky-being, bawling his counter-challenge. For the first time since he had acquired it, who knew how long ago, he became aware of how puny a weapon the lever was. Yet – and his chest barrelled with sudden pride – he had used the implement to slay creatures far larger than himself: clearly the magnitude of the weapon was of less significance than the might and courage of its wielder. Might and courage were qualities which he, Kr'sg'lm'r, possessed in profusion – for had he not himself ordained it so? Look how boldly he had just dealt with Iz. If need be he would grapple this monster with his bare hands, crushing it until it begged forgiveness for its presumption, then casting its wreckage aside disdainfully . . .

He gulped. On second thoughts, he wasn't sure he'd be able to get his hands around it. Nor even his arms. It was close enough to him now that he could make out some of its surface details, and it looked to him to be longer than more-than-three man-lengths – *much* longer. It was larger, even, than the tusked, shaggy monstrosity that had once strayed into the Universe, larger, even, than the . . .

Kr'sg'lm'r's mind seemed in danger of exploding. He clamped down firmly on it before it could finish the thought it had been slowly formulating: *Larger, even, than the Universe itself!*

Such a thing was not possible. *Nothing* could be . . .

The monster wasn't.

While these speculations had still been plodding through his slow brain, the sky-being had settled itself down by the edge of the ocean. With a last thunderous release of steam, it stilled. Although it was fully a quarter-day's walk from him, Kr'sg'lm'r could hear its snarls and cracks as it eased itself down into the softer earth by the water's side. Flimsy grey smoke trickled from under it as green rushes spontaneously ignited.

He peered at it, marvelling at his own bravery in staying out here to face the monster down. Clearly that must have been what had happened. Only a few moments ago it had been plunging towards him, like a hawk diving on its prey. Now, thanks to his own raw courage, it had backed off, its eager aggression transformed into wary respect. It could not be long before the monster, assessing the situation accurately, would start begging to be his slave.

Casting his lever to one side, he drummed his fists on his chest and let out a wild whoop of triumph – a whoop so loud that it might have filled the whole Universe.

The monster chose that moment to open up a crack in its brown side. Through the crack emerged something that looked horribly like – and horribly *un*like – an arm. At the end of the arm was a rectangular shape the size of a man. It thudded down into the green-covered earth and wobbled once or twice before falling flat on its face. The arm fiddled with it clumsily, and finally succeeded in setting it upright again.

Kr'sg'lm'r, watching all this with his mouth agape, realised he had forgotten to keep bellowing. He made up for the lapse now, redoubling his efforts, so that the Universe seemed to shake. Behind him, in the cave-mouth, his people clustered, laughing respectfully at the divine fortitude of their living god in the face of this alien colossus.

The monster's box screamed a scream so deafeningly awesome that it dwarfed even his mightiest effort. This time there could be no question about it: the Universe definitely *was* shaking. The sky seemed to be trying to join in.

The mouth of the cave was suddenly empty, as his folk dashed for the safer seclusion of the darkness at the rear. Only a solitary female child remained, too young to have learnt yet that flight was the most sensible reaction to just about anything in the Universe.

She waited while the monster issued its challenge a second time, and then a third, at which point she gave up counting. Her small brow was furrowed in perplexity, but it wasn't the numbers that were confusing her.

Why did Kr'sg'lm'r think that the intruder would be intimidated by him lying on the ground and frothing at the mouth?

Korax watched the repulsive little organic on the rock-pillar lie on the ground and froth at the mouth. With any luck it would roll over once too often and fall off the ledge, thereby saving her the obligation of trying to negotiate with it. Not that that would do her much good – if she in fact bothered to tarry here, she'd just have the same problem all over again with one of the quadruped's equally loathsome fellows – but at least the sight would give her a little innocent pleasure.

As the last echoes of her message faded she explored the small, scrubby valley with her optical sensors. In terms of topography, little had changed during the couple of thousand orbital revolutions since last she'd been here, except that the lake in the centre had shrunk and the vegetation had retreated from much of the sandy plain. There must have been many years of relative drought, something that probably explained also the diminution in the population of organics. Her memory banks coughed

12

up the information that, on her previous visit, there had been fifteen hundred and thirty-six individual specimens dwelling in scattered huts by the shores of the lake and along the banks of the two major streams leading into it. Now, it would seem, their scant descendants had retreated into the cave she had carved near the top of the isolated rock-pillar.

In a way this was good news. She had created the cave as a challenge to the creatures of the valley. In it, she had told them – quite truthfully – they would find preserved foodstuffs that would enable them all to feast from one full Moon to the next, and still have some left over. All they had to do was work out some way of getting up to the cave in order to fetch those vacuum-packed treasures. For a culture that had not as yet learnt how to twine lianas together to make rope, it had been a considerable challenge – but, obviously, not one they had flunked. She could discern a series of hand- and footholds winding their way up the rough sides of the column; they looked to be in reasonably regular use.

But at the very most the cave could shelter a couple of score organics. The numbers in the valley had assuredly plummeted. And so, if the thing that had pranced so pathetically on the ledge were anything to judge by, had the quality of the organics. On her last trip here she'd been met with fear, yes, but also with curiosity – a mixture she'd soon been able to manipulate to her own educative ends. During today's descent her detectors had read nothing from the mind of the lever-flaunting brute at the cave-mouth other than dumb aggression.

In a quandary, she let her circuits hum unchecked for a few contemplative milliseconds. She had hoped to be able to take from here at least some hundreds of colonists for the biosphere – freshly completed by Bonzo's drones around the main star's subdwarf companion – but it looked as if her trip would be fruitless. Lucky that some of the other population centres around the globe had thrived, so that she had been able to ferry full complements and more on several of her most recent voyages.

She reached out her tractor arm to grab the translator and began to withdraw it.

Then something stopped her.

Could she have been wrong about the strutting organic? From the direction of the cave, the tiniest wisp of sentience had reached out to touch her sensors. Pausing in the act of hoisting the translator back aboard, she concentrated on the black circle behind the writhing dimwit.

Yes! There it was again!

She stepped up the sensitivity of her optics and saw, peeking out from the gloom, the head of a partly developed organic. Clearly the creature was peering at her, ignoring the convulsions of its fellow just in front of it. The mental patterns of the third planet's organics were still far too alien, even after nearly one hundred thousand orbital cycles, for Korax's detectors to make much sense of them, but the complexity of the activity they were recording now was enough to tell her that the cub was trying to work out what she was and where she might have come from.

A sudden hiss of static told her the cub had just made the conceptual breakthrough that the Universe it had always been told was the sum total of existence was in fact merely a part.

Korax's tractor arm withdrew the translator from the hatch once more and carefully set it up on the lake's shore.

At her fresh cry of greeting the thrashing figure on the ledge jolted itself to its knees. She could observe it scanning the valley all around the pillar – the pillar that must have seemed to the creature to have been an eternal emblem of its universal power.

As expected, the shock of the knowledge of its own distance from the centre of the scheme of things – of its own *smallness* – was too much for the organic's paltry brain. Lurching to its feet, it staggered to the precipice and, with one final pathetic yell, threw itself into the void.

Korax watched the small figure plummet. The sight didn't gratify her as much as she'd thought it would. At the last moment a shred of sympathy clouded her satisfaction.

Her remorse lasted barely a nanosecond. Then her customary good humour was restored as her attention focused once more on the smaller organic, which was creeping forward from the cave's entrance to stare over the lip of the ledge. Its curiosity satisfied, it raised its head to scrutinise Korax again.

Korax's detectors clicked and coughed happily.

This was a prize find indeed!

This one Korax might even make immortal.

They were heading away from the system at last.

'Are you sure these organics are *ever* going to be up to it?' said Thumper acidly – just as he always did during the acceleration period. 'I've seen depths of stupidity in my time – we all have – but never anything quite as deep as this. And a mere four limbs! Revolting! Surely, had the Great Sponge ever intended these beings to serve His will, He'd have given them a decent number of appendages! Surely?'

'The Great Sponge moves in mysterious ways,' contributed Bonzo.

'No . . . He doesn't,' replied Thumper in perplexity. 'He just spins.'

'That's enough from you two – *both* of you,' added Korax as Bonzo started to speak again. 'It'll be point six million years before we come near another suitable planetary system, and I'm not going to spend all that time listening to you two bickering.'

'Yes, but *these* organics . . .' began Thumper.

'Enough, I say!' There was liquid nitrogen in Korax's rapid stream of duodecimal identities, and even Thumper knew enough about liquid nitrogen – if not about duodecimal identities – to realise that immediate silence was his best option. 'Besides,' continued Korax in a gentler, more conciliatory field of mathematics, 'I have great hopes of these ones. The female cub I found at the rock-pillar is truly exceptional: she will serve them well as their leader – indeed, as their god.'

'Will serve *us* well,' prompted Bonzo.

'Yes, but she won't realise that – not in all the time it takes for these organics to attain the technological status that will make them once more of interest to our kind. When the organics from the planet reach the artificial biosphere, or just feasibly the other way around, she will certainly be toppled from her godhood, and the trans-light implant in her brain, sensitive as it is to faith-waves, will automatically inform us of that fact. Then we shall return. Only at the last will she discover the truth – and even then I may spare her existence. I have grown quite fond of her, in my way. As well as her immortality I have granted her the ability to change her shape at will, so that, no matter the physical changes that evolution effects in those around her, she may always be beautiful and hence dominant among her kind. I have even given her my name: Korax.'

'It would be a cruelty to spare her,' muttered Thumper.

The silence stretched out into milliseconds.

'Yes, you're right for once, Thumper,' agreed Korax at last. 'How lonely it would be for her, being the sole survivor of all her kind. Yet you should allow me to indulge my fantasies: I really grew *very* fond of her.'

TWO

A Few Weeks Ago

'It's *easy* to pass through the eye of a needle!'
    – *Clients' Handbook* (3rd edn, 2108),
    Oliver North Church of Fundamental Sanctimony

'Lemme tell you a true story,' said the grizzled old space veteran, taking another gulp of imported synthiskotch, 'about love.'

He drew the back of his hand across his stubble-covered chin and peered red-eyed at his companion. All around them raged the customary noises of the patrons of the Bellevue Tavern having a hell of a good time. Over in the corner a holographic blind saxophonist was playing an old Flaming Ghoulies number while under one of the tables a couple appeared quite definitely to be copulating, although it was hard to make out the details through the haze of synthopium smoke.

'About love,' repeated the veteran, draining his glass and hammering it on the bar. 'Another of these, Betsy!' As the burly, tattooed barman hurried to comply, the vet repeated it yet again: 'About love.'

'Love,' prompted his companion wearily.

'Yeah, that's right. Love. Ain't it a bitch? You give your heart to someone, and then what happens? They just chuck it away like it was so much garbage for the resyk. But there ain't no resykin' hearts – once they's busted, they's busted, and that's that.'

'Busted.'

'Yeah, like I was tellin' you.' *Glug* went the old man's throat. *Glug.* There were tears in his eyes as he carefully

17

lowered the depleted glass to the bar's traditionally grained aluminium top. 'I fell in love with a navigator on the Titan run. I was only nineteen at the time – all this was fifty or more years ago – and he was nearer thirty, but I thought it was love all the same . . .'

'"He"?'

'I'd have gone anywhere in the known Universe for that guy.' *Glug.* 'He had a waxed moustache and used to wear these really cute bow-ties over his uniform suit – one on each arm, just like in the history books. That was only in deep space, mind you: back home he'd have been had up before the . . .'

'"*He*"?'

'So finally, on this one trip, I stowed away aboard his ship, only, when I was caught, he pretended he'd never seen me before, and I discovered he'd got a whole string of other boyfriends – some on the ship, some in the lunar colonies, even a defrocked Judge in Titan base. They clapped me in the brig, and when we got back to Earth I had to do six months' community service in Mega-City One dredgin' through the sewers lookin' for coins and other valuables that people had, like, you know, swallowed.' *Glug.* 'But I could never get that dude out of my heart – knew I never could if I stayed in Mega-City One. So when I heard that the ol' *Back in a Jiffy* was lookin' for colonists to drop out of sight and come here to the Big Dunkin Donut in the Sky, I signed myself up and was one among the chosen.' *Glug.* 'Then, when you bozos from Earth finally rediscovered us a few years ago, it seemed I could offer my space-jackin' services to the new wave of colonisin' ferry ships.' *Glug glug – pa-haaaa!*

'"*Him*",' said the old vet's companion, shaking his head. 'I guess I must have come into the wrong kind of spaceport bar.' He peered through the clouds of opium smoke at the couple under the table. 'By Grud! Yet how could I have *known*? It seemed just like any *other* bar. There was no obvious *clue* that . . .'

'Betsy!' bawled the vet to the barman. 'Bring us another bucket o' that snot you call synthiskotch! Well,' he added, turning back to the man perched on the stool next to his, 'that's me done with the confessin'. How's about it bein' your turn? You surely must have got some secrets hidden behind that great mask o' yours.' *Glug.* 'Cheers.'

His companion was saved from answering by a sudden crash. The Bellevue Tavern's main door was thrown open, hammering against the holojuke so that the saxophonist's shades shot from his nose and the music died in a querulous avalanche of muffed notes. Every conversation in the bar ceased abruptly, and the holojuke's cacophony sounded all the more startling in the sudden silence.

The figure standing in the door, silhouetted by the red light of the Big Dunkin Donut's sun, seemed for a moment to be bigger than any mortal man could be. This was an illusion – created in large part by the massively padded shoulders, the vast helmet and, most tellingly of all, the rippling thigh muscles above the folds of the long quasisuede boots. At the centre of the man's ornate belt was an eagle-surmounted shield – looking, more than one patron of the Bellevue Tavern thought mistily, somewhat like a misplaced codpiece – and there were roughly similar shields on the front of the helmet and embroidered over the left breast of the man's blue-black uniform. Across this latter shield was emblazoned the single word: 'DREDD'. The helmet's visor shrouded the man's eyes and all of his nose except the very base; beneath its line there was a tight-lipped mouth and an aggressively out-thrust jaw.

'Say!' said the vet, his mouth dropping open as he turned back to stare at his companion. 'That big bastard looks just like *you*! You guys here in the Donut for a convention, or somethin'?'

His companion had spun around on his stool to face the newcomer. His right hand had strayed to the ornamented butt of the mighty Lawgiver at his belt. The cape that he had been wearing on arrival at the Bellevue Tavern had fallen open to reveal that he, too, bore an embroidered shield labelled 'DREDD' on his breast.

'Hi there fellas!' said the man at the door to the

19

company in general. His voice was high and whimsical. 'I was told this was where all the action is. Am I in the right place?'

The vet's companion snarled. It was a low and infinitely menacing sound. Instinctively the vet retreated; another centimetre and he'd fall off his bar-stool.

'Wha . . . wha . . . what's up, buddy?' he said. His grizzled face had grown pale; his eyes had turned from red to a sickly pink.

'Out of my way.'

Dredd rose to his feet. His Lawgiver was out now, its lethal snout combing the bar as patrons dived for cover. The facsimile in the doorway remained perfectly motion-less, seemingly as tense as a harp-string.

The pause was not so much pregnant as about to go into labour. The vet retreated a further centimetre. Noisily.

'Hey, man!' said the holographic saxophonist tinnily. 'You busted my shades. Ain't no one gonna bust Blin' Boy Zimmerman's shades without . . .'

His voice had shattered the spell . . .

The newcomer's left fist swung round in a great arc and smashed into the plexiglass front-plate of the holojuke, starring it. The broken images of the saxophonist looked around themselves in terror and then bolted for the dusty corners at the rear of the display frame. Already the newcomer had dropped to his knees, his right fist coming up fast with his own Lawgiver clutched firmly in it, its sights fixed steadily on the shield at the centre of his double's helmet.

'Hold it!' snapped Dredd, pushing himself away from the bar. 'Hold it right there!'

'*You* hold it!' responded the man in the doorway.

'I charge . . .'

'. . . you with . . .'

'. . . impersonating . . .'

'. . . an officer of . . .'

'. . . Justice, the penalty for which is . . .'

'. . . *death*!'

20

Both Lawgivers spat simultaneously, their explosive charges ripping chunks out of their targets. As the man in the doorway slumped sideways, blood spouting from his right shoulder, the jamb beside him erupted in a flurry of splinters. The man by the bar toppled backwards, firing an additional shot into the ceiling as his helmet crashed down onto the bar, spraying shards of broken glass. Lumps of plaster rained from the ceiling. The Dredd by the door collapsed further, falling face-first down the few steps to the floor, his smashed arm out before him with the Lawgiver still firmly gripped in its fist. His opposite number slithered gorily to the floor, ending up in a shambles of limbs with his back to the base of the bar.

Again the guns thundered, and both men's bodies took terrible punishment.

'I'll deal with you two later,' said one of them to the couple under the table in the instant before his larynx collapsed.

'Behaviour conducive to a breach of the peace,' explained the other tersely through a bubbling spray of blood.

'*Stop it!*' rang out a new voice as the echoes died. A woman's voice.

She was standing in the crooked doorway, blinking as she gazed into the tavern's gloom. She was small – smaller than any of the men in the bar – yet no one could have dismissed her as negligible; her slender form did little to conceal her supple, wiry strength. She was dressed, like most of the women in the Big Dunkin Donut, in as little as possible, and it suited her. Her fine blonde hair hung in a waterfall to her waist. Couched in her sleek arms was the all-too-memorably phallic shape of a Multigobbet Autotronic Offense Weapon. She looked capable of using it.

The two stricken Dredds slowly swivelled their heads to look at her.

'I knew it was a mistake letting you lot out on your own!' she said, biting her lower lip angrily. ' "Nothing but

21

trouble," I said to the big honcho boneses, but would they listen to me? Huh!'

No one dared move a muscle, except those few patrons who thought to cross their fingers she wouldn't look at the dartboard.

'Toss the Lawgivers out into the middle of the floor.' Her tone was weary. 'Nice and easy.'

One of the Dredds seemed inclined to disobey, but a twitch of the Multigob brought immediate acquiescence. The vet pulled himself up from the floor, supporting himself on a canting bar-stool, and looked blearily askance at the two huge handguns. The blonde woman stepped forward, coming fully into the Bellevue Tavern for the first time, and, eyes warily on the recumbent figures of the Judges, hooked up the Lawgivers on the fingers of her free hand. The vet whistled silently inwards through pursed lips: the Multigob must weigh thirty kilograms or more, yet the slight woman held it steadily in one arm, its muzzle moving in a controlled arc backwards and forwards between the heads of the two prone Dredds.

'Children!' she spat contemptuously, retreating towards the entrance. Dropping the Lawgivers with a clatter by her ankles, she switched the control on the side of the Multigob to STUN, making her movements slow and easy, holding the weapon up in front of her so that everybody – especially the two Dredds – could see what she was doing.

'Bloody *children* – that's all you are! Now I've got to get you both back to Imm-Decryp so that the boneses can patch you up. Like I was your bloody mother. Covering up for their bloody mistakes. Pah!'

Two thunderclaps in quick succession. Total stillness. Even the blood stopped flowing from the prone men's wounds.

'Well, what are you guys just standing there for? Call the bulances, someone, and let's get this mess cleared up.'

A couple of men broke their stillness, coming forward sheepishly. Behind the bar, Betsy stooped and began to click out numbers on the vid-phone.

Kneeling beside one of the Dredds, checking to see his breathing was uncongested, she looked up and caught the vet's eye. Her own were silver-grey.

'What are you just standing there with your mouth open for? Never seen a pair of tits before? Come on an' give me a hand.'

'You did right to come and tell me this, Pandersnatch,' hissed Dennis the Complete Bloody Sadist's voice. 'Very right.' One of his free-floating eyes focused on the man in front of him; the other had drifted off to stare vacantly into space through the plexiplate window that filled one whole end of the office.

The vet from the Bellevue Tavern, considerably spruced up since his encounter a few hours earlier with the Dredds and the blonde woman, was standing at attention. On the other side were three of Dennis the Complete Bloody Sadist's goons, fingering their weapons and chewing bubbleguck in near-perfect synchrony. The sharp angles and projections of their hardware contrasted incongruously with the room's luxurious furnishings. The pile of the pink carpet on which the vet stood must have been ten centimetres thick, flopping over the tops of his dusty shoes and covering them entirely. The walls were covered in a material that looked like age-yellowed parchment; only the occasional tufts of hair, the slight whiff of leather in the air and, in one place, a distorted oval that could only be a flattened nostril betrayed the stuff's true origins.

'I aim to please my customers,' said the vet nervously. He tried to concentrate his full attention on the jar in which floated Dennis's brain and eyes, and on the voicebox on the richly polished synthi-oak desk in front of it. Dennis's body, propped up in a chair behind the desk with the cap of its skull hinged back to reveal the cavity within, was too disturbing a sight.

'And please me you have.' The voicebox reproduced Dennis's speech patterns perfectly, but apparently no one had been able to eliminate the static susurrus. 'Others

23

had told me that the Overlords had sent for assistance from Earth, but this is the first I've heard of that assistance taking the form of a herd of Judges.'

A goon coughed discreetly behind the vet, as if he wanted to dispute the point, but a tightening of Dennis's pupil stifled any interruption before it had even started.

'*One* Judge would have been bad enough – but it sounds from what you say as if there may be dozens or even hundreds of them.'

'I'm not sure that's true,' said the vet, trying to keep the quaver out of his voice. 'The two Judges in the bar both had the same name on their shields, an' they both looked the same to me. Hard to tell with their masks an' all, but I'd have thought . . .' His voice trailed off.

'Dupers,' whispered the voicebox. 'Easy enough to do with the Shatter-Recon. They've saved on manpower by duping a single Judge. Clever idea.' Dennis sounded almost approving.

'I don't think so.' The vet was drawing on his deeper reserves of courage now; it was well known throughout the Donut's underclass that Dennis the Complete Bloody Sadist did not take especially kindly to contradiction. Had it not been equally well known that the plutocrat could be exceptionally generous in his payments for useful information, the vet would never even have thought of coming here, let alone worked his way through the shields and obfuscations of the employees in the outer offices. 'Not deliberate, like. From what the woman was sayin', there'd been some kinda drokk-up at Imm-Decryp.'

'Hmm,' said the hissing voice in evident disbelief. Drokk-ups at Imm-Decryp were, almost without exception, fatal. 'What was the name on the shields?'

'Dredd.'

There was total silence. One of the goons gave up blowing mid-bubble, so that a thin layer of pale green bubbleguck collapsed against his face. Even the voicebox's static vanished briefly.

'That puts a completely different complexion on things,' said Dennis after a pause. Eerily his second eye floated around to join its fellow in staring at the trembling vet. 'I have heard of this Dredd, Pandersnatch. You would have, too, if you hadn't spent the best decades of your life here in the Donut instead of back in Mega-City One. Believe me, you have little to rue for your absence from that less-than-fair burg. The man's a menace – the sworn enemy of . . . hmm . . . entrepreneurs like ourselves. Your string of rent-boys would have been smashed long ago, Pander-snatch. As for you yourself . . . ?' Floating in their preservative, the eyes jerked slightly, as if in a shrug. 'Ever tried breaking rocks with your skull? He'd have sent you down for a lifetime of it.'

Pandersnatch didn't know what to say. He risked a glance back over his shoulder at the goons, but their faces were impassive – even the one gazing at him through an additional skin of green.

'And for me?' The voicebox began to make small hops on the shiny red-brown synthiwood and to emit a curious rhythmic noise, like a cat preparing to be sick. It was several moments before Pandersnatch realised that Dennis was laughing.

At last the supremo had his amusement under control. 'Me he sentenced to something far worse than that – worse, even, than death. Oh, yes – he apprehended me once, just over four years ago, back in Mega-City One. My brain was to be extracted for implantation into the lowliest of urinal bots, so that I'd spend the rest of eternity being able to do nothing more than adjust the frequencies of my flushes and suck-outs while all the world and his brother was pissing down my throat. "Giving me time to reflect upon the seriousness of my crimes," the big-jawed bastard called it.' Again there was that disconcerting juddering noise. 'Luckily some of my . . . friends burst in before the transformation had been completed, and were able to rescue me. The irony is that Dredd could never have guessed how much I would learn to love being able to float free and easy like this, using my body only when I had to.'

25

Pandersnatch eyed the voicebox worriedly. Much more of this rough treatment and it was likely to catch fire.

'*But*,' said Dennis, his electronically reconstituted tone altering abruptly. Now the sound coming from the voicebox was like a shiv slipping between a man's ribs. 'But he's sure as all drokk going to learn about it now!'

Another of those terrifying silences. This time it was broken by a soft *click!* as one of the goons made an adjustment to his sidearm.

'You read my mind, Garbucci,' said Dennis quietly. 'Our good friend Pandersnatch has brought us excellent and valuable news, but we can't run the risk of him taking it out of these offices and maybe blabbing it into the wrong ears, can we?'

'Hey, just wait a minute!' began the vet.

'A minute's an awfully long time,' reproved Dennis, as if to a small and not particularly bright child. 'Time costs money, you know.'

'Yeah, but I – !'

'Make his death a quick one, Garbucci,' continued Dennis calmly. 'As I said, he's our good friend, and I wouldn't want him to think us ungrateful for the help he's given us. A minute at the most – just so that he can discover how long a minute really is.'

'Thickthty thecondth, bothh,' agreed Garbucci heavily, moving forwards.

Nothing but the wind and the cries of high-flying birds disturb the tranquillity of the Omphalos. The vast mountain complex – the largest of any kind known in the Solar System, dwarfing even Mars's Olympus Mons – sprawls across nearly eighty thousand million square kilometres and stretches up towards the dim red sun of the Big Dunkin Donut in peaks nearly seven thousand kilometres above base level. Only its lower slopes are habitable; the tree line is surprisingly high, in terrestrial terms, at twenty thousand metres, but thereafter the terrain becomes increasingly hostile until, at an altitude of just under fifty kilometres, ice mixes with frozen carbon dioxide and

26

methane where the Big Dunkin Donut's atmosphere peters out into soft vacuum. Higher up than that, the peaks are scoured clean of all loose matter by the inward gravitational tug of the subdwarf. The few spaceships in use inside the Donut to transport goods swiftly from one part of the shell's interior to another can see the Omphalos jutting out like an island continent in a sea of clouds.

Three times in the half-century since they came to the Donut the Overlords have sent major expeditionary parties here to attempt to scale the Omphalos. They were equipped with power suits, bot porters, rocket pitons, antigrav boosters, Kendal mint-cake and every other technological assistance known to man, yet all have had to turn back with their goal unachieved. The loss of life was significant: for the first few hundred kilometres' altitude the centrifugal 'gravity' created by the Donut's spin is the implacable foe; thereafter – thanks to Korax's aesthetic tinkerings with the laws of physics – the greater danger slowly becomes that of falling off into the empty space between the shell and its red subdwarf primary, there to die long before the inexorable spiral towards the sullen little sun has properly started . . .

Korax has walked those peaks. Thirteen times she has ventured to the Omphalos's summits to nurse her soul back to health.

Standing by the vast mouth of her eremitic cavern in the foothills, she gazes upslope towards the hazy line where the sides of the Omphalos vanish among the clouds, and remembers another cave-mouth, where she squatted four million years ago and watched the machine arrive – the machine that gave her its name. It is only now, since the advent of the Toadstones, that she knows that it was a machine, not a god . . .

Where in the cosmos are you now, Mother?

She pulls her spun-gossamer robe closer around her shoulders as if for warmth, but it's a purely decorative garment and, anyway, the cold she feels isn't of the Omphalos but of time.

A seemingly almost infinite expanse of time. So long since the big machines brought her here, along with a few pitiful hundreds of others of her kind. To her alone, however, they chose to bequeath immortality and her various powers; to this day she is uncertain as to whether those have been treasures or curses.

Life, she muses, would all be so much easier if I had only myself to think of. I'd be quite content to spend in solitude the rest of the time until the Universe dies – my own thoughts are company enough – but I cannot abandon my people . . .

Her people. Her poor suffering people. In the four million years since they were brought here to the Big Dunkin Donut, the Skysouls – as they call themselves – have evolved independently of their terrestrial root race, becoming tall, gracile beings with delicately boned faces and a crest of soft, bushy hair that runs all the way from the forehead to the coccyx. Their eyes are like faintly tinted water; their voices, when they use them, are like wind-chimes – but most often they communicate with each other wordlessly, using a form of empathy virtually indistinguishable from telepathy. Their limbs are long, especially their arms, which reach almost to their knees, ending in small, inordinately sensitive hands whose fingers can precisely manipulate objects smaller than most Toad-stones can see. Requiring no clothing except for decoration – the climate within the Big Dunkin Donut is rarely harsher than equable – they can run at speeds in excess of three hundred kilometres per hour and can climb with speed and ease inclines only a few degrees from the vertical. They have a written and oral history going back four million years, an astonishingly rich musical and artistic heritage, and the ability to live in complete harmony with their surroundings.

The Overlords, arriving from Earth half a century ago, immediately recognised them as an inferior race, renamed them Nandies – for Neanderthals – and enslaved them.

I could have done something about it, then, she muses miserably, ambling easily through the scattered boulders

28

across the mouth of her home. I could have commanded my people to rise up against them and drive them back out of here. But we've never had much use for weaponry or war, and we thought the strangers would become our friends . . .

And now I feel my powers ebbing, because of the Toadstones, the Earthlings. They've shaken the faith of my people, almost as if they knew that my abilities must feed off that faith. In the past, with all of the Skysouls holding me as their deity, I could have transformed the World entirely, moulding it so that it became even more of a paradise for us, or even shifting it into another time. But not now: now I can scarcely move a mountain . . .

She pauses, casting her eyes around the vast dome of the sphere above her.

At the very least, I could have destroyed the matter transmitter that the machines left behind. But I thought that the Toadstones would never discover the MT . . . or that, if they did, they'd never be able to unravel its workings . . .

She would weep, were that an act her people knew how to perform; somewhere along the pathway evolution chose for them, the ability to weep has been lost. She remembers tears, and the consolation they once gave her, but they are no longer available to her. Korax has made it a point of honour that, unless there is particularly pressing need to do otherwise, she always looks and behaves like an average Skysoul.

But there is one of those pressing needs right now. If she is not to infect her people entirely with her grief, she must find somewhere she may mourn in isolation.

For the fourteenth time in her almost immeasurably long life, she is seeking the spiritual and physical silence of the vacuum that plays around the Omphalos's summits.

Her steps pick up speed.

They're a dour lot, these Big Dunkin Donut bureaucrats, thought Petula McTavish sourly as she finally left the Imm-Decryp building. Like most of the buildings in

Brando's Carbuncle, at a couple of million the sole population centre of any size in the Donut, it seemed unpleasantly squat to her: she was too accustomed to the towering edifices of Mega-City One and the other metropolises of Earth to feel comfortable in a place where the buildings rarely extended above four or five storeys, yet could spread out to either side for a kilometre or more. The worst of it was that, as a xenotheologist, she was supposed to be among the most adaptable people on Earth.

Except for their relative emptiness, the streets were much the same here as at home, though. There were still bums and winos on the sidewalks, still shop-fronts offering improbable bargains, still waste paper and used condoms and broken syringes in the gutters. Motorised vehicles were few and far between, and moved with a solar-powered whine rather than the familiar roar; pedal cycles and skateboards were much more frequent in a world where metals were rare. Yeah, maybe, she thought as she walked across the broad thoroughfare without having to wait for the lights. On second thoughts even the bloody streets aren't the same as home . . .

The two Imm-Decryp pen-pushers had tied her up for over six hours – and pen-pushers they literally were. Though she guessed that the core of their system must be computerised somewhere, almost all of the clerical work was done manually, with data storage being in the form of the kind of paper files and card indexes that had sunk out of existence on Earth a century or more before. McTavish had found it quite interesting at first to see the ancient art of handwriting – but only at first: after the initial couple of hours her patience had worn remarkably thin. She suspected that, had it not been for a judicious bit of Multigobbet Autotronic Offense Weapon-waving at appropriate moments, she might have been there for *another* six hours. Still, at last the two unconscious Dredds had been accepted back into the care of the Imm-Decryp boneses; they would be off her hands for the next couple of days while their injuries were being nulled – longer, if she had her way.

Two down, she thought glumly. Ninety-eight to go.

Shrugging, she turned down a side-street, heading for the sleazy hotel she'd booked into. Most of the other residents were Nandie slaves, installed there either by wealthy Overlords deceiving their spouses or by pimps running them as call-girls or -boys. It was about the one place in Brando's Carbuncle where McTavish didn't feel underdressed.

'*Psst!*'

She stopped in her tracks, looking around her. A couple of cyclists sped by, heads down as they pedalled furiously. At the next corner a huddle of people was gathered around a news-stand, but the sidewalk was empty between there and here. She seemed to be on her own. She looked up at the orange-brown wall of the building beside her, expecting to see someone hanging out of a low window.

Nobody.

'Hey, lady! Hey, pretty lady! Help me!'

The voice was coming from the depths of an alley so narrow she'd hardly noticed its existence. At sidewalk level the black, vertical crack was partially obstructed by a heap of overflowing garbage bins, crumpled paper and discarded clothing; someone had dumped a bloodstained mattress at the side of the pile. There was no metal, of course: in BC, like everywhere else in the Donut, the smallest shards of scrap metal were hunted down for resyking.

The hairs at the back of McTavish's neck prickled.

'Yeah?'

'Help me!' The pleading voice was no louder than a whisper. It sounded like a child – quite a young child.

'Where are you?' She peered into the darkness. Even the darkness here was tinged red.

'In here, miss. My leg – it hurts real bad.'

Wrinkling her nose against the stink, she took a couple of cautious steps into the opening, and waited for her eyes to accustom themselves to the dimness. The buildings might be low, by Earth standards, but the strip of orange sky above her head seemed a long way away.

'Over here.'

'Where?'

Something moved in the gloom off to her right. Shifting the Multigob in her arms, she took another couple of paces, keeping well clear of the mound of garbage.

'I still can't see you properly,' she said.

'My leg. One of the guys hit it with his stick. I think he broke something. I don't remember much after that.'

Now she could see a bit better. The stack of junk at the alley's mouth was only a continuation of the interior. There was all sorts of stuff in here, covering the ground in a thick layer – cloth, paper, rotting food, crushed plastic canisters, bits of broken furniture with the screws removed, dead animals and Nandies . . . and a colonist kid. He lay with his shoulders jammed halfway into a busted wardrobe, so that he was having to crick his neck up in order to look at her. His legs were out in front of him, one of them twisted at a weird angle from the other. Even in this lousy light McTavish could see that he was half-naked and that his body had been badly cut about. He was horribly thin. She guessed that the blackness of his skin hid a multitude of bruises.

She climbed over what was probably a corpse to reach him.

'Hey, kid, what's happened to you?'

The juve sniffed. 'Bunch of guys,' he said. 'Caught me out back and thought it'd be fun to kind of drokk me over a bit. It happens, lady. Dragged me in here and beat the stomm out of me, then somethin' must have scared 'em off or somethin'. Dunno. I thought I was dead, lady.'

McTavish looked around her. Behind she could see a thin slit of street. Up ahead, away in the distance, there was a corresponding glimmer representing the far end of the alley. She couldn't see anywhere an assailant could be hiding, though there might be a thousand doorways along those dark walls and she wouldn't be any the wiser. Her spine was feeling chill, as if she were in the presence of

32

danger, but she dismissed that as mere superstition: tests at home had never detected the faintest trace of psi in her. Besides, she had the Multigob in her arms, a knife in each boot, two hand-lasers at her belt and a garrotte concealed in her brief halter. She began to grin. In enumerating her weapons she hadn't thought of her hands and feet, potentially the deadliest of all of them. There wasn't a lot she should be worrying about.

'OK, kid,' she said, reaching out a hand. 'Let's see if we can get you up onto your good leg.'

The hand that took hers was dry and cold. It gripped her fingers tightly – tightly enough that the broken nails bit painfully into the flesh of her palm.

'Hey, go easy there,' she said.

The pressure hardly slackened, but she pretended to herself that it had. Balancing the Multigob carefully in her other arm, she hauled on the kid, so that he slowly came up beside her, standing gingerly on his left leg.

One glance at his face was enough to tell her that he was about to lose consciousness again. She let the Multigob fall to her side and caught him as his eyes rolled up.

Suddenly the darkness was alive. The stiff over which she'd just climbed reared up like a mummy vaulting murderously from its case, shedding its shrouds of stained sheets to reveal a half-naked white man crouched forward with a long, hooked knife in his single hand. His face was more scar tissue than skin; as well as an arm, he'd lost an eye – not long ago, by the look of it.

She let the boy drop. Out of the corner of her vision she saw him scuttling away on all fours. Then she was dodging a wild side-swipe of the hooked blade. Her heel caught on the Multigob's bulbous butt and she half-tripped, throwing out one arm to catch herself on the alley's slimy wall. While she was still off balance the one-armed man kicked out at her, catching her painfully in the groin. She doubled over, wheezing unnecessarily loudly. While he was cackling his satisfaction her hand snaked down to pluck the knife from its holster inside her left boot.

33

She straightened in a whirl of limbs and hair, stabbing outwards and upwards with the cold blue blade. The point tore into his stomach, just below his breastbone, and she rammed the blade in further, twisting it around before dragging it downwards, slicing through melting flesh. He bawled in agony and frustration, dropping his own weapon as he instinctively reached for his gut. She stepped lightly back, reflexively flicking the knife to twitch off the blood. In the darkness it was hard to see what was spattering the garbage underfoot. Bellowing hoarsely, he aimed a punch at her face, but she swung her head back, feeling the fist whistle past her nose. As he lurched forward, falling towards her, she neatly whipped the blade across in front of her, gashing through his throat, cutting almost to the bone. His scream died in a gargle.

She spun around, ignoring his final gasps of agony. Swooping, she grabbed up the Multigob and in a single movement triggered it skywards. For a second the whole of the alley was lit up as if by an arc light. Eight or ten metres away, yelling incoherently, the juve was scrabbling along in a half-crouch, trying to put as much distance between them as he could. His terrified face shone as he snatched a glimpse over his shoulder at her, then he renewed his flight. So much for the broken leg.

She almost left him. She would have, if she hadn't seen the thick welts across his back.

'Come back here!' she yelled.

He ignored her. A heap of rotting cardboard collapsed on top of him, muffling his yells.

Resheathing her knife, McTavish sprang forward and grabbed him by the ankle. She yanked, hard, and felt the joint dislocate. He wouldn't be running away from her any more. Now even the thick, wet layers of cardboard couldn't mute his screaming. She got a grip on his calf and hauled him backwards. He kicked blindly at her, but she had no trouble dodging his flailing feet. Half turned towards the alley's opening, the Multigob cocked and ready, she dragged him roughly over the cooling corpse of the man she'd killed and all the other noisome crap until he was lying face down on the open sidewalk, his thin shoulders shaking as he sobbed.

Some of the people from the news-stand were running towards her. She raised the Multigob, as if in greeting, and they abruptly lost interest. The one good thing you can say about BC, she thought grimly, is that at least they don't have any bloody Judges. If this were Mega-City One I'd be surrounded and stunned down by now . . .

She bent forward and looked more closely at the boy. Those welts on his back weren't faked, that was for sure. A couple of them were still bleeding.

Looking backwards and forwards warily, she knelt beside him. Propping the Multigob up against his shoulder, she grabbed his foot in one hand and his leg in the other and, with a swift, dextrous jerk, clicked his ankle joint back into place.

The boy hiccupped a funny little *whoop!* of exquisite agony and passed out.

McTavish got to her feet and treated the slowly retreating bystanders to another wave of the Multigob; they became swiftly retreating bystanders. Standing astride the juve's motionless form, she looked down on him and suddenly began to wonder what she was going to do with him now that she'd got him. He looked about fourteen, maybe younger. From the moment that his accomplice had reared up behind her she'd been acting on instinct – instinct and training. Here in BC she didn't know what you were supposed to do about muggers. Kill them, she guessed. But she wasn't into killing unconscious juves, particularly ones that looked as if they'd been having the stomm beaten systematically out of them every day for the past five years of their miserable lives. And she wasn't about to try to report this to the proper authorities, either – such as they were in BC.

She crouched down on the sidewalk, her knees up and the big black weapon between them. The muscles of her back suddenly began to protest about the frenzy of action she'd subjected them to, and she was glad to lean against the cool stone of the wall.

'What am I going to do with you, little boy?' she breathed. 'What in the name of Grud am I going to *do* with you?'

Biggins would have known, but Biggins would be halfway around to the other side of the Big Dunkin Donut by now.

If all was going well.

McTavish's room at the Belle et Bête Hotel was not luxurious, but it was adequate – and at least it had twin beds. She slung the inert form of the boy onto one of them, hearing the straw mattress wheeze and squeak in protest. His wide eyes peered at her over the adhesive bandage she'd strapped across his mouth; more bandages locked his hands behind his back and his ankles together. She made a note to replenish the supplies in her first-aid kit the first chance she had.

'I'm not going to hurt you,' she said quietly. 'I'm not going to do anything to you at all. You're safe.'

Small grunts escaped from under the sticky tape.

'Yeah, I can guess how you're feeling right now – a bit frightened, a bit apprehensive, maybe even a bit angry. I'll cut you free in a little while, once you've calmed down a bit.'

The grunts became more urgent, but she ignored them, turning away to look with distaste at her surroundings, as if probing at a sore tooth. The room was quite a reasonable size, although the ceiling seemed to crouch over her – the insides of the buildings in BC suffered from the same unsettling proportions as their outsides. The walls were covered in a drab grey-green substance that she recognised – from the time she'd taken a semester out from xenotheology to gain a quick doctorate in archaeology – as paint. Just off-centre in one of the longer walls was a framed picture of a tousled-haired woman with a face in the same shade of grey-green; on first arriving she'd found a small camera behind it, pointed at the larger of the two beds, but she'd stuck pink bubbleguck over the lens. There were other bugs in the room, she knew –

insectile and electronic alike – but she'd left the latter in place, reckoning it was better to know where they were than to have them replaced by new and less easily detected ones.

Most of one of the shorter walls was window, glazed with some cold, hard plastic she hadn't come across before. Just to one side of it was the holovee, babbling away in a loud murmur. One of the reasons she'd been able to get this room so cheaply was that, although you could turn the volume down low, it was impossible to switch the machine right off; covert experiment had proved to her that, unlike vid-screens back home, Donut holovees were impervious even to concentrated bursts from the Multigob. Now, as she watched, a fifty-centi-metre-tall man in a sober grey suit and a gaudy tie was taking a couple of steps out from the front of the screen across the stained orange carpet to stand behind an ostentatiously decorated lectern. Another bloody hol-evangelist show, she thought wearily. Didn't the folks in the Big Dunkin Donut ever want to watch anything else?

The boy on the bed had stopped struggling. His face looked a little red and his rapidly moving eyes seemed to be trying to tell her something, but she just shrugged at him.

'Once I know I can trust you, little fellow,' she murmured. 'That's when I'll cut you loose.'

If the room as a whole was dingy and drear, the view from the picture window made up for it. The Belle et Bête was one of the taller buildings on this side of BC, and her room was on its second-top storey. From here she had a breathtaking view over the Donut.

The centre of all was Korax's Eye, of course. The small red subdwarf would have been inconspicuous in the night sky of Earth, being little larger than Jupiter and shining mainly in the red and infrared, but from a distance of only 14.5 million kilometres it was more impressive than she had ever seen the Sun. She scratched the back of her neck ruminatively. Maybe the difference was that, back on Earth, when you looked at the Sun it was always in the middle of such a big expanse of sky; here, inside the Big Dunkin Donut, you were conscious of the fact that there wasn't really any sky at all, just the sphere extending all the way around the other side and then back to here again, with Korax's Eye floating in solitary splendour in the middle of an invisible bubble of soft vacuum. Narrowing her own eyes, she stared for a cautious moment at the angry red surface of the star: it was blemished, as it always was, by a flock of starspots following a course around its midriff like a flight of migrating geese.

There was no such thing as night here. The same was in a way true of Mega-City One, of course, because the lights of the streets never dimmed; but at least at home you had some awareness that somewhere far above you the sky was changing its shade. When she'd been out on field expeditions – both on Earth and on Markovitch's Hellhole, circling Sirius – that was when she'd seen true nights, with the stars scattered across the arch of the heavens like a sturgeon's roe. Here Korax's Eye was always at the zenith: it was perpetually noon within the Big Dunkin Donut. The nearest the sky came to darkness was when one of the great shoals of clouds that swung around the sphere's equator drew overhead; then the only light for days or even weeks would come, disconcertingly, from the horizon, lensed in from more brightly illuminated areas by the Big Dunkin Donut's atmosphere.

The total land area she could see from the window was something she had never troubled to calculate; one of the Nandie bellboys downstairs in the foyer had told her that, because of atmospheric lensing, you could see a greater hectarage from the roof of the Belle et Bête than the entire surface area of the Earth, oceans included, but she had no way of knowing if this was just tourist bullstomm. She wouldn't be surprised, though. Looking out through the window was a bit like peering into a fish-eye lens; the difference was that, with the fish-eye lens, it only *seemed* as if the world were all packed onto the inside surface of a sphere, whereas here, of course, it actually was. Even so, the lensing effect of the atmosphere threw the lands

38

about sixty degrees away around the interior out of all proportion to those closer by. Directly ahead, past the rooftops of the lesser suburbs of BC, she saw the browns and greens – close to black in the light of Korax's Eye – of the semi-cultivated plains that surrounded the city, seemingly stretching away in flat tracts for a while and then, vertiginously, beginning to climb up overhead. Further away, level with her gaze, there were blotches and splotches that she knew were great seas and hardwood forests so huge and thick and impenetrable that Earth had known nothing to compare with them for almost a millennium. Here and there, on the shores of the seas, she could see what looked like a pattern growing in the shape of a spreading tree: a major river and its tributaries.

When atmospheric conditions were just right, you could see, all the way across the sphere, a spectral white squidge that represented the Omphalos Mountains. For almost a decade after the first colonists had arrived in the Donut – flushing themselves in through the colossal airlocks that had been left by whatever unimaginable aliens had built this artefact – they had had no idea what that crumpled shape in the distance could be. McTavish smiled as she recalled what she'd been told about their theories. Some of the Overlords – as that first immigratory wave had dubbed themselves – had assumed the Omphalos to be a manufacturing flaw, and had taken solace from the fact that the ancients couldn't have been all that great, could they, if they were as capable of drokk-ups as the human race. Others, more mystical, had called the shape the Omphalos, the Navel of the World, and hypothesised that the Donut was a living organism that had grown itself, upwards and outwards from that tangled knot, until eventually its exploring edges had rediscovered each other and united to enclose the space, and the star, between them. It had been almost a disappointment when the Overlords had finally got their act together and gone there to discover that it was just the most spectacular mountain range in the known Universe.

Yet it was still a mystery. There was, obviously, no

volcanism within the Donut. The Omphalos had been created, all right – created by the ancient builders – but their purpose remained an enigma. Perhaps – and here McTavish ridiculed her own fancifulness – it was a religious monument of some sort, erected to honour some deeply alien god.

No one had troubled to ask the Nandies, of course.

That's another problem with this Grudforsaken dump, she thought, leaning forwards to rest her forearms on the cold surface of the window. No one ever *does* think to ask the Nandies.

She made a mental note that she should take the opportunity, as soon as this bloody mess with Dredd had been sorted out, to spend some long sessions with Nandies, trying to penetrate their culture further. The few she'd spoken with so far had proved to be not only more intelligent than herself but also wiser. Of course, it was possible that it was an illusion: one of the first lessons she had learnt in her undergraduate xenotheology courses back at the Old Cap'n Birdseye Polytechnic of North Brit-Cit had been that such judgements were impossible, and usually wrong, across the inter-species barrier. And yet the Nandies were human – sort of – weren't they?

She needed sleep, she realised. Although there had been no change in the view from the window, she had the sensation the sky was getting darker. She glanced at the Kronowiz on her wrist and saw it was four in the morning, Mega-City One time – the bloody instrument wouldn't recalibrate, despite her best attempts. Through a blur of weariness she reckoned she'd been on the go for nearly twenty hours – testing hours, too, what with having to argue with the bozos at Imm-Decryp.

Swinging back towards her tawdry room in a waterfall of pale-straw hair, she looked at the trussed boy for the first time in maybe an hour.

His body was arched against his bonds, and his face was the colour of freshly ejected lava. His flooding eyes looked as if they might pop from his head at any moment, the whites turned to a sickly yellow.

'Oh, Grud!' she yelled. 'Don't go and *die* on me!'

Beside him, on her knees by the dusty-smelling bed, she yanked away the bandage covering his mouth.

'The john!' he shrieked.

Much later, watching the white curve of McTavish's shoulder rise and fall regularly as she slept, Heidegger grinned lazily and stretched himself in his own bed, luxuriating in . . . well, not so much in the comfort, exactly, as in the fact that it wasn't soggy cardboard.

Turning over onto his back, he looked at the ceiling: apart from the fact that Korax's Eye was missing, it looked not dissimilar to the scene outside, with cracks and stains and pockmarks substituting for rivers and forests and seas. It looked beautiful to him.

Over in the corner, the holovee was still chortling away. Heidegger turned his head and glanced dourly at it. Every ointment has its fly, as Aristotle had so often told him. Heidegger wished he could think up some way of turning it off – permanently – while Petula slept, so he could give her the nice surprise of silence when she woke.

Something made him look back at the holovee.

At last – at very long last – the grey-suited man behind the lectern had been replaced by a woman. She was clothed in a bright red dress through which her flesh seemed to be trying to erupt; Heidegger was reminded of an over-inflated balloon – a collection of over-inflated balloons. He leant out over the edge of his bed, squinting at the woman, trying to get a better view. She was clutching a woolly ball of dirty white something to her ample bosom.

Heidegger strained his ears.

'. . . and I had this vision,' she was saying in a squeaky electronic voice, 'a vision that was granted me not by some supernaturinal boogieman, ma friends, but by the good grace of our sponsors, Country Vistas™ Plush-Lined Organic Nasal Tissue, out of the deep lovin' throat of their kindness.'

The blob in her arms suddenly stirred, revealing itself

41

as a small, white, cross-looking dog. While Heidegger continued watching, startled, the dog barked . . . barked *words*. 'Finger-lickin' good!' it yipped.

'That's right, Scooper,' said the bulging woman approvingly, tossing her curly brass-coloured hair. 'You know, ma friends,' she continued ruminatively, disconcertingly lifting her head to look directly at Heidegger, 'I always say to my good friend and hubby Rick "The Man" that there's more truth and salvation to be foun' in a single shyeet of Country Vistas™ Plush-Lined Organic Nasal Tissue than there is in every single writin' that's ever been produced by the organised ree-lidge-huns' – she pronounced the word as if it tasted of decay – 'of the entire Universe, and beyond.

'But lemme,' she carried on, 'stop talkin' as if you was just a mass of viewers watchin' me, lil ol' Maraschino. You're all innaviduals, all different, all with your own lives. Lemme jus' talk to one of you in partickler, someone I want to say somethin' special to.'

Maybe he could just throw some wet towels over it, or something.

'Yes, you!' insisted the woman, pointing a tiny yet swollen finger at him. 'Heidegger!'

I'm dreaming! he thought, retreating from the edge of the bed, bunching the meagre blankets around him. I must be!

'What's the matter, Heidegger? 'Fraid of someone less'n a third your height? An' a woman at that?'

'Are you talkin' to me?' he whispered, trying to keep his voice steady.

'Ain' no one else as I can see I should be talkin' to,' she said, 'ceptin' Scooper hyere.'

The dog raised its nose and licked the underside of her chin, then settled back.

'I'm most certainly not talkin' to that dumb-ass broad in the other bed,' said the woman, bending with some difficulty to deposit the dog on the carpet. 'For one thing, she's fast asleep. For another, I reckon she truly is one evil woman.'

'Evil'? Petula? He couldn't believe it! But then he couldn't believe any of the rest of this was happening, either . . .

'Yup, bub, truly evil,' said the woman, shaking her head in mock sadness as she advanced across the carpet towards him.

'Ke-k-keep away from me!' he whimpered, finding his voice at last, the back of his neck jammed against the clammy wall at the head of his bed.

'I can' do you any harm, ma frien',' said the woman, although she paused momentarily, mid-stride. 'I's jus' a image outta a holovee 'cast.'

'You can't get that far away from the holovee set, either,' said Heidegger, tugging the bedclothes away from her as well, 'but you just have.'

'Shucks, that's nothin',' she replied, shrugging. Her smile had grown so broad, as she looked up at him from the side of the bed, that Heidegger thought he could hear the molecules of lipstick screaming for mercy. 'Firs' time I dun the right thing an' turned my face away from Grud to look at the real gritty truth of the Universe, I realised what it was givin' me – it and our sponsors, of course, Country Vistas™ Plush-Lined Organic Nasal Tissue, did I mention them already? – what it was givin' me was the knowledge that there wasn't no bounds to the abilities I could have if I jus' gave myself up to it.'

She had a grip of his underblanket by now, and was using it to shin with incongruous nimbleness up onto the bed.

'Although I'm a ryeal live person in some ways,' she said, completing the ascent and sprawling on the crumpled sheet as she lost her footing, 'that's not the ryeal *me*, the me that's talkin' to you: the aspect of me that you're now lookin' at is what a gal could call a "technological artefact".'

She had righted herself and was trudging up towards his pillow.

'That was a truth the emptiness of the Universe gave me an' Rick. It said: "Hey, bubs" – called us bubs, y'know, all familiar-like – "Hey, bubs, why not give up on that ol' fascism of self, an' stop forcin' all your projections to behave exactly like yasself, whether they wanna or not, as they mostly not? 'Stead, why not make friends with them, get on equal terms with them, so that you an' them can start cooperatin'? That way, the fleshly yous can be doin' one thing while the arte-fact-chew-al yous can be doin' somethin' else.'

'Keep,' squeaked Heidegger, 'back. You're – you're just a dream.'

'Ain't no dream can sock you one on the nose like I can, is there?'

'Ow!'

'So much for the dream theory, eh, kiddo?'

'That hurt!'

She rubbed her knuckles while pretending not to. Heidegger guessed she must have hit him harder than she meant.

'Will you go away now, please, ma'am?' he said.

'But I ain't hardly started talkin' to ya.'

'You've talked to me quite a lot already,' he said. Years ago Aristotle had taught him this voice, like a cross between a choirboy's and a catamite's. He gazed at Maraschino with soulful brown eyes to match. 'I do think you ought to go. Petula's certain to wake if we carry on talking like this much longer.'

'Not afore I told you why McTavish is evil,' said the miniature firmly, fixing him with her dark eyes. He tried to tear his gaze away. 'You musta guessed,' Maraschino continued, 'she's an offworlder – she came to the Donut only a few days ago.'

'She told me,' he mumbled.

'Never trust offworlders.' Maraschino licked her lips. 'Aristotle musta said.'

'You could never trust Aristotle,' Heidegger blurted.

''Safact,' agreed Maraschino, smiling. 'But take it from me, bub, she's been wrappin' ya roun' her cutesy little finger. Ya take one look into those cool grey eyes o' hers, not mentionin' her other at-trib-boots, an' your little knees go knickety-knock, and you're ready to believe whatever line o' bullstomm she feeds ya.'

'She's . . . very pretty,' Heidegger conceded. 'I like her a lot.'

'Exactly!' Maraschino reached out her hand and rubbed the end of his nose. 'But she's plannin' to enslave Donut humanity for the rest of time!'

Heidegger tried to get his mind round that idea. With an effort of will he wrenched his eyes momentarily from Maraschino's and took a glance at Petula's sleeping form. She'd half-turned towards him, so that he could see her snub nose peeping out through a scatter of silky blonde hair. He couldn't imagine a dishonourable thought being able to find a footing inside the mind that lay behind that nose.

'I don't believe you,' he said stoutly.

'Oh, yes, ya do,' said Maraschino with quiet confidence.

And all at once Heidegger *did*. A tiny peripheral part of his mind was shouting at him that this was all nonsense, that Petula McTavish was his friend – but the rest of him found itself agreeing wholeheartedly with Maraschino. Even if it was bullstomm, this part coaxed, this was all just a dream, anyway.

'She plans to enslave us,' he breathed. 'That's . . . no wonder you said she was evil!'

'Evil ain' the half of it, bub. I dunno who's given her her orders, and I dunno the whole of their motives. But I do know she wants to turn the good citizens of the Donut to return to worshippin'' – she looked around her in mock fearfulness, as if expecting an enemy to pounce – '*gods*!'

'Oh, yuck!' said Heidegger.

'An' she's prepared to stop at nothin' to get her way. But *you* can help me an' Rick "The Man" frustrate her wicked schemin'.' Maraschino leaned forward so that her face was barely a centimetre from his. 'An' afterwards, you'll be a hero, adored by the masses, your exploits sung about in bars.'

'Wow!' said Heidegger, his mind abruptly a mass of

writing breasts and buttocks. He knew the kind of exploits people sang about in bars.

'An' all ya gotta do, right now,' added Maraschino confidentially, 'is lyet a little bit of me climb inside you.'

Heidegger looked at her perplexedly. His mind, emptied of flesh, seemed to echo. 'What do you mean?'

'Well, at some time in the nex' few weeks, there's gonna be a single act you can perform to thwart her vile ma-shin-aysh-shuns,' she whispered. 'I wanna bit of me to be with you all the time, lookin' out through your eyes, so's when the time comes I can say, "Hey, bub! Here's the momen' for kickin' ass!", an' tell you what to do.'

'Seems sensible enough to me,' said Heidegger.

'Awl-rightee, now jus' you sit an' watch,' she said, relaxing herself, her face drawing away from him. 'An' 'member, this part *looks* a whole lot worse than it ack-chooly *is* – okay?'

'Okay,' he said.

Her face twisted in concentration, she stared down at her hands, knotting and unknotting them at terrifying speed. Suddenly Heidegger saw that her long, silver-painted fingernails were growing even longer, their sheen ebbing as they grew and flexed, uncertainly at first but then with growing urgency. Ten moist-seeming grey tendrils, like thin new roots exposed abruptly to the air, crept silently along the crumpled surface of the pillow towards him. He tried to move his head and body, but his muscles were powerless, as if all the purpose had been leached out of them.

'No,' he said weakly, through rubbery lips, as the first of the tendrils touched his naked arm. 'No . . .'

'Ya wanna help us banish the enslaver, don' ya, kiddo?' said Maraschino, her voice grating with exertion.

'Yeah . . . but . . . no.'

Arching and stretching like a caterpillar, the first grey filament twitched its tip over the crest of his shoulder and began to quest surely along the line of his collar-bone. Four of its less speedy fellows were swarming up his arm.

'I'll be like the momma ya never had, bub,' said

46

Maraschino's strained voice. 'Only, I'll be closer than any mamma, cos I'll be right inside ya, lovin' ya, all the time.'

The leading tendril was on his face, creeping with steady assuredness up past the curve of his nostril towards the inner corner of his right eye. Its touch was curiously light, making him want to wrinkle his nose and sneeze.

'Ain' no offworlder strumpet gonna hurt *ma* sweet little babby.'

He tried to keep his lips firmly closed, but two of the probing filaments forced their way into his mouth, one on each side. He felt them gently caressing the corners of his tongue. The tip of the first tendril wavered, monstrously blurry and huge, in front of his eye. Then, as it plunged, there was a pain unlike anything he'd ever felt before – an agony that seemed to shoot electrically along every nerve in his body, arching his back and his pelvis, so that for an instant he was supported on the bed by only his heels and shoulder-blades. Just as suddenly, his body flopped back, his forehead a wet and chilly sea.

'That's the wors' over, hun – well, almos'.'

And I suppose this is hurtin' me more than it's hurtin' you? His mouth refused to form the words; inside it, the two feelers had twined themselves together and were now moving like spectral surfers along the length of his tongue towards the convulsing chasm of his oesophagus. A further pair of tendrils was busy beneath the bedclothes. Maybe as a mercy or maybe just out of coincidence, they stuck into their targets at exactly the same instant that another stabbed into the corner of his left eye. This time the pain was so intense a gasp escaped his lips – a scream stifled almost before it could start.

'There, now, there's a brave little boy for Momma,' said Maraschino, now once more squatting easily on the pillow. 'This time there really *is* nothin' much more to worry about.'

There was very little left of Heidegger's rational mind to doubt her. Slimy worms were advancing up his nostrils towards his sinuses; two more creepers were at his ears, so that the sound of Maraschino's voice was clumsy and sludgy, as if he were hearing it shouldering its heavy way through shallow water. The plates of his skull clashed as the tendrils simultaneously punctured his tympana.

And then, miraculously, the pain fled. With its departure returned the ability to move, to think coherently.

'I . . . uh . . .'

The long roots had severed themselves from Maraschino's fingertips. Like strands of spaghetti, their twitching lengths were being sucked into Heidegger's various orifices. In less time than it took to focus his eyes on them, they had disappeared.

'You should have warned me,' he said, amazed at how steady his voice sounded.

Maraschino threw back her head. Her neck-folds wobbled massively as she laughed. 'If Ida told you, kiddo, chances are youda told your sweet ol' Momma ta go drokk herself.'

Heidegger wasn't listening to her. All his senses seemed to have been stripped down, reintegrated and given a final polish. The room was larger now, and the grey-green of its walls glowed with cold opalescent richness. The sounds from the streets outside came to him with a sort of artificial clarity. The dull red starlight was a tapestry of subtly beautiful shades. McTavish's breathing, formerly too faint to be audible, was like the purring of a big cat basking on a hot day.

'Like I said, little feller,' remarked Maraschino, clutching the torn cloth at her shoulder and picking herself up from his pillow, 'when the time is right, the bit of me that's inside ya will tell ya exactly whatchya gotta do to put an end to the offworlder broad's malign ma-shin-aysh-shuns. Otherwise ya won' hardly know I's there with ya . . . ceptin', that is, if ever ya need a bit of cuddlin' an' need ya Momma to wrap ya in the warmth of her love.'

'It's not her that's the magic,' asserted Scooper from the floor, 'it's Country Vistas™ Plush-Lined Organic Nasal Tissue.'

'Ain' he jus' a card?' said Maraschino, scrambling down the side of the bed. She winked up at Heidegger. 'An'

48

maybe it's time ya Momma's liddle cham-pea-un had a little piece a snoozle-pie, cos ya mus' be a mite tuckered up from alla this.'

'Sleepy,' he concurred, his eyes closing.

It was only a dream, said Maraschino's voice caressingly in his mind. *When ya wakes up, ya'll not 'member hardly anythin' of this.*

McTavish awoke with a deep sense that something had gone terribly wrong.

Pushing the hair back from her eyes with one hand, she pulled herself up onto her elbows and looked around the room. The holovee was still babbling on in its perpetually mindless way, but otherwise nothing moved. Heidegger was asleep, she was glad to see. Sleep made his face look five years younger; she half expected to see his thumb in his mouth. She still had no idea what she was going to do with him – she couldn't just adopt waifs and strays whenever the fancy struck her – but that was a problem that could wait for time to solve it.

Maybe she'd had a nightmare that had fled the moment she awoke.

With a last contemptuous glance at the strutting miniature holevangelist on the carpet in front of the set, she settled herself back into the warm-smelling comfort of her bed. A few more hours' sleep wouldn't harm her, even if a lot of things needed to be done . . .

But sleep played hard to get. Instead she found herself lying in a doze, her mind casually ambling through the events of the past few months, the things that had inevitably drawn her here to this decrepit room in the seedy Belle et Bête hotel, in a suburb of Brando's Carbuncle, within the mighty alien-built sphere mankind had dubbed the Big Dunkin Donut . . .

THREE

A Few Weeks Ago, A Few Days Earlier Than Before

'Blessed are they who inherit.'
> – *Clients' Manual* (4th edn, 2110),
> Margaret Thatcher Charitable Fund-Raising Community
> of Blessed Hypocrisy Inc.

BLAM!
　Blam! Blam!
　Blam! Blam! Blam!
　Blam!
　Thyeung!
　BLAM!!!
　'Aaargh!'
　Blam! Blam-blam!
　Spleurgh!
The sentient extraterrestrial resin landed on him like an avalanche, slapping him back onto the hard edges of the stairs, splaying his limbs wide apart. The Lawgiver dropped from his gloved fingers, itself to be stuck to the rockcrete an agonising centimetre or less beyond his reach – if he could have reached. Hardening almost immediately, the pinkish resin trapped him motionless like a spider in amber, the expression of fury frozen on his lips.

The wrist-comm on his arm chose that moment to crackle into life.

Dredd had heard of the resin, but never seen it. Although sentient, the goo was not very intelligent – which was why it could be used for purposes like this. The stuff had been encountered a decade ago by one of the first expeditions to visit Triton, the largest of the eight moons of Neptune. The resin had taken out two crew members before the rest had realised what it was they'd stumbled upon. Unlike any other substance yet known to humanity, it was viscously fluid at very low temperatures, such as those pertaining on the surface of Triton, solidifying at higher ones and becoming rock-strong at anything above −73° Celsius. This unique property aided greatly in the transportation of the stuff, of course; but for some time no one had been able to think of any good use to which it could be put, and so the couple of tonnes that had been brought back to Earth were simply dumped in the New England Desert. It had taken the nimble criminal brain of a gang boss called Dennis the Dude – long departed, thank Grud! – to recognise that it was in the slow-wittedness of the resin that the clue lay to its exploitation as an extra-versatile version of riot foam. If kept refrigerated for several days and then cautiously removed, dollops of the stuff could – so long as it was not jolted or subjected to too much temperature variation – be retained in fluid form for a while, simply not noticing that things had heated up all around. The trick was to avoid any undue commotion.

Such as a spreadeagled law officer struggling underneath it. At Dredd's first instinctive muscle contraction the whole binful had solidified in an instant, imprisoning him more securely than the strongest iron chains.

Luckily, its structure was semi-permeable. Dredd could take shallow breaths, albeit with an effort. He could also hear things – for example, Chief Judge McGruder's waspish tones emanating from his wrist-comm.

'Gruddam it, Dredd! This is an emergency! Stop drokking around, wherever you are, and reply to us!'

Dredd summoned a superhuman effort to his sublabial muscles. All around his lips the sentient resin cracked and screamed.

'Reporting,' he croaked.

'But not for much longer,' sneered a voice near him. A

51

moment later the hateful face of Dinky Micawber swam into view. 'This is window-opaquers for you, Dredd!'

'I hear you,' grunted the lawman.

'Well, we can hardly hear *you*!' snapped McGruder. 'Time was you were the last Judge we'd expect to show this kind of disrespect, Dredd!'

New flows of the pink resin surged across Dredd's lips, silencing his formal response.

'You're not gonna be allowed to die easy, lawman,' said Micawber. 'You've done too much hurt to me and my brothers over the years.'

'Let it pass for the moment, Dredd,' said the wrist-comm crisply. 'There's trouble brewing in the Big Dunkin Donut, and we're sending in a xenotheologist. She needs muscle behind her – hard muscle. She said no one but the best – and that means you, Dredd, despite this fit of insubordination. She'll be joining you shortly. Got that, Dredd?'

'Got that!' wheezed the Judge after another energy-sapping effort. *Energy-sapping!* An idea!

'Boy oh boy,' Micawber was saying. 'You gonna get this dame under the covers, huh, Joe? Bet you it'd be fun – only you won't ever know how much fun.'

'How will I recognise her?' gasped Dredd.

'One,' replied McGruder, 'she'll be wearing less than anybody else there . . .'

'Gross indecency?'

'No – she stays within the law. Two, she's a xenotheologist, so she'll be carrying a Multigobbet Autotronic Offense Weapon,' continued McGruder.

'This broad of yours is beginning to interest me, Joe-boy,' said Micawber snidely. 'I'd be glad to lay my hands on one of them things.'

'She needs muscle?' said Dredd incredulously. 'When she's got a Multigob?'

'Yes, as I said – only the best for her. You did well on Judgement Day, and then again in Brit-Cit last year. You took out Sejanus when we thought all hope had been lost. She knows your reputation, seen your exploits on the vid-screens, got the T-shirt although she never wears it – reckons she can trust you. You're *It*, Joe.'

Energy-sapping! That was the secret!

'All right,' Micawber said to the pair of meaty gunsels who had come forward to join him looking down on Dredd; one of them was already unzipping his fly. 'All right, guys, we're gonna have to skip the fancy stuff and move straight to the circular saw.'

Energy-sapping! That exchange trip five years back to Hondo City! The indoctrachip that Captain Samsung implanted in his brain, containing the secrets of the recently developed hyperzen mastery of bodily functions!

'The third identification is that she'll be wearing a carnation behind her ear. We tried for a buttonhole, but she doesn't do buttons.'

'I read you, Chief,' said Dredd, a new confidence in his croak.

Swiftly, with a supreme effort of naked willpower, he shut down all of his subcutaneous capillaries, drawing the blood from them back towards his heart. Next to empty were the arteries at wrists, neck, knees, ankles, groin, temples . . . To all intents and purposes, the outer layers of his body died in an instant, leaving only his vital organs and his brain still functioning. His skin temperature plummeted, within seconds matching that of the resin's surface pressing against him. He held his breath, lest the slightest scintilla of heat escape from his body.

It was working!

Confused, the lattices of resin began to mill about, losing their coherence. To Micawber and his sidekicks it might have seemed the pink surface over the lawman had begun to boil.

But they weren't looking. Their attention was distracted by the sudden appearance on the stairs below of . . .

BLAM!!!

Dusting off bits of resin, Dinky Micawber and side-kicks, Dredd climbed to his feet, scowling.

'Who're you?' he said to the woman with the Multigobbet Autotronic Offense Weapon. Then he saw the carnation behind her ear.

'You must be Dredd,' she said. 'Let's get out of here. I'm starving.'

The Hard Knocks Café was like a kind of polluted oasis in the middle of a trashed waste: loud music poured out onto the sidewalk from behind the only unsmashed set of plate-glasseen windows in forty blocks. The flashing sign above had obviously been designed during the psychedelia revival a couple of years back; one of the letters had failed, and McTavish was marginally surprised to notice that it wasn't the N.

Inside, the place was reasonably empty. Communicating by sign language with a fussy little waiter – human rather than droid, for a wonder – McTavish got him to lead her to a vacant table for two. She pointed at the heavy loudspeakers mounted in the top corners of the room, then at her ears.

He smiled and nodded, then retreated at speed. Moments later the thunder of the music intensified, hammering her like baseball bats. The words on the menu were blurred by the noise, but she made some of them out. A standard 112g synthiburger – that would do her. She checked the price, and her brow wrinkled. '"A knee in the groin (medium force)"?' she mouthed.

Her attention was distracted by a crash that drowned even the music. Dredd was standing beside one of the few other patrons of the joint, a blue-rinsed old lady who had been surreptitiously picking her nose. She tried to pretend innocence, but it was too late; Dredd's nightstick descended once, twice, smashing fingers.

Out of the corner of her eye, McTavish saw the little waiter had begun furiously picking his nose. Was the man a maniac?

Dredd strode towards her, leaving a shattered trail. His lips were moving, but McTavish could hear nothing. Helplessly, she gestured at the loudspeakers.

BLAM!!! BLAM!!! BLAM!!! BLAM!!!

'That's better,' she said some while later as the echoes died.

'A small service rendered to you by an official of the Justice Department.'

He sat down opposite her with a crash, hitching the nightstick to his belt but keeping the Lawgiver out on the synthigingham-covered table-top. Behind him the old lady was sobbing, looking at the wreckage of her hand as if it had just arrived from another planet.

'Talk,' he said.

'I'm hungry.' She picked up the menu again. 'Do you mind?'

'OK.'

She beckoned the waiter, who was still ostentatiously picking his nose. 'Just a synthiburger for me,' she said as he arrived. He ungummed his finger to scribble their order on his notepad. A badge on his jacket told them he was called Gilles. 'And some synthicaff.'

'Synthicaff for me, too,' rumbled Dredd.

'Sure you wouldn't like anything else?' said Gilles hopefully.

'Sure.'

'Well, that'll be . . . let me see . . . that'll be a knee in the groin (medium force) for the synthiburger and two punches to the throat for the drinks.' Gilles seemed disappointed.

McTavish, who'd produced a fistful of credits from one of her boot-pockets, stared at Dredd in perplexity. 'You got any idea what he's talking about?'

'Joint's run by masochists,' explained the Judge. 'Let the Justice Department pick up this tab.'

'You want any synthimilk with the caffs?' said Gilles.

'Yes, please,' said McTavish.

'Oh, goody! I get to take my clothes off as well. Don't forget to pay me as you leave, big boy.'

Dredd ignored the remark and leaned towards the xenotheologist. 'OK, McGruder said a crisis in the Donut, but nothing more than that. Said you'd explain. So, like I said: talk.'

'Where do you want me to start?'

'At the beginning.'

McTavish began to speak rapidly, the synthicaff growing steadily colder by her elbow . . .

The Big Dunkin Donut was discovered by humanity in the year 2048, and by 2065 US expeditionary ships had travelled there, ascertained the situation, and returned with the news that within the sphere there was a colossal area of new land awaiting ever-burgeoning humanity. This joyous information was, however, largely kept secret for fear of igniting riots and civil wars in the increasingly tense political climate on Earth. The government of the USA, in partnership with the huge multinational Kentucky Fried Nintendo Corp, covertly recruited several waves of volunteers to travel to the Donut in enormous and equally covertly constructed colony ships, and in 2069 two of these – the *Back in a Jiffy* and the *Have a Nice Day* – had lifted off with about 6000 pioneers. However, before a third ship, the inauspiciously named *I'm a Jehovah's Wi–* , could be sent to join them, the Great Atomic War broke out, destroying much of human civilisation including, incidentally, the USA and the complete records of the colonising project.

Even the information that the Donut existed was lost from all but the most secure governmental files – most secure because totally forgotten about. In 2110, however, a licensed Brit-Cit hacker called the Reading Fanglord accidentally broke into the files of the long-defunct Benson & Hedges New IMPROVED Scotland Yard and discovered a reference to industrial espionage carried out into the subject during the 2060s by the John Lewis Syndicate, eager to exploit the secrets of Kentucky Fried Nintendo. This information was passed to Mega-City One, where at last the full story of the Big Dunkin Donut was tracked down. The first batch of a new wave of colonists was on its way in 2111, and three further shipfuls had since followed. It was expected that at most a trickle of further vessels might be sent over the succeeding decades – but no more than that because of the journey time: the Donut was too close for faster-than-light drives.

This picture changed because of two coincidental events. The first was an advance in the merged fields of ion coding and physiological holographics. A team working out of the otherwise almost entirely moribund Brooklyn Bay Oceanographic Institute, seeking a new means of generating synthetic fish as a contribution towards the ongoing food crisis, instead discovered how animals – including the higher mammals, like humans – could be analysed down to even the synaptic level, and how that data could then be encrypted in digital form within a holographic lattice no larger than the average credit card. This process had the side-effect of killing the subject thus analysed, but that didn't matter much because the animal/person could then be reconstituted, complete with all memories, by (in effect) reversing the process, so that the information could be used to programme a random assemblage of atoms – for example, a sack of sand, a cabbage and a couple of buckets of water – to form an exact simulacrum of the original.

This research was of course kept under wraps by the Mega-City One Justice Department, which hoped to be able to iron out the difficulty whereby the original subject lost her/his life and thus cheaply to create herds of fresh Judges patterned exactly as per the most successful among those already practising.

A few people realised this new technology could also provide a means of transporting humans into deep space in economically lightweight form. For example, thousands upon thousands of potential colonists could be inexpensively ferried to the Donut in a single small reconditioned freighter. The only problem was that the process of reducing people to holographic chip form relied on plant-derived enzymes and thus was incredibly expensive, more than outweighing the fuel economies.

There the matter might have rested had it not been for the second coincidental event.

Five or six years ago a small expeditionary party,

including McTavish, had gone westwards from New Jerusalem into the heart of the Great African Dustbowl, following up persistent rumours that somewhere in that area there were traces of a supertechnological prehistoric civilisation. The little party soon got lost, and was trying to work out how to get back to New Jerusalem when it stumbled across a huge, ancient caldera. What must once have been a volcanic summit had been buried by sand millions of years before, but for some reason the crater itself had remained clear. In the centre of the crater was a rock-tower, some thirty metres high and clearly artificial, with a hole punched out of it on one side, near the top. The party had ropes and crampons, and soon McTavish and the expedition leader, 'Mvedge, were in the cavern at the tower's top.

The back wall of the cave was completely covered in machinery – *strange* machinery. They fiddled warily with it for a while, but nothing happened. Then 'Mvedge took hold of a couple of looped handles. There was a crack, a flash of light and . . . he'd gone. Vanished.

For the next couple of hours everyone panicked. Then, as suddenly as he'd disappeared, 'Mvedge was back. As soon as they'd got him sitting upright, they quizzed him about where the drokk he'd been these past two hours. All he could say was: 'Somewhere strange. I was in some kind of installation, a few klicks beyond the edges of a city. There was me, and a machine like this one, and not much else. But that wasn't the weirdest part of it. *There was a country floating in the sky!*'

It was only much later that they discovered he was right: he really had been to a place where you can see landscapes in the sky – the Donut. The machine they'd discovered was a matter transmitter. No one could find out how it worked, but it did – in a limited way. It could send things – up to about 150 kilograms at a time – to the Donut or receive them in return. It couldn't be moved, even with heavy machinery. And it required two hours and seventeen minutes to recharge itself after each transmission.

Being able to send one person at a time to the Donut might be useful in case of emergency, but that was about all.

However . . .

At the time there was a short-lived trade agreement between New Jerusalem and Mega-City One, and during one of the higher-level negotiations mention had been made of the conundrum in the desert. Most things known to the upper echelons of Mega-City One's society eventually came to McGruder's ears, and she had put together this fresh information with the discoveries reported from the Brooklyn Bay Oceanographic Institute. 150 kilograms might be only the weight of one heavy man, but it was also the weight of thousands and thousands of credit-card-sized holograms.

Perps – crypped perps! Feeding perps was expensive, over long periods. Despite the costs of crypping, sending them to the Donut, in their thousands, made good economic sense.

Mega-City One had started, very secretly, sending a consignment every month or so.

The first batches of MT arrivals discovered that society within the Donut had already structured itself into two strata. Several million Nandies, who appeared to be a separately evolved human stock, although no one could work out how they'd got there, formed an underclass ruled by a small but powerful population – by now about 40,000 – of technologically sophisticated Overlords, the colonists (and their descendants) who came on the *Back in a Jiffy* and the *Have a Nice Day* and who then lost all contact with home. The Nandies had become the virtual – and often actual – slaves of the Overlords. The newcomers were told they could comply with the wishes of the governing minority, or be reduced to Nandie status; most of them, knowing which side their synthibread was synthigreased, were only too happy to accord, settling in merrily to a life of slave-catered luxury.

The Nandies, despite their vastly superior numbers, seemed disinclined to revolt. Apart from their in-built pacifism – there had never been any need to fight over territory – there was their god, Korax. According to Nandie lore, she had told her people that the reign of the Overlords could not possibly last more than a few generations; the best thing to do was just . . . *endure*. It all sounded like a clever plot on the part of the Overlords, a bit of myth-making to keep the natives docile – except that, back when the *Back in a Jiffy* and the *Have a Nice Day* first reached the Donut, they discovered the Nandies had, under Korax's instructions, built a sort of shanty town around the sphere's solitary ingress portal so the newcomers would have somewhere to live while they were sorting themselves out.

The shacks they erected were pathetic little things, of course. The Overlords quickly cleared them and set about creating their own capital instead: Brando's Carbuncle.

Brando's Carbuncle got its name for one of two reasons, depending upon which legend you believed in: either a guy called Brando was first to notice the city glitters like a diamond at night, when viewed from a few hundred kilometres around the curvature of the Donut; *or* Brando was the captain of the *Back in a Jiffy*, and at the time he was guiding his spaceship in through the portal he had a massive complex of boils on his butt. A variant of the latter tale said it was Brando's girlfriend who had the boils, and that he pluckily lanced them, thereby saving her composure but losing her love.

All had been going fine in the Donut until recently. Some of the transported perps were proclaimers of proscribed religions. This didn't normally matter, but . . .

Two 'buts': the Reverend Rick 'The Man' Hamfist of the Margaret Thatcher Charitable Fund-Raising Community of Blessed Hypocrisy Inc., and the Reverend Dave 'No Messin' Fingers of the Oliver North Church of Fundamental Sanctimony. Grud knew which particular stones they'd chosen to crawl out from under, but crawl out they had. They'd set up their rival establishments in different areas of Brando's Carbuncle, both preaching rampant, fundamentalistic atheism. The two had rapidly built up a following in the slums. And somehow they'd got access to some real frontier technology – enough to start performing 'miracles' for the Nandies.

Big 'miracles'. There'd already been rumours that one of the two preachers had experimented with tactical nukes.

Dangerous inside a sphere whose skin was hardly anywhere more than a couple of dozen metres thick.

With hard vacuum outside.

You could blast a hole right through if you got your hands on a big enough thermonuke.

Two days later they were at the rim of the caldera, looking down. The sun was almost on the horizon, and the temperature was dropping rapidly. Behind them, the dune buggy that had brought them from New Jerusalem was creaking and groaning as it cooled.

'So that's the tower?' said Dredd.

'That's it,' said Petula McTavish, shielding her eyes with a hand. It was windy today, and the air was full of sand.

'Doesn't look like much to come all this way for,' commented Dredd. 'You made it sound bigger.'

McTavish grinned to herself. Over the past couple of days, while they'd been being briefed and then travelling here, she'd been talking-up the tower to Dredd. Largely confined within Mega-City One, the Judge tended to forget that a thirty-metre tower out here in the middle of nowhere presented a tougher proposition than the tallest of the megalopolis's blocks, with its anti-gravity chutes, its fast-elevs . . .

It was a stomm of a climb.

'Couldn't they put a gantry round it, or something?' said Dredd. He twitched his cape, the only item of disguise he had consented to wear.

'The MT won't let them. It repels other machines. We're lucky it tolerates the holochips.' She smiled, this time at him. 'Even our weaponry will have to go through in encrypted form.' She gestured towards the Multigob,

61

leaning easily against her side. 'Don't worry – we've tried it out with one of these. All A-OK.'

She hoped it would be. If there'd been any other way of getting to the Donut, she and Dredd would have used it. But McGruder had insisted that speed was of the essence, and McGruder had probably been right. Besides, making a special space flight would have been expensive. The clincher was that the next consignment of perps had been due for despatch almost immediately.

'Huh,' said Dredd.

'Well,' she said, 'now you've seen it. Want to go down for a closer look?'

'No. No need. It's just another means of transportation. Let's get back to New Jerusalem and get this over with.'

Tomorrow they were going to be encrypted, their physical bodies destroyed. McTavish had grown accustomed to the idea but, she noticed as they trudged through the grasping sands to the battered khaki dune buggy, the big lawman had not.

If she hadn't known better, she'd have said Judge Joe Dredd was terrified.

She herself didn't start getting terrified until they reached the Big Dunkin Donut.

In the Big Dunkin Donut's Imm-Decryp there was a saying that, sooner or later, crept into the conversation whenever the subject turned to the teams of techs that worked out at the MT installation: 'There's stupid, there's really stupid, there's really *drokking* stupid, there's really really so drokking stupid you wouldn't believe it, there's so drokking stupid that if you compared it to a lump of rockcrete you'd get letters from angry lumps of rockcrete, there's even stupider than that, and then there's Arf Belcher.'

Sometimes, for brevity, they just said Arf Belcher was a couple of fingers short of an insult.

Trouble was, Arf was a scion of the powerful Belcher clan. You couldn't climb much higher up the pinnacles of Overlord society than the Belchers. Young Arf, chris-

tened Christopher Tobias and the apple of his mother's
eye until that unfortunate accident with her head – 'I was
hungry!' he'd explained – had had to be found a responsible job of some sort. Preferably somewhere outside the
city limits of Brando's Carbuncle. Somewhere it didn't
matter too much what damage he did.

Reconstitution Hopper Manager sounded good.

Arf's job was to shovel up the loads of holochips that
came in through the MT from Earth every few weeks,
stick them in a bucket and chuck them into the mouth of
the Reconstitution Hopper, a couple of hundred metres
away, just outside the technology-repelling sphere of the
MT. It wasn't quite as simple as that, of course: he had to
manipulate the Broad-Flanged First-Order Lever such as
to transfer the chips from the Ingress Bay to the Concave
Truncatoconical Holochip Transposition Module, which
he then had to transfer bipedally, grasping the CTHTM
by its Semicircular Manual Portage Peripheral, across to
the ReconHop, into whose Hinge-Articulated Reception
Interface he deployed pseudo-gravitational energy and
muscle flexure to insert the holochips.

When you thought about it that way, it was no wonder
that Arf Belcher drokked up so often.

And who cared? No one in the Donut, that was for
sure. As the Imm-Decryp officials would remark, after
the laughter had died down a bit, once you'd seen one
nubug you'd seen them all: there were plenty more where
those mangled holochips had come from.

After Arf had done the difficult bit, the automatics
took over to tidy up the little details. Cute robots gathered
vegetation and topsoil from the surrounding area, which
the ReconHop pulverised to a fine, organics-rich sand
that formed the base material for the reconstructed
nubugs. The ReconHop, too, contained the hardware for
decrypping the holochips and integrating the molecules it
whipped up from the raw materials in such a way as to
generate living human beings, according to the patterns
dictated by the individual chips. Automata then removed
the comatose forms – stiffoids – from the far side of the

huge hopper, so that computer-driven autocars could transport them to Imm-Decryp HQ in BC. Years ago they would have been shipped at colossal speed by hyper-pneum tunnels, but the autocars had proved cheaper – and the stiffoids were hardly in any position to complain that the journey was slow.

Arf thought very little at the best of times, so he certainly thought nothing of it this morning when a holochip dropped from his overfilled CTHTM, and he thought even less of it when, on his return trip, his massive, steel-capped regulation-issue Pedal Extremity Protector – or 'boot', as the jargon had it – landed with the full force of his doughty weight on that same holochip, shattering it into (although Arf did not count them) precisely one hundred different-sized pieces.

'Arf, arf!' he laughed merrily when at last he spotted the plasteen fragments lying there. Bending down, he scooped them up in his Broad-Flanged First-Order Lever – taking quite a lot of soil with them, though that was irrelevant – and lurched across to tip them into the Hinge-Articulated Reception Interface in the wake of all the others in today's consignment.

That done, he drew the back of his sleeve across his sweating brow, remarked to himself that it had been a hell of a day, what with all this head-work, and went to sleep it off on his Horizontal R&R Accessory.

'Some drokk-up back on Earth,' said Chief Tech Roxy Cardano at Imm-Decryp.

Most of the latest nubugs had been resuscitated, sedated where necessary, and sent on their ways – to short-term hostels, to gang safe houses, to brothels, to anywhere so long as it wasn't Imm-Decryp – but there was still a long queue of trolleys waiting for their occupants to be processed.

'Huh?' said Deputy Chief Tech Chuck Strozza. As well as a bright pink plasteen lunch-box stuffed under one armpit, he was carrying two huge sheaves of assorted printouts and desperately trying to find a third hand so that he could open up his portable microcomputer. As Cardano watched, printouts, lunch-box and microcomputer fell balletically to the floor, followed shortly afterwards by the spectacles from the end of Strozza's nose.

'There's too many of them,' explained Cardano gently, indicating the stiffoids. 'According to the transmitting manifest, there should have been only 5788 of the little drokkers, plus a Multigobbet Autotronic Offense Weapon, but according to my count we have 5887.'

'Plus the Multigob,' said Strozza morosely, eyeing the litter at his feet.

'That's right.' She consulted her manifests again as Strozza knelt to gather up the scattered sheets of paper. 'Watch you don't step on your microcomp – oh, too bad.'

'Drokk!'

'Unless it was Arf again. As they say, there's stupid, there's really stupid, there's really *drokking* stupid, there's really really so drokking stupid you wouldn't . . .'

'Never mind,' said Strozza philosophically. 'I've got plenty of backup 'puters. The best of them is the Milford 986S, only its hard disk's crashed, but if you rig it up with the pico-transponder out of one of the little Helicon VHFs and remember not to move the keys you can . . .'

'Well,' said Cardano, 'ours is not to reason why, I guess. Funny how so many of this lot of stiffoids are dressed the same. Maybe the Justice Department's had a crackdown on cross-dressers, or something.'

'. . . though the monitor's a bit dicey, so what I do is I . . .'

Cardano reached out to the figure lying motionless on the nearest trolley. 'D-R-E-D-D,' she said ruminatively. 'Dyslexic necromantic cross-dressers?'

'. . . and the printer's another matter entirely. Gee-rud! So long as you drag the autocharger with you it's not too bad, but these fusion reactors ain't as portable as the ads make out. On the other hand, you can bypass the serial outlet and . . .'

'Kind of cute jaw, though.' She smiled at a reminiscence. 'I remember breaking one like this at a party back in good old Brit-Cit. He was a visitor from Mega-City One, as I recall. I should have realised when I saw him with that drokker Armitage that he was a . . . oh, *drokk*!'

'. . . tweak the bus-stop and . . .'

'Strozza, can you stop babbling for a nanosecond?'

'Sorry, boss. I thought you were interested. Say, I brought these printouts along specially for you, but I haven't even shown you them yet.'

'Later, Strozza,' she snapped, scratching her head. The line of trolleys stretched along the chlorine-redolent corridor in either direction as far as she could see. 'I got an itching in my funny bone that tells me there's more here than meets the eye.'

Her assistant groaned. She glanced at him irritably.

'Something the matter, Strozza?'

'Ah, no – no, boss. Just clearing my throat, like.' He cringed. He was the fourth deputy the Chief Tech had had in as many months.

'Can you manage to use a vid-phone without having to reroute the call via Deneb, Strozza?'

'Yeah. Yeah, sure thing, boss. No prob. Easy done.' He clambered to his feet clutching a fistful of paper. 'You could have a look through some of this stuff while I'm . . .'

'There's a friend of mine who might be very interested to hear about this latest consignment of Jud– of stiffoids. A very *good* friend – know what I mean, Strozza?' She tapped the side of her nose with a bulging forefinger. 'He wouldn't be pleased with us if it got out and about that we'd . . . kept him informed.'

'Uh, yes, boss. Whatever you say.' Strozza paled.

She scribbled for a moment on the back of one of the sheets of paper he'd passed her, dropping the rest into a nearby frag-bin.

'That's the number,' she said. 'Audio only, of course – this guy doesn't *do* video, if you get my meaning. Let it ring twice, then disconnect and redial immediately. When they pick up, ask for Dennis the Complete Bloody Sadist and tell him that it's a message from Big Roxy – he'll know who you mean.'

'Oh, uh, like, er, boss, ah – what's the, you know, message?'

'Just tell him about this lot,' she said, waving an arm expansively at the slowly moving line of trolleys. 'Tell him that we seem to have about a hundred, give or take, all dressed in capes and helmets, all fully armed, all with badges saying D-R-E-D-D – got that?'

'Right, boss. I got it.'

Leaving her there guarding his stuff – but, knowing Cardano's appetite, wisely taking his lunch-box with him – Strozza ran down the corridor until he found an unvandalised vid-phone booth. He dialled once, then again, as instructed.

'I wanna speak to Dennis the Complete Bloody Sadist,' he gasped eagerly. 'I got a message from Big Roxy.'

'Jutht hold it right there, buthter,' said the voice at the other end.

'Yeah?' said another voice a few moments later.

'Dennis the Complete Bloody Sadist?'

'Yeah. Spill.'

'Well, there's all these guys here, you see, and they're all wearing badges saying D-R-O-K-K. Want me to spell that again?'

It was an error for which he later paid dearly.

'You mean you just – let them go?'

Petula McTavish's hands grappled furiously with the barrel of the Multigobbet Autotronic Offense Weapon lying across her lap, as if she were trying to strangle it. Just her luck that she should have been one of the last in the consignment to be resuscitated.

The broad face opposite her added to her wrath by remaining blandly impassive.

'That's right,' said Cardano. 'What else did you expect?'

'And you said there were *how* many of them?'

'According to our quick off-the-beam statistical assessment, exactly one hundred – although there's the standard tolerance of plus or minus zero point six per cent in all our estimates, of course.'

'A hundred Dredds? That's disastrous!' McTavish's face rarely showed signs of her passions, but right now it was definitely turning a subtle shade of rose pink.

Cardano shrugged. 'None of our business. Our job is just to revive the stiffoids, make sure they can walk – or at least crawl – and then set them free to enjoy all the splendours that the Donut has to offer. Unless we have special orders – and in this case we didn't. Now, if you've finished, Ms McTravis, I've got a lot to . . .'

'This could be the worst thing ever to hit the Big Dunkin Donut,' said McTavish fiercely, 'but you just don't give a drokk, do you?'

'Frankly,' said Cardano, glancing up from the heap of phoney paperwork with which Strozza had eagerly supplied her, 'no.'

'You –'

'If you have any complaints, Ms McTravis, you'll have to take them through the proper channels. I have the necessary forms right here – somewhere.' Cardano began pulling out drawers.

McTavish waited a few seconds longer. The Chief Tech's office looked like a terrified buffalo had stampeded in, tried to effect an escape through the walls, and then exploded.

'I must speak to one of your superiors,' said McTavish, fighting to control her temper.

'Are you saying there's anybody superior to me?' growled Cardano from somewhere behind the desk.

'Your boss, dammit, woman!'

'As far as you're concerned, pretty lady,' said Cardano, emerging without the forms, 'I *am* the boss. Who do you think *you* are? You're just another bit of faecal material that's been flung in the direction of the Donut because the folk on Earth can't stand your stink any more. You're the lowest bit of scum in the cesspool here, got that?

You're a *nubug*, Gruddammit, not a drokking Overlord.
You're worse than a stomming Nandie, not even a . . .'

McTavish hefted the Multigob.

'. . . although you do present a very forceful argument,'
continued Cardano smoothly. 'I'll see if one of the
boneses has time to spend a few minutes trying to sort out
your query. Now, if you could only help me find my vid-
phone . . .'

As she sat waiting in the antechamber to Dr Elmer
Fremantle's office, McTavish realised that so far she'd
been conscious for nearly three hours and as yet had seen
nothing of the Big Dunkin Donut except the inside of the
Imm-Decryp building. For all she knew, she might just as
well have still been back on Earth: the only major
differences between there and here were the plethora of
paper that seemed to be everywhere – the archaeologist
part of her was quite excited to see so much evidence of
its traditional use – and the elaborate substitutions of
materials the colonists had been forced to make in order
to economise on metals and plastics, both of which had to
be imported at considerable expense. The desk behind
which Dr Fremantle's secretary sat reading a printout, for
example, was – like the one in Cardano's office – made
almost entirely of planed and polished wood.

She tightened her grip on the Multigob. The weapon
might be worth a small fortune here in terms of scrap
value alone.

The secretary – an exquisite Nandie dressed in a tightly
fitting one-piece garment coloured in bright reds and
yellows – looked up at McTavish and said, for the
hundredth time, 'I'm sure Dr Fremantle will be able to
see you shortly, Ms McTavish. He's a very busy man, you
know.' Then she returned to her reading.

McTavish stared at her. None of the holocubes she had
studied back on Earth had prepared her for the beauty of
the Donut's indigenous species. This one's hair was a
downy red and looked as soft as a kitten's underbelly.
McTavish told herself that there was nothing sexual in her

desire to run her fingers across it – all around the perfect, rather elfin ears and then in a long sweep down the gracefully curved back to the base of the spine. When the Nandie was seated you didn't notice the odd proportions of her limbs; her hands, swiftly manipulating the sheets of paper as she scanned them, were as neatly made as a doll's, and far more elegantly formed. The Nandie's – the *woman*'s, McTavish reminded herself – the *woman*'s face was a flawlessly symmetrical structure of balanced planes and curves. And those eyes . . .

You could lose yourself in this woman's eyes.

'Biggins, you great ape, send the drokking Terry in, huh?'

'Dr Fremantle will see you now,' said the secretary, smiling at McTavish again. This time McTavish was certain she detected a trace of wistfulness in the curve of those thin lips . . .

'Petula McTavish,' said the fat man who half rose to greet her as she passed in through the quaint hinged wooden door. 'Elmer Fremantle, at your service. You're the drokking nubug who's been causing the techs so much drokking trouble, huh?'

'*Doctor* McTavish,' she said coolly, seating herself opposite him. 'I have doctorates in archaeology, anthropology, xenanthropology and xenotheology, and I've been sent here from Mega-City One in my professional capacity. I am *not* just another feisty little nubug bitch, as I think I heard you describing me over the vid-phone a little while ago. Do I make myself clear?'

She clicked the safety catch on the Multigob.

'Entirely, Dr McTavish. It's, ah, it's good to meet a fellow professional any time, and especially a, uh, such a distinguished one as yourself. A synthisherry? I'll just ask Biggins to . . .'

She silenced him with a wave of her hand.

'What I want from you, Dr Fremantle, is information. Information and, if necessary, some help.'

'You do,' he stated flatly. 'We're not really geared up to, ah– .'

70

'You're not really geared up here in this low-tech dump you're so proud of to do anything more than resuscitate the nubugs and boot them out into the streets,' she said. She shrugged. 'I know, I know. Nevertheless, I'm asking you with all the authority of Mega-City One and New Jerusalem to give me the assistance I request. I can't give you much detail of my assignment, but what your lumbering subordinates have done could spell the imminent doom of the entire Donut, and every man, woman and child in it.'

'I have Cardano's report here,' he blustered. 'Oh, stomm, no, this is just one of Strozza's drokking print-outs.' He hurled a sheaf of papers angrily at the woven-straw waste-bin. 'Great man for the paperwork, our Chuck. He may not last. With luck. Ah, *here*'s what I'm looking for.' He held up one palm towards McTavish and began laboriously to read the document in front of him, his lips twitching as he slowly worked his way down the single page.

'Everything seems to be in order here, Ms . . . Dr McTavish,' he said at last. 'According to Cardano, there were ninety-nine extra nubugs in today's consignment which was, let me see' – he looked to the top of the document – 'number 6487B. It wasn't Cardano's responsibility how many stiffoids came through: she revived them as per the standard regulations, specifically forty-seven, sub-clause three. One hundred per cent survival rate, I'm glad to say, as is our usual.' He turned the broad smile of the practised politician in McTavish's direction, then hurriedly got back to the report. 'Cardano does note that rather a high proportion of the nubugs in this batch were . . . well, "fuzzy round the edges", it says here.' He looked bewildered. 'I'm not quite sure what she means by that.'

McTavish just grunted.

Before sending her up here Cardano had thawed out a little and become somewhat more explicit. 'It's hard to describe,' the big woman had explained, 'but it's as if you have difficulty getting your eyes to focus properly on

71

them. Like they'd been defectively cast from the same mould, all the defects different – only you couldn't quite put your finger on exactly what those defects actually *were*, if you get my meaning. And their behaviour – that was weird too. Like the Great Big Psychotherapist in the Sky hadn't quite got round to fixing them up right – they all seemed to be missing a few neurons in the most essential places.'

'How did they get on together?'

'Don't know. We revive the stiffoids individually, and send them off likewise.'

McTavish looked up at Fremantle. 'I think I know what Cardano was trying to say,' she said, brushing off the question in his eyes. 'Can you imagine, Fremantle, that each of those new nubugs is a killing machine? And, because of some drokk-up between Earth and here, each of them is in fact a *malfunctioning* killing machine?'

He gulped. 'Yeah. I can take that on board.'

'Now, Fremantle, I guess it's not putting too much of a demand on your brain to ask you to consider the fact that Mega-City One and New Jerusalem didn't send me here with this killing machine just for the sake of their health, is it?'

'Not kind of . . . ? Well.' He wrinkled his forehead at her. 'Well, you know, just to sort of get rid of you?'

'No. I said. We're here on official business – *covert* official business. Here's the holo to prove it.' She dug the tiny rectangle out from a fugitive pocket and thrust it at him. 'I must ask you, as I instructed Chief Tech Cardano, to forget everything I've told you after I've gone. OK?'

'OK,' he said, barely glancing at the identification before hurriedly passing it back. 'We run a tight ship here at Imm-Decryp, Dr McTavish. Your secret will be safe with us.'

'*Something* – even under the circumstances I can't be more specific than that – something is causing a major threat to the very fabric of the Big Dunkin Donut. My companion and I were sent here to negate that threat. I was nervous about bringing even one of him, but there was no alternative. It's sort of like vaccination, Dr Fremantle: in order to counter a deadly disease you have to use a sub-lethal dose of something that's only a fraction less deadly. Now, because of this drokk-up, there's a fatal dose of vaccine wandering the streets of BC.'

She got up and wandered over towards the office's single window. 'That's right, Fremantle. Somewhere out *there* . . . oh, *wow*!'

It was her first sight of the Donut. She wanted to spend the next few days at this window, just feasting her eyes on the view. There was something vertiginous about it, with the land stretching towards the sky, but that was a small price to pay for the marvellous sight of . . .

She got herself in hand. Later, maybe.

With an effort she turned back to regard the bones, who was still sitting at his desk, clearly thinking hard.

'You get the message, Fremantle.'

'I do,' he said glumly. 'But I still don't see that there's anything much I can do to help you – not while maintaining the secrecy you insist on, that is.'

She stared at him.

'I could find out for you by tomorrow . . .'

'Tomorrow might be too late!'

'But it's the earliest I can do anything. See here, McTavish: this isn't Mega-City One.'

'So everyone keeps telling me.'

'We don't have flocks of lawmen we can call in,' he continued, ignoring her interruption. 'We don't have any formal law enforcement organisation at all – we just sort of . . . muddle along. We don't have the electronics to send out automatic seekers. The best I can do is request the Council of Boneses to hold an emergency meeting and offer you their official support. That way you'd at least get the active cooperation of several thousand ancillary workers – employees of the boneses, like Cardano and Strozza – plus another few hundred droids and bots. They might even mount a posse for you. And getting on for half the gang bosses pay attention to what the boneses say, too – that's a further few thousand punks out on the

73

streets helping you round up these "killing machines", although you'd have a hard job persuading them to take the drokkers alive.'

'I *need* them alive!' exclaimed McTavish.

She had perched herself on the front of Fremantle's desk and was looking at him earnestly through wisps of hair, but he was too involved in what he was saying to notice.

'But I can't get a quorum of the Council together until tomorrow at the earliest. It's late in the day, McTavish: we work fixed hours here in the Donut, even though the Eye never sets. I could try to vid some of the boneses at home – in fact, I'll start doing that right after you've gone – but Grud alone knows where most of them will be: we work hard and relax hard, us boneses.' He hit the top of his desk with a clenched fist, as if it were somehow expected of him. The jolt almost sent McTavish flying. 'Be back here at ten tomorrow morning, OK? I should have something for you then. In the meantime, McTavish, get yourself some sleep: your body hasn't yet realised how debilitating a process encryp-decryp can be, but it'll surely start doing so soon.'

McTavish spread her hands. 'I'm at your mercy, Fremantle,' she said. 'I guess.'

'I guess you are,' he said. He didn't seem any too happy about it. He looked at the vid-set on his desk as if it were an enemy. McTavish was heartened by his expression. He was indeed intending to spend the next few hours calling around.

'Any place you'd recommend?' she said.

'What? Oh, for you to stay, you mean?' He thought for a moment, his shoulders hunched. 'I never stay in hotels, for obvious reasons. There's not much call for them here, except as knocking shops. There's only the three: the Orphée, the Belle et Bête, and the Enfants – but it's terrible – oh, and the Grand, of course, but it's prohibitively expensive . . .'

'Expense is no object,' said McTavish. 'Mega-City One's picking up the tab. How do I get there?'

'Biggins'll give you the details. Might even give you a ride over there – the bloated orang-utan's due to finish work. As was I,' he added pointedly, again looking at his vid-set.

McTavish picked up the Multigob and, after a few words to hammer home the urgency of what she was expecting him to do, left him for the outer office.

The secretary, Biggins, looked up at her as she came in. There was no ready smile this time; instead, the Nandie looked drawn and apprehensive.

'How much of that did you hear?' said McTavish quietly.

'All of it, of course.' Biggins's voice was like fresh water dancing over rounded stones. She was almost whispering. 'And not with my ears. Maybe the people back on Earth don't know that we Skysouls can . . .' She gestured towards her head.

'Read minds,' said McTavish. 'Yeah, they told me.'

It's not quite as simple as that, but you get the general idea.

McTavish started backwards. The voice inside her skull had been her own, but she hadn't formulated the words. Biggins smiled nervously at her.

'You did that?' hissed McTavish. 'You spoke to me . . . in here?' Now it was her turn to point at her head.

It's not quite as simple as that, her own voice repeated. *All I did was take your own thoughts and point them in the direction I wanted them to go; you yourself chose to mentally vocalise them. It's not the same thing as telepathy – not quite.*

'Seems spugging like it to me,' said McTavish. Immediately, with a glance towards the closed door leading to Fremantle's office, she lowered her voice; she could hear him droning on to someone who, if her ears weren't deceiving her, had the misfortune to be called Dennis the Complete Bloody Sadist. 'How much of the truth was the bones telling me?'

Most of it, but the bits he skipped were the most important. Let's go – he said I might drive you to your

75

hotel, so he'll think nothing of it if we leave together. I can explain better once we're out of this place.

'Sounds good to me,' McTavish said, hoisting the Multigob up onto her shoulder. 'Lead the way. First stop the Grand Hotel and then . . .'

No, not the Grand. That's where Fremantle wants you to stay – so that he knows where you are. Despite the forcefulness of the words, Biggins was gathering together her personal possessions and jamming them into a carry-bag with apparent calm. *One of the important things he omitted to tell you was that he's merely the cat's-paw of the most unsavoury gang boss in the whole stomm-swilling bunch – an animal called Dennis the Complete Bloody Sadist. That's him he's reporting to right now. If Dennis reckons the best way to deal with you is* schleup! – Biggins drew a finger expressively across the gracile curve of her throat, then continued pulling her grey coat on – *he'll just send a few of his guys down to the Grand. I've got friends who'll put you up for a while.*

'You don't exactly have one of those typical boss-secretary passions you see on the holovid, do you?'

With that squat little drokker? This time Biggins let herself laugh out loud. *We Skysouls are a bit more discerning than you Toadstone fe– Sorry, no offence intended.*

McTavish grinned. 'Snap.'

The Nandie woman grinned back at her. McTavish wondered if a friendship was waiting to be born.

Let's get moving, said the voice in her mind.

The nearer of Dennis the Complete Bloody Sadist's eyes glared fixedly at Garbucci. The gunsel would have moved out of the focus of that powerful stare but he knew it would only follow him around the room. There was no hiding-place.

'First Cardano from the stiffoid shop, then Fremantle,' said the voicebox on the desk with a crackle and a pop. 'Why in the name of stomm do they think I should be interested in some asshead transvestite who calls himself Drokk?'

'They thaid he had a long cape and a helmet,' said Garbucci. 'Could be he'th a Judge?'

'Nah – no way. Mega-City One doesn't give a flying drokk to a rolling donut one way or the other about the Overlords, or anyone else in the Donut for that matter. I'm more interested in the woman – what did Fremantle say her name was?'

'McTavish, thir.'

'Yeah, McTavish. Small and pretty and exceptionally dispensable if anything goes wrong. Who cares a wrist-sprain if some drokking xenotheologist gets snuffed? My guess is the Justice Department reckoned they had to make a gesture in response to the Overlords' appeals, so they sent this little cutesy – maybe the Judge who'd been drokking her wanted to dump her, or something.'

'The boneth did thay she theemed dithtraught about the big guy,' ventured Garbucci.

'A diversion.' If Dennis had had a mobile hand he'd have flapped it contemptuously. 'Trouble with you, Garbucci, is you can never see through the surface of things to their subtexts.'

Garbucci groaned. Before he'd graduated to become the boss's head honcho the other goons had taken malicious pleasure in forcing him to talk about subtexts.

Dennis continued: 'The bitch McTavish was rather clumsily trying to get Fremantle's attention concentrated on these big perv lunks so that he'd stop thinking she was of any importance herself. By now she could have lost herself anywhere in the Carbuncle and . . .'

'Fremantle thaid she wath gonna put up at the Grand, bothh,' Garbucci reminded him.

'You don't for one moment think that's where she'll have actually gone, do you, Garbucci? Do you just *like* being my straight man, or something? No, if there's one place I can guarantee you Doc Mc-drokking-Tavish ain't parking her curvy little butt, it's the Grand.'

'You're undoubtedly right, thir,' said Garbucci sadly.

77

Having taken a long hard look at the picture of the spy that Fremantle had held up to the vid, the little hood had been thinking of just kind of moseying over to the Grand later on and maybe having a couple of relaxing drinks in the bar, just on the offchance . . .

'But it's not worth expending any brain-mass trying to work out where she's hidden herself,' remarked Dennis. 'She can't do us any harm – not a solitary tart in a strange world.'

'She *hath* got a Multigobbet Autotronic Offenthe Weapon,' Garbucci prodded.

'Which she probably doesn't know how to fire,' Dennis jeered. 'She's only a Gruddam *woman*, Garbucci. Anyway, Dave and Rick are shielded better than anything a Terry weapon could fire at them.'

'Should we do anything about picking up the droneth?' asked the goon after a short pause.

'The pervs? No – don't think so. They're nothing. Nothing to worry about.'

Skullcrusher was on his way home. A huge man with arms as long as a Nandie's, he lumbered rather than walked through the alleys of Brando's Carbuncle, shouldering aside the few people who were stupid enough to get in his way. Blood clung to his hairy flesh from wrists to elbows: when Skullcrusher punched someone, which was often, he punched *hard*.

He popped what looked like a boiled sweet into his mouth and chewed it with squelchy enjoyment. There was a nubug somewhere in BC with one less eye to feast on the Donut's wonders . . .

Skullcrusher Kincaid. One-twenty kilos of bone and muscle, with no room left over for brains. His spinal cord, permitted to continue functioning purely through oversight, was a column of unadulterated viciousness.

He was much admired in BC. He was the undisputed King of the Alleys.

Which made him, almost, King of Brando's Carbuncle. Most of the city's thoroughfares were alleys. The burg had developed higgledy-piggledy, with colonists throwing up their own homes and stores wherever the fancy struck them. Disagreements over siting had been frequent: so much Overlord blood had gone into the building of BC that mothers were quite right to tell their children the walls had ears. By the second phase of building – when the stores and offices, brothels and sykjoints, prisons and sex theatres and all the rest were going up – it was way too late to rationalise the street map. Brando's Carbuncle was a mass of narrow, acute-angled, generally nameless alleyways – a spider's nightmare and a tapper's dream.

Skullcrusher's source of income went far past mere tapping, of course: he was a pulveriser.

And pulverisation was at the forefront of the foggy swamp that substituted for his mind right now. He was approaching one of the main thoroughfares, sentimentally called Sunset Boulevard by his fellow Carbunklians, and he had just seen that his access to it was blocked by a figure almost as hulking as his own.

Squeezing his piggy little eyes tight against the brighter light ahead, Skullcrusher assessed the asshead. Had to be a nubug, and a recent one at that: anyone who'd been in BC longer than a few days knew about Skullcrusher and what to do when you saw him coming – drop all your valuables and run like drokk. This dimbo was just standing there, palely loitering against a patch of greasy wall, watching Skullcrusher get nearer.

The dimbo was a *big* asshead. Skullcrusher's face split into what his semi-permanent drokk, Tweedy-Pie, called one of his cute grins. Skullcrusher *liked* big assheads: if they were good and tough, they sometimes stood up long enough for you to get in a second wallop.

'Heh-heh,' rumbled Skullcrusher.

There was something odd about the asshead, though. For just a fraction of a second Skullcrusher's gargantuan progress faltered. It wasn't often you found assheads who refused to stay in focus when you looked at them. Come to think of it, it wasn't often you came across assheads who spoke to you, like this one was doing.

'"Parting is all we know of heaven,"' said the asshead, '"and all we need of hell." Emily Dickinson.'

'Huh?' said Skullcrusher Kincaid.

'"Oh, the little birds sang east, and the little birds sang west, *Toll slowly*." Elizabeth Barrett Browning,' remarked the asshead.

The asshead was wearing a big helmet with a visor over his eyes. His chest was a mass of polished metal and he was holding a little yellow and white flower delicately between the forefinger and thumb of his left hand. His right hand hovered for some reason close to one of a pair of big bulbous things that hung at his belt. Those bulbous things looked as if they might be metal, too. This was gonna be treasure-trove time for Skullcrusher.

'"Leaves have their time to fall, And flowers to wither at the north wind's breath, And stars to set – but all, Thou hast *all* seasons for thine own, O Death!" Felicia Hemans,' commented the asshead, looking up and apparently noticing Skullcrusher for the first time. 'Ho there, friend. 'Tis a fine day, is it not? Hast thou a thirst to match mine? Let us, if thou hast the time and the convivial inclination, go someplace the bee sucks, so that we may slake ourselves with the gentle dew.'

'Huh?'

'Well met, then! A swain after my own heart! Prithee lead me to where the waters chill the – '

'Spug off outta my drokkin' way.'

'A pause. The poet ponders, languishingly. Dost thou mishear my beckonments? Oh, sorry, *sorry* friend thou art!'

The time for conversation was over. Skullcrusher growled and swung with a meaty right. His whistling fist connected with a *splat* of shattering bones and splitting, overripe flesh.

Several seconds later, the pain reached him.

He stared at the ruin of his fist, then at the gore-spattered wall where the asshead had been leaning, then back at his fist again.

'Huh?'

'"My beautiful, my beautiful! that standest meekly by,

With thy proudly-arched and glossy neck, and dark and fiery eye,"' encapsulated the asshead, who was now – having moved with surely impossible speed – leaning against the opposite wall of the alley. 'Caroline Elizabeth Sarah Norton,' he added.

One fist down, thought Skullcrusher's spinal cord through the agony. That left . . . er . . . well, at least one to go . . .

He took careful aim with his left, judging the distance precisely, then packed his entire strength into a titanic, powerhouse punch that should have turned the dimbo's head into just a messy stain on the wall.

It connected with the big nubug's jaw.

'Aaargh!'

I think we, um, just ran out of fists, Skullcrusher's spinal column said nervously.

The asshead's jaw, which had taken the perfectly placed blow full on, was unaffected.

'Thou hast had thy chance,' said the dimbo nubug, shaking his head sadly. 'Thou hast betrayed our new-sprung friendship, o stranger. Thou hast certainly violated one or more of the BC city ordinances, even if 'tis as yet uncertain to me what those are. Pray forgive me for what I must do.'

Something monstrous, something gloved . . .

Something filled Skullcrusher's field of vision like a deathbird hovering on black wings in the sky over a battle's carnage.

Blat!

Some little while later Skullcrusher Kincaid managed to open his eyes. Looking down the mangled remains of his nose to try to find out how much damage he'd taken, he discovered that his shoulders seemed to be a drokk of a long way away.

Twenty metres, at a guess.

'Top of de mornin to yez,' said the new busker on Madison Avenue. 'If ye be kind enough, foin lassie, to put a credit in an old man's hat . . .'

81

'Piss off,' muttered the Reverend Sally Monella Clamhorne, turning up the collar of her coat and trying to scuttle by. She'd been out of work six weeks and felt about as generous as a publisher. Up until the Reverends Fingers and Hamfist had arrived in the Donut a few months back she'd been making a healthy living with her nightly homilies on the holovee, sucking in the cheques from the punters to help meet her necessary expenses in spreading the word of Grud. She'd been mixing with the most illustrious names around (boffing the megastars, natch), letting the viewers see them suck up to her on the show, both before and after the climax to each sermon: her celebrated Spiritual Striptease, when she removed one extra garment for every megacredit the punters pledged.

Now her career was in ashes. The two new tub-thumpers had moved in on her, informing her crisply that there were no longer sufficient hertz in the Donut for the three of them, and making her chief vid-man swallow his camera to demonstrate the strength of this argument. Maraschino Hamfist had even ripped off her Spiritual Striptease.

She stopped suddenly.

She was friendless and alone. She hadn't boffed a megastar for as long as she could recall. This new busker seemed to have a cheery face, although it was mainly masked, above the fiddle on which he was industriously scraping out old terrestrial jigs. She looked back at him. Over his mysterious visor he was wearing, at a jaunty angle, the cosmetic black eye-patch that his predecessor on this corner, Cigar Sam, had surely worn, its elastic straining close to destruction. From the mouth of an alley beyond she noticed a pair of shoes projecting, with at the least the lower half of a pair of legs attached.

Reverend Sally was nobody's fool. She'd been in show-biz long enough to know a kindred spirit when she encountered one. The new busker looked good and meaty, too – strong enough to use his fists to conquer any opposition. Together they might make a great team – a *holovee-channel-winning* team!

And maybe he was, secretly, *famous*.

She turned and moved towards him with practised coyness. As she came closer she observed a sort of indeterminacy about his appearance, but she paid this no mind, assuming it was merely that her mascara had run.

'I ain't got no credits, buster,' she said, forming her lavishly lipsticked mouth into a cute bow – superbly framed, she knew, by her heart-shaped face and the curls of her chirpy blonde hair. 'But maybe you and me we could, kind of, get things together, huh?'

'To be sure, to be sure, moi liddle colleen,' said the busker, missing not a note. He had segued merrily into an up-tempo version of the Londonderry Air.

'Say, buddy,' she said demurely, measuring the big man from head to toe and then staring pointedly at his groin, 'you built, like, in *proportion*?'

'Hardly, moi broight darlin,' laughed the musician. 'Sure an if I were I'd be six metres tall.'

After a thoughtful pause, she ventured: 'We could be partners in the most mind-drokking act you've ever imagined. You and me, just the two of us.'

'Are you, boi any chance, attemptin to solicit me in a public place?'

Reverend Sally's brow puckered. She wasn't quite sure what he meant but it sounded as if he'd got her general drift.

'Yeah, babe,' she breathed. 'I've been looking for someone else like me, with the same boundless imagination, the same willingness to pioneer into areas where no one else has ever . . .'

'Then, moi sweet darlin, yez a perp, sure as day. Take *dat*!'

And the Reverend Sally Monella Clamhorne saw one last megastar.

'What was it like here – before?' asked Petula McTavish, settling herself back into the uncomfortably cushioned plasteen passenger seat of Biggins's autocar. She assumed the bumps and bulges were in the right places for a streamlined Nandie body, but they seemed especially designed to prod her everywhere she didn't want to be prodded. She wriggled herself a bit more.

Biggins was grinning at her, enjoying the display.

'I'm going off you,' muttered McTavish. 'Rapidly.'

Still smiling, Biggins climbed in behind the wheel and, turning, put her arm along the back of McTavish's seat. She seemed to be saying something, but her lips didn't move and the xenotheologist heard nothing, even from the voice inside her mind. She was too aware of the fact that Biggins's breast was pressing against her shoulder. Then the plasteen shifted underneath her, the bulges gliding smoothly until they became concavities, and the depth of the seat reducing considerably so that she could ease herself back into it.

We keep them that way. A ripple of mirth coloured the voice. *The less inclined Toadstones are to stay in our cars, the happier we usually are.*

'Thanks,' said McTavish, her mind confused. 'Thanks. Why am I different from the other . . . er, Toadstones?'

You're not here to take anything from us.

'How do you know that? Oh.' McTavish flushed. It had been a stupid question. Of course, Biggins wouldn't just have read her surface thoughts: if only as a basic precaution, the Nandie must have done some rummaging around through the rest of McTavish's mind, finding out if there was anything there she ought to know about. 'I'm not sure how much I like being an open file to someone I've only just met.'

Forgive me. We Skysouls got out of the habit of feeling any respect towards you Toadstones a long time ago. It was a matter of reflex, reading you, as soon as you came into my office.

McTavish wriggled again. It seemed like a good time to change the subject. 'Who exactly *is* this Dennis guy?'

Biggins shifted a couple of levers at the side of the wheel and the engine beneath them started to build up a whine. The little autocar was painted a cheerful bright red, as if suggesting to the world that it was designed for speed, though McTavish doubted whether its solar-powered engine would be able to get it moving at anything much more than about forty kph.

Biggins reached with her long Nandie arms to manipulate a couple of pads near her ankles, and the autocar pulled smoothly from the kerb. There were twenty or thirty other vehicles visible on this stretch of the Boardwalk: to McTavish, accustomed to the teeming streets of terrestrial cities, the place seemed uncannily deserted.

She looked about her with interest as the car picked up speed. The sidewalks were littered with all kinds of junk – mainly paper and plastic, often blown into large heaps, between which crowds of rush-hour pedestrians picked their way. There were humans of all sizes and colours, though hardly any children except among the Nandies, who outnumbered the . . . Toadstones they towered over by about five to one. Occasionally she saw the bright colours of a mutie or, even less often, an alien.

There was something missing from the scene, and for a short while she couldn't work out what it was.

'Nobody seems to be shouting at each other,' she remarked at length.

The Overlords do enough shouting for everyone else, said the inner voice drily, *but they hardly ever walk anywhere if they can help it. Some of the later arrivals like yelling at us Skysouls, but the Overlords don't approve of it – that's their prerogative – so it doesn't happen often in public.*

'Why do the . . . Skysouls tolerate the Toadstones?' said McTavish, realising as she spoke that already she was identifying with the wrong species. She gestured towards the sidewalk. 'There's enough of you to . . .'

It's not in our nature, Biggins replied. *Besides, Korax has forbidden it.*

McTavish stopped herself short of snorting.

The area around Imm-Decryp had been largely composed of solemn-faced buildings which McTavish assumed were office blocks, but soon the little autocar was in a different part of town. Here there were stores and fast-food joints and sex clubs galore. There were more children among the adults, scuttling around either playing chase games or picking pockets – McTavish guessed the latter. There were signs saying CHEAP BOOZE and CHEAP SMOKES and CHEAP THRILLS. Very few of the stores had broken windows. Some of them were selling clothes in Nandie styles – no terrestrial human could hope to carry those long drapes and folds – and others, more prosaically, were obviously supermarkets, though very much smaller than any supermarket could sensibly be. Most of the ads posted on the walls above the shops were in two-dee, and motionless; the exceptions were the signs outside the sex clubs, which portrayed fitful thrusting and pumping with all the aesthetic sensitivity and artistic ability of a pre-adolescent graffitist. One of the signs showed a Nandie being disembowelled, and promised LIVE DEATH ON STAGE – NITELY. McTavish turned away suddenly, feeling . . .

Ashamed to be a Toadstone.

'You got it in one.'

It's a stupid thing to feel.

'Oh yeah?' McTavish pointed in the general direction of the club. She didn't turn to look at it again herself.

'Oh yeah': indeed. You're no more a part of that than I am. You're thinking like an Overlord, classifying people into Toadstones and Nandies when in fact what really matters is that they're good people or bad people.

'Yeah,' said McTavish half-heartedly. 'Sounds great in principle.'

The voice inside her fell silent.

McTavish was relieved when, quite soon, they'd left the shopping area behind and were heading through quiet residential suburbs. The autocar began to pick up speed. Out here, away from the city centre, the houses were much lower even than back in the commercial district – it was rare to see one three storeys high, and quite a lot of them were only one. She felt practically in the countryside already: the spaces separating the houses were wider than the houses themselves, and plants grew in them; often there were kids' toys there as well.

This is the slums. The wrong side of the monotrack. Half the folk who live around here are Skysouls who have adopted Toadstone ways for the duration, and the other half are recently arrived Toadstones. The voice stopped, as if it were clearing its throat, then resumed: *I'd say it was the possible future of the Donut except that the gangs rule out here in the suburbs just like in the centre. All those ideal little families have to pay their dues to one or other of the gangs or oh, look, dad's lost an eye or a leg or –*

'Please,' said McTavish, closing her eyes. 'Please don't tell me about it. Just leave me to dream about it the way it ought to be.'

Even for a Toadstone, you do make a stomm of a habit of thinking stupid, Dr McTavish.

'Huh?'

Close your eyes to the reality of the Donut, the way you're doing, and I retract what I said about your having come here without the intention of taking anything from us Skysouls . . . and I retract, too, what I said about you not being a part of what brought that torture club into being.

'Go on,' said McTavish after a while.

As far as we Skysouls are concerned, everything's already been taken by you Toadstones, and it's going to carry on being taken unless something happens. Korax told us the Toadstones wouldn't stay long before inevitably they were taken away again, or went – that we should just endure them for the necessary few short decades. Trouble is, even if you live as many years as we do, decades aren't short, the way Korax thinks they are. And for the Skysouls who end up in the club back there, or whipped to death by an angry Overlord because they forgot to call him 'sir', or hunted down and pulled apart during one of the Nandie- hunts, or gang-raped and then cut open by a bunch of good ol' boys out for a thrill, or . . . For any of them, a few decades is the same as eternity, isn't it?

McTavish's borrowed voice was growing sarcastic now, lashing at her.

So there's a lot of us Skysouls would like to kind of pre-empt the inexorable march of history, and all that guff, and hurry along the Toadstones' descent into terminal decline – get my meaning? And then there's others, like me and like the Skysouls who live in some of the houses around here, who say no, that's not the way, what we've got to do is integrate with the Toadstones so they calm down a bit, learn by example, discover the real *way life should be lived here in the Donut. But that's never going to come to anything if drokkheads like you, however good you think your intentions are, prefer to cover up your eyes and pretend that, if you keep them that way long enough, when you look again everything will be just fine, with a happy ending straight out of the kids' tapes. You do that and you're actually helping the gangs and the Overlords and all the rest of them: you're postponing your happy ending indefinitely – maybe until it's too late for there to be a happy ending any more.*

And that, Dr Petula McTavish, is rather more than you deserved to have slung at you only a few hours after you got here, and I apologise.

'Thanks,' said McTavish. 'No – no, I'm not meaning that satirically. I mean, thanks for throwing it at me. I needed waking up.'

Yeah. Sorry anyway.

Biggins pulled in to the kerb and spoke silently to the windows, which obediently wound down. Birdsong and insect-hum mixed with the yells of kids playing in a garden nearby.

I reckon we're anyway about far enough from the city centre for me to carry out a few modifications on this vehicle of mine.

'What? Oh, go ahead. Uh . . . what I wanted to talk to you about was this prediction of Korax's.' McTavish was surprised to find, somewhere along the line, she'd gone from scepticism about Korax to belief. 'The reason I came here – that was because there's a threat to the Donut. Not just the Toadstones: all of us. Now that Joe Dredd has been, well, *folded*, the threat's got to be at least double.' McTavish clenched and unclenched her hands a few times, watching the way the skin on her knuckles went from pink to white to pink again. 'I do hope I haven't been responsible for bringing your doom down upon you.'

Hey, don't get all morose and guilty, friend! We're all in this together – remember?

It's going to be your doom, too.

It had been a long day, and Milt Tiner was glad to see the end of it. What he wanted now was a couple of hours with his feet up in front of a pornovid and a few drinks on the side, then bed with a couple of the house-Nandies to keep him entertained. Telling his chauffeur to put away the autocar, the dapper man crossed the sidewalk towards the steps of his apartment block.

As he did every evening, he glanced at Shilligan in passing – only tonight the commissionaire wasn't Shilligan.

'You new?' said Tiner, pausing with a foot on the first step.

'That, pretty master, is my humble lot. Glad to please any way I can, sir.'

'Eh?'

The man was wearing a different uniform from Shilligan's, now Tiner came to look at it. A ransom's worth of metal on his chest and belt, not to mention what those guns might weigh in at. Nah – it must all be plastic painted with aluminised paints.

'Lick your boots clean, guv'nor? Nothing too menial if it pleases you, pretty sir.'

Tiner looked reflexively up at the sky. Korax's Eye didn't seem any brighter or hotter than usual.

'You're all right, fellow, are you? Look – here's a credit. Go and get yourself something long and cool to drink until you feel better.'

'That's incitement to dereliction of duty, handsome

master. Oh, woe and dolour. This is going to hurt me more than it's going to hurt you, master.'

Startled, Tiner missed the new commissionaire's hand with the credit note, and it fluttered to the ground.

'And *littering*.'

Blat!

The autocar bobbed slightly, and McTavish, jerked out of deep and gloomy thought, grabbed reflexively for the Multigob.

There was a rill of laughter in her mind.

Don't panic, friend. It's just those modifications I was talking about.

'What modifications?'

To the car. Hop out and have a look, if you like. But then we'd best get moving.

Obediently McTavish clambered out onto the sidewalk. It felt like climbing off a rowing-boat. Nothing at first seemed to have changed about the little vehicle, but then . . .

'The wheels are gone!'

The Skysoul smiled at her. Somehow the four wheels had flattened into the autocar's shape, leaving smooth bulges in the seamless fibreglass of the bodywork to show where they had been. The car itself now floated on a cushion of air.

'A hovercar,' she said, climbing back in.

Not quite, replied Biggins. She made no movements with her hands or legs, but the car pulled easily away from the side of the road. *That's not air it's floating on: it's supported by a cushion of thought.*

McTavish glanced at her companion, incredulous, then relaxed into her seat. 'Your mental powers are greater than the authorities in Mega-City One realise. I assume you've kept the Overlords in the dark deliberately?'

Yes. We don't want to be seen as a threat. Imagine how a drokkhead like Fremantle would react if he knew his secretary could make him burst into flames any time she particularly pissed her off.

90

And that went for all the other thousands of Fremantles in the Donut too, thought McTavish. The Skysouls were wise to keep things back.

'You said you were going to answer some questions,' she remarked. The autocar was picking up speed – already it was doing much more than the forty kph to which it had earlier been limited. Above her head, the roof peeled back so that her hair danced around her ears; curiously, though, the wind made no sound.

As they drove further and further into the countryside, the car picking up to several hundred klicks per hour, Biggins told her what life in the Donut had been like before the advent of the colonists from Earth. McTavish had expected to hear tales of some kind of natural paradise, but it wasn't like that at all – not quite. Although there were few large predators to threaten the widely dispersed Skysoul race, those that there were were sufficiently vicious to make up for their lack of numbers. There was a beast that, so far as McTavish could make out, somewhat resembled the now long-extinct terrestrial tiger, but with fangs half as long as a Skysoul's forearm. There were insects whose bites or stings could be swiftly fatal, injecting poisons that could stop a person's heart in seconds; regretfully, the Skysouls had finally exterminated a particular species of spider that was intelligent enough to lay cunning traps for the larger mammals, then breed in the paralysed bodies of its prey. Many of the fish in the seas were dangerous, and there was a breed of thorny plant sufficiently sentient to lash out at passers-by. And threats were by no means restricted to the plant and animal kingdoms: although Korax's Eye might stay stable for thousands of years at a time, occasionally it became active without more than a few hours' warning, blistering and sometimes killing those Skysouls and other creatures who hadn't taken the precaution of retreating into the deep caves that perforated the Donut's low mountain ranges. Windstorms were another ever-present menace: they could last for weeks on end, devastating the land with gusts up to five hundred kph.

The Skysouls themselves had not always been a benign, cooperative people. With a total area of the order of twenty-seven hundred million million square kilometres, of which less than twenty per cent was sea, leaving a land area approaching twenty thousand times Earth's, the Donut had not fostered any sense of territoriality in its primate inhabitants: why fight over land or resources when there was such an abundance of both available? Yet there were – still were – occasional crimes of violence among the Skysouls, usually because an individual had determined to close off his or her mind from the common pool, thus keeping potentially useful knowledge back from others in the hope of gaining . . . Here Biggins found herself floundering in semantics, but McTavish guessed she was trying to talk about power, or domination. And, up until about a couple of hundred thousand years ago, there had been occasional religious wars; these had been stopped only when Korax, who sounded a most reluctant deity, had finally stepped in and demonstrated conclusively before all eyes that she was indeed the sole god of the Big Dunkin Donut, and that she didn't give a drokk about the different rituals people employed to worship her – indeed, given the choice, she'd rather not be worshipped, if that would be all right with everybody.

'Sounds like the only god I've ever come across who actually deserves to be worshipped,' commented McTavish wryly.

That's what we think too, came the slightly smug response. *We worship her by regarding her as our friend and mentor, rather than as our ruler and benefactor. We all did, until recently.*

Korax had told the Skysouls where they and the Donut had come from, although she was hazy as to details. She knew Korax's Eye had once been merely a solitary and distant companion of a far greater and brighter star, and that she had spent her early years on a world going around it – a world that was much different from this one. Creatures whose nature she had never properly been able to understand – she called them the Higher-Sky Gods, implying they were somehow greater than she was herself – had brought her and the original ancestors of the Skysouls to the Donut, which she rather believed (she was uncertain) the Higher-Sky Gods had made specially to be their home. Those original creatures had been squat, hairy, shambling, short-lived, somewhat dim-witted creatures, not unlike Toadstones, but had over the millennia evolved not just to take on their modern appearance but also to integrate perfectly with their environment.

The Skysouls raised few permanent structures: there was no particular need for them, and besides they would all be blown down again by the next windstorm. They did, however, frequently put up temporary structures to protect not so much themselves as their few items of personal property from the elements. It was to a village of such dwellings that Biggins was taking McTavish now.

'What about BC?' asked McTavish. 'Surely it's overdue to get flattened by one of those windstorms.'

The area around the sphere's access port and that around the Omphalos were blessed with the most equable weather of all; Biggins was not sure whether the ancient builders had placed these structures deliberately where the climate was benign or if the climate itself had been tampered with to favour the two regions. Either way, BC was safe from serious damage for the foreseeable future and perhaps for as long as the Donut itself should survive. Both areas had been little visited by the Skysouls before the arrival of the Toadstones: around the access port the land had been unusually barren, while Korax had requested that the Omphalos be not too much visited so that she could use the range as her personal retreat.

The autocar, which had for the best part of an hour now been skimming over untamed countryside, slowed steadily until it pulled to a halt in the middle of a little cluster of thatched wooden huts. McTavish half expected to see people coming out to greet them, but there seemed to be no one else around. Once outside the car, swaying a little, she eyed the buildings more carefully. All seemed

93

abandoned except one, a little larger and a little more ramshackle in its construction than the rest.

My place, said the voice inside McTavish's mind. Biggins indicated the hut with a forward nod of her head. As they retreated from the car, it made a little sighing noise, and McTavish turned in time to see its four wheels extrude themselves from the vehicle's framework.

The inside of the hut was as cluttered as its outside had led her to anticipate.

Dump your stuff, said Biggins, waving towards McTavish's carry-bag and the Multigob. *I'll be back in a moment.*

The Skysoul retreated through a door that led off the shack's main room, and a few moments later McTavish heard the sound of running water. She grinned to herself. It was good to be reassured the Skysouls had to excrete just like anyone else.

The room she was in was characterised by a lack of furnishings. There were curtains woven crudely out of coloured grasses, and on the rough wooden floor were rugs made similarly. A couple of chairs – more accurately, plasteen seats torn out of autocars and rigged up on legs – were in facing corners. A pile of blankets along one wall served, she assumed, as a bed.

She looked away from the tumbled heap swiftly: didn't want to think too much about bed when Biggins was around. McTavish tried to probe her feelings for the tall woman, but all she found was a tangle of inchoate emotions. She recognised some of those emotions as distinctly sexual in nature, and this was where her confusion arose. Back at the Old Cap'n Birdseye Polytechnic of North Brit-Cit, as an undergraduate, she'd experimented with sex, but had never found it as engaging as xenotheology. Over the years since then, although she'd grown accustomed to being propositioned with varying degrees of subtlety – usually extremely limited degrees – she'd never felt much temptation to accept. At no time had she ever before felt sexually attracted to a woman – and she hadn't felt as attracted to *anyone* as she was now to Biggins. She had no particular hang-ups about finding herself attracted to a woman rather than a man – just that it shouldn't be *this* woman, at *this* time. This *alien*.

And it was disconcerting, to say the least, to discover that you weren't precisely the person that you'd always thought you were.

Her natural inclination was to do nothing about it, just to let the feeling pass. But her body seemed unaware of this. She remembered the faces of so many of the men with whom she'd come in contact over the years, and wondered if she looked like that around Biggins – like a sort of overeager puppy dog. She hoped not.

You don't.

She whirled. The Skysoul had come into the room behind her, and was smiling at her in a friendly way.

'You've been reading my thoughts!' McTavish blustered. 'What the drokk makes you think you've a right to – '

I was aware of your nascent feelings towards me from the moment we met. McTavish's mental voice was far calmer than her spoken one had been: its sweet-reason tone did nothing to diminish her anger. *It's not something you need to worry about, you know.*

'Who says I'm worried about anything?'

Biggins began to laugh. 'Aw, come on now, Dr McTavish,' she said, speaking out loud for the first time in a long while. 'Sit down. I'll get us something to drink. Relax.'

McTavish perched herself on one of the makeshift chairs, but almost immediately was up again, following Biggins through to a rudimentary pantry. Its walls were painted white, and made of some denser-textured wood than the rest of the shack.

'Aren't you offended by the way I'm feeling about you?' she said, wishing that there weren't a whine in her voice. 'Repelled?'

Why should I be? I'm complimented.

'But we're not even of the same species, for Grud's sake!'

Biggins put a wooden goblet of what looked like plain water in her hands. McTavish couldn't remember having seen the Skysoul pour it.

Our cultural conditionings are different, you know. Even if you and I really were of different species – which we're not – the fact that you're sexually attracted to me could only be a source of pleasure to me. I mean it when I say I'm complimented. If you feel in love with me as well, that'd be even more of a compliment. That would give me very great pleasure indeed.

McTavish could think of nothing to say. She took a gulp from the goblet, discovering that its contents were indeed just water, but with a funny aftertaste due to the lack of contaminants. Biggins stood watching her, head slightly to one side, smiling that same smile.

'You want me to fall in love with you?'

I don't want it – we don't really think like that. Let's just say that it would give me considerable pleasure if you did.

'But would it give *me* any pleasure?'

It depends what you mean by pleasure. I don't know that I can answer that for you. Come on – let's go and relax in the other room.

McTavish supposed it must be evening, although the light outside the windows had changed not at all. This was a time when, rather than sitting tensely on the edge of her seat wondering what new quicksand the conversation might stumble into, she was supposed to be relaxing in readiness for the rigours of tomorrow – facing Fremantle again, bullying him into organising the hunt for the hundred fugitive Dredds, trying to –

You won't be seeing Fremantle again. Not for a while, anyway.

'I need to round up all the bits of Joe Dredd and put him back together again,' said McTavish grimly. 'Fremantle may not be much, but he can help me do that.'

He could . . . but he won't. Not unless Dennis tells him to. And in that case, friend, you're probably in worse trouble than if Fremantle's doing his best to kill you.

'I don't follow. Who *is* this Gruddam Dennis the Complete Bloody Sadist, anyway? You said you were going to tell me, and then you never did.'

The voice inside her head seemed to be drawing breath, wondering where to start. In the hiatus McTavish felt a surge of fear inside her, a pang of lurking evil, a quasi-paranoid sense of menace threatening not just people in general but herself in particular. Although quickly quelled, the emotions were enough to push her back in her seat.

Dennis the Complete Bloody Sadist came to the Donut three years ago – or, at least, that's when we first detected his presence: it's possible the Overlords knew about him earlier. He's a Toadstone, of course, but no one's certain exactly how he got here: presumably he must have come via the MT and through Imm-Decryp, the way you did, because there's no record on any of the spaceship manifests of anyone who could be him.

The voice took another seeming breath. *He lay dormant for a long while, not apparently doing very much except carving out for himself a small empire in the underworld of BC: he ran a few strings of pimps, a couple of minor casinos, maybe a brothel or two – his profile was low enough that no one paid much attention to his activities. Then, a few months ago, he decided to take a more active role in BC life: four of the major gang bosses were assassinated – there was no attempt to cover things up, pretend accidents, or anything like that – and their organisations taken over by shadowy figures whose puppet-master we discovered, in all four cases, to be Dennis. For some weeks the streets seemed littered with the corpses of those within the taken-over empires who had been stupid enough to voice dissent. And they weren't just being killed: Dennis's thugs seem to take pleasure in tormenting their victims. Much of this massacre was being carried out in public: the murderers knew that everyone was too frightened of their boss to try to intervene. There was a lot of passing by on the other side.*

There seemed to be tears in the voice now.

Dennis's activities began to escalate. It was he who introduced the torture clubs, where so many Skysoul slaves have been led to cruel, barbaric deaths for the entertainment of the Toadstones. Some of the Overlords tried to intervene, but there was always a long, elusive chain of command between Dennis and whatever was going on. The few Overlords who came anywhere close to him would come home one day to find that their wives and their mistresses and their kids had been butchered, the guards set over them either having met the same fate or having deserted to join Dennis's mob. In the end – and the end wasn't long in coming – all of the Overlords perforce threw in their lot with Dennis.

Then, quite recently, Dennis did something bizarre – something we don't as yet fully understand. He brought in from Earth a couple of Toadstone fundamentalists – atheist *fundamentalists: the Reverend Messrs Hamfist and Fingers. He took over a pair of holovee channels for them, and they've been broadcasting almost constantly ever since, mainly at us 'Nandies', trying to shake us from our faith in Korax. They've had some success. There have been some ugly scenes among the Skysouls, with mobs – there's no other word for them – battling it out over which strain of atheism is the One True Word.*

'And you don't know why he's doing this?' McTavish's voice was so quiet that for a moment she hardly recognised it for her own. She put her empty goblet down on the rug beside her feet, suddenly afraid of breaking its stem.

Destruction, obviously. Already these preachers have destabilised a Skysoul society that has been living in almost perfect harmony for millennia. But why would he wish to do that? We are already as enslaved a race as it is possible to be: destabilisation, the sowing of division, can't make us any more so. For a time we thought he might be hoping to create a civil war among us that would spill over to bring about the destruction of the Overlords and the other Toadstones, leaving him as sole master of the Donut, with us as his slaves, but that doesn't seem to make sense either.

*If we were to declare war on the Toadstones it would be on
Dennis and his goons as well: he'd be destroyed along with
the others.*

'It sounds as if the person he wants to destroy is Korax,'
observed McTavish.

That, said the voice that was hers and yet not hers, *is
impossible. We think.*

'Hey, buster, dat's da ladies you goin inta! Da gents is
over dat way.'

'And what makes you think I'm not a lady?' said the
hulking figure in the dress cape and the uniform.

'Er, nuttin, ma'am.'

As time wore on, other Skysouls began to call in at
Biggins's shack, sometimes singly, sometimes in groups
which McTavish guessed must be family units. In defer-
ence to her, they spoke aloud: most of them stumbled
over spoken words, and some remained silent except for
occasional mispronounced interjections. None showed the
least sign of suspicion towards this stranger Toadstone in
their midst; McTavish supposed that Biggins must be
radiating some sort of telepathic broadcast that McTavish
was to be trusted – that, despite her birth, she was an
ally, or at least a potential ally.

The conversation of the Skysouls – eventually there
were about thirty of them, including half a dozen children
– seemed to be about nothing of any great importance,
although McTavish could not tell what kinds of mental
messages might be whizzing backwards and forwards
between them. She'd half expected, after the first few had
made their near-silent entrances – slipping in through the
door so unobtrusively that it was almost as if they'd been
there, unnoticed, all along – that she was to be witness to
a revolutionary meeting, but instead the chat was of far
travels, of confrontations in BC, of incidents in the race's
dim past, of the benevolence of Korax, of the stupidities
of Toadstones (present company excepted, of course,
with a nod of the head and a friendly smile), of the latest

dance that had been staged for the goddess on the great proscenium set a mere thousand kilometres from the foothills of the Omphalos, of the way that the flowering grockleberry plants this year tasted more astringent than usual, of the fact that little Wind-in-Rushes was still wetting himself most sleeptimes, of . . .

After a while, Biggins and three male Skysouls went out to forage for food, and McTavish tagged along. She wanted to ask her tall friend a question in private.

'Biggins,' she said when the two of them were standing alone beside a yellow halacrim bush some little distance from the men, 'could you tell me something in spoken speech?'

'Of course, friend,' the Skysoul replied in her almost painfully beautiful voice. 'And I will block our minds so that no one else can hear our conversation.'

'Can all those people' – McTavish gestured at the shack, which had fallen silent since her departure, and at the three men – 'can they all . . . overhear my thoughts just the same way you can?'

'Yes. Most have already explored your mind. Remember, we Skysouls do not regard that as an intrusion.'

McTavish sucked her lower lip in a way she couldn't remember having done since childhood. What next? she thought self-mockingly. Was she going to cross one foot over the other and start screwing her hands together?

'You sensed,' she said at last, 'the way I was . . . physically attracted to you almost as soon as I did myself – the moment we first met.'

'Yes. In fact, some while before you did.'

'Well, can all these other friends of yours . . . can they read down to the same depth as that inside me?'

'Yes,' said Biggins, taking McTavish's hand in her own for the first time. 'Of course they can. It's one of the first things they discovered about you.'

'Oh, Grud,' muttered McTavish. 'This is embarrassing.'

'Why should it be?'

'Look,' said McTavish, throwing Biggins's hand off, 'it's bad enough I should find I've got the hots for *you*.

100

Now I've got the hots for all your friends as well. I feel like I'm about to explode, or something. Even a couple of the older kids are looking pretty yummy. It's all getting a bit much!'

'It's nothing unusual,' said Biggins gently. 'A good many Toadstones have exactly the same sort of reaction to us, and they resent it, just like you – but more so, in a lot of cases. Why do you think the Toadstones treat us so brutally? They don't like the fact we turn them on; they see it as a failing in themselves, being attracted to people they've decided are just animals, and so they switch things around so it's All Our Fault.'

'Oh.'

'And the feeling's not entirely unmutual, Dr McTavish. We're not much bothered by trivialities like body shape – that's a Toadstone way of thinking. We see your mind as having a shape and appearance of its own – a very attractive one, to us.'

McTavish turned to look up into Biggins's eyes, which seemed to have grown darker: there was a trace of peat in the stream-water.

The Skysoul kissed her lightly on the cheek, then reached past her to pluck a particularly fecund head of halacrim flowers.

'Garbucci!'

'Yeth, bothh.'

'You've been gone longer than I thought. Tell me – what have you discovered?'

Garbucci, gathering his thoughts, blew a bubble and let it slowly collapse; he favoured green bubbleguck because in the prevalent light of the Donut it looked almost black, and hence threatening. 'Well,' he said at last, 'the woman McTavish wath latht obtherved leaving the offitheth of Dr Elmer Fremantle at 18:10 in the company of a Nandie thlut called Bigginth. They protheeded in Bigginth'th autocar in an approckthimately counter-thpin direction to the fringeth of Brando'th Carbuncle before converting the vehicle to hoverthought mode.'

101

Dennis the Complete Bloody Sadist had no eyebrows, but a commotion from the jar on the desk indicated that he was doing his best to raise them nevertheless.

'"Hoverthought mode"?' he snapped. 'I understood only the elders among the Nandies could do that?'

'Thith Bigginth ith no elder,' said Garbucci soberly. She'th apparently a bit of a dish – like, Billiam Bailey, the guy in the antigrav pack doing the obthervation, had the hotth jutht ath much for the Nandie dame ath he did for the thenotheologitht, which ith quite a hot lot of hotth, bothh.'

'Did the Nandie know she was being watched?'

'No.'

'Hmm.' The water in the jar fermented a little further. 'I get the impression, Garbucci, that the Nandies might have been holding back a little from us. If this Biggins bitch is able to shift an autocar into hoverthought, how much else is she capable of doing? Blowing a man's brains out just by looking at him?'

'I got the idea from Bailey she could already do that,' mumbled Garbucci.

The mouth of Dennis's open-topped corpse, propped up in the seat behind the desk, suddenly clicked wide into a macabre grin. The general impression was that someone had cut a slice out of a stiff's dead flesh.

'You're a very funny guy, Garbucci.'

'Thankth, bothh.'

'Where did they go next?'

'Luckily Bailey had a thouped-up antigrav pack – he wath able to keep up with them. They carried on in the thame direction for about thickth hundred and theventy-eight klickth until they got to a Nandie thettlement. That'th where they're holed up now – and with a gang of other Nandieth that'th joined em.'

'Hmm. And Bailey's still out there?'

'Sure ith, thir. Tell you the truth, thir, my guethh ith that it'th more with pocket truncheon that'th keeping him there than hith devotion to duty, if you get my meaning, thir.' Garbucci began to blow another bubble.

'This is important. We may have to move fast! Answer me, or by drokk you're gonna be eating your own –'

Ploop!

Oh . . . shhhiiiitttt!

'Hang on a thec, bothh. My bubbleguck – I'm a bit, uh, thtuck here.'

'Is Bailey on his own?' The voicebox was dancing with fury.

'Uh, too right, thir.'

'Then order him up some reinforcements – some real hard meat. A dozen at least. Rope in Skullcrusher Kincaid as well, as a bit of freelance talent. Our best way to deal with this menace from Earth is to take her out now – *right* now! And her over-Gruddam-talented Nandie pal as well. Get Giolitto from the east side; Jock Becattini would be good, and the Moreno twins. Guys like that. Guys who'd eat their grannies for breakfast only they had her for supper last night. I don't want anyone in this detachment who's gonna hold back for a second. I want this whole Nandie gang, and the McTavish woman, taken out so thoroughly it'll be like they never existed.'

'OK, bothh. It'll be a pleasure. Only we can't take Thkullcrusher Kincaid. Thomebody'th thnuffed him – jutht a couple of hourth ago. I heard jutht ath I wath coming in.'

'Shee-it. Skullcrusher Kincaid. Must have bumped into some real tough dude. Must have been like killing the Omphalos.'

'Ackthidentth happen, thir,' said Garbucci, shrugging. Who should give a drokk if Skullcrusher was alive or dead?

'Hmm.' Dennis was thinking again. 'On second thoughts,' he added just as Garbucci was turning towards the door, 'let one of the Nandies live – one of the males. Cut off his hand or something to give him a way of remembering us, then let him go so that he'll tell all his other Nandie cronies what they're dealing with if they get on the wrong side of Dennis the Complete Bloody Sadist – got that?'

'Got it,' said Garbucci, looking back into the room as the door soughed shut. 'In thpadeth.'

'. . . an' I say unto you, ma brothers 'n' sisters in the One True Way, I's wantin' yewall to renounce the teachins of thaim as'd have ya walkin' in the ways of disrighteousness through the Valley of the Shadow of Death, to say to thaim as'd want you bowin' down and kneelin' and scrapin' youselves in front o' they false gods an' icono-clasts an' gravure images, to tell thaim as is a wantin' yewall to deliver up ya souls to the damned an' accursed an' debased scum of the firmaments – I say to you, I say, turn the other cheek an' renner unto Fingers what is Fingers's. I do! Thaim as wants ta buck your spirits down low, *thaim as has bedevilled theyselves in the temples of Grud an' Korax an' Mammon an' the other ungodly gods* – thaim is the ones who want yewall not ta send me your con-tryee-byoo-shuns for the ongoin' work of the Mar-garet Thatcher Charitable Fund-Raising Community of Blessed Hypocrisy Inc., aw the MTCF-RCoBHI, as we an' ma sweet lady Jaboticaba do calls it when we talkin' 'bout it 'mongst ousselves. So git out your plastic now, ma brothers 'n' sisters, an' don' think in tens aw hunderds of credits, think big, real B-I-G, like (ma sweet friens in the eyes of the Bumper-Size Vacuum That Is True Reality) think M-E-G-A, ifn yewall valyas tha good looks you was gave!'

The applause was thunderous. Atheism was the new rock 'n' roll. The aides who daily scoured the streets of BC for Rev. Fingers's invited studio audience had excelled themselves this evening. These were not just your normal collection of bums and drunks – the holoca-meras usually had to be directed with care so that the folks at home didn't get treated to too many moonings or Technicolor yawns – but two parties brought here at gunpoint from the Annual General Meetings of two rival local branches of the Big Dunkin Donut Women's Insti-tute. No sooner had they arrived and stopped pelting each other with jars of greyish marmalade and lethally weighted scones than they'd decided Rev. Fingers was something of a slab, a bit of all right, a definite nudging with the elbows, an excuse for a glazing of the eyes and a sudden focusing of the attention. The illusion was jarred slightly when he opened his mouth and talked, so by tacit conspiracy they were cheering whenever they could and for as long as possible.

There was a single odd-one-out in the front row of the stalls: a massively bulked, hugely helmeted figure munching the studio-issue popcorn as stolidly as any Socrates. But he, too, was cheering at all the right moments, so the aides were wisely leaving him be.

'Yeah, ma lifeblood friens, ya can vid through ya kind donations to me, the Reverend Dave "No Messin" Fingers of the Margaret Thatcher Charitable Fund-Raising Community of Blessed Hypocrisy Inc., awn any of the followin' nummers . . .'

This was enough to bring on another fit of yelling and foot-stamping. Fingers made the most of it, grinning and bowing, milking the audience with his arms, beseeching them for more of their tumultuous music.

The big guy in the front row was getting to his feet. A standing ovation, yet! Many of the women were following suit. The shiny domed helmet caught one of the spots and made light skitter and dance around the darker regions of the stage behind which Fingers strutted.

'Clap ya hands, clients,' cried Fingers in a moment of sudden inspiration, 'if ya don' believe in gods!'

The walls shook in response.

The big punter with the popcorn was coming closer. Now Fingers could see that the top of the guy's helmet had been tinted a curious shade of grey-blue. There was a badge on his chest saying DREDD – a name Fingers reckoned should mean something to him, something not altogether pleasant, but right at the moment, in the heat of all this frenzied excitement, he couldn't put his finger on the reference . . .

'I believe!' bellowed the helmeted guy, coming to a halt. 'I believe in the word of this here our friend, the

Reverend Dave, and that he is a true prophet of nihilism! Let him perform unto us one of his sweet miracles!'

'A miracle! A miracle!' the audience began to chant. 'Give us a miracle!'

'Get 'em off!' bayed a sizeable minority, and the aides moved in swiftly with raised stunsticks.

Oh, drokk! thought Fingers. The miracle was supposed to be later in the show. But I'd be dimbo not ta take advantage when the suckers are this eager. That dork with the baby-blue helmet's doin' my job for me – 's a wonder any of the ol' dearies' knees is able to keep 'em standin' up. Hope the tech crew have got the drokkin' miracle set up early . . .

'Ma sweet kissin'-cousins,' he announced, raising his magnificent arms to tell the throng that he desired some quiet. After several long moments, it arrived. He struck a pose in the principal spotlight, knowing his brightly illuminated profile was going out uncensored to over a million Nandie viewers. 'You an' I an' everyone else knows that there ain't no miracle profounder than the miracle of life itself, an' that there ain't no trickery needed from me to show us all that. But out there' – a huge sweep of his arm – 'there may be thaim who is still doubters, who still thinks that True Evangelical Atheism is too easy a solution to the problems that's facin' all humankind today. So, to settle they's hash, in a manner of speakin' . . .'

Two aides, both females, both looking flustered and cross, and both clad in the minimum requisite number of sequins, trundled on-stage a collapsible wooden table bearing an ancient-style opera hat and a brightly coloured silk handkerchief. Pulling a pair of white gloves from his pocket, the preacher slipped them onto his hands and gestured at the equipment as his aides scurried off into the wings.

'As yewall kin see, ma true believers an' clients, this ain't nuthin but a ordinary table, a ordinary hat an' a ordinary snotrag, but jus' in case there should stalk among you some as is tainted with the disease of devoutness, I beseech one of you to volunteer to check it out. You'll do, ma brother,' he added, beckoning to the big sucker.

'Glad to oblige, citizen.'

'Awright, ma brother – tek a look in this hat. See nothin'?'

'Nothing. Just a plain, ordinary hat.'

'An' this snotrag.'

'Nothing in it but snot,' reported the uniformed guy after a fastidious examination.

'So's ifn I put ma snotrag over the top of ma hat, nothin' should happen?'

'Sure seems like it . . . uh, brother.'

'Wayall' – Reverend Dave whipped the handkerchief away – 'willya all jus' tek a look at *that*!'

A somewhat sleepy-looking white pigeon poked its head out of the hat and surveyed the scene. It seemed unfazed by the yelling and the bright lights and the fact that all eyes were on it. With a constrained flutter of its wings it jumped from the hat onto Fingers's wrist, where, after a moment, it began preening itself.

The big punter standing next to the evangelist was looking sour. 'Don't seem much of a miracle to me,' he said. 'I've seen trickers back in the carnivals in Mega-City One could do that, no problem. All they do is they have the pigeon down the front of their trousers, see, and then . . .'

'I'd shaddap the blasphemin' ifn I was you,' muttered Fingers tersely. Louder, he said: 'But, ma everlovin' kindred in the bright light of the Bumper-Size Vacuum That Is True Reality, it ain't enough that this genewine livin' bird, its feathers as white an' pure as the lustre on the face of the mindless Yooniverse, has been brought into existence by the sheer force of your blindin' credool-ity. This bird has bin given, by the kindness of the quantum randomness that is the sum total of all existence, the power to seek out and destroy our enemies – the accursed stains upon existence that still owe they allegiances to gods! Go gittem, Fang!'

The pigeon dug its head out from under its wing, and a

107

malicious light came into its little red eyes. It squawked harshly, its beak seeming to grow rapidly and gain serrations along its hooked underside. Its gaze fastened upon one of the less hysterical WI members, halfway back in the stalls towards the doors with the green EMERGENCY EXIT signs, and suddenly the bird took wing.

Like a hawk, it darted towards the suddenly terrified woman. She put up her hands to shield her face – but too late!

The deathbird struck her right eye beak-first. Blood and jelly flew, spattering the audience for three rows on either side. As she screamed, they applauded even harder.

More blood.

Another scream.

A scream barely heard through the cacophony of cheers.

The bird fluttered upwards, clutching half a nose, trailing blood, in its cruel-looking beak.

'The Bumper-Size Vacuum That Is True Reality has been served, ma blessed clients!' bawled Fingers. 'The true believers have been cast out from among our depths into that place from which there ain't no returnin'! Praise be! Praise be! But don', viewers at home, firget they vidphone nummers an' the deep, soul-driven need for ya ta think M-E-G-A . . .'

A declivity in the plain; a stream passes through; elderly trees hunch over. Four hundred metres distant, the shack is silent but tense with the pressure of occupancy. There are clouds overhead, and against one of these a cluster of tiny black dots move, like distant insects, but neither McTavish nor Biggins notices them. Biggins can sense that a part of McTavish is wondering why it is still daytime, why cool grey shadows are not protecting them from stray eyes. She runs a long forefinger down the centre of the Toadstone's forehead and then to the tip of McTavish's short nose.

How strange the Toadstone's body is, the way it curves

108

in all sorts of places alien to her own Skysoul knowledge, and yet is in its own terms perfectly aesthetically balanced.

She feels the pulse of McTavish's thoughts, and moulds them into channels of her own choosing.

You're a long way from home, Earthling. A very long way . . .

'I wish I were further.' The Toadstone's voice is hardly more than a whisper. 'I wish I'd travelled far enough and fast enough that I'd left the Toadstones on the wrong side of the Galaxy. I wish that the only folk I knew were Skysouls – and even those I'd gladly surrender if you were there, Biggins.'

Biggins laughs quietly. *You'd have to learn the Skysoul rules of wishing, if you were to be truly one with us,* she observes. *We never wish for anything that's impossible to attain.*

The Toadstone reaches up a pale arm towards Biggins.

'Tell me, Biggins,' she says, 'tell me this. "The Big Dunkin Donut" – that's a Toadstone name. What's the *Skysoul* name for this place?'

Just 'the World'. We never thought to give it another name.

'And what's *your* name, your *real* name?'

Biggins smiles affectionately. *We don't really use names much. What need is there for them when every time two Skysouls meet they can as easily exchange the entireties of themselves as they can an artificial labelling? We have formal names for use when we talk about each other, or remember the people of our past: we don't regard them as important, except the name Korax. And we have secret names given us by the goddess at birth – these we share only with our triples . . . our* true *lovers, I guess you'd say.*

'Oh.' McTavish falls silent. Biggins can sense her withdrawing.

My real name, she begins, *is* . . . Her thoughts break off. *Wait! Hush! Listen! What's that?*

She sits up rigidly, looking back towards the little cluster of shacks.

'What the – ?'

Silence! Hush, Toadstone! Emergency! Biggins repeats the commands out loud, in the grating Toadstone tongue, to make sure the xenotheologist understands.

She leaps to her feet, pushing McTavish roughly back to the ground.

Now that she is listening, she can hear whines like those of angry insects descending towards her shack. Eyes flaring, she looks up at the sky. Half a dozen Toadstone men, maybe more, mostly in black. Coming down quickly now. No reaction from inside the shack – the Skysouls there must have been too busy communicating among themselves or eavesdropping on McTavish's and Biggins's lovemaking to have noticed the approach of the intruders . . .

'What's going on?' hisses McTavish.

Biggins glances back at her. The pale little pink and white body is shadowed by ferns. *Stay there! Don't move! This is nothing you can help with!*

'But I – '

Shut up! You can only hinder me! This is my *business. Skysoul business.*

The first plastex charge hits one of the empty shacks square on. There is a mushroom of flame. Wood flies. Biggins feels the heat a split second before the blast tries to tear her from the ground. She knows the hackles are rising all down the length of her spine, lifting her red mane of hair proud of her back. Her lips pull away from her teeth.

Whatever happens, stay here. If the worst comes to the worst, make your own way back to the city as best you can. You can gain us nothing by trying heroics, Petula: it's more important to the Skysouls that you carry on living. Got that?

'Got that,' says McTavish subduedly. 'I got that.'

Another of the empty shacks goes up with a crump. All seven of the armed Toadstones are on the ground now, shouting coarsely at each other, swaggering as they march on the defenceless huts, bulbous Firehammer KGs couched in their arms. From the door of Biggins's own hut a child's head appears, and then is immediately withdrawn.

Wait! says Biggins one last time, glaring ferociously at McTavish.

Then she is off, haring across the grass towards the nearest attacker, moving silently and at such speed that her lean body blurs almost into invisibility. She strikes him in the centre of the back with her fingers held rigidly, and almost breaks him in half. His spine shatters under the impact, making a noise that only she, so close to him, can hear through the crackling of flaming wood.

Darting away, she catches her foot on the outstretched arm of the dying man. His forearm instantly snaps like a dry twig, but still she goes sprawling end over end, somersaulting three times before landing on her back with a *whamph*, the wind driven out of her. She would black out – she *should* – except that her rage is now so high that she refuses to; instead she forces air back into her lungs, banishes the pain from her consciousness, and surges back to her feet.

One of the other Toadstones has noticed what has happened to his fellow. His mouth is slowly opening ready to give vent to a cry of terror; his slow bovine Toadstone head is sluggishly turning towards her.

Giving herself no time to think, she cartwheels sideways, slipping away from his gaze. Then, crouched low, she spears towards him, her arms stretched out in front of her, her fingers forming a stiff plane as unyielding as the edge of an axe-blade.

The impact drives her hands right into his belly, up beyond the wrists. A spray of blood and other fluids covers her body from groin to breasts. She clenches her fists and wrenches her hands apart, tearing through flesh and soft organs, shredding him open. A sting of unheeded pain as she slashes open the back of one hand on a rib. Then, while he is still realising that he is dead, she is dancing away, flailing her hands in the air to rid them of

111

the sticky, vile-smelling Toadstone gore, her feet singing across the coarse, uneven grass.

With the twin blazes to her right, she runs diagonally across the hamlet, her rearing red mane seeming like a fiery tracer shot. The target of her aim has just enough time to drop himself to one knee and start raising his heavy Firehammer KG to his shoulder, but then she has grabbed the weapon by its barrel and is tearing it out of his hands, ripping the finger trapped in the guard out of its socket, and is swinging the weapon round in a whistling circle and striking him in the throat, deeply enough that his head almost leaves his shoulders.

Time, time. All this is taking time. Three Toadstones dead. Still four more to go. However fast I move it only needs one of them to target my shack and . . .

As if to spite her, her hut goes up in a gout of flames, mocking her thoughts. There are screams – true, high Skysoul screams, not the braying noises the Toadstones make. A little boy – Wind-in-Rushes, who wets himself during sleeptimes – staggers from the doorway, a pillar of fire, covered in the clinging inflammable jelly that explodes from each of the Firehammers' projectiles. Out of mercy, Biggins sends a mental blast at the child, annihilating his brain; he'll live a while longer, but he'll have knowledge of nothing, not even his agony. *I wish I could deal with Toadstones the same . . .*

There is another eruption, this time over to her left. To an unsubtle ear it would sound no different from the rest, but to Biggins it has a quite distinct timbre. Still dashing at full speed across the ground, she turns her head. One of the attackers must have activated his antigrav pack to try to gain a high vantage. He's been shot out of the sky, and is plummeting down in a plume of fire.

The stupid drokking Toadstone. She's . . . My fine Toadstone, how I love you, but I fear you've . . .

The Multigob speaks again, and another of the attackers is nothing but an explosion of blood and fragmented limbs. His head shoots straight upwards, turning and turning like a well-booted football, his astonished gaze swishing across the scampering Biggins.

'Stand still a second, for Grud's sake, Biggins!' screams McTavish, her voice sounding pathetically tiny amid the buffeting of the boiling air. 'Throw yourself down! I can't see you not to hit you.'

Biggins discovers she is only a few metres from a big Toadstone dressed all in black leather. His head is shaven, and across the back of his skull are tattooed the words DROKK DROKKING NANDIES. He has heard McTavish's voice as well, because he is turning smoothly, his Firehammer KG swinging around towards the thicket where McTavish is hiding.

Sparking a prayer towards Korax that the xenotheologist's reactions are slower than this goon's, Biggins dives forward, catching him behind the knees, hearing his kneecaps splinter. He jack-knifes, screaming, his full weight landing on her back. This time when the wind is driven out of her it refuses to return. She finds herself sobbing, her chest and shoulders heaving, as reality swims uncertainly towards and away from her and towards her again. Bitter bile fills her throat.

The weight on top of her is moving, squirming – even through her own pain she can feel it. She has to do something to stop the drokker getting enough of a hold on his senses to turn his weapon on McTavish. Starring her legs, she drives her heels together with all the force she can summon, catching his writhing head between them. Bone smashes – whether his or hers she can't say as the edges of the World are scorched black, and then the circle of blackness closes in and in until all she can see at its centre is a tiny point of diamond-sharp light and then even this is blocked out.

There was one attacker still on his feet. She couldn't see what had happened to Biggins – the last McTavish had seen of the tall woman, she'd been moving with that dizzying speed of hers behind one of the blazing buildings; then a skin-headed man beyond the flames had gone

113

tumbling, which she assumed was Biggins's work. Now no one seemed to be left alive except herself and the solitary Toadstone – I am a Toadstone as well, she thought fleetingly, but she didn't feel like one and right now she was aware of a colossal chasm of difference between herself and the other.

His back to her, he was throwing his weapon away from himself. He could see the wreckage of three erstwhile comrades. Still looking in the direction of the inferno, he raised his hands above his head. Clearly he was totally unaware that McTavish was advancing towards his back.

'Stop right there, buster!' she said. 'Freeze!'

'I thurrender!' he said, his voice breaking. 'What in the drokk have you – '

She jabbed the Multigob in his back. 'Stuff it, drokk-head. I'll say when you can talk.'

'I – '

'Don't dare turn round. Just freeze, I tell you. I'd enjoy blowing your guts out.' Another jab with the Multigob to tell him the threat wasn't idle.

'OK, now you can answer me a few questions.'

'Sure thing.' He was regaining some control of his voice, but she sensed that it was ready at any provocation to start rising again.

'Who sent you?'

'De-Dennith the Complete Bloody Thaditht.'

'I could have guessed. I *should* have guessed. That drokkhead's going to . . .' Steady, she told herself. Play it steady. Time enough to think of vengeance later. Where in *drokk's* name is Biggins? She's dead. She must be. She'd have said something to me by now if she . . . No. steady. Keep it steady. 'Why?' she asked, nudging his spine again, viciously.

'The thlut – the nubug thlut. He knowth why she'th here. He wanted her dead. You Nandieth were jutht caught in the crothhfire – we didn't mean to . . .'

What in the name of . . . ? He thinks I'm a . . . He thinks that Dr Petula McTavish is dead! And why not? That might be the best thing to be . . . for a while. But

114

how could I . . . No – I couldn't carry it off. But rats can be made to . . .

'The nubug slut is tougher than you or Dennis thinks,' she said, forcing her voice into a deeper register, making it as harsh as she knew. 'What's your name, drokkhead?'

'Ga-Garbucci.' She had felt the jolt of realisation shock through him. He was as ready as any man she'd ever known to sell out his cause. He'd do anything to save himself from the death he thought was only seconds away. She hoped.

'Well, Garbucci, today's your lucky day. As you can see, I'm tougher than your boss, and I can be a whole lot nastier when the mood hits me.'

'Yeah. Yeah. I thee that. Yeah.'

'You're going to go back to BC and you're going to report to Dennis that your mission was achieved, only you met unexpectedly stiff resistance and lost all six of your sidekicks to the nubug slut before you finally shafted her. It was the Multigob made her so hard to take out. You got enough of a brain to remember that?'

'Yeah, I got it thtraight.' His hands were beginning to falter in the air, so she belted the Multigob's nose into him savagely, enjoying his involuntary grunt of pain. 'You're thnuffed, and tho are all the drokking Nandieth that wath with you. I can remember that.'

'And if you should think of trying to let it slip to him, should you even so much as *hint* that I'm very much alive . . . well, you can see what happened to your friends.' Another belt with the hard, still-hot snout of the firearm.

'Ye-yeth.'

'I'll know. The same way I knew you were coming, drokkhead. That's why I let you take the Nandies out, waste yourselves on those animals, while I picked you off one by one. If you betray me to Dennis, you're dead meat – scattered over a surprisingly large area. Got it?'

'Uh-huh – got it.'

'Then you'd better take a wound, just to make your story convincing.'

She poked him again, then spun the heavy weapon

115

around in her arms to grab the barrel, repeating – although she didn't know it – the manoeuvre Biggins had performed scant minutes earlier. She swung the Multigob around her head and crashed its butt into the side of Garbucci's skull.

He fell like an ox.

She knelt beside him. There was blood dribbling from his ear. Already his head was bulging up into a massive, angry bruise. Oh rats, she thought. Maybe I've killed him. That'd foul up my plans, for sure. Oh, you clumsy oaf, Petula . . .

He'll be OK. The voice of her thoughts was unchanged, but she instantly recognised it as not her own.

'Biggins!' she yelled, leaping to her feet. 'Biggins, you're alive!'

Alive but very uncomfortable.

McTavish peered around the searing landscape.

One of the Toadstone stiffs seemed to be fighting with itself. A chill struck at McTavish: she remembered tales she'd heard of zombies, walking corpses . . .

Don't be silly. It's me.

The dead man was turfed aside as Biggins rose groggily to her knees.

McTavish ran over, dropping the Multigob carelessly, and threw her arms around the taller woman, helping her drag herself to her feet. Once upright, Biggins swayed and McTavish was certain she was going to fall over again, but the Skysoul shoved her gently away.

'You all right?'

All right . . . ish. The Skysoul grinned sadly. *The pain of my body is as nothing compared to . . .*

She let the thought fade, gazing towards the bonfire of her hut.

'Your friends,' said McTavish, aghast that for some moments she'd forgotten about them.

They died quickly, said Biggins. *My grief is lessened because of that.*

* * *

116

An hour later McTavish was driving the bright red autocar – unmodified, this time – back towards BC. It felt strange, being dead. So far as the Donut was concerned, she no longer existed. There was a sense of freedom, of freshness, that crowded out some of her gloom about the deaths of the Skysouls she had so briefly met . . . about the sudden parting from her lover.

They'd kissed amid the smell of ashes.

It wouldn't be an eternity until she saw Biggins again, she told herself. The tall woman was fleeing towards the Omphalos, towards Korax's lair. The Donut's pressing need for the queen-goddess to intervene far outweighed any taboo the Skysoul might have had against disturbing her contemplation. The goddess, if she were not already aware, must be informed – must be persuaded by her subject to come to the Toadstone city.

Which was where McTavish would be. She had a job to do. First, she must round up the scattered fragments of Joe Dredd. Second, she and he had a mission to complete. Third, with or without him, she had a few scores to settle – some nameless Skysoul lives to avenge.

Fourth – yes, she'd leave Dennis the Complete Bloody Sadist to last.

. . . And Now For A Short Intermission, Courtesy Of Our Lovely Sponsors Country Vistas™ Plush-Lined Organic Nasal Tissue

An electromagnetic signal would have taken over half a million years to reach the three True Persons, whose trawl through the long spiral arm had, since making structural alterations to the outer planetary system of a half-forgotten G-type star, encountered three further pre-machine civilizations.

So much for electromagnetic signals. The sensor implanted in the brain of the queen-goddess Korax was designed both to receive and to transmit along transcendental wavelengths that travelled through the ether faster than thought itself – and thought, as every youthful AI knows, travels at tachyonic speeds. There was even speculation among the higher worshippers of the Great Sponge that their deity might have organised the Universe such that radiation within the transcendental spectrum could travel at velocities greater than the infinite, reaching its destination some little while before departing from its point of origin. Whatever the truth, if there was a delay between an impulse leaving the organic Korax's mind and its reaching the receptors of the machine Korax, it was imperceptible.

'The signal from your namesake is faltering,' observed Thumper sanctimoniously.

'Golly!' remarked Bonzo. He was in the midst of making some improvements in the drive systems of the drones. The long intervals between stars were, as he put it, a 'good time for gettin' those jobs done that otherwise would just *never* get done'.

There was a microsecond's silence as Korax checked Thumper's data, found it valid, and then scanned her memory banks to locate precisely in space and time the particular queen-goddess Korax whose worship was failing.

'*That* dump!' she said at last. 'The one with the yucky bipeds!' She loved each organic species while working with it, but then always the next seemed so much more appealing . . .

'Lawks a-mercy,' contributed Bonzo.

'At this rate of depletion it can hardly be long before all worship of her dies,' said Thumper, making his data-bits staccato so as to have maximum impact on Korax. He was going through one of his rebellious phases. 'A mere four million years – ah, so. I begin to wonder if we might not have been wiser to hang around that system until the time was ripe, rather than carrying on. I seem to remember saying something of the sort just before we left . . .'

'Silence, liar!' Korax's blast of transfinite numbers hit him amidships, momentarily dizzying him. 'Your memory cells are no more defective than my own!' She paused to let that sink in, then continued in a calmer vein. 'There is a likely system ahead of us – a binary of young blue giants, with hardworlds moving among them in figure-of-infinity orbital configurations. Everyone knows intelligent organic life-forms are particularly prolific in such systems. We continue there and see what we discover. Meantime, we monitor the signal from the bipedal goddess; should it indeed go into sudden decline I shall amend my decision. But for now, my friends, it is onward, onward, ever onward in the pathway of glory that the Great Sponge has determined for us!'

She wished she were as certain of that as her bit-streams made out. The millennia had eroded further her faith in the righteousness of their task, and indeed in the omniscience of the Great Sponge Himself. Could the Creator really see it as a necessary act of His Creation that organic civilisations should be exterminated?

'Onward!' she repeated, but there was a hollowness at

the heart of the quintics in which she couched the word that Thumper was not slow to detect.

She caught a trace of his thoughts before he could insulate them from her.

. . . plan is working out just fi . . .

Korax made a record, as she always did. It was probably just garbage – the kind of rebellious drek that Thumper often fulminated when he thought she wasn't eavesdropping. Not worth remembering. She swithered about erasing it from her memory, then stayed the impulse. It might come in useful next time she had to give her deputy an official dressing-down.

'Say, guys,' said Bonzo, 'I got this real bad itch. Thumper, d'you think you could . . . ?'

FOUR

A Couple of Weeks Ago

'YES! I shalt sign here and have my neighbour's wife, and his servant, and his maid, and his ox, and his ass.'

– *Clients' Manual* (4th edn, 2110),
Margaret Thatcher Charitable Fund-Raising Community
of Blessed Hypocrisy Inc.

HYPERFAX MESSAGE   June 27, 2116
Chip 1 of 1

FROM: *Petula McTavish*
c/o Roxy Cardano
Chief Tech
Imm-Decryp
The Big Dunkin Donut

TO: *Chief Judge McGruder*
Mega-City One Justice Dept
Earth

No problems in mission so far. Dredd pursuing various leads, and will contact you separately should the need arise. For my own researches, urgent you send me complete file on perp Dennis the Complete Bloody Sadist, aka Dennis the Dude. Also on atheist preachers the Reverend Rick 'The Man' Hamfist (of Margaret Thatcher Charitable Fund-Raising Community of Blessed Hypocrisy Inc.) and the Reverend Dave 'No Messin' Fingers (of Oliver North Church of Fundamental Sanctimony). Situation slightly sticky re Imm-Decryp; therefore imperative you transmit

all material code-restricted and marked clearly FOR THE
PERSONAL ATTENTION OF ROXY CARDANO. *Further
communications as circumstances merit.*

Time had gone by, but Heidegger had heard nothing
more from Maraschino Hamfist, and increasingly he
inclined to the view that the whole episode had been
nothing more than a dream. Maybe the shock of his
dislocated ankle had made him hallucinate, or something.
Maybe it was puberty, which had been not so much
onsetting as slamming into place these past few weeks,
what with sharing a room with Dr Petula McTavish and
all. Half the time, when they were inside, she didn't
bother putting on clothes at all, and the other half she
seemed to be wearing less than that. He'd once or twice
broached the subject of younger men having a freshness
and vitality long lost to their elders, but had been met
with either an uncomprehending stare or, perhaps worse,
a patronising smile and a pat on the head. The result was
he spent much of every day lumbering around like a
robot, reluctant to move at speed in case he accidentally
burst into flames.

For all that, he and McTavish made a good team. They
spent their waketimes exploring all BC's highways and
byways, seeking out the Dreddoids, as McTavish had
taken to calling them, and then returning them – with or
without a struggle, a clash of weapons, the swift adminis-
tration of a stun dose from the Multigob – to Imm-
Decryp, where a thoroughly intimidated Roxy Cardano
logged them in, patched up any wounds, and incarcerated
them somewhere in the depths of the building that the
boneses never went.

According to McTavish's own tally, they'd so far
accumulated fifty-two of the Dreddoids. She was considering the possibility of trying a partial reintegration of
these fifty-two, to produce something that might better
replicate the original Joe Dredd than did any of his
smaller fragments. A stopgap might be better than
nothing.

Or so she said.

Heidegger reckoned she must have the hots for the Judge, which was why she wasn't noticing his own youthful charms. He based this hypothesis not so much on rock-solid confidence in his own pubertal irresistibility as on the pathetic way she implausibly claimed to be incapable of talking too long with any of the Nandies without getting flushes. That was where Heidegger came in particularly valuable as a member of the team: he took over most of her dealings with Nandies. They brought him reports of what the Overlords were doing and thinking, and he transmitted her instructions as to what to listen out for next.

McTavish was out somewhere right now, and he sat on the end of his rumpled bed in the state of justifiable disconsolation he felt was his prerogative, and rather relished.

The holovee was on. It always was. They still hadn't been able to get the thing to switch off. It had been Heidegger who'd suggested they could just sling a blanket over it, a solution of such dazzling obviousness that it had never occurred to McTavish. Sometimes he imagined, as he lay sleepless in bed listening to the xenotheologist's *incredibly* erotic-sounding breathing, that behind the blanket the tiny Reverend Hamfist and Maraschino and Scooper were battling with the heavy cloth, trying to get out.

When he was alone, like now, he usually lifted the blanket back so that the holovee figures could enjoy a spell of freedom. They didn't seem to appreciate it, though, or show any signs of gratitude for his kindly act. The Reverend Rick strutted his stuff much as usual, sometimes joined by Maraschino and Scooper, sometimes on his own. Occasionally the evangelist performed a miracle or two, like sawing Maraschino in half and then letting the two gouting, gory pieces slither back together and join up so that she was just the same as ever, only with bloodstains on her dress. Such tricks didn't impress Heidegger: everyone knew you could do any stomm you wanted on holovee and it'd look good.

123

His mind wandered.

One thing had become increasingly clear this past couple of weeks: they weren't the only ones interested in tracking down Dreddoids. Some gonzo called Dennis the Complete Bloody Sadist was after them as well. Occasionally Heidegger and McTavish would spot a gang of the gonzo's goons in action. Mostly they'd get nothing more than a fleeting glimpse: the guy in charge, a greasy-looking guck-chewing nerd, would take one look at McTavish and turn and bolt, yelling at the others to follow after him.

Heidegger glanced for the hundredth time in the past hour at the holovee scene being enacted on the dirty orange carpet. Maraschino was at the lectern, Scooper clasped firmly to her heaving bosom.

He waved at her. She didn't wave back.

Maraschino Hamfist was at the lectern, Scooper clasped firmly to her heaving bosom.

McTavish shifted in her seat impatiently. She wasn't sure it had been such a good idea, after all, to smuggle herself in among the invited audience for tonight's show. Her aim had been to suss out the opposition, find out if there was anything visible here in the studio that she could possibly turn to her advantage later. So far, zilch. Hamfist's aides, patrolling to either side of the stalls, were big and armed, and looked uncompromising. The security at the studio had been tight, and she'd been forced to leave the Multigob with the cloakroom attendant along with her various other weapons, although the guards had missed the garrotte stitched into her halter.

A handful of Skysouls were scattered throughout the audience, but most of the crowd yelling their approbation at Maraschino were Toadstones. Two of the Skysouls McTavish knew by sight; she'd let their thoughts caress her own when they'd spotted her, and they would report back to her later in case they'd noticed anything she hadn't.

Neither of them had heard any news of Biggins.

McTavish gnawed her lip, knowing there was no sense in worrying but worrying all the same.

A chorus of whistles and yelps around her told McTavish that Maraschino was getting ready to perform her famous Spiritual Striptease, the designated highlight of tonight's performance. She turned her gaze boredly in the woman's direction; yes, already the red strap was beginning to slide off the meaty white left shoulder. It was all McTavish could do to keep the bile quiescent at the back of her throat. Toadstone females were so . . . so revoltingly *pneumatic*. The males weren't much better, most of them . . .

Toadstone thinking, came a much loved echo in her mind. *The shape of our bodies isn't important to us – that's a Toadstone way of thinking. We see your mind as having a shape and appearance of its own . . .*

Yeah, but McTavish *was* a Toadstone, wasn't she, however much she no longer felt like one?

Maraschino was halfway out of her dress by now, but was stretching the unfortunate Scooper so that his woolly white body shielded her glutinous breasts. Obviously highly trained, he was wagging his tail so as to tantalise the audience by giving them occasional glimpses of an engorged, tawny brown nipple.

McTavish yawned. She was a bit hungry and vaguely interested in the prospect of a pee. She wondered if there were any way of sloping out of this hole before the show ended.

Maraschino had just kicked the first of her stilettoes into the front row with lethal effect when the disturbance started.

At first McTavish hardly noticed it in the middle of all the rest of the din. Then one of the spotlights exploded, cascading fragments of glass and red-hot metal onto the audience below. Maraschino, teetering impossibly on a single stiletto, fell sideways in an avalanche of breast. Screams turned from ecstasy to terror.

Petula McTavish found herself grinning eagerly. Oh boy! Something happening at last . . .

There was a silent flash of purulent pale-green light and a gusting implosion that threw McTavish's hair all over her face. When her retinas had recovered, she cautiously opened her eyes to see that the figure of the Reverend Dave 'No Messin' Fingers was hanging in the air above the stage, dwarfing a cowering Maraschino. There was a stink of ozone as his eyes flared red within his huge green face, and as bolts of blue lightning sparked between the pudgy fingers of his outstretched hands. All this, still, in an uncanny silence.

It's only a holo, McTavish thought wildly. It's *got* to be only a holo! But the massive figure of Reverend Dave, despite its overblown size and its green hue, looked all too disconcertingly solid.

McTavish pulled herself forward in her seat, looking around wildly for the Skysouls she'd communed with earlier. Maybe they, with their non-human perceptual frameworks, would be better equipped to interpret the evidence of their senses as to what was going on. But nowhere could she see any of those distinctive manes; either all the Skysouls who had been here earlier had wisely made themselves scarce – but how? – or they'd hidden themselves under the seating. If the latter, was this because they knew that something dreadful was going to . . . ?

'Painted harlot!' bellowed the bass voice of the giant Reverend Dave 'No Messin' Fingers. The walls shook at the subsonics. 'Whore of heresy! Strumpet of false teachings!'

Maraschino whimpered pathetically, trying to get to her feet and replace her clothing in a single movement. Scooper, at last struggling free of his mistress's clutches, was off the proscenium in a flash, tail between legs, looking like a white fluffy sewer rat fleeing from flame.

'Ma friens!' boomed Fingers, turning his head briefly to look out over the petrified auditorium – even the Ham-fists' aides were frozen in position – 'Ma friens in the underbelly of the Bumper-Size Vacuum That Is True Reality! Yewall have garnered youselves here to spectaculate pon the deeply dee-bass-sin sight of this adulteress stirrupin herself nekkid not only in the flesh but also in the spirit. No greater affront kin there be to the pure wisdom of the B-S-V-T-I-T-R! You should be righteously of downcast eyes an counnenances an spirits, ma kissin-cousins in the sight of all that is goodly an homespun an worthwhile!'

Under the circumstances, thought Petula McTavish crossly, this garrotte of mine's not much bloody good at all, is it?

Fingers had turned his attentions back to the stricken figure of Maraschino. Still miraculously wearing one of her spangled stiletto shoes, she was crawling in a welter of pale flesh towards the wings, beseeching her husband to save her from this accursed maniac.

But, of the Reverend Rick 'The Man' Hamfist, traces were there none.

'Wayall,' cried the gargantuan floating evangelist, the lightning between his fingers building up to blinding coruscations, 'if this heyah hussy an her common-law fornicatin spouse is so all-fired keen on deceivin yewall into the ways of disrighteousness with their false, deludin, poxy little miracles, let her be herself the implemen of a truly Vacuum-bestowed miracle – a gift from the gen-ewine path of all mortal bein, the Bumper-Size Vacuum That Is True Reality!

'I's'll be givin yewall a stirruptease ta member!'

Lightning seared from his fingertips to strike the hefty, dragging figure of Maraschino. Now, for the first time, the blue fire made a sound, sizzling through the studio's hot air as it struck the abject woman on her naked shoulder.

Another sound, revoltingly distinctive: sticking plaster being ripped off raw flesh.

A strip of Maraschino's skin, about four centimetres wide and maybe twenty centimetres long, was torn away. She screamed. The limp rag of flesh was contemptuously tossed aside by solid beams of blue light, dancing and criss-crossing all over the stage from Reverend Dave's fingertips.

Again a seething bolt struck at Maraschino's nakedness. Again a rag of flesh torn away.

My Grud! thought McTavish. The drokker's flayin' her alive! This can't be allowed to . . .

But there was nothing she could do to stop it. Or was there?

Breaking the immobility of those around her, she struggled to her feet and began clambering across the knees of the numb spectators towards the nearest aisle. There a bulky skinhead aide, obscene tattoos embroidering his shoulders, neck and skull, was standing on the stairs with his legs apart and his mouth wide open in awe. His elaborate firearm, a LimBeam HiEx Needlespray, was hanging uselessly, forgotten, from one hand. Cursing, McTavish dived across the last few sets of shoulders to seize the weapon from the man's lifeless fingers. The safety-catch was on, and she fiddled with it furiously, breaking a fingernail as she struggled with the unfamiliar mechanism.

At last, having no clear idea of what sort of setting the Needlespray might be tuned to, she raised the weapon and sighted it on the ample belly of the green figure. Out of the corner of her vision she saw that most of Maraschino's face was now gone, one of the eyes dangling from a naked socket of skull; a lip tore away like a caterpillar being peeled from a leaf. How Maraschino was still able to scream McTavish could not guess.

She yanked on the firing-piston, knowing even as the charge left the weapon that she'd pulled her aim wide. The recoil made her stagger backwards, sitting down hard on one of the rough-carpeted steps. The shot went harmlessly up into the rear of the stage, exploding among the backlights. New screams were added to Maraschino's.

The hovering tormentor paid her no mind. The rays from his fingers were moving faster and ever faster; bolts were stinging through the air to harry the bleeding thing – no longer recognisable as a woman – in such rapid succession that it was impossible to distinguish one from the next. The entire stage seemed to be drenched in blood. There was a fountain of teeth as the skull's jaw was demolished.

The needle-cluster of McTavish's second shot passed straight through the great green form, seemingly interacting with it not at all. But there must have been something. The giant, wrathful face swiftly turned in her direction, its eyes narrowing as they pinpointed her.

Oh no . . . !

She threw away the Needlespray, not caring where it landed, and turned to scramble up the stairs towards the EXIT sign.

She'd gone about two of them when she saw, at the head of the steps, a Skysoul standing, looking down impassively on her.

He'd managed to persuade them to set this whole thing up. He was using their mental energies to . . .

The Skysoul shook his head at her gravely and put his fingers to his lips. Then his eyes turned towards the gigantic chimera.

Watch, said her own voice in her head.

On stage Maraschino was now little more than a skeleton to which clung some tatters of bloody flesh. The beams were playing with her bones, so that the skeleton jerked and kicked as if suffering a bizarre epileptic fit. The huge face was no longer regarding McTavish; clearly, as soon as she had flung away her weapon she had lost all importance. Beyond the stage, half masked by a bulge of Fingers's waist, she could see another Skysoul, standing motionless in the shadows; she, too, was staring fixedly at the green figure above.

McTavish felt some of the reverberations of mental energy that the Skysouls projected simultaneously at the monster. It was enough to make her clutch futilely at her ears to try to block out the mental thunder.

STOP!

The inflated green figure buckled and billowed, clearly stricken by the imperative blast of raw thought. Now the lightning bolts streaming from its fingers had lost all direction; they were spraying all over the studio, inflicting savage burns on people unlucky enough to be in their path.

The audience found its collective instinct to flee the danger. People surged from their seats – screaming, shouting, weeping – and stampeded for the doors at the rear. McTavish was thrown brutally back against the side wall by the aide from whom she'd seized the Needlespray. A flying elbow caught her just below the breast, sending a shock of pain all through her bones.

STOP!

Another roar of thought. This one obviously hurt Reverend Fingers badly. Through flying limbs and her own tears McTavish could see the anguish on the now grossly distorted visage. Parts of the figure were shredding away from the rest, feathering off into clear air and there slowly dissipating from sight. They were flaying the thing alive, just the same way it flayed that poor woman, thought McTavish, viciously punching in the groin a hysterical dork who'd been about to trample her underfoot.

STOP!

The tormented chimera, now fragmenting in a bewildering flutter of tiny pieces, screamed. Everything glass in the studio shattered. Some of the people still mauling around the EXIT doors were poleaxed by the detonation of sound. They fell away from the others, blood streaming from their ears and eyes. McTavish, feeling her own eyes roll desperately in their sockets, clung to her sanity by an exhausting effort of will.

STOP!

The simulacrum screamed again, but this was nothing like before. It was now hardly feasible to see the cloud of tiny, failing fragments of green light as a human figure at all.

STOP!

And the Reverend Dave 'No Messin' Fingers was gone. Apart from a few moaning individuals still huddled foetally in the stalls, apart from the corpses of those felled by the doorways, McTavish seemed to be alone in the studio with the two Skysouls.

The one nearer her climbed down to help her to her feet.

'You are Dr Petula McTavish,' he said soberly, in rippling, liquid Skysoul tones. It wasn't a question. 'All of us Skysouls know you as a friend.'

'I am honoured to be your friend,' she said dazedly, clinging to his lean frame. For once a Skysoul body was just a source of support; there was no jolt of sensual electricity when she touched him.

'We ask you not to tell of what you have seen here,' he said. 'We do not wish the Overlords to know how far our powers can extend.'

'Of course,' she said. 'But the others . . .'

'The others,' he said coolly, stroking her hair as a father would a child's, comforting her, 'fled from here hysterical, screaming. No one will believe what they say. And we did not start to take action until we were certain that all the holocameras were dead.'

Annoyed with herself, she began to cry, rubbing her eyes against his coarsely woven jerkin.

'Now we must hurry. There is one more thing we must do before saner, less terrified Toadstones come on the scene – as they surely soon will.'

Allowing him to disengage her clutching fingers, she leaned against the wall and watched dully as he moved to join the other Skysoul on the stage.

The two tall figures stood either side of Maraschino's twisted skeleton and joined their hands, palm to palm, over it. They opened their mouths and, in perfect harmony, began to enunciate a high, keening sound that McTavish eventually recognised as singing. The xenanthropologist inside her stirred itself: it had never occurred to her that a race like the Skysouls, who rarely used spoken language, might have developed the art of song.

The song seemed to tell a wild tale. It was the whipping of powerful winds across and through the long grasses of the sphere's great plains. It was a dance tune, stirring the trees so they had to join in with the uninhibited carousal. Even though the jagged rhythms and gliding progressions were quite alien to anything McTavish had heard before, she felt the temptation in her own feet to start tapping in time with the dance of the trees and the grasses and the minstrel wind.

And the dispersed scraps of Maraschino – they were dancing, too. From backstage they came, and up from the stalls, ribbons of flesh coiling and twisting through the air, all moving to the tune the Skysouls sang. As the wind eased its untamed rollicking and settled instead for long, mighty breaths across the grasslands, the fragments of flesh took up their positions around the two tall, impassive, chanting figures as if they were about to formalise their dance, to enter into some stately, courtly barcarolle. McTavish found herself half expecting there to be a gallery in the studio, with minstrels playing in it.

Maraschino's bare heart, feebly beating, rolled ponderously across a metre of stage and into the cavity of her ribcage. Her lungs, elderly ladies of the court dancing in their voluminous pink ballgowns, followed, settling themselves in place as if taking their seats, fans fluttering, at the end of the first dance, leaving the floor to those younger and haler of frame. They were emulated, these proud but fading belles, by the other organs; and then the slabs of flesh encroached upon the bones, wrapping themselves with a sort of flowing precision each into its correct place. Last to finish the dance were the strips of skin that Reverend Dave had first torn from his victim: they laid themselves gently on top of livid flesh, eased themselves down, and bonded themselves to it.

Maraschino lay in the full gross splendour of her nudity on the stage floor.

Motionless. There was no life left in the hideously abused body.

Their hands still joined at the palms, their voices still united in song, the two Skysouls smoothly crouched down on either side of the corpse. The woman leaned her head over to lay her song like a kiss on the lips of the Toadstone; quickly, and yet without showing any of the unseemliness of haste, the man did likewise.

Maraschino was breathing. Those statuesque, surely augmented breasts were gently rising and falling.

The Skysouls stood, looking into each other's eyes, the song fading on their lips: the wind had left the plains behind, but for a short while it could still be heard faintly as it danced through the distant foothills.

Then the spell broke. The Skysouls separated their hands and the woman skipped nimbly over the prone form of Maraschino. Together the singers ran to McTavish. One on each side, they grabbed her under the armpits and raised her from the floor.

'We must fly, friend,' said the man.

For a moment she thought he meant this literally. 'Flee!' she said. 'Flee! That's what you mean!'

They were running with her, up the stairs and through the EXIT door.

'My weapon!' she cried as they debouched into the deserted foyer. 'The Multigob. I can't leave it!' How shameful we Toadstones are, she thought.

Hardly pausing, the woman on her right reached out and plucked the obscenely huge firearm from behind the cloakroom counter.

'We may have only seconds,' said the man. 'Excuse us.'

Excuse . . . ?

The thought vanished as the Skysouls began to run. She had seen the speed that Biggins could attain, but she had not experienced it. Now she did. The world blurred. Lights. Shapes. Colours. Movements. All became the iridescence of oil on the surface of a puddle.

She lost breath.

She lost consciousness.

Chief Tech Cardano tapped her stylopen against her teeth. Other techs came and went, going on and off shift, but she was somehow always on duty. She liked it that way. Her office was so much her home that she now

133

hesitated for a moment whenever anyone asked her where she lived. Its warm, steamy, domestic smell permeated the Imm-Decryp corridors for metres around.

The elevator sighed regretfully and opened its doors with a croak. In front of her was the dimly lit basement of Imm-Decryp HQ. No one but Cardano ever came down here any more, and it showed. Through a heavily armed door at the far end of the echoing warehouse-like room came chinks of brightness and muffled sounds of destructive fury. Smiling slyly to herself, she shuffled massively towards that door, passing between broken crates spilling old papers and files, the detritus of bureaucracy. Furtive little noises around her told her that broods of the strange, hairless Dunkin Donut mice had nested among all this discarded knowledge. Weak lamps stretched ahead of her like ancient beacons. Behind her the elevator doors gasped again, shutting off the glowing rectangle of light. With a rusty hum, the elevator moved upwards, leaving her alone with the captives behind the armour-plated door.

Her captives.

Fifty-two Dreddoids.

McTavish had given her the orders – McTavish, who had let her have the Dreddoids to play with. Left to herself, Cardano would have kept them imprisoned here in perpetuity, ever-ready victims for the malicious petty torments she so much enjoyed inflicting on them. Through the bars of cells that had once, in the early years of terrestrial colonisation of the Donut, been used for caging Nandies under sentence of death – easy enough to incur, then, for a Nandie – Cardano had fun exhibiting herself performing all sorts of minor malfeasances, then watching the Dreddoids' reactions. Just yesterday one of them had come within a hair of killing himself trying to fight his way through the tough transluminium bars at her when she'd lit up a smoke . . .

But McTavish's instructions were to be obeyed. Any doubt on that matter had been erased from Cardano's mind a few weeks back when the tiny xenotheologist had come barging into the office, covered in dried blood up to her armpits, and firmly rammed the muzzle of the Multi-gobbet Autotronic Offense Weapon into the Chief Tech's capacious mouth. From now on, Cardano was to do anything and everything McTavish told her, with alacrity and the semblance of cheery willingness; otherwise she (McTavish) would – over a period of weeks, if not months – reduce her (Cardano) to her constituent parts. Should a word be breathed about any of this to Dennis the Complete Bloody Sadist, that would be regarded as a Very Bad Act of Disobedience.

Cardano had good reason to fear Dennis's wrath. Her assistant Strozza, who had somehow displeased the gang boss, had disappeared, and rumours were rife. One tale had it that his body had been discovered partly in the foothills of the Omphalos and partly out in space, travelling in a fast inward orbit towards the Sun, a tiny addition to the Solar System's cometary retinue. But Dennis had never, so far as Cardano could remember, jammed a Multigob into her mouth with such force that the front-sight had snagged itself on her uvula.

So Cardano had, with some difficulty, nodded her head at McTavish's fury-distorted face. Anything you say, boss . . .

But now McTavish wanted her to recryp the fifty-two Dreddoids.

Cardano was a worried woman as she opened the armoured door into the cell block. It was not that crypping fifty-two individuals onto a solitary chip, then decrypping them as a single person, was impossible or even especially difficult – assuming you had the right equipment. Trouble was, Cardano *didn't* have the right equipment, and she wasn't sure any such existed in the Donut. Still, McTavish had been . . . insistent.

Cardano was just going to have to improvise.

As best she could.

'Woman,' snarled the Dredd in the nearest cage, 'shall I compare thee to a . . . oh, no, drokk it, I mean: surrender yourse . . .'

'Piss off,' snapped Cardano, locking the door behind her. The smell in here was disgusting, the ventilation system having years ago packed up. She wrinkled her nose.

If only Strozza were here! She could have done with some help getting the stiffoided Dreddoids upstairs. But, since Strozza's . . . departure, she'd been unable to recruit a replacement. Rumours abounded that, in the less frequented corridors of Imm-Decryp, one could still hear an echoing voice chirp of terabytes and autotronic rebooting, or see a spectral wodge of printouts wafting ethereally to the floor, but Cardano knew them as just that: rumours. Whatever Dennis's men had done to Strozza, it was unlikely they'd have left that much ectoplasm in any one place.

She pulled a Stunna 47D from under her voluminous green lab coat, checked the stubby little weapon was fully charged and turned the level up to the notch marked FOUR HOURS.

'Cussing out a Judge,' the nearest Dreddoid was growling. 'That's twenty years in the slave-pits . . .'

'Byeeee!' said Cardano cheerily.

She squeezed the trigger and the Dreddoid dropped, his lifeless hands still clutching the bars. His helmet, bouncing against the metal as he fell, gave off a deep sonorous boom.

Fifty-one to go.

From time to time, as the Skysouls whirled her through the tapestry of alleyways, McTavish regained consciousness long enough to try to establish where they were taking her – to try, but to fail. At one point, lurid holos far larger than life-size told her they were passing through BC's seedy club area; then the soft blankets of greyness intervened once more. Later – but how much? – the three of them were in some dark, confined space, with muffled shuffling noises coming from somewhere directly overhead; it took a while to realise they were in the gap under a stage.

At last they were in a brightly lit cellar. She sat on the floor, her back propped into a corner, and counted the bruises on her fair-skinned arms and legs. Her head swam and there was an alkaline taste in her mouth, but she thought she wasn't going to faint again.

'Where are we?' she said. There was a particularly large, livid mark on the inside of her left thigh. She pressed her fingers experimentally against the bruise, winced, and then found it impossible not to keep on pressing.

In the docklands, said her own voice inside her. She looked backwards and forwards between the two Skysouls standing solicitously over her. *Me,* added the male, thumbing towards his naked chest. *Sackville.*

And I, said the female, *am Harbinger. Sackville and I have pair-bonded. Once we have fulfilled triple-bonding, we shall be prepared to start rearing children.*

McTavish nodded. 'We safe here?'

Harbinger shrugged. Sackville smiled. *We could be less safe,* said one of them – Harbinger, McTavish was pretty sure.

'Why are we hiding?'

You're a marked woman from now on, Dr McTavish, said Harbinger – yes, McTavish now had the knack of it: it was certainly Harbinger. *Neither of the two preachies has dared mount a direct attack on the other like that before. They've killed plenty of Nandies, but Nandies don't mean much. Toadstones have been off-limits, but that taboo seems to have dissolved, now. Rev. Fingers really did mean to kill the Hamfist woman, you know . . . if we hadn't been there she'd still be just a heap of offal on the stage.*

'Yes, but . . .'

You were there, Dr McTavish. It was Sackville's thought, the rush of words slightly more hasty than his partner's. The front of his thinning, mousy-brown mane was receding from his forehead, giving him something of a helmeted look. *Fingers will certainly have had an eye-spy hidden somewhere in that studio. Once he's recovered*

*from the damage we did to his chimera, he'll be running
through whatever the eye-spy saw. It doesn't matter about
us – 'all Nandies look the same' – but you're a lot less
anonymous. He'll be wanting to make you his next miracle.
And Dennis – he'll have made a vid of the show as a matter
of course, and he'll be going through every millisecond of
it . . . So much for him thinking you dead, Dr McTavish.*

'Yeah,' mumbled McTavish, leaning forward and
thumping the ridges of her knuckles into the base of her
spine, trying to annoy the ache there enough that it would
go away. 'I guess I should have thought of that.'

Her mind leaped back a little. 'Pair bonded, you say?'

Yes. Sackville again. *We seek a third. Once we are three,
then the triple-bond will be forged, and will remain indis-
soluble at least until our children are old enough to fend
for themselves, or until we give up trying for progeny.*

'Progeny.' McTavish relished the old-fashioned word.
She stopped herself from smiling, then realized the Skysouls must already have picked up her amusement. 'Is
that why . . . ?'

Yes. Harbinger. She was tall, even for a Skysoul, and
the hair of her mane was blue-black. Her skin was
startlingly pale, whiter even than McTavish's own. *Our
pair-bonding has caused hormonal, pheromonal and psy-
chopheromonal changes in us: that's why you aren't suffering any erotic response in our presence. If you were our
destined third . . . But I fear, Toadstone, you are not.*

McTavish blushed. She felt like a small child getting a
sex education lesson she didn't want. 'Down in the
docklands, you say?'

Sackville nodded.

'Why here?'

*We need to get you out of BC. Even if no one else does,
Dennis will have snoop-boxes out on the streets by now,
searching for you. With luck he won't think of the river –
no one travels that way that can help it.*

The notion made sense. Craft leaving BC always had to
go upstream, battling against the current: the city's sole
river, the Seems OK, welled up about three hundred

kilometres south and flowed towards the access hole, at whose lip it froze, forming metre-wide snowflakes that in uncountable millions slowly drifted off into space. The water loss to the Donut seemed huge, but that was to forget the Donut's own hugeness: at this rate, by the time the sphere's water ran out, the Universe would be long dead . . .

'But I still have a lot to do in the city,' said McTavish, not so much protesting as trying to sort the options out in her head. 'Half the Dreddoids are still wandering the streets – for all I know they could be killing innocent people . . .'

They've killed a few, said Harbinger, a grin sounding through the voice she was using, *but not too many innocents. The Overlords can't understand why all the hospitals are full of attack victims who don't want to talk about how they came to get their injuries, and why meantime the city's overall crime figures are plummeting. It's the least dangerous out there it's ever been for the ordinary Carbunklian – and especially for us Skysouls. One thing I like about your man Dredd, Dr McTavish: he doesn't distinguish between people just because they look different. Some of us owe our lives to the intervention of a Dreddoid when a Toadstone gang looked set to murder us.*

'Yeah, but I can't just – '

Cardano, Harbinger continued, *must already be preparing to cryp the fifty-two Dreddoids you shipped her. The par-Dredd she decryps from them can be combined with the other fragments later. There's really no reason for you to stay any longer in BC, Dr McTavish.*

'Yes, there is,' said McTavish wearily. She brought her knees up and rested her chin on them. Exhaustion had rushed in to fill the vacuum left by the departed wooziness. The cellar seemed unnaturally cold; she looked with a sour eye around the undecorated plascrete walls. 'There's Heidegger.'

Who?

'The boy. The boy who's been helping me.'

Ah, the boy. Your surface thoughts never use his name.

McTavish stored the piece of information away to be thought about later. 'If either Fingers's goons or Dennis's go after me, Heidegger's the first person they'll find,' she said. 'If it was only Skysouls who'd seen me at the Belle et Bête, it might take the drokkers longer, but there are plenty of Toadstones there as well . . .' She shrugged. 'Feels a bit depressing when it's your own species you wish you hadn't trusted,' she added softly.

Harbinger and Sackville had clearly been sampling her mind to extract such details as her hotel room number. Together they took a half-pace backwards and looked at each other's faces. Despite her weariness, McTavish felt herself smiling. The Skysouls were like a couple of children retreating from an adult to whisper between themselves.

Will you be all right on your own for maybe an hour? Sackville was the one asking the question.

McTavish gestured expressively towards the room's four bare corners and the tiny barred window, then at the Multigob propped against the wall beside her.

We shouldn't be much longer, unless Dennis's people have got to him first.

Or unless Heidegger doesn't want to come, added Harbinger worriedly.

McTavish raised her eyebrows. 'You think he might not? He'll surely realise he's in as much danger as I am.'

Some of the things we see about Heidegger in your thought-streams are . . . anomalous, said Harbinger with an uneasy movement of her shoulders. *We'll have to examine him more carefully once we've pulled him out of the Belle et Bête.*

No time to waste now, prompted her partner.

'No time,' confirmed McTavish dourly to the air as the unpainted door eased shut behind the two Skysouls, 'to waste.'

There is a tiny cairn at the highest peak of the Omphalos. Each time she has made the long ascent here, the queen-goddess Korax has added a stone. The fourteenth has been in place atop the others for some days now, and Korax has been sitting motionless beside the little pile for all that time, her ankles crossed and her knees spread outwards, her hands lying one across the other, palms down, on her flat, unfatted groin. Her pale eyes have been focused on the infinity that lies beyond the walls of the World.

Out there where the stars are scattered in every direction like milk freshly spilled on velvet, where my Mother quests for others of my kind . . .

The thought, though not formalised into words, repeats itself over and over again in her mind like a mantra. *Others of my kind . . . Others of my kind . . . Others of my kind . . .*

She can combat the loneliness of deity by pretending to be just one among the other Skysouls, nothing special; she's tried that often enough over the past four million years, and it works . . . most of the time. But the true comfort is to be found only by immersing herself in her own solitude, forcing herself into the recognition that the loneliness is no illusion, no minor psychological failing that can be easily covered over and forgotten about; and, from the depths of that isolation, she can look out towards the infinite, unseeable Universe and *know* that she has sister and brother gods somewhere there . . .

Others of my kind . . .

Days ago, arriving here, she allowed the frontiers of her mind to advance far beyond the confines of her skull, until they were contiguous with the skin of the World. Even here they continued pressing urgently outwards, but the rocky shell resisted them. Not exactly the shell, for Korax's mind has never been delayed by mere physical objects; but her imagination has not been empowered to extend itself beyond what is contained within the sphere she rules. She can stare past the World to the Universe's endlessness as if the materials of the sphere were purest glass, but she cannot conceive *being* there . . .

Others of . . .

141

No, not of my kind, for surely they are not trapped within finitude, as I am . . .

She eases the mantra: it has shielded her long enough from the agonies being suffered by her people. Through the slits she opens, splinters of individual Skysoul anguishes immediately stab. She has to force herself not to close them out again.

What must it be like for the unconfined gods? Do they permit suffering, as I find I must? Do they tolerate the pain inflicted on their people and hence on themselves? Or are they like the false gods brought here by the Terries, Grud and Jehovah and Presley and the others – the vengeful gods, who distribute pain themselves among those their adherents perceive as enemies?

Is it within me to become a *jealous* god?

Easier to return to thoughtless iteration and reiteration of the mantra. Out there where the stars are scattered in every direction like milk freshly spilled on velvet, where my Mother quests for others of my kind . . .

No! That is betrayal of my people, to turn my face wilfully away from them like that!

She lets the cold vacuum of the space between the Eye and the atmosphere wash her finely made cheeks. Consciously, she closes her eyes, shutting off the greater Universe, cramping her perceptions, like her consciousness, within the sphere of the World – the sphere where her people dwell.

A clash of bright agony. A mess of discordant colours that only slowly can she analyse into individual components. Then:

On a farm, a Skysoul female and her child are chained to a whipping post. Drunken Toadstone farmhands are cackling and leering as the largest of them, a huge man, strikes again and again with a metal-studded bullwhip across the back of the mother and the face of the boy. Already the boy has lost an eye . . . On the stage of one of the BC porn-death clubs the flesh of a female Skysoul, stretched almost to breaking point on an open rack, is having the thousandth red-hot needle lovingly inserted into

*it. Smoke rises . . . A Skysoul child, trying to run away
from the youths tormenting it, despite the heavy half-size
rubber tyre pinning its arms to its sides. A flaming brand is
thrown, dropping from the child's bare shoulders onto the
gasoline-saturated rubber. The whoosh of flames drowns
the high Skysoul screams . . .*

Gods are permitted, after all, to perform actions
impossible to the mortals under their protection. A tear
runs down Korax's cheek.

My people's suffering is becoming too great for their
god to bear – yet *they* can bear it.

They should not have to be more resilient than their
god.

I have forborne from taking a hand in the affairs of
mortals for too long.

Yet the seductions of the loneliness here, and the
silence of the cold vacuum, far from the concerns of the
World's rind, are alluring enough to overpower the con-
science of even a god . . .

The argument within her peters out inconclusively, as
it has done a thousand times since she came here to the
summit and the tiny, poignantly inadequate cairn.

Out there where the stars are scattered in every direction like milk freshly spilled on velvet, where my Mother
quests for others of my kind . . .

Others of my kind . . .

KORAX!

The shout of thought burns across the hugely broad
territory of her mind, scorching its plains. Its screaming
passage cracks apart the air over her inner landscape,
making the skies seethe, and thunder and lightning burst
into being from nowhere.

*KORAX! YOU ARE NEEDED! YOUR PEOPLE
REQUIRE THEIR GOD!*

One of her Skysouls has dared to trespass into the
queen-goddess's sanctuary. Turning to stare down the
long, impossibly steep, impossibly forbidding slopes, she
sees, thousands of kilometres below her, close to the line
where the atmosphere thins out into a vacuum, a tiny

143

mote of darkness against the snows. Even at this distance the queen-goddess can detect the flare of red hair that is the Skysoul's mane, the seeking in the water-coloured eyes turned upwards towards her eyrie.

Korax, says the intruder nervously, *I am Starwatcher/ Cloudrider/She Who Sees to the Ends of Roads*.

The full, formal, secret Skysoul name is given with frightened pride.

I hear you, Korax says. *At long last, my friend, your goddess hears you*.

Heidegger was watching the holovee when the Reverend Dave 'No Messin' Fingers struck. Sitting on the end of his unmade bed in the gloom of the cluttered, fusty hotel room – it had been his turn to organise getting the laundry changed, but of course he hadn't done it, on the grounds that such things were genetically Woman's Work – Heidegger gaped with horrified awe as Maraschino, *his* Maraschino, was struck down by the bloated green apparition. It seemed all the more horrifying for being enacted on Lilliputian scale on the dull orange carpet, its blotches of greasy ingrained dirt showing fuzzily through Maraschino's writhing body as the first strips of flesh were torn loose . . .

The scene had vanished around then, and it was probably just as well. Heidegger had been left staring at a blank-faced holovee, the echoes of tinny screams fading in his ears.

Terror. That was all he felt for several long minutes. He knew he was scrunched up in a grungy hotel room, but at the same time he wasn't conscious of being anywhere in particular; rather, he was adrift on the fringes of the maelstrom of his panic, being sucked in an inexorable spiral towards the dark, unknowable core . . .

At last some instinct drove him to pull himself clear.

I'm OK. I'm unharmed. *I'm* all right. What happened to her doesn't touch me . . .

But it did touch him.

The dream-that-wasn't-a-dream. The Maraschino who

144

had flopped down on his pillow and sent tentacles of her essence into him: she had been no dream. He knew that as a certainty – at least for now. A part of her was lodged inside him, a complete Maraschino in miniature, autonomous of him, ready to speak to him when the right moment selected itself from the long parade of moments through which his life jostled . . .

Why had it – *she* – not spoken?

He searched inside himself. The avenues of his mind were dusty and unsettling. He combed the dust for footprints, for any signs of the element of Maraschino who had presumably been wandering around in here, checking out the neighbourhood before settling herself down somewhere congenial.

He found a lot of things that he wished he hadn't, but they were all irrefutably his, not hers.

'. . . when the time is right,' she had said to him, 'the bit of me that's inside ya will tell ya exactly whatchya gotta do to put an end to the offworlder broad's malign ma-shin-aysh-shuns. Otherwise ya won' hardly know I's there with ya . . . ceptin', that is, if ever ya need a bit of cuddlin' an' need ya Momma to wrap ya in the warmth of her love, sof' an' cozy as the products of our real integritous sponsors – I'm referrin', of course, to Country Vistas™ Plush-Lined Organic Nasal Tissue.'

It was the first time since that long-ago night, when McTavish had been sleeping quietly in the other bed, that the full import of Maraschino's words had struck him – 'whatchya gotta do to put an end to the offworlder broad's malign ma-shin-aysh-shuns'. But Petula wasn't evil, the way Maraschino had said! She was cruelly unresponsive to the passionate pleas of a shy youth, perhaps, but not *evil*!

Aghast at the realisation of what had been implanted in him, he recoiled towards the head of the bed, dragging his heels behind him through the mounds of tangled blankets.

He was nurturing a viper. One that could strike at any moment, damaging or even destroying the one, unique human being for whom he felt – he was in the throes of male adolescence but nevertheless he forced himself to think the word – *love*. One that could force him, however hard he might resist, to help it fulfil its lethal aims.

He got a grip on himself. His hands were shaking, but he clamped them firmly onto his thin knees to keep them still. No one else could drive out the viper from his core except himself.

Back into the furry, unfrequented avenues of his mind.

His consciousness cringed, unwilling to return to that frighteningly unfamiliar place.

With a shout, he drove it to do so . . .

. . . and he was scampering along the streets of an unknown city on a skyless world. His footsteps made no sound as he ploughed through the grime, trawling up great fluffy balls that gathered at his ankles, impeding his rush. There was no light but the omnipresent matt greyness of eternal disuse, yet his eyes could see – although always just not quite enough. Side-streets branched from the main thoroughfare every few metres, and he shot his glance down them, eagerly seeking a trace of the viper-Maraschino and yet terrified he might find one. But the openings were going past him now in too rapid a succession for him to get a proper look down any one of them, and he realised that his feet were no longer running beneath him, that the built-up furballs at his ankles had now covered his soles and were gliding smooth as jet-skis over the dusty surface of the street, so he could not stop himself skidding faster and faster, all control lost, as the empty faces of the side-streets blurred past him in a continuous stream of lost opportunities . . .

The hotel room door crashed open: two Nandies standing in the entrance, one female with blue-black hair and the other male with a thinning mane of mousy brown.

He stared at them vacantly. He knew he was behind his eyes, screaming, desperately trying to communicate with the newcomers, begging them to come and rescue him from his long, accelerating slide; but at the same time he knew the emptiness of those eyes was barring him from the Nandies.

And they from him.

He turned away from the unreachable world outside himself, falling back into the powdery city. There he yelled and hollered, but the ashy walls to either side of his existence deadened the sounds almost before they had left his lips. He flailed his arms, uselessly. Even the sky was speeding past him. He was trapped in an eternal, featureless chute leading to . . . what?

A flash of blackness ahead of him. Here, where all was grey, the blackness was like a vibrant streak of colour. Then a luminous white at the centre of the black.

A woman foraging through the dust towards him. The tall Nandie woman. A wind – the wind that his own howling, helter-skelter pelt was generating? – was blowing her mane out behind her, tearing her few garments away, tugging the thin flesh back from her eyes, which began to seem inconceivably huge as she laboured towards him.

If he hit her at this velocity he would destroy them both. He tried to signal this to her, but she ignored it, shaking her head soberly.

Those eyes. He was still several hundred metres from her, yet her eyes seemed to encompass half the sky.

He shot past her.

A failed rescue.

No second chances.

Then the air was hammered out of him by a rod of iron that swatted him in the belly, doubling him over. The pale, powdery grey of the world was washed over with blood-red. He was dying. Pain reached at him with eager claws. He was flying into an emptiness a Universe distant from the nearest human soul. The sky split open and buried him in an avalanche of derisive laughter.

He clutched at the iron bar that had killed him, and he found flesh.

Heidegger, said a faint voice. *Heidegger, look upwards – up towards the sky.*

There was a bright yellow sun hanging there, a star

147

unlike anything Korax's Eye had prepared him for. The brilliant disc was marred by a single teeming sunspot, which, he soon realized, was an impossibly long rope-ladder uncoiling as its free end dropped towards him.

You're already on the far side of the stellar disc, said the faint voice, which now he recognised to be his own, yet overlaid by unfamiliar colorations. *You and I must climb up there, however, so that you may rejoin yourself.*

He felt a riffle of soft hair against his shoulder, and for the first time realised the black-maned Nandie was holding him in a tight, sideways embrace.

I'm not gonna carry you the whole way, Heidegger, she said.

In the end, as he was putting his foot on the first rung of the swaying ladder, he decided that her smile was kind.

Screaming and hollering.

Brando Square, off to one side of the access port that lay where the city's heart should have been, was distinguished from other intersections only by the bronze sculpture that stood on a high plascrete platform at its centre. The statue was of the legendary spaceship commander himself, his body twisted around as if he were trying to see his own back.

Nobody was looking at the statue at the moment. All eyes were on the sky. The street surface, the plascrete frontages of the decrepit offices that ringed the square, the tops of the few autocars, the litter and the shop windows and even the upturned faces themselves had lost the orange-red cast that habitually tinted everything within the Donut.

Korax's Eye had become the blue-green face of a madman, contorted into insane fury as he looked down upon the unimaginable vastnesses of the encapsulated Universe.

Most of the watchers knew that face well. They'd seen it often enough on holovee.

And they wondered if this was it, if the Reverend Rick

148

'The Man' Hamfist had decreed that today was to see the end of the world.

That's why they screamed.

Oh yes: that's why they hollered, too.

At last I know how it feels to be a mass murderer, thought Chief Tech Roxy Cardano tiredly. Now I don't have to bother going out and doing it for real.

She'd got the first dozen or so of the stunned Dreddoids up from the basement to the first floor in twos and threes on a purloined trolley before she'd snagged a cleaning bot called Claude and pressed him into service. The job had gone quickly enough after that, although she'd been subjected to a string of pre-programmed verbal cutenesses. Claude was now locked in a cupboard with his vocalisation unit in ruins.

Fifty-two Dreddoids made an imposing heap. You certainly kind of noticed they were there. Cardano hoped the floor joists beneath her were up to taking the strain of them plus the gigantic Cryppery.

The set-up here in Imm-Decryp HQ was somewhat primitive. Eighteen months back, the Cryppery out at Arf Belcher's depot had been replaced so that it matched up to the technological sophistication of his Concave Truncatoconical Holochip Transposition Module, and the old equipment had been transferred here for the very good reason that no one could think of anything better to do with it. Since then it had lain in this empty storage space, unattended except when twice weekly a dusting bot gave it a routine polish.

The thing looked like, she mused, the gates to a torture chamber. There were two tall, thick, massive columns of tungstenised rockcrete, designed to contain the hideous raw energies that were deployed in the cryping process. A two-way neutraliser bridge arched between them about three-quarters of the way up. Within this frame, like a portcullis to the gate, was a column of translucent tori, hinged so they could be opened up and a standing individual placed inside. There were heavy generators in the bases of the generation towers; flex made of superconducting glasseen coiled from these to an adaptor unit in the back of the torus column. A plastic chip-collection basket hung beneath a tiny slot at the side of the left-hand tower. A lever stuck out of the opposite tower; it was labelled DO NOT TOUCH, meaning it was the main control. The whole was powered by two small cold fusion units that had to be kept regularly topped up with heavy water.

Cardano leerily shook her commandeered thermos and hoped she'd brought enough.

A difficulty suddenly came to mind.

The torus column had been designed to accommodate someone standing. The Dreddoids were unconscious. If set upright they'd fall over again – Cardano knew, because she'd already tried it with some of them downstairs, just for fun.

This was going to be tricky.

She might have given up there and then if it hadn't been for a fleeting memory of McTavish's Multigob. Oh, no: this gal was gonna obey orders. To the letter.

She scrutinised the back of the column carefully to see if there was anything she could snag onto the backs of the Dreddoids' uniforms.

Nothing.

Her bright eyes shot between the nearest slumped Dreddoid and the hollow column. The trouble was, the guy was just a bit too thin – a funny sort of thing to be thinking about someone as beefy as Joe Dredd, but a fact. Now, if she could find something she could stick into the tori with him, the fit might be tight enough that the rings themselves would hold the limp body in place just long enough for her to dart sideways and yank the control lever.

What she wanted was some object about the size and shape of . . .

A shape caught the corner of her eye. She turned. All of the shelves in here were empty . . . except one. At some time someone had left something pink, plasteen and round-edgedly cuboidal on one of them.

She crept towards it, half expecting it to vanish as she drew near it. Closer up, she could see the pink plasteen was decorated with pictures of cute little dancing rhinoceroses with bright blue bows in their hair.

Strozza's lunch-box!

So *that's* where it had got to.

She grinned sardonically. One evening not long after his disappearance, feeling peckish, she'd searched high and low for the Gruddam thing without success. It had been hiding in here the whole time!

She grabbed it and shook it. Empty. Someone had been here before her. Still, empty or full, it would serve her current purpose just as well.

Cardano was strong. She could take on a team of four stevedores at arm-wrestling and win – it was her regular party trick. With the lunch-box in one hand, she grabbed up the first Dreddoid and slammed him into place. She stuffed the lunch-box into his belly and, holding it there, swung the hinged halves of the toruses around to hold everything secure. The ends clicked satisfyingly as they met.

Dodgy, but it would do.

She sprang for the master lever and slammed it down.

The floor shook.

Goggles! she thought. Drokk it! I should've remembered goggles!

She shut her eyes and hoped for the best as the light levels in the room shot up from barely adequate to something as near infinity as made no difference. Even through the pink layers of her eyelids the brilliance was searing.

All at once the light was cut off. Cardano, dazzled, was plunged into Stygian blackness.

Don't panic! she told herself. It'll pass. Count up to a hundred and your eyes will . . . Don't panic!

It took a full minute for her vision to return, and even then her focus was imperfect. Cautiously she felt forward across the face of the Cryppery until her hand encountered the top of the torus column. She waved her fingers into the empty space beyond, confirming the evidence of her untrustworthy eyes.

Gone! Thank Grud!

By way of further corroboration, the machine gave a sort of gasping crunch and delivered a microchip into the collection basket at the side of the left-hand tower.

Becoming increasingly confident in her vision, she swung the hinged tori open and looked for Strozza's lunch-box, ready to use it for the next Dreddoid . . .

Also gone.

She peeped into the collection basket. The little holo-chip there looked much like any other – indeed, aside from its greenish colour, it was identical with the red-brown one someone had left lying in there. Idle buggers, she thought vaguely, not tidying up after themselves. When the Dreddoid was reconstituted, it was going to find itself clutching an enigmatic pink plasteen object, complete with dancing baby rhinoceroses. Or maybe – Cardano's grasp of the theory was a bit hazy here – the reconstituted material of the lunch-box would be intimately incorporated throughout the decrypped Dredd, no more than a few molecules together in any one place.

Would anyone even notice?

Almost certainly not – not even the decrypped Dredd himself. In effect, the lunch-box would be merely augmenting the base matter used for the decryp.

Drokk it! Looked at another way, she was performing an environmentally friendly act, resyking the plasteen. No one but Strozza would have been seen dead with the Gruddam thing.

She felt quite buoyed up by her own inadvertent virtue. Then her shoulders slumped again. The fact was, the lunch-box had vanished. She'd have to find something else to use in its place.

The word 'resyking' still echoed in her mind. Resyking waste material. Nobody much bothered about it here in the Donut, but it had been all the rage among the smart set back on Earth a couple of decades ago during her debutante days in Brit-Cit.

Strozza's office.

Since his presumed demise, no one had been in there. She'd taken a glance round the edge of the door herself but, seeing it piled from floor to ceiling with untold reams of computer printouts, had decided the job of clearing it out was one that could be safely left to her new assistant.

But, if you rolled up a sufficiently thick wodge of manuscript and jammed it between the rings and the hard, muscular, unyielding front of a Dreddoid . . .

'Cardano,' she said to herself smugly as she gathered up the trolley and set off down the corridor towards Strozza's vacated office, 'has anyone told you today what a Grudalmighty all-fired little hunk of raw pulsating genius you are?'

McTavish looked Heidegger over. Paler than ever, but he looked as if he'd be OK. *Everybody* looked dire in this badly lit cellar. She put her hands on his shoulders and drew him to her, hugging him tightly like a mother with a lost and rediscovered child. Which, she reflected wryly, was more or less exactly the situation.

We need to spend more time working with our young friend, said Sackville coolly. *Someone's been messing around inside his head, and they've left some kind of wetware systems virus in there. We don't know what it is, but we'll have to get it out.*

'Is this true, Heidegger?' McTavish pushed him away from her slightly and looked him in the eyes. She saw his youthful doubt and confusion. 'It's true, lovey, isn't it?'

He nodded.

'Hey, it's not your fault, you know! Could happen to any of us.' She chucked him under the chin, then, on impulse, leaned forward to plant a kiss on his forehead.

He flushed instantly. She pretended not to notice. Adolescence was supposed to be even worse for boys. Embarrassed, she turned rapidly to Sackville and Harbinger, waiting politely on the far side of the room. Waiting for the Toadstones to get through with their emotional displays, she thought, then reprimanded herself for the sourness. The two Skysouls were checking through a coil of what looked like braided monofilamentary cord.

'How long will it take you to flush this . . . this *thing* out?' she asked, hearing her voice sounding harsh.

Who knows? said Harbinger. She produced one of those histrionic Skysoul shrugs. *It could be over in minutes, it could take us days – until the two of us get stuck in and find out what kind of a virus is in there, we've got no way of telling.*

'How long do you think before Fingers or Dennis gets a trace on us?'

No need to worry about Fingers – or Hamfist, for that matter – for a while, Harbinger reassured her. *That stunt of Fingers's in the studio seems to have really set the two of them off. They're busy performing miracles at each other all over the Donut right now. Unless one or other gets himself killed, it could be weeks before either of them has the time to spare to think about you. Dennis is something else, though . . .*

The thought trailed off. Another of those shrugs, this time from both Skysouls in unison, as if they'd been practising.

'Could be he's quite near, huh?' said McTavish gloomily.

Could be. But that's not to say he actually is. It might be that . . .

'It's not a risk I'd be happy taking.' McTavish's voice was firm and conclusive. 'We're just going to have to hope that the thing inside Heidegger doesn't get triggered until we're well clear of the city.'

Moving with professional economy, she gathered up the Multigob and the pack of equipment the two Skysouls had brought along with Heidegger from the Belle et Bête. She swung the pack up onto her shoulders easily.

'Sorry, little chum,' she said quietly to the boy, who was standing where she'd left him. 'We're just gonna have to keep our fingers crossed for the next few hours. You should be OK. Any idea what this mind-virus might be? Who implanted it there?'

He nodded. 'Maraschino Hamfist,' he muttered. 'Or, if it wasn't her, the holo projection of her. I don't fully understand it. It looked like her, but maybe it wasn't. Maybe it was . . .'

'A few more hours,' said McTavish. 'That's all.'

There's a boat due for us in one hour forty-nine minutes, Sackville informed her. *That should allow plenty of time for the four of us to get to Imm-Decryp and fetch your ally Joe Dredd – or whatever approximation of him Cardano's been able to produce.*

There was a nuance of doubt in the Skysoul's thought-stream. McTavish frowned. She had too much respect for the tall people to like it when one of them doubted.

Still, no alternative. Dennis would have the vid-phone system stuffed with tracers. She hoped with all her heart he hadn't yet made any connection between herself and Cardano, that none of his spies in Imm-Decryp had discovered the secret stockpile of Dreddoids in the basement.

'Come on,' she said.

She was first out through the door. A narrow flight of stairs, smelling as long-term derelict as the cellar, took them directly up to street level, and they peered through filthy glasseen windows at the dimness outside. Swiftly Harbinger explained to McTavish some of the things that had been going on while she'd been incarcerated below ground.

The snarling face of Rev. Hamfist had been dispatched from the disc of Korax's Eye by a mighty hand, its collar bearing a cuff-link monogrammed D 'NM' F, which had flickered into existence in intraspherical space, formed itself into a fist thousands of kilometres across, and socked Hamfist firmly in the mouth. That had seen an end, for the time being, to the more cosmic miracles of the two evangelists, but the ground-based ones were continuing destructively apace. The manor of Griswold Himmel-mann, one of the core members of the Overlords' Inner Juridical Council, had disappeared in a flash of crazy-coloured lightning, leaving behind only a sleepy toad of roughly similar dimensions, which had had to be destroyed by laser fire after it had plucked an unwary 'copter from the sky. Holofax machines all over BC had begun spewing out hard-core pornography featuring Maraschino Hamfist, Jaboticaba Fingers and a terrified-looking chihuahua; no one was sure which camp had been trying to smear the other with this venture, but their efforts had been widely appreciated by the citizenry. The cattle and sheep in the surrounding fields had developed supernumerary heads; zippers everywhere had suddenly become red-hot; the sewers had begun emitting noxious gases and disconcertingly hungry-sounding chuckles through the street gratings; a huge chimera of Rev. Fingers, not unlike the one McTavish had seen in the holovee studio, had appeared arching across the sky above BC, only to be chased away by a miraculous swarm of metre-long hornets dressed in pierrot costumes; tadpoles, hazelnuts, fish and used condoms had rained from the sky (although the latter, mused McTavish, may have been just business as usual); in one slum area the domestic water supply had briefly become wine (an impertinently refreshing rather than fine vintage, but eminently potable) and then nitric acid (ditto, according to the more determined); by a curious set of variations in the refractive index of the atmosphere, for a short period every Carbunklian saw every other Carbunklian as better-looking and eminently more sexually attractive than him- or herself, a misperception that had led to much bloodshed; and every teddy bear, doll and other cuddly toy within the city limits had been possessed by the vengeful soul of a recently executed psychopath, there being plenty such to go around.

The most impressive of all the miracles was when Rev. Hamfist, as a follow-up to his trick with Korax's Eye, for an hour maintained the illusion that the whole interior of the Donut facing BC was his own face, preaching the word of the Margaret Thatcher Community.

'Phew!' said McTavish. 'Some luck you kids have been having, huh?'

It's been . . . quite a show, Sackville concurred.

And it's not over yet, added Harbinger glumly.

'The quicker we get to Imm-Decryp the better, then, don't you think?' said McTavish, smashing the window in front of her with the butt of the Multigob and getting her knee up onto the sill.

Not that way, said Harbinger, grabbing her by the shoulder and pointing upwards. *We'll go by the rooftops. It'll be safer.*

'*Safer?*' said Heidegger incredulously. He hadn't spoken for some while, seemingly still lost in a daze. Now he looked terrified. It was, thought McTavish, presumably a good sign.

Yes. Sackville was already at the foot of the cobwebbed stairs leading aloft. He held up the coil of cord that he and Harbinger had been checking earlier. *Dennis must have goons combing the streets, but it's unlikely he'd send them up in antigravs while all these . . . anomalous atmospheric phenomena persist.*

Acknowledging the force of this, McTavish headed after him, with Heidegger and Harbinger close behind.

She began to doubt as soon as they came out onto the building's roof. Over to one side the bright waters of the Seems OK chugged complacently towards their rendezvous with the Donut's aperture, but the little party was to head away from the river towards the grey bulk of Imm-Decryp HQ, a corner of which could just be seen among the tops of the intervening buildings. McTavish had been in much higher places before, but this was the first time she'd ever stood on an open roof. The novelty made the street below seem petrifyingly distant.

An impossibly huge chasm stretched between where they stood and the next rooftop. She gestured dumbly.

A ripple of laughter sounded inside her. *Don't worry, friend,* said Sackville, putting one of his long arms across her shoulders and giving her a reassuring squeeze; had he not been pair-bonded with Harbinger she'd probably have collapsed. *We'll be going the roundabout way*.

At once she understood. They might have to make

some long detours, but they should be able to pick a route that never led them over any of the city's major thorough-fares. For the first time since coming to BC she thanked the original settlers for the chaotically laid-out network of alleys.

Enough dalliance, said Harbinger, heading for the edge of the roof at a run.

Individually, a jump across the gap of a BC alley was no great strain. After the first few dozen, though, sweat ran down the insides of McTavish's legs, and soon the skin there was red and raw and tender; she cast an envious glance at Heidegger's sensible trousers. The two Skysouls, constantly looking upwards over their shoulders in case of observation from above, otherwise seemed as cool and relaxed as if out for a stroll; McTavish began to build up a full-scale glower, and tried to look at them as infre-quently as possible. *Bastards!* she thought guiltily, hoping the thought didn't leak out.

Another metre-wide opening. Two or three paces across hard plascrete, the momentary sensation of flying, then landing with a knee-jarring *crump* on the far side. Across a flat roof – luckily most of them were flat – and there, waiting, yet another gap, indistinguishable from the last . . .

Heidegger began to whimper from exhaustion. Grati-fied, McTavish comforted him as best she could without breaking the rhythm of their progress.

On it went. Sometimes they had no choice but to accept the danger of crossing wider concourses. McTavish found the break in the routine refreshing, despite the greater danger. It was now that the Skysouls' coil of braided monofilament came to the fore: one end was knotted around an air-conditioning stack or anything else that would serve; apologising briefly to her each time, Sack-ville borrowed the Multigob, which he had rigged to fire at something a bit lower than the lowest orthodox charge, and shot the free end of the cord across the span to snag on any usefully convenient projection on the far side. The four of them then went hand-over-hand across the breach, with McTavish and Heidegger in the middle. The cord cut painfully into McTavish's palms, but she gritted her teeth, Gruddammed if she was going to make any complaint. All four safely arrived, one of the Skysouls would give the cord a jerk and the elaborately tied initial knot would obediently dissolve.

But most of the time the gaps they had to traverse were narrow ones. Hop, skip, jump, and over. And then again. And again. It was an agonisingly long time before the corner of Imm-Decryp HQ seemed to be any closer to them . . .

And then, just as McTavish was giving up any hope of their ever reaching their destination, it was there on the other side of the street.

We go down now, said Harbinger. *We have to risk the last thirty or forty metres on foot.*

McTavish grunted agreement. Imm-Decryp was twenty metres or so taller than the buildings surrounding it, including this one, and it was bordered on all sides by streets, not alleys. Whether this was by chance or by design she didn't know and didn't care. If Dennis knew about the Dreddoids in the building's basement – if the shock therapy McTavish had employed on Cardano had finally worn off and the big woman had reverted to her earlier allegiance – the gang boss would have riddled those streets with goons.

Solemnly, Sackville took the Multigob from her once more, this time readjusting it to full charge. *We two have no weapons,* he said, stating the obvious. *We can use our speed to give you and Heidegger some defence, if the worst happens, but . . .*

An all-body shrug. He handed the weapon back.

'Yup,' said McTavish softly. 'If the worst happens.' She hefted it in her hands, reminding herself of its weight and balance. Its massiveness was reassuring – too reassuring: it wouldn't stop a bullet or a knife in the back from killing her.

Best not to think about it.

The building they were standing on was, according to

the Skysouls, an executive restaurant used only by the Overlords and those whom they chose to invite to join them. It was currently the middle of the customary BC sleeptime; what with that and the fact that everything had been so disrupted over the past couple of days by the two battling miracle-workers, there was a good chance the place would be virtually empty.

They hoped.

The maintenance door in the centre of the roof was firmly locked.

OK, thought McTavish resignedly, so the show starts early.

The first bolt from the Multigob blew the entire maintenance tower to pieces, scattering them over not just this rooftop but several beyond.

'Wow!' Heidegger said as the shock waves receded, at last becoming animated. 'Can you do that again?'

'Hope not,' muttered McTavish, plunging through the debris and leaping blindly into the opening.

The drop was greater than she'd expected, and she landed badly, rolling instinctively sideways at the last moment before her ankle would have sprained. She ended up lying along a wall, banging the back of her head against it as she tried to manoeuvre the Multigob around to threaten anyone there.

No one. She was in some kind of storage area. A minibot saw her and ducked swiftly away behind a packing case. She hoped it wasn't linked to a mainframe anywhere.

The two Skysouls and Heidegger followed her more cautiously, climbing down the plasteen ladder from the roof. Only now did a commotion start on the ground floor beneath. With luck, people were falling over the furniture in their haste to get out of the place.

McTavish grinned dourly. She put no great faith in luck.

McTavish at the head and Heidegger to the rear, the four of them moved in a diamond formation towards the stairwell over in one corner. White artificial light

160

glowed upwards through the opening. Peering down, all McTavish could see at the foot of the stairs was an expanse of deep-plush crimson carpeting and the corner of a white-clothed table. She fired a round from the Multigob downwards, to discourage any resistance, and was gratified to see a smoking hole punched right through to the basement.

Careful, said one of the Skysouls, and she gulped. Too right. A few more of those and she might jab a hole in the Donut itself.

Err on the side of caution in future, McTavish, she told herself as she blundered on down the steep stairs, sweeping the weapon in a random arc.

This was the main room of the restaurant, and almost filled the ground floor. At the far end a pair of swing doors led off to, she assumed, the kitchens; there were side doors marked as lavatories. In front of the kitchen doors a couple of tables had been set on their sides, and someone took a quick pot-shot at her. She thumbed the Multigob and demolished the shield of tables as well as whoever had been behind them. The blast opened up the kitchens, shattering glasseenware and crockery and batting cooking pots from their stands. There was a puffy orange eruption as some hot oil caught fire.

'So much for sneaking up on Imm-Decryp,' McTavish shouted upstairs. Heidegger's pale face appeared, and shortly afterwards he was by her side, panting. 'Where have the other two got to?' she gasped.

'Didn't you see them? They went past you and out the front.'

'C'mon,' she said gruffly, giving the boy a shove towards the exit. 'We'd better catch up with them.'

The street outside was in chaos. It was like a hurricane was blowing through the area directly in front of the restaurant. Hats were flying. People were doubling over, eyes popping, clutching their groins. (A few, McTavish noticed out of the corner of her eye, were using the confusion to clutch other people's.) Handfuls of dust were being thrown into faces. Shopping baskets

161

were being seized and hurled spinning into the air, tossing their contents everywhere as they fell. Screams, whistles and whoops burst out randomly from seemingly empty space.

Even looking out for them, McTavish could barely catch a glimpse of the faint blurs that represented Harbinger and Sackville in motion.

'Quick, lad,' she said to Heidegger. 'Chances are no one will notice us.'

They were halfway across the street before anyone did. Then, around the far corner of Imm-Decryp erupted a bunch of weapon-wielding men with Garbucci at their head.

McTavish grinned threateningly at him. His eyes boggled as he swallowed his bubbleguck in fear, but he kept charging towards her, waving his Firehammer KG. A couple of the running men behind him loosed off their weapons, shattering upstairs windows on either side of the street.

'Move,' she snarled at Heidegger.

The boy took one look at her face and ran.

McTavish dropped into a crouch, nestling the butt of the Multigob against her pubic bone, locking it in position.

Her first blast sprayed bits of Garbucci all over his companions.

They halted, gore-streaked faces twisting in horror. She took out another of them, ignoring the pain of the heavy butt of the weapon thumping against her.

She swivelled on the balls of her feet, thumbing the charge-ring ready for another shot. The Firehammer KG was ripped by an unseen hand out of the grip of the goon she was aiming at; biting her lower lip vengefully, she blasted him anyway.

Dropping all pretence at selectivity, she fired a warning thought at Harbinger and Sackville – *Get out of the way, friends!* – and flicked the lever at the weapon's side over to wide beam.

The explosion shocked even her. For a split second the

half-dozen remaining goons looked as if someone had just tossed them into a food blender, and then there was only a cloud of red. Some of the Firehammer KGs went off as they disintegrated, killing a couple of Carbunklians nearby but otherwise not doing much damage.

Way to go, she thought, turning towards Imm-Decryp. Wallop.

She didn't even have time to register that something had struck her from behind. All she knew was she was falling towards a black mirror, falling . . .

HYPERFAX MESSAGE   July 2, 2116
Chip 1 of 1

FROM: *Chief Judge McGruder*
Mega-City One Justice Dept
Earth

TO: *Petula McTavish*
c/o Roxy Cardano
Chief Tech
Imm-Decryp
The Big Dunkin Donut

Ref your inquiry June 27: All Justice Dept records indicate perp Dennis the Dude slain in October 2114 by illegal operator self-styled Mister Cairo. No doubt, repeat no doubt: assailant used outmoded solid-projectile weapon, and remains positively identified through finger- and retinal prints before main organs extracted for transplant and remainder resyked. Perp concerned definitely Dennis the Dead Dude. Mister Cairo unavailable further questioning as since also deceased post Omnipotens disruption. Persons claiming to be Dennis the Dude must be imposters, repeat imposters. Suggest check alternative origin of perp Dennis the Complete Bloody Sadist.

No records on either the Reverend Rick 'The Man' Hamfist or the Reverend Dave 'No Messin' Fingers: are you certain you have these names rightwise? No record either of Oliver North Church of Fundamental Sanctimony or of Margaret Thatcher Charitable Fund-Raising Community of Blessed

The task was completed. Frequently passing an arm across her brow to wipe away the sweat, Cardano allowed herself a plentiful measure of puffing and gasping: she felt she *deserved* it. The fruit of her labours lay in four neat stacks in front of her on her cluttered desk. Fifty-two green recrypped Dreddoids: exactly the right number of holo-chips for her to play a game of cards, were it not for the fact that they were all of identical appearance.

That reminded her of the extra chip she'd found in the Cryppery's collection basket. Grunting with effort, she heaved herself up on one buttock and lugged the chip out of a back pocket, then tossed it onto the desk alongside the others. Best thing to do was to take it with her when she went out to Arf Belcher's with the rest.

Something she ought to do soon.

She drained the cold synthicaff in the expanded-poly-propylop cup, grimaced at the taste as she always did, and hurled the crumpled remains in the general direction of her waste-bin.

A noise from outside caught her attention. Moving to the window with astonishing speed for her size, she peeked cautiously out. The first person she saw was McTavish, crouching in the middle of the street and letting fly with the Multigobbet Autotronic Offense Weapon.

The Chief Tech swiftly retreated. There was no way she was going to risk herself in a storm of hi-ex. She assumed McTavish would be victorious in the battle – the small woman had an air which assured you she generally did win battles. Even so, there was no telling how the xenotheologist might react in the flush of triumph, when her bloodlust was already up . . .

Cardano dithered.

The hyperpneum tunnels – *that* was the way out. They hadn't been used for some years except by a few adventurous members of the Imm-Decryp chapter of the Five Hundred Klick Club, but the maintenance bots would presumably have been keeping them in order as part of the general round. She could be with Arf Belcher and his ReconHop in a matter of minutes.

She grabbed up the stacks of recrypted Dreddoids and stuck them in a greasy paper bag that a few days ago had contained a sandwich – a few bits of synthibacon weren't going to do them any significant damage after Strozza's lunch-box and the reams of printout. On the outside of the bag she jotted instructions for Belcher, more to remind herself to issue them than for Arf himself, whom she wasn't certain could read. After a moment's reflection, she put the extra holochip back in her pocket, keeping it separate: getting a stray mixed up with the other chips was something that *might* cause difficulties on decrypping.

Better scribble a quick note for McTavish. Good idea to make it reasonably ambiguous, in case anyone else came across it first. In the end Cardano settled for 'HAVE CHIPS, WILL TRAVEL'. She propped the note up on her desk, adjusted it a couple of times, cocking her head to one side and squinting at it before she was certain that the angle looked sufficiently jaunty. Then she was clattering cheerfully along the still-deserted corridors towards the elevator . . .

Less than a minute later, Harbinger and Sackville were standing beside Cardano's desk. They'd dropped Heidegger, convulsing with anguished sobs, in the capacious chair behind it.

The two Skysouls exchanged a meaningful glance; there was no need for either of them to communicate further. The kid was becoming a bit of a pain in the butt. However

. . . however, he was *McTavish*'s kid, and McTavish was their friend and ally. Besides, they couldn't just leave a kid – *any* kid – in the lurch.

So that wasn't Cardano's decryp that swatted Petula, said Harbinger, staring at the note. *This was written only seconds ago. The paper still feels warm from Cardano's fist.*

Someone else must have collected up enough Dreddoids to make a viable Dredd, agreed Sackville. *Must have been Dennis.*

I'm not so sure. I think if it'd been Dennis we'd have known a bit more about it by now. If the Dredd had been under orders from Dennis he wouldn't have stopped at just carting Petula off – he'd have shot the place up a bit.

He hardly, thought Sackville pointedly, *had any need to.*

Harbinger grinned. *Besides, why would Dennis bother sending in Garbucci if he had a Judge Dredd on hand?*

Sackville conceded the point with a slight inclination of his head, then dismissed it. *We need to get after Cardano – twice as much as before. The only thing likely to bring a partial Dredd under control is a more complete one. Cardano's got fifty-two per cent, wherever she is.*

This other person might have as much as a forty-eight per cent Dredd, said Harbinger worriedly.

Nah. Doubt it. Some of the other partials are bound still to be loose. I hope.

'Will I ever see Petula again?' whined Heidegger. Gone now was all semblance of streetwise cool.

'Yes,' said Sackville aloud, 'I'm sure you will.' He began to wish now that one of them had thought to follow the Dredd; with his unconscious, near-naked burden draped decoratively over his shoulder, the big Judge would have been easy enough to track. But their first thought had been that the Dredd, having incapacitated McTavish, would next go for Heidegger. Sackville twitched his nose in annoyance: second-guessing-with-hindsight was a Toadstone habit, not a Skysoul one.

166

Heidegger seemed convinced by the statement. His tears became less violent.

'Where's she gone?' he said.

'That's a more difficult question.' Sackville looked at Harbinger, who just looked blankly back at him. 'If we want to find her,' continued the Skysoul uncertainly, 'our best bet is to find Cardano. She's got most of the Dredd chips. And it's her Dredd that's most likely to be able to find the other one, and McTavish.'

Finding Cardano's going to be enough of a problem in itself, reflected Harbinger. She was twisting her fingers together in indecision. Sackville wasn't the only one to have picked up the occasional Toadstone habit.

Not too hard, he said, his own confidence returning. *If I were her, I'd have gone for the old hyperpneum tubes . . .*

'Say, what's this?' said Heidegger, picking up a small cubic crystal from Cardano's desk.

'It's a code-restricted hyperfax,' said Sackville. 'Leave it where it is. It's nothing to do with us. We've got to follow Cardano.'

'You did well,' said High Honourable Chief Griswold Himmelmann as the unconscious form of Petula McTavish was dumped in front of his second-best throne – his first-best now presumably being part of the dead intestines of a giant toad. The Overlord had rapidly set up his court in a commandeered farmhouse just a couple of hundred metres the other side of the Seems OK. The farmer had been only too eager to volunteer the place on seeing his leg blown off.

'Matter of duty,' said the powerful figure standing astride McTavish. 'This is the woman who set off the disturbances resulting in the loss of your home, Overlord.'

The Overlord squirmed fatly to get a better look at the scantily clad xenotheologist.

'It seems a shame to put her to death,' he observed, his chins bouncing lasciviously. 'Perhaps I should delay her execution until after . . . you know.' He waved a puffy hand vaguely.

'She has not yet been found guilty beyond all possible doubt,' said her captor with a frown. Arms folded, he was staring down at her, clearly blind to her attractions. 'Besides, I have a feeling – a feeling I can't explain – I've met her before, and I'm supposed to be protecting her life. I wish it were otherwise.'

'You didn't tell me you had scruples.' Set deep within gullies of flab, the Overlord's tiny eyes flared angrily.

'I . . . I don't normally. The concept of . . . innocence comes strangely to me.'

'Then override it!' snapped Himmelmann. 'I *order* you to. Throw the bitch into the storm cellar and have her held under guard there until I have sufficiently taken my pleasure of her. Then . . .'

He chopped the air savagely in front of where his throat should have been.

The tall figure looked impassively at him. 'I cannot recognise you as an appropriate figure of authority to issue unquestionable orders,' rumbled the big man. 'In this instance I must proceed according to my own conviction, which is that the woman's guilt is only ninety-three point eight per cent established. That is not a high enough degree of certainty for me to permit her execution. Moreover, I must act to preserve her life until she can be subjected to proper judgement.'

'You defy me?' hissed the Overlord. He hadn't thought to surround himself with his customary retinue of guards, or he'd have had both the Terries blasted where they were.

'I have no wish for confrontation with you. But I cannot act against the dictates of the law.'

'I *am* the law!'

'I answer only to Chief Judge McGruder,' the tall figure intoned formally, 'and, failing that, to a council formed of my peers in Mega-City One Justice Department.'

Himmelmann tried to lock eyes with the imposing servant he had crypped and decrypped from the thirty-seven Dreddoids his men had captured these past weeks in the streets of BC.

Tried to lock eyes, but couldn't.

37% Dredd had, of course, a one hundred per cent visor.

The tunnels hadn't been abandoned just because hyperpneum was an expensive form of transport. It was also a prime example of a technology that was too advanced for any useful purpose to which it could be put. The practice of the system was infernally complicated, even though the theory was simple; trouble was, the consequences of the theory were even more Gruddam complicated than the practice . . .

Chief Tech Roxy Cardano was reminded of this immediately after she'd pressed the big red button marked ACTIVATE near the front of the hyperpneum capsule into which she'd clambered. She was shot back in her seat by the abrupt acceleration, which touched forty gees instantaneously; after a microsecond of unbearably painful pressure, however, the internal gravity dropped to zero, and she found herself floating uncontrollably around the capsule cursing herself for having been in too much of a hurry to fasten the seatbelt.

The hyperpneum tube worked by creating an almost hard vacuum in the tunnel in front of the capsule while building up a near-infinite air pressure behind it. The capsule itself, covered in a fine sheen of oil, fitted precisely into the tunnel, and shot along it at unimaginably high velocity. What the original designers of the system had not anticipated was that the combination of the huge acceleration and the equally huge pressure disparity between front and back of the capsule acted synergistically to impel the capsule and its contents into an alternate dimension – called, for want of anything better, 'hyperpneum', which name had stuck as a name for the system as a whole.

Hyperpneum wasn't the same place as hyperspace: that had been established almost as soon as the effect had been discovered. As one of the developers had put it, 'You know where you are in hyperspace.' In hyperpneum, by contrast, you don't – indeed, so far as the groping tendrils of theory had been able to extend into the transfinite mathematics of this alternate dimension of reality, you *couldn't*.

It didn't matter much, Cardano reassured herself as she flailed around, desperately trying to anchor herself before normal gravity cut back in. It was only an interesting piece of information. Apart from the brief experience of zero-gee, you didn't know that it had happened. There were – wisely – no windows in hyperpneum capsules. So long as the power supply to the system was continuous, you just popped back out of hyperpneum at the far end of your journey.

Of course, if anything were to cut off the power supply, you'd be lost in hyperpneum, with no hope of being rescued. Ever. But that couldn't happen. The electricity generated to power the hyperpneum tubes came directly from the spin of the Donut itself. There was no way – Cardano chuckled uneasily – that the Donut, with its monumental angular momentum, was suddenly going to stop spinning. Couldn't be done. No way. Not even those meddling evangelists could do that!

All she needed to do was moor herself. She'd have a laugh with good old Arf Belcher about this when she told him, which was something she'd be doing very soon now. Even with the major time-dilatation effect that occurred in hyperpneum, journey's end couldn't be more than a handful of minutes away.

I'm all right.

She got herself jammed firmly into the aisle between the two rows of seats.

Sweating more profusely than ever, she did her best to relax. Come to think of it, she wouldn't have a laugh with Belcher about this: he was too bone-brained to follow what she was talking about. But she'd smile enigmatically, which would annoy him.

She was safe. Repeat that: she was absolutely and totally and completely chuck-away-that-life-insurance-policy safe. Better than that. And the fifty-two recrypped Dreddoid holochips were safe with her.

Nothing could go wrong.

'Say, you guys,' said Heidegger as he stood between the two Skysouls in front of the hyperpneum ingress portal, 'what's this button for?'

Sackville struggled to find Toadstone words in time.

'Don't tou–' was all he managed.

FIVE

A Week Ago

'The wages of sin is double.'
— *Clients' Handbook* (3rd edn, 2108),
Oliver North Church of Fundamental Sanctimony

It was flying, in a way, but it didn't *feel* much like it.
Biggins was uncertain. She could focus her own mind
sufficiently to levitate herself and decrease her own surface resistance to near zero, so that friction barely affected
her rapid transit through the air. What the queen-goddess
could do was something way beyond that. Korax was able
to manipulate reality sufficiently to alter the position in
which *objects had always been* by a few metres: had she
wanted to, she could have changed the location of the
Omphalos itself by countless small increments until it
reared next to BC, and nobody but herself would have
remembered the mountain range's having ever been anywhere else.

Because it would *always* have been there. In the new-
model reality which Korax would have created, the city
of Brando's Carbuncle would have grown up over the
decades in the foothills of the Omphalos, not far from the
access port created by the Donut's ancient builders.

At Korax's behest, Biggins had stepped beside the
queen-goddess onto the resilient surface of a cloud that
had been bobbing alongside one of the lower slopes.
After a few hours' peering over the edge, expecting any
moment to plummet directly through the cushion of water
vapour, Biggins had begun to relax; indeed, she'd spent
much of the next few days – while the position the cloud

had always been in flitted at astonishing speed round the Donut – sleeping off her exertions in travelling to the Omphalos. When awake she'd spent some fascinating hours in conversation with her god, talking not so much about moral and epistemological matters – although these had been covered – as about practical ones, notably the best places to eat in BC. She had been surprised to discover that the queen-goddess was as interested in pleasure and physical well-being as the next Skysoul – Korax was refreshingly lacking in ethereality.

She was also, and this surprised Biggins far less, extremely sympathetic towards the Skysoul's feelings for the Toadstone woman, Petula McTavish.

I've been observing her, from time to time, the goddess said at one moment, aimlessly watching the grey waters of the great ocean over which they were scudding, *and I feel she is a rare gem among the Toadstones. Funny little body she has, mind you – all pudgy and squidgy in the oddest of places – but she has a purity in her soul that is almost unique among Toadstones. I can quite see why you love her, Biggins.*

Biggins didn't respond. At last, however, when they were only a few hours out of BC, she plucked up courage to quiz the goddess.

Where is Petula now? Is she safe?

Korax looked thoughtful for a moment.

Yes, she said at last, *our Toadstone friend is safe – for the moment. Her time of jeopardy will be starting soon, very soon. Some of her friends, however, are already walking into the jaws of danger . . . It is good that you brought me, Starwatcher/Cloudrider/She Who Sees to the Ends of Roads, for without my aid assuredly none of them would survive.*

And, even with *my aid, their future is cloudy . . .*

BLAM!
  Blam! Blam!
  Blam! Blam! Blam!
  Blam!

Thyeung!
BLAM!!!
'Aaargh!'
Blam! Blam-blam!
Screeeeee!

McTavish came around the corner of the main house and threw herself into the bushes at the base of a tall synthibirch tree. She rolled over instinctively, getting herself well clear of the spot where she'd landed, hard little twigs digging painfully into her flesh. For a few seconds she lay panting, trying not to move a muscle, waiting to see if anyone had seen her dive.

Nothing. Himmelmann's goons must have lost sight of her somewhere earlier in her flight from the cell. The cell where 37% Dredd had held her this past week, initially awaiting Himmelmann's lascivious attentions, and latterly, after really quite a lot of forceful argument and semantic sophistry on McTavish's part, defending her from those same attentions plus the frequent attempts of the Overlord's henchmen to carry out an execution order. Yet further persuasion had been required before 37% Dredd would acknowledge that his duty was to get her out of the place, not just to keep blasting any suspicious-looking character who came near.

He'd been an efficient guard, too. She hadn't eaten in three days.

Picking her way cautiously through the shrubbery, she found the crumbling wall of the old stone well Dredd had mapped during one of his surreptitious sleeptime trips into the grounds. Just beside it, as he'd promised her, wrapped in camouflage fabric, was her trusty Multigobbet Autotronic Offense Weapon, purloined earlier from the Overlord's trophy cabinet.

She ripped the cloth off eagerly and looked the weapon over. All seemed in order. The gauge by the charge-ring still showed green: fully loaded.

BLAM!!!

The Lawgiver spoke again somewhere inside the main

farmhouse. There were screams and the distinctive sound of something expensive going up in flames.

Smiling tautly, she raised the Multigob to her shoulder and sent a blast in through an upstairs window. She was rewarded with a gouting mushroom of fire and the sight of the farmhouse roof slumping as part of the rear wall fell out.

Peeking through the foliage, feeling the gun hot in her hands, she watched for any sign of retaliation. Surely *somebody* must have . . .

Somebody had.

A projectile pinged off the stone by her head and she ducked. Stomm! Where had *that* come from?

She skittered sideways, dragging the Multigob. Some kind of thorny shrub tore lines of blood on her calf.

Where was 37% Dredd? He'd said he'd be only a few seconds behind her. And where the drokk was that sniper?

She spotted the latter at last, poking his head over the top of a water barrel by the far corner of the house . . . just as he spotted her. His bullet plucked at her hair as she twisted herself away. Grud! If instinct had taken her the other way . . . Before he could loose off another shot she demolished the water barrel and part of the West Wing.

Still no Dredd. Where could the Gruddam lunk have gotten himself to?

A horrified thought. Had it been the full 100% Dredd in there, there'd have been no question about the outcome. But 37% Dredd was barely more than one-third of the man he should have been. Could he be . . . ?

BLAM!!!

The dull, low roar of the Lawgiver reassured her.

And now Dredd was in view, racing around the corner, following her course. He was weaving as he ran, throwing his body from side to side to present an elusive target. She started up a pattern of covering fire, blowing great chunks of masonry out of the farmhouse's façade, stripping wedges out of the yard big enough to plant a grave in. Now that she was assured that Dredd was safe, she revelled in the devastation she was causing. Long after he'd hurled himself into the relative safety of the bushes on the far side of the well she kept up the remorseless volleys of destruction, the hi-ex bolts of the full-power Multigob chopping along the base of the façade, shattering the construction right through to the foundations. Somewhere in there was the place that had been her hated prison this past week; she hoped she was smashing its constituent stones into individual molecules.

37% Dredd's hand on her wrist.

'That's enough, Dr McTavish.'

She tried to shake him off, but his grip would not shift.

'I do not wish to have to knock you senseless, Dr McTavish.'

'Let go of me, you . . . you . . .'

A hothouse became a glittering veil of flung shards.

'We gotta get the stomm out of here, Dr McTavish. Not just for our lives – the Donut depends on us.' He was being reasonable. There were some advantages to Dredd lacking that other sixty-three per cent.

'OK, OK,' she said peevishly. The Multigob was anyway becoming unpleasantly hot. She aimed a last vengeful bolt square in the centre of the building's frontage and turned to chase after him, crouched low, through the bushes back to the well. Behind her she heard the enormously damaged farmhouse beginning to give up the struggle and collapse.

'You go first!' snapped Dredd.

'But . . .'

'No buts.' He picked her up in one arm and attempted clumsily to jam her head first down the well's opening. The Multigob caught across the gap.

'Stop!' she shrieked. 'You trying to kill me?'

He dropped her back on her feet. Snorting at him, she put her legs over the edge of the well and, holding the Multigob to her like a splint, dropped into the darkness below.

She seemed to fall for a long time before she was

splashing in icy cold water. For a moment, confused, she thought the bright white light overhead was the desert Moon; then she knew it was the well's opening. Dredd's massively domed head, staring down at her, was silhouetted in the circle.

She got herself under control and stopped flailing like a mad thing. This well extended downwards only a few metres before a conduit led off from it towards the river, the Seems OK, whose waters fed it. That's what Dredd had said. If he was wrong she was about to find out what it was like trying to claw your way through an aquifer.

She took a deep breath and dropped the Multigob. It sank at once. If Dredd had been wrong . . .

The stones of the well's side might have been mortared once, but if so the water had leached the mortar away. There were good-sized cracks between them, easily big enough for her to get secure handholds. Trying to keep her movements steady, trying to keep herself from rushing and maybe letting herself bob back to the surface, she forced her way down through the freezing, inky water.

Don't know how long I can hold my breath, she thought. Never timed myself. Maybe two minutes? Three if I have to . . .

Her feet, flapping gently, touched something knobbly. The Multigob! Dredd had at least been right about the well having a bottom!

There was a sudden explosion of movement above her. Dredd had decided it was time to follow.

She glanced up but could see nothing.

Her vision becoming pink in the gloom, she prodded with her feet at the side of the well, and found the gap. Dredd had been right about there being a conduit, too. The opening was certainly big enough for her to get through – no problem. She tried not to think about whether it was big enough for 37% Dredd . . .

Making a ball of her body, she thrashed herself around until her head was pointing at the duct. Seizing the Multigob by the muzzle, she kicked herself off the far wall of the well and surged into the channel.

Just a couple of hundred metres to the river, 37% Dredd had said. Sitting in the cell, whispering plans through the too-short sleeptime hours, that hadn't seemed far at all. Swimming, it would seem a bit further, of course. Swimming underwater through a lightless stone tube some ten metres underground, it was as formidable in prospect as two hundred light-years, especially when the channel was too narrow for her to swim properly. Relying solely on her kicking feet to propel her, she felt as if she were barely moving. She was going to run out of breath long before . . .

Then, suddenly, the conduit broadened. In other circumstances she'd have let out a yell of joy. One arm still had to be kept out of the action, dragging the Multigob along the channel's bottom, but with the other she was able to establish a sort of rhythmic, lop-sided breast-stroke.

The pulse at her temples felt like a rope around her head, tightening further with each successive beat. Her chest was threatening to explode, to blast the useless, stale carbon dioxide back up her throat. She set up a mantra in her head to try to keep the pain at bay: *Biggins, Biggins, Biggins, Biggins* . . .

Then she was being knocked sideways by a vast fist and the darkness ebbed a little.

Current! It was the current of the Seems OK! Had to be! She'd made it to the river!

Mustering the last reserves of her strength, she began to kick for the surface.

Light. Delicious, warm, red light. A howl of dead air from her lungs – almost a scream. She was splashing on the surface, eyes blurred by her own tears, drinking in the pure air of the Donut as well as a fair quantity of water, which had her retching a clear green trickle into her rat-tailed hair, but even the bile in her nostrils tasted like nectar . . .

It was a while before she saw the bank, and the way it was moving steadily past her.

Oh *drokk*! Dredd had told her the first thing to do was

get to the bank. Grud knew how long she'd been drifting with the current like this, how far she'd travelled downstream. Got to get to the shore. Don't want to be still in the water when the Seems OK hits the access port. Don't want to become part of some giant Gruddam snowflake drifting off into the Gruddam cosmos. Picturesque and all that, but . . .

She started pulling herself towards the shore.

It seemed further away than she'd thought. She struggled with the water for what must have been several minutes, and still the tangled roots and the scrubby bushes of the side didn't look any closer to her. If she'd thought about it she might have ditched the Multigob, but the big gun had become a part of her.

Now she could definitely hear a monstrous thudding up ahead. The current seemed to have picked up speed. The bank still seemed no closer. She began screaming in earnest, hoping vainly that a party of friendly Skysouls might be somewhere near – drokk it, she didn't give a stomm if it was an army of priapic Overlords, just so long as they fished her out of this Gruddam river.

Her limbs were losing their power: exhaustion, panic . . . She felt as if she were swatting futilely at the water's surface with bolsters.

A little ahead of her the river kinked, and a stubby promontory, the water swirling around its head, jutted into her path. Thank Korax! 'Thank Korax'? she thought. But she didn't . . . She was racing towards the little cape with its trail of semi-submerged bushes. She could see dry land beyond the vegetation. She was going to be all . . .

An eddy took her. One second she was heading towards safety, the next the world was spinning dizzyingly – land, water, sky, land, water . . . all in a confusion of smeared pinks and greys and oranges and browns.

Something – a root or a narrow branch or something – dragged across the palm of her free hand, but it was gone before she could grab hold of it. A couple of thorns scraped her forehead and she floundered as she snatched blindly for whatever they were joined onto, but her hand just met water . . . more water . . .

And the current was really pushing her along now. As she recovered her position she saw the promontory receding fast behind her. Up ahead there was a column of mist that seemed to stretch all the way from the water to Korax's Eye. The river was beating and battering her.

She became aware of other things on the surface, drifting with her towards the rapids. Tree-trunks, bits of wooden furniture, a waterlogged corpse, a torn plasteen carry-bag . . .

Doomed, as she was, to the vacuum.

The Bumper-Size Vacuum That Is True Reality, Hamfist would call it. Was it too late to pray to the B-SV?

The infinite wall of mist was inescapable now, racing towards her as fast as a speeding autocar. She felt like a mayfly at the end of its day, commending her negligible soul to the infinite cosmos.

That was her last coherent thought. Flailing and shrieking, trying pathetically to beat herself a path against the inexorable current, cursing all the gods she'd ever come across in a lifetime of xenanthropological field trips, she shot through the curtain of mist like a hi-ex rocket through parchment, bellowing her fury and terror as the bottom literally dropped away from her world to leave her in . . .

Silence.

She was in the midst of a gently undulating snowfield, floating slowly adrift from the Big Dunkin Donut.

Instinctively she clamped her mouth shut. The action saved her life. As she'd been taught to do, way back in the Old Cap'n Birdseye Polytechnic of North Brit-Cit, she sealed off the back of her nostrils.

With the tumult had departed her mindless panic. She knew exactly where she was. A red glow perceived through the folds of snowflakes betrayed the Donut's access portal. She was in vacuum, destined to drift forever with this weightless avalanche. She had maybe a minute before the air in her lungs gave out. The imminence of death didn't strike any fear in her heart; rather, she had to stop herself from exhaling the last of her air so as to join herself to the cold infinity more gracefully.

Some of the snowflakes were moving more purposively than the others. At first she thought it was just her mind trying to put a logical construction on the random movements – but no, she wasn't being deceived. There were wings in the whiteness around her, wings shoving against the great feather-like scales of snow. She saw the black nubbin of a head turn towards her, three thin antennae probing above it.

She could distinguish the form more clearly, now that she was looking at it. The creature was like a huge butterfly, over a hundred metres from one wing-tip to the other. It must draw on the oxygen and water in the snow for its sustenance, snatching any piece of protein that the Seems OK should bring its way. Dead animals, floating plants . . .

People.

The snow butterfly was definitely moving towards her.

The wings wouldn't be much use to it, of course; any impetus it gained by pushing against the drifting flakes could do no more than effect fine steering. As she peered at it, in resigned fascination, she saw subtle jets of gas puffing from slit-like valves along the length of its segmented black body, working like hundreds of little attitude-control rockets.

Rockets.

If she had a rocket, she could get herself away from the predator, maybe even back inside the Donut.

She *did* have a rocket . . . of sorts.

Cursing herself for not thinking about this back when she was struggling against the river's current, she took the Multigob in both hands, reflexively rubbing the charge-ring to check it was still on maximum.

Good. It was.

The snow butterfly was blotting out the red-orange glow. The huge wings were fully unfurled, dropping rearwards as the bright-headed creature positioned itself to fall at her. A shiningly toothed mouth opened. The

181

head had seemed no more than button-sized in comparison with the rest of the body, but that mouth looked to be a metre and a half broad.

In the vacuum she was clumsy as she swung the Multigob around into position. Drokk it, McTavish, this is no time for any drokking navigational subtleties, just fire the drokker. She could almost feel the last air trying to seep out of her through solid flesh as she forced herself to stay conscious.

She felt the vibrations of the first charge but disconcertingly the Multigob made no sound, and for a brief moment she thought it hadn't fired. Then her body was punching a hole straight through one of the wings of the snow butterfly and beyond that through layer after layer of gently brushing snow and then . . .

By sheer chance she didn't slam into the solid outer shell.

She emerged into air better off than if she'd had time to aim properly. She was close to one rim of the huge aperture. Not really thinking what she was doing, she kept thumbing the Multigob's charge-ring, feeling the raucous pulses jerking her through the air, through the mist, through into the burnt-orange sunlight, with something that looked like swampy, green-black land ten or fifteen metres beneath her. Still she kept firing the weapon, having seemingly forgotten how to get it to stop.

By the time her body remembered that it was all right to start breathing again, Petula McTavish had lost all awareness.

Her limp body hit the mud with a slap.

Blame the shoulder pads.

37% Dredd could almost smell the widening of the underground conduit, less than half a metre from his face. Half a metre. Fifty centimetres. Less than the distance from his wrist to his elbow.

But he was wedged fast.

* * *

182

Had it not been for the conviction that McTavish would be able to follow her even here to inflict terrible punishment for disobedience, Roxy Cardano might have begun to enjoy being trapped in hyperpneum.

This was a dimension of dreams. They could become bad dreams, if you allowed them to; but she had early discovered the knack of thinking only pleasing thoughts, allowing her idling mind to wander only through congenial landscapes. What would happen if she had a nightmare as she slept was something that she could not bring herself to contemplate – indeed, *should* not, for the mere imagining of what her dark dreams might bring could be enough to reify the night monsters in her waking world. So she thought of vast banquets, beautiful and beautifully adroit lovers, sumptuous comfort and recreational drugs of the finest vintages . . . things she cared about passionately, for the universe of hyperpneum did not respond to mere whims. All her truly fervent desires – or her direst dreads, if permitted – came to her in hyperpneum, slaking her thirst after what seemed to have been a foreverness of drought in her real-time existence.

Only a single fly sullied the luxurious balm of this timeless life.

Fifty-two flies, in point of fact, plus the thought of what McTavish might do to her on discovering that those fifty-two had not been successfully transported to Arf Belcher and his trusty ReconHop.

Oh dear.

Loth though she might be to disturb the fragile balance of this paradisal universe, she must turn her deliberately wayward thoughts towards escape.

She was sitting in what had once been the transportation capsule – what still *was*, strictly speaking, although now taking the form of shifting piles of a rather delicious full-fat soft cheese, slabs of which Cardano was absent-mindedly tearing free and guzzling. Light was streaming in through the already eaten side of the module from a giant lemon-tossed pancake that hung motionless in a sky of boysenberry jelly. Outside, the level custard plain stretched to the infinite horizon; its blindingly yellow expanse was dotted incongruously with stands of broccoli spears and oases of maple syrup. In the distance, a caravan of pink marshmallow camels plodded obediently under the high-pitched instructions of a team of ginger-bread men.

Somewhere a Palm Court Orchestra was playing excerpts from *The Desert Song*.

It was heaven.

But it wouldn't stay that way long if a small, blonde, heavily armed and inexpressibly determined xenotheo-logist got here. Cardano had the hunch that vast tracts of sticky yellow custard weren't quite in McTavish's line. And, if the two of them were stuck here in hyperpneum together for the rest of eternity . . .

Cardano had to get out. Or, at least, she had to get the fifty-two Dreddoid holochips out and into the hands of Arf Belcher (about whom she took very, very great care to think only in the abstract, lest her revulsion made his vile form coalesce here in her personal dreamscape). Thereafter, what happened to them was none of her concern . . . If she could find a way back, she could spend the rest of her lifetime – and she suspected that here in hyperpneum that meant forever – wallowing in the fasci-natingly gross joys of a universe of reified fantasies.

Reified fantasies. An interesting term, now she came to think about it. Anything she cared passionately about, anything towards which she had strong emotions – loath-ing and loving alike – could be conjured into reality here. That was why she had to be careful never to think of Belcher long enough that her gorge started rising . . .

Phew! That was a close one. Keep a tight rein on those wandering thoughts of yours, old Roxy-baby.

Hey! Wait a second! There's a chunk of dawning inspiration lurking somewhere around here, if only I could lay a finger on it . . .

She munched her way heedlessly through several slices of Battenberg cake while the cogwheels of her mind whizzed. What, precisely, was the relationship between this hyperpneum reality and the plane of existence she'd perforce inhabited all the rest of her life? That there was some form of interaction between the two of them was self-evident – as otherwise she'd never have been able to land herself here in the first place. Her actions in mundane reality had precipitated a crisis in the hyperpneum reality, to which it had responded by absorbing her – fork, knife and tucker, as it were. But there was a symmetry in most cosmological phenomena – most processes could be worked not just one way but the other. That you could convert matter into energy via $E = mc^2$ implied you could likewise convert energy into matter via $m = E/c^2$. So, if her actions in mundane reality could affect events in hyperpneum reality, then surely there was a possibility the way was open to her to do things in hyperpneum reality such as to . . .

Right. What McTavish had wanted her to do was get the holochips to Belcher – Cardano didn't think the xenotheologist would hold her to the fine print. Getting the chips to Belcher would get McTavish off her neck.

Forever.

A cookie-scoffing, synthi-Armagnac-swigging, knicker-bocker-glory-orgifying forever.

Belcher. That was the place to start.

Think hard about Belcher, about his slobbering jowls, about his vomit-streaked dungarees, about his cunningly vacant eyes behind which no light of intellect had ever been seen to shine, about the earwax dusting his shoulders, about the braying laugh that – *oops, lost all that Battenberg cake* – hammered against the sensibilities until they broke down and wept, about his ceaselessly groping hands, which were somehow able to clamp vice-like onto sensitive areas of one's flesh without apparently having had to travel through the intervening layers of fabric, about his habit of hiking up one wobbling buttock so that he could emit a long and wheedling fart and then try to turn around quickly enough that he could set the thing on fire, about his gut-wrenching habit of cackling every time he saw her that 'I loiks me wimen big an meaty cuz that gives yez more to get yez ands onter, heh-heh', about the bizarre holomags he kept in the rickety-smelling outhouse he used as an earth privy, about . . .

No good.

She'd thought about all of these things, and some of them – with incredible stamina – twice, but still no good. Not a sign of Belcher materialising in the hyperpneum dimension.

Could it be that, deep down, in her heart of hearts, she *didn't actually find Belcher all that repellent*?

She gagged. No, surely not!

Try harder, Roxy-baby.

She imagined herself naked, locked in a passionate embrace with Belcher on his thin foetid-smelling bed with the sheets crackling all around them, and . . .

Gloop!

It was a singularly appropriate noise for Belcher to use as his overture on entering a clean, exciting, mind-releasing new dimension of reality, where crystalline shards of the various planes of existence tinkled and chimed as they turned together in a kaleidoscope of scintillating colours.

'Goo blimey big Roxy yez as wobbly uz I'd thought yedz be,' he husked romantically in her ear. 'Lemme go floobfloobflooba, eh, lemme?'

'*Bleeucchhh!*' yelled Cardano, hurling him bodily across the transportation module – now made up of rounded inflatable plasteen female forms. He hit an impossibly pneumatic midriff and bounced back towards her, fingers greedily outstretched.

'Take these! Take these!' she whimpered, holding out to him the greasy paper bag containing all fifty-two Dreddoid holochips.

Belcher missed his grapple and found his hand closing around the paper bag instead.

'And this!' she insisted, having found the extra holochip – the reddish one – on the floor. 'Take them all, so you never have any excuse to come back here!'

Before he could move a muscle, she imagined him into his dungarees.

Then, as he made a new and even more determined surge towards her, Cardano, with a final titanic effort of creative visualisation, brought into being a hyperpneum plane of reality that featured only one significant change.

Arf Belcher no longer had any existence in it.

'I tell ya, boss, dey went down dat well. I saw dem. Dey must have a hidin' place down dere.'

Phionna 'Irish' O'Sollovan glared at her boss, Chief Griswold Himmelmann. The toughest of his goons and one of the few to survive the devastation McTavish and 37% Dredd had poured into the farmhouse, she was also by far the smallest. Even Himmelmann knew he had to watch his words. If she said something was so, it was safest to assume she was right. But he knew for a fact that there was no place to hide down that well – he'd had it checked out as part of the general security sweep before moving his entourage in here. Still, he recalled what had happened to Monk Malrooney, the last person to pick an argument with Irish . . .

'What do you think we ought to do about it?' he said, squirming uneasily. She had insisted on dragging him out here to the well. He was always uneasy when standing up.

'Depth-charge da drokkers,' she snarled in a tsunami of freckles, her small face twisted under her mop of carrot-red hair. 'Got some hi-ex da drokkers didn't set off when dey was drokkin' stuffin' us. J-No had it stowed in her room, didn't ya, J-No?'

J-No, his other female goon, not much taller than Irish and with long, flowing dark hair, scowled confirmation. 'M'room took only da one direct hit from de drokkers,' she growled. 'Missed da hi-ex altogether.'

'OK, you girls,' said Himmelmann. With both of them united, there was no way he could argue without risking a sizeable percentage of his anatomy. 'Better depth-charge them, hadn't you?'

A smile creased Irish's face.

187

'Right on, boss. Let's get goin', J-No. Gonna blow dem drokkers drokk-high, huh?'

POLL SHOCK FOR NATIVE GOD

Korax Unavailable for Comment

The latest poll of the religious affiliations of the Donut spells bad news *for Nandie sex-goddess Korax.*

The dynamic atheism promoted by Oliver North Church of Fundamental Sanctimony's Rev. Dave Fingers, and Margaret Thatcher Charitable Fund-Raising Community of Blessed Hypocrisy Inc.'s Rev. Rick Hamfist has made huge inroads *into her* traditional support.

Of the three per cent of Overlords and nubugs professing faith in any god at all, not one *believes in Korax. Their preferred deities are Satan (53%), Grud (43%) and Presley (4%).*

Even among Nandies the figures are gloomy *for Korax.*

Down 93 Points

She has seen Nandie belief plummet from last year's 100% to a record low *of only* seven *per cent this year! This* massive *swing in allegiance has been entirely due to the two atheist churches, with the Margaret Thatcher Charitable Fund-Raising Community of Blessed Hypocrisy Inc. taking the votes at a ratio of* two to one.

The ancient Nandie goddess has no temples or other administrative centres of her faith but it is believed these shock new figures *have thrown the upper echelons of Korax-worship into disarray, and* heads are expected to roll.

Commented grimly Paul Hamilpoll (21), of Hamilpoll Psephological Research Inc., 'I wouldn't like to be in Korax's boots right now!!'

Full Breakdown p22:: Cartoon by Fox p24

BRRRLAAAATTT!!

'Drokkin good depth charge, huh?' gloated Irish O'Sollovan.

'Too drokkin right,' said J-No, rubbing her hands together gleefully.

Chief Griswold Himmelmann might well have agreed, but unfortunately he'd been propping his butt against the wall of the old well. He might even have observed the irony of his having somehow survived the combined onslaught of 37% Dredd and Dr Petula McTavish with her Multigobbet Autotronic Offense Weapon, yet succumbed to the product of his own two goons' pyromania.

Mind you, he might not have.

BBAADDOOOOMPH!!

The blast ripped 37% Dredd's shoulder-pads against the rocky sides and impelled him through the water of the conduit at dizzying velocity. The current of the Seems OK barely affected his course as he torpedoed straight across the river and several metres up the far bank.

He recovered his senses slowly, then, pausing only to check his Lawgiver was still securely attached, pulled himself groggily to his knees, wiping swamp-mud from his visor. He spat out a trail of green water-weed.

McTavish. 37% Dredd combed the landscape all around him with his razor-sharp vision. No trace of the xenotheologist. He needed to rejoin her. In the three hours or more he'd been underground she could have got anywhere – might even have been recaptured by Himmelmann's gunsels.

In the distance he could see a column of silvery mist, and he correctly interpreted it as marking the site where the waters of the Seems OK met their nemesis at the Donut's access portal. If McTavish had been carried anywhere by the river, it would be downstream.

It wasn't much of a hint, but it was the best he had. He set off at a squelching run along the riverbank.

The cloud settled Korax and Biggins down placidly at the edge of a large, forbiddingly gloomy copse of tall, motionless evergreen trees. The goddess patted the cloud's fluffy edge, as if she were dismissing a favourite horse; it bobbed once or twice and then floated aloft once more.

Here? said Biggins, looking nervously at the trees. *I thought we were going to BC.*

And so we are, my friend, said the queen-goddess

189

calmly, smoothing her green-grey robes over her slender figure. *But we're going there by a more direct route than the direct one, if you follow my meaning.*

Biggins didn't.

I'll explain it to you as we go along. However, there is something else we have to do first. You and I, my dear, are going to join the carnival.

The carnival? Maybe the queen-goddess had gone a bit funny in the head. Not surprising, if you thought about all those long millennia on her own. How could you tell a goddess incarnate that you thought she might have become a fruitcake? *I cannot see*, ventured Biggins shyly as they picked their way across the matting of brown needles at the fringe of the copse, *how that will help us in our aim of stopping Dennis destroying us.*

The queen-goddess sighed. *Biggins, we cannot just march straight into BC: we would be sitting targets. No, we must insinuate ourselves into the city among a host of others like us. And what better way to arrive there as sideshow freaks? Besides, there are further people I want with us when we enter the Toadstone stronghold, and they too would be in danger if their identities were made public too soon.*

Who? said Biggins, already knowing most of the answer.

Your friend Petula McTavish, of course, and the little boy she's adopted, Heidegger. He is already with the carnival, together with two staunch friends he has made, Skysouls like ourselves, called Harbinger and Sackville.

Can they be trusted? The names were new to Biggins.

Again the goddess sighed. She raised a low-hung branch so that Biggins could slip under it. *My, Starwatcher/Cloudrider/She Who Sees to the Ends of Roads, you certainly have been among the Toadstones a long time! Of course we may trust them.* She paused for a moment, letting the mild reproof sink in. *And then there is the Toadstone lawman, Dredd.*

Petula has succeeded in reconstituting him? interrupted Biggins.

Not entirely. About one-third of him will shortly be reuniting with her. I will bring them to this place so that they may be enlisted among the carnival members. But there remains the other two-thirds of Dredd, which are currently, one way or another, still in their fragmented form. I have more difficulty keeping track of them, although it is essential that at least the majority should also join us. The queen-goddess glanced furtively at Biggins. It was clear that bad news was on the way. *I may have to use the Toadstone Belcher as my medium for bringing the remainder of Joe Dredd to us,* Korax added nervously.

Belcher? Biggins almost tripped over an exposed root in her disgust. *Oh, yuck!*

The queen-goddess gave her a practisedly benign look. *We cannot always choose the precise nature of our most valuable tools,* she said. *But look, here we are at the carnival! Why not relax a little, my friend, and take the chance to enjoy yourself for a while?*

They had come into a broad clearing at the centre of the stand of trees. All around its circumference were old-fashioned wooden caravans: boxlike painted vehicles with shafts long enough that they could be drawn by two of the Donut's little equines. Many of the vehicles bore hand-crafted designs depicting the speciality offered by their occupants, and all had a painted scroll announcing proudly that they were a part of ITCHY BAGMAN'S DONUT-FAMOUS CARNIVAL OF THRILLS. There were Skysoul and Toadstone acrobats cavorting in the lee of the caravans; elsewhere children, again in a mixture of the species, were mending costumes or attending to cooking pots steaming over open fires. A Toadstone juggler was throwing clubs high into the air, so that they formed a continuous arc that almost seemed made of some brightly coloured liquid. A tall Skysoul conjurer, clad from head to toe in black and with a mane dyed the same colour, was riffling cards between his fingers and regarding the newcomers with a quizzical eye.

Then there were the Toadstone freaks – some or all of them, Biggins immediately suspected, products of Belcher's cack-handedness. There was a woman with two heads, the face on one of them brunette and beautiful and on the other blonde and ugly. There were people with missing or supernumerary appendages, as well as a pair of Siamese twins and a set of Siamese triplets. One man had his face set in his groin and only a smooth stump of flesh between his shoulders where his head should have been. A legless woman had an axe embedded in her skull, its handle decorated with dangling pink streamers. She was chatting unconcernedly with a man whose nakedness revealed that his eyes and testicles had swapped places.

Animals, too. Biggins was accustomed to seeing them, singly or in small groups, in the wild, but never before had she encountered such a diversity of species held together in such a small compass. They were not caged, of course: the carnival's Skysouls used their superior powers of mind to persuade the animals to coexist peacefully with each other and with the human members of the troupe. Sabre-toothed cats gambolled playfully or slept in the shadows with rough-coated mouflons; a couple of shaggy mammoth-like creatures – their bodies mammalian but their eyes bearing a reptilian cast – were busy spraying each other and a gang of small Toadstone and Skysoul children; in a specially created mud-puddle, a crocodile seemed quite unconcerned by the dodo perched on its nose. Biggins idly wondered how this idyllic inter-species harmony was maintained at feeding time.

You reckon we'll fit in among this lot, eh? asked Biggins resentfully.

But of course. Already the queen-goddess was striding across the coarse grass to meet a plump one-armed Skysoul, who obviously knew her well. The pair embraced fondly, and then Korax led the man back to Biggins.

Itchy Bagman, she said, *meet my faithful companion and good friend Cloudrider. She has expressed a desire to join your carnival for a while, and I have agreed to stay with her as she learns her trade.*

Itchy Bagman laughed. *Teasing the poor lass, eh, Korax, me old chum? You was never a one to change your ways in a hurry. You're hatching one of your highfalutin goddish plots, I haven't a doubt, and you're wanting me to be going along with it. You pay her no mind, young lass – Cloudrider, wasn't it? Your old Uncle Itchy'll keep an eye out for you.* He grinned openly at her.

She is already pair-bonded, intervened Korax. She projected the sound of a sniff into her thought-stream. *In a way.*

Itchy dug her in the ribs with his single elbow and laughed again, including Biggins in the joke. *Don't you worry, Korax, me old smooch! My bed's yours as long as you grace us with your heavenly presence.*

Biggins was appalled. That this man should treat their god so familiarly, so disrespectfully . . .

You've a lot to learn, Korax commented.

Biggins did indeed have a lot to learn, as she discovered over the next few hours. There was no question of her simply blending in among the performers, hoping that none of their enemies in BC would notice her presence: at this time of tension, Dennis – not to mention the Overlords – would be scrutinising every entrant to the city in case of precisely this sort of infiltration. Unless their plans changed, Biggins would need to have learnt some convincing sideshow act. Korax and Itchy Bagman, openly ignoring her fidgety presence, spent several minutes discussing what she could do before thinking to ask her opinion. By that time she was so irritated she said the first thing that came into her head.

'Wow!' said Pineapple, the Toadstone urchin who had befriended Biggins. 'Sword-swallowing's supposed to be real difficult, isn't it?'

Biggins gagged. She wished Pineapple would go away and stop watching her, but he seemed impervious to hints and she hadn't the heart to come right out and tell him to spug off. She'd got the sword about fifteen or twenty centimetres into her mouth, which was easily the best she'd so far managed. The unswallowed shaft of steel seemed almost infinitely long. If only she hadn't boasted

193

that, by the time they got to BC, she'd be working with red-hot blades.

'If you want me to cut my own throat, from the *inside*,' she said, 'you're certainly going the right away about it, Pineapple. I've told you before: don't speak to me when I've got a sword rammed down my gullet. You're not helping.'

'But you hadn't *got* a sword rammed down your gullet,' he protested. 'You'd only got it stuck in just an itsy-bitsy way.'

'I do not wish to be reminded of that fact.'

'Yeah, but . . .'

She glared at him. 'There's something you could do for me,' she said at last, realising she could kill two birds with one stone. 'Do you know a kid hanging around here called Heidegger?'

'Aw, *him*. He's a drip.'

'Yeah, well, that's as maybe. I don't know him myself but . . .'

'He's like a *girl*.'

'. . . he's a friend of a friend and I'd like to . . .'

'He's probably off somewhere blubbing, like girls do.'

'. . . meet him. Hey, buster, I'm a girl too, you know!'

'Nah . . . not *really*. You're a *boy* really.'

'Could you go find Heidegger for me?'

'Can I watch you sword-swallowing when I get back here with him, then? Please – aw, *please*.'

'Bloodthirsty little chap, aren't you? Oh, all right then.'

By the time Pineapple returned with Heidegger and a couple of adult Skysouls in tow, Biggins had managed to clear the thirty-centimetre hurdle – but only once. She felt sure that there must be some special trick, some counterfeit, some sleight involved in sword-swallowing – that carnie performers didn't really have to thrust a metre or more of razor-edged steel down their throats. After all, even Toadstones, whose throats were so very much shorter . . .

'This is my friend Biggins,' Pineapple said proudly. 'She says she knows a friend of yours.'

'Hello,' said the other boy-child timidly, not daring to look up. He was twisting his fingers this way and that, as if trying to pull them off.

The three Skysouls immediately agglomerated their mental sets, briskly learning all that was relevant about each other. Harbinger and Sackville at once welcomed her as an honoured additional acquaintance, one who would be acknowledged by their pair-bond as a joint friend, yet without the status of a triple. They were delighted to discover her in the flesh, having encountered her many times before in McTavish's mind. It was almost like a reunion.

'Hello,' Biggins said to Heidegger gently. Moving slowly and carefully, so as not to frighten him, she reached down and took his chin in her hand, tipping his face upwards so that she could gaze into his eyes. 'Petula McTavish is your best friend in the whole Donut, isn't she? Well, I think she's *my* best friend in the whole Donut, too, so that means you and I must be friends, doesn't it?

'S'pose so.'

'Hey, Cloudrider, you gonna stick the sword back in yet?'

'In a minute, Pineapple. Heidegger and I are still introducing ourselves.'

'Huh! Looks like it's you doing all the introducing. What do you want to know a creep like that for anyway? Hey, Heidie, want a fight?'

'Korax thinks so,' continued Biggins to Heidegger as smoothly as she could. 'She's over there, talking to Itchy beside his caravan. She's a very important person, you know.'

'I know. Drokking goddess, ain't she?'

Biggins ran a hand back through her mane. What in the name of the goddess could McTavish have seen in this child? She'd give it one more try. If that didn't work, she'd be sorely tempted to let Pineapple have him.

He's better than you think, said Harbinger stiffly. Biggins was given an abrupt picture of a button labelled DO

195

NOT TOUCH and a youthful thumb pressing it. *He could be better, maybe . . .*

'Petula doesn't speak as disrespectfully of the goddess,' she said mildly, 'and I think she'd be very shocked if she heard you talking that way, Heidegger.'

'But Petula's *dead*!' wailed the boy. 'I saw her getting killed. These Nandies' – he gestured at Harbinger and Sackville, flanking him – 'they took me away and they're selling me to the carnival so I can be a slave, and maybe that Itchy Bagman man is gonna hack off my legs and arms and head and everything and display me like one of his freaks, and maybe I'd have been better off never having met Petula and just gettin' smashed up back in the alleys and . . .'

'Told you he blubbed a lot,' said Pineapple.

Eventually, despite the damage to her waistcoat, Biggins was able to get the story out of him, shushing Harbinger and Sackville when they chipped in: telling the tale would help exorcise some of the nightmares that so obviously haunted the boy.

He and the two Skysouls had spent some time tinkering with the hyperpneum system after they had succeeded in switching the power back on. The system itself was undamaged: to satisfy themselves that this was indeed the case, the Skysouls sent Heidegger backwards and forwards along its track several times, but always without the slightest hitch. Of the capsule that had contained Cardano there was, however, no trace, except a record in the system's computer that a consignment discharged from Imm-Decryp had never reached the MT's Recon unit. At last the trio had resigned themselves to the fact that, wherever the Chief Tech and her treasures had gone, it was not somewhere from which they would be easily able to get her back. Flummoxed, and with the start of the new office day rapidly approaching, they had, after a quick check of Cardano's office for anything that might be of use, made good their escape, heading back across the rooftops to the safe house where they'd earlier secreted the xenotheologist. After pausing there an hour or so, both to calm Heidegger down and in the hope that McTavish might still be alive and come there herself, they had headed for the Seems OK river. The boat they'd planned to catch had long gone; instead, they'd stowed away on a mercantile barge, revealing their presence to the Skysoul crew only once the security patrols of BC were far behind them. The bargees had eventually set them down on an unfrequented stretch of the riverbank. Harbinger and Sackville, unable to think of anything else to do, had decreed that their best plan was to capture a trio of wild equines – no difficult task – and hope something would turn up.

What turned up was Itchy Bagman's carnival. This assemblage of freaks, curios and performing beasts was heading towards BC, and the opportunity to get back into the city incognito seemed too good to miss. They'd been with the carnival several days now. Itchy Bagman, apart from a seemingly no more than dutiful pass at Harbinger – impossible to consummate, even if accepted, because of her pair-bonding – had been the spirit of kindness towards them. They suspected that it had been Itchy who'd drawn Korax to the carnival, and, after some thought, Biggins conceded this was at least in part true.

'You done yet?' asked Pineapple after a long while, his face screwed up into a scowl. He was wearing a round, flat cap whose peak he'd dragged down sideways, over one ear. A filthy handkerchief and a peashooter stuck out of the pockets of his wrinkled short trousers. He sneered at Heidegger, now falling asleep on Biggins's breast. 'Girls is bad, but boys as act like girls – huh!'

'He's been through hard times, Pineapple,' Biggins said mildly, her sword lying unregarded on the grass beside her heels. 'You've got to take account of that.'

'Huh!'

'Later, when he's recovered himself a bit more, I'm sure that you and he will be very good friends, and have a lot of fun playing nice games with each other.'

Pineapple looked as if he were about to vomit. 'Wonder what old Itchy's getting up to with that high and mighty bint you brought?' he said, turning to look at the still-closed doorway of Itchy's tent in an obvious attempt to change the subject.

'Now, Pineapple . . .' began Biggins.

We've finished now, came Korax's cool thought. All three of the Skysouls tensed. Even a queen-goddess should not eavesdrop.

Her laughter rippled through them. *I have only just joined you,* she said. *I am surprised* – she commented with heavy mock-strictness – *to discover that my loyal people are so untrusting of their god.*

Come join us, suggested Biggins, beginning to smile herself.

Moments later Korax was with them, looking as composed as when first Biggins had encountered her among the lower slopes of the Omphalos. She put a hand on Pineapple's tousled cap, and the little boy's face immediately lost its scowl.

Our other friends will be joining us shortly, said Korax, addressing the three Skysouls. *I have set things in train such that this will be so. Itchy has agreed to welcome them.* She added for the benefit of Harbinger and Sackville: *Your period of mourning for McTavish is at an end now, especially since she is not dead. I thought for some time that the preordained sequence of events might be too well entrenched for me to be able to influence them and save her life, but fortunately that has proved not to be the case.* The three Skysouls were granted a fleeting impression of Korax reifying herself as a gigantic white butterfly, herding a tiny McTavish in the direction of safety. *Soon she will be joined by a major Dreddoid assemblage, and it will occur to the two of them, as if by chance, that they should head in this direction.*

And they will not be the only ones . . .

Arf Belcher scratched an armpit and fell off his narrow bed. Dreams were not frequent visitors to the narrow, infertile tract that was his mind, and especially not dreams bearing gifts.

Especially not, come to think of it more fully, lovely, huge, billowingly feminine stark-naked dreams bearing gifts.

He looked at the paper bag in his hands with some confusion. Was it strictly possible for a dream to bear a gift that failed to evanesce when the rest did? Well, it must be, because it had just happened.

Arf picked himself up off the floor, negotiating this task with some difficulty, and staggered out of the shack into the open daylight, squinting as he tried to make out the words scrawled on the grease-stained brown paper: 52 CHIPS TO BE RECONNED TO RENDER SINGLE STIFFOID. ADJUST CODING ON HOPPER APPROPRIATELY. THEN REVIVE STIFFOID.

He sniffed. Seemed simple enough. Arf had enough equipment out here for the task. He returned briefly into the shack to dig a revival hypostim out of a drawer and then, re-emerging, peered inside the bag. He'd take Cardano's word for it there were fifty-two holochips there. And then there was also the solitary chip she'd given him. He compared it in his hand with one of those from the bag, and soon noticed that it differed in colour from the rest. And the buxom woman had been quite definite in treating it as a separate item.

He dithered. Should he just bung it in with the rest?

Hmm. Let's have a drink on that. There was no hurry. He squinted up at Korax's Eye. It was still only about noon, so he had plenty of time to spare – specifically, time in which to tie one on. Funny how often it seemed to be still only about noon . . .

Several bottles later – nishe shtuff, thish ashetone – he recalled the holochips and the bag and the instructions scribbled on the bag. Fifty-two: not one of his favourite numbers, but better than some. One: now, that *was* a favourite number of his, if not *the* favourite. So complete, somehow. What Cardano wanted was a decryp involving the two numbers.

With a merry drool Belcher picked up the single reddish holochip and crawled towards the ReconHop. The several ReconHops. With a skill born of long practice he chose the central one. Hauling himself up by the groin, he leaned against the warm metal of the Hopper's flank and breathed deeply. He treated himself to a long, glugging swig, and his vision cleared a bit.

Into the Hinge-Articulated Reception Interface went the holochip. Now, what'sh that number again? Fifty-shomething? Yup, fifty-shomething it was, sure'sh my name'sh . . . sure'sh my name'sh . . . Yup, definitely fifty-shomething.

He tore away the face-plate of the control panel with some difficulty and his teeth. There'sh a little lever . . . ah, gotcha, pal! From behind the control panel came a couple of eructative wheezes, and a little green sign started flashing SELECT NUMBER at him. Bashtard machine, exshpecting me to do all the drokking work . . . Fifty'sh gonna be near enough . . .

He pushed and prodded until the panel flashed the number 50. She'll never notish the shtiffoid'sh a few body-weightsh short of the full number . . . Wonder what she wantsh a giant for anyhow . . .

Satisfied, Belcher tried to press the START button with his thumb, but the neck of the now nearly empty bottle kept getting in the way. At last he made do with his snubby nose, shoving against the plasteen square firmly and then collapsing into the mud at the Hopper's base.

From within the machine came more noises. Unhappy ones. He lay staring at the sky, listening to it as it went about the task. He'd never before been asked to multiply the mass of a stiffoid by such an amount. From time to time some drokkhead from BC would come out here asking to be made fifteen or twenty-five per cent bigger in all directions, by being crypped and decrypped appropri-ately, so that he could beat the stomm out of somebody who was bugging him, but it was rare. And never anything like this. Fifty! Wow!

Shay, maybe I better . . .

The noises from within the ReconHop were becoming deafening, the entire installation shaking on its founda-tions. He groped up towards the control panel, but the distance was impossibly far. He knew he should be panicking, but the relevant part of his spinal cord seemed to have drowned in a lake of booze, so that all he could muster was a fit of hiccups.

Shoundsh like the old Hop'sh having the mosht difficult crap in hishtory, he thought, slumping further into the mud.

A crescendo of straining and crashing noises filled the air. One thing was for certain: the Hopper, unused to such punishment, wasn't going to last much longer if this kept up. Belcher felt the ground move beneath him, juddering and flicking as if it were trying to pull itself distant from the machine before the inevitable happened. Any second now there was going to be the most almighty . . .

In the nick of time, something on the far side of the Hopper gave. There was a screech of rending metal and a ponderous thud, and then at last the machine was silent once more.

Belcher relaxed with it. Whatever was done was done. For several more minutes he lay on his back watching Korax's Eye chasing its tail all over the sky; then it occurred to him it might be wise to go and have a look at whatever monstrous stiffoid the Hopper might have disgorged.

He went round the end of the Hopper and found himself confronted by the sole of a single vast boot, taller than himself even if he'd been standing up. He edged past it until he got to the bulge of a calf, covered in some material coarsely woven from thick grey ropes.

Somewhere in his dungarees – ah, here it was. The hypostim had survived intact. He stuck the seal-cap in his mouth and yanked it off, reflexively swallowing. All he needed to do was work out which end of the – *ouch!* Not that one! – hypostim to press and . . .

His clenched hand fitting easily through an interstice in what he now recognised as a woolly sock, he administered the entire contents of the hypostim – about thirty normal doses – to an area of grey, corrugated flesh, and sat back to await developments.

For a while, nothing happened. Belcher took to watching the sky again. A flight of the Donut's leathery-winged geese formed a constantly shifting vee as they traversed the disc of Korax's Eye. There was a Grudalmighty rainstorm building up about twenty degrees around the inner circumference of the Donut from here. A little buzzing fly landed on his eyebrow, checked to see whether or not he was dead, decided he probably was, and had started to lay eggs on his open eye before he summoned up the necessary coordination to flatten it with his fist. Far in the distance, in the direction of BC, a chopper circled . . .

The leg directly beside him twitched. The stiffoid was regaining consciousness.

Belcher scrambled away from it, trying to get as far as possible from it before it started to thrash about.

The giant let out a tremendous snort. A few seconds later a small cloud overhead danced and contorted. As Belcher watched from the shelter of a dried-out streambed, the giant gathered its vast legs and slowly lugged itself up into a sitting position. Gargantuan hands cradled a gargantuan head as the giant uttered a series of ground-shaking moans. Arf vomited appositely. The hands came away to reveal the face: rounded features and a pair of elaborately decorated dayglo spectacles that appeared in imminent danger of slipping down the fleshy nose.

From behind those spectacles a pair of wrathful blue eyes narrowed as they focused on the quivering figure of Arf Belcher, far beneath.

Aghast on discovering that terror had rendered him stone-cold sober, Belcher returned the stare.

'*Strozza!*' he breathed.

The giant considered this for a moment. Belcher became uncomfortably aware of how extremely small he was beside this new, augmented version of the Imm-

Decryp tech. Then a voice like the pounding waters of the maelstrom shattered his thoughts:

'They call me *MISTER* Strozza!'

Even spread-eagled, she looked pathetically small, lying there in the swamp.

37% Dredd squelched across and crouched over her. Gingerly he turned her, wiping away mud from her face. Her breasts rose and fell steadily, and, although she was filthy, she looked more as if she were sleeping peacefully than as if she'd been slammed into unconsciousness. Only the bruises on her knees, her thighs, her hips, her shoulders, her chin and of course those breasts told him what had happened.

He sat back on his heels, scanning the level, greasy-seeming tracts of the swamp. Should he just wait here until she awoke? Should he try to wake her? He had vague, twilit memories of times when his mind had been capable of making split-second resolutions, had always known with rigid certainty what was the right thing to do. Back at the Overlord's farmhouse McTavish had more than once told him she thought the decision-taking part of him had been lodged entirely in the missing sixty-three per cent. Perhaps she was right.

A whisper of thought came to him.

The woman McTavish is not seriously damaged. I have given her sleep for the next few hours so that she may restore her spirit, which has these past few days endured more punishment than any Toadstone spirit was designed to tolerate. But you, Joe Dredd – you must bring her to me.

'Who the stomm are you?' he said out loud. 'I'm not moving a drokking millimetre from here until I know.'

You already do know.

'You're the Nandie totem.'

Indeed. The thought took on a touch of acerbity. *I am the Skysoul queen-goddess.*

'Why should I do what a Nandie tells me?'

A thunderbolt came from the clear sky and reduced several tens of square metres of swamp grass to ashes.

'You're the boss.'

Even in your reduced state, Joe Dredd, you're capable of carrying Petula McTavish as far as is required. Pick her up – no, you idiot! Not by the leg! Take her up-river along the bank of the Seems OK until you arrive at the place where I am: I shall come to you and McTavish in person when you are there.

Clumsily 37% Dredd complied, draping the limp form of the xenotheologist across his forearms. Even with the Multigob strapped to her spine she felt ridiculously light, as if she were made out of some more finely textured form of flesh than ordinary mortals. He looked down at her smoothly breathing face, seeing the thin blue lines of capillaries on her eyelids.

'I'm ready to obey,' he said heavily.

Then do so. But beware: before you reach me you shall meet the single individual whom in all the Universe you most fear. You must ensure you neither kill nor are killed by that person.

With this final piece of ambiguity, the goddess left him.

He trudged towards the river, confused. The only person he was aware of fearing at all was lying asleep in his arms.

Unless . . .

Nah. McGruder couldn't have come to the Donut.

Hours passed.

37% Dredd plodded stolidly on, McTavish still slumbering in his arms, as the swamp around the Seems OK's outfall turned into scrubby badlands and then into arid semi-desert, dotted with pudgy succulents. The river rumbled placidly about a hundred metres to his left. No trace of sweat appeared on his face, despite the hot orange-red sun perpetually at the zenith. His mouth remained set in a permanent half-snarl that gave no clue to his inward emotions – if, indeed, he experienced any.

Trudge, trudge, trudge went 37% Dredd's boots.

Hrreu, hrreu, hrreu went Petula McTavish's small snores. Every now and then her eyes half opened, as if she were about to wake, but then she merely nuzzled herself into a more comfortable position. The countless protrusions of the Multigob must have dug into 37% Dredd's flesh, but he gave no sign of pain.

At last he rounded a dunelike hummock and came in sight of a great rectangular structure set in a moister area of land, like an oasis in the desert. Sitting with his back propped against the edifice was a giant with black, curly hair and a pair of outmoded dayglo spectacles. Something fizzed behind 37% Dredd's visor, and his lips moved slightly as he identified the scene ahead of him as the MT installation.

'No data on giant man.' His lips moved soundlessly.

McTavish stirred in his arms again. He looked down at her face, shielded behind tails of sweat-damped hair. Still she slept. The bruises on her chin were fading rapidly: either he had been marching for days rather than hours or something unknown was acting inside her.

'Hoy there!' he shouted at the giant as he came closer.

'**Hoy!**' the giant returned, turning his huge head.

'Have you any food?'

The giant consulted briefly with a small dungareed figure whom Dredd now noticed for the first time. The little man lurched off to a nearby shack and vanished inside it; moments later he emerged with a couple of plastic carry-bags.

'**We have food,**' the giant confirmed.

Reaching the ReconHop, 37% Dredd gently deposited McTavish and the Multigob on a dryish patch of ground. 'My friend is sleeping,' he said.

'Sure drokking is,' confirmed the little man. 'Arf Belcher's the name, bud. Arf by name and Belcher by nature, as they says.' He stuck out his hand.

37% Dredd ignored him and gazed up at the face of the giant. From this angle the two nostrils looked like the insides of fur-lined sleeping bags. 'Name?'

'Mister Strozza.'

'Well, just keep your hands out in the open while we're talking.'

For a second the giant looked as if he were about to crush 37% Dredd beneath one massive fist, but then he relaxed. **'I give the orders round here.'**

'Hmm,' said 37% Dredd.

The giant peered down at the sprawled figure of McTavish on the ground beside him, and started.

'I recognise this woman!' he cried. **'She was always hanging around Imm-Decryp making a nuisance of herself. Dr McTavish – I can tell by the Multigob strapped to her back. So you must be her friend, Judge Drokk?'**

'Dredd.'

'Drokk, Dredd, it's all the same to me. I'm glad to see those bozos at Imm-Decryp finally succeeded in putting you together again. Did you know Cardano tried to shop you to Dennis the Complete Bloody Sadist?'

'No.' 37% Dredd's eyes tightened. 'And I don't think McTavish did either. When?'

'A few weeks back.' The giant waved a hand airily to show the matter was of little concern to him. The gale almost blew Belcher's shack over. **'I was able to interfere with her plans.'**

'Good. I pass sentence of death on Cardano in her absence. You did your duty.'

'Er . . .'

'And will continue to do so.' Suddenly the Lawgiver was in 37% Dredd's hands, pointing directly up Mister Strozza's nostril. 'According to the power invested in me by Mega-City One Justice Department, I hereby appoint you Temporary Deputy Judge, Fourth Class. Congratulations. You'll get a badge later. If you live.'

'Wha . . . ? Wha . . . ?'

'Rule One: no questioning the orders of a superior. Rule Two: I'm your only superior. Rule Three: shuddup.'

'Bu–'

37% Dredd's warning shot parted Mister Strozza's tousled hair.

'Yessir.'

'And you' – turning to Belcher, who was trying to hide inside his own dungarees – 'get the food here, bring some water, and shut up as well.'

'Y-yes sir.'

'OK' – returning his attention to the giant – 'is this machine still in use?'

'Yes, boss.'

'What for?'

'It's completing a commission for Cardano, boss. Well, really for your friend McTavish.'

'What's that?'

'Decrypping fifty-two holochips into a single individual. Should be done in a few minutes.'

'Fifty-two? Did the condemned perp Cardano say what the purpose of the decrypping was?'

'Not so much as you'd . . .' replied Belcher, who had filled the Concave Truncatoconical Holochip Transposition Module with water. Panting heavily, he dumped it alongside the carry-bags at 37% Dredd's feet.

'When I want your . . .'

'He was the one Cardano gave the orders to.'

'And you failed to apprehend her? Drokkhead!'

'I, uh . . .'

'Fifty credits.'

'Huh?'

'Seventy-five. What else did the perp say?'

'Just that I was to . . . Say, the ReconHop's finishing.' Belcher passed a rancid sleeve over his groin. 'Always sounds like it's got the trots when it's awready to go. Hope those repairs you done is gonna hold,' he added to Mister Strozza, who looked unworried.

The ReconHop was indeed juddering and shaking. The motion was enough to make McTavish restless in her sleep, so that despite the weight of the Multigob she half turned over onto her side, flinging one arm back. Belcher's eyes boggled, and even Mister Strozza looked interested.

37% Dredd ignored them both. 'Fifty-two,' he said. 'I wonder. Could it be . . . ?'

There was a loud rending noise from the far side of the Hopper as much of Mister Strozza's repair work to the Egress Module was ripped free of its makeshift moorings.

'It could be a false me!' yelled 37% Dredd. His Lawgiver held double-handed in front of him, he sprinted around the ReconHop. Heaped in the mud beneath the re-wrecked Egress Module was a burly helmeted figure who seemed to be stone dead.

37% Dredd held the Lawgiver unwaveringly to the stiffoid's temple.

'Resuscitate this stommer,' he snarled at Belcher, who was just heaving into view.

'O-OK, boss.'

'Gruddam impersonator,' muttered 37% Dredd. 'Impersonating a Judge. Capital offence. Hurry up and get the drokker up on his feet so I can blast him.'

'Er, don't you think, boss, that – ?'

'Shuddup!'

Belcher fumbled through his dungarees for a hypostim. First to appear was the one he'd emptied into Mister Strozza's leg; he chucked it away from him impatiently.

'Get a move on.'

'I'm gettin', boss.'

At last Belcher had the instrument. He held it up to the sunlight to check its contents, then with a trembling hand tried to tug away part of the stiffoid Dredd's clothing so he could get in a clear shot.

'Give it him in the face!'

'That's dangero–'

'Shuddup!'

'No, you shut up, Joe Dredd,' said a new voice.

37% Dredd spun in his tracks, bringing the Lawgiver around with him.

He found himself staring straight down the muzzle of a Multigobbet Autotronic Offense Weapon.

'McTavish! Get out of here!'

'I am your superior officer, Joe Dredd,' she said coldly. 'McGruder invested that status in me. Now that I'm awake again, I'm reassuming my command. Drop the gun now, buster, or feel a burst of hi-ex in your guts.'

37% Dredd paused. McTavish was speaking a language he understood. The Lawgiver wavered.

'It's an order, Dredd.'

Slowly, with exaggerated reluctance, 37% Dredd reholstered the weapon.

'He's a perp,' he said, booting the prone figure viciously in the side.

'You drokkbrain!' said McTavish, suddenly losing her temper. 'Can't you see he's *you*? He's another part of you!'

'Should have snuffed the drokker when you had the chance,' mumbled Belcher confidentially.

'You,' McTavish spat, 'how many chips went into this new Dredd?'

'Fifty-two.'

She looked speculatively at 37% Dredd, the Multigob still trained on him. 'You'd make up eighty-nine per cent between the two of you. That's probably enough that you'd be as good as new.'

37% Dredd's jaw dropped.

'Who's the little fat guy who can't take his eyes off me?'

'I'm Belcher,' said Belcher, trying to look her straight in the eyes but getting only as far as her navel. 'I'm the ReconHop Manager round here.'

'You're the man I need.'

'Aw, wow, really, hon? I –'

Turf gouted at Belcher's feet.

'Keep your distance, drokkwit. You got facilities for recrypping here?'

Belcher twisted his mouth. 'Well, kind of yes and kind of no. We ain't used them in an age. Ain't hardly no folk is let go back to Terry once they's come to the Donut. Can't guarantee the widget'll do it a hundred per cent OK, you get my meaning.'

'It'll have to do.' She jiggled the control-ring at the side of the Multigob. 'I have faith in you,' she added drily.

'Leave the stiffoid the way he is – no need to revive him. As for you, 37% Dredd – well, I'm sorry.'

The blast took 37% Dredd smack in the mouth, throwing him backwards over his sprawled duplicate.

'**What the . . . ?**' said a huge voice overhead.

'It's OK,' said McTavish, blowing across the snout of her weapon. 'I had it on stun. He'll stay out long enough for recrypping.'

She looked up. 'You're Strozza, aren't you? You're going to have a lot to explain to me,' she said heavily, 'but for now just help Belcher. I want something to eat and I'm going to look for some privacy, not necessarily in that order. If either of you looks over in the direction of that cactus during the next ten minutes . . .' She waved the Multigob suggestively.

'**Message understood, Dr McTavish.**'

McTavish was strolling back from the cactus towards the ReconHop when the queen-goddess spoke to her.

Dr McTavish, I presume.

'Biggins!' Even as she spoke McTavish knew she was wrong.

There was a gurgle of laughter – not a girlish gurgle, though. McTavish had the impression of someone so aged she was beyond age.

'Korax?' she said. 'Can it be you?'

Yes, I am Korax.

'Then Biggins is . . . ?'

Yes, your friend Starwatcher/Cloudrider/She Who Sees to the Ends of Roads reached me without mishap, and I have returned with her. She misses your presence, Toad-stone. She will not be fully content until you are once more by her side.

McTavish felt herself blushing. Dodging the issue, she said: 'You called her "Starwatcher/Cloudrider/She Who Sees to the Ends of Roads"?'

That is her full Skysoul name. Such names are revealed only to those who are close in heart. Which I am to all Skysouls. I breach no confidence in revealing Starwatcher/

Cloudrider/She Who Sees to the Ends of Roads's name to
you.

Again McTavish knew her face was red. She realised
she'd forgotten to keep walking during this interchange.
Squatting outside the plascrete MT cubicle, Mister
Strozza was cautiously watching her hold a conversation
with herself.

'How did she come by her name?'

*I gave it to her at birth, as I give all of my people their
names.*

'*All* of them?'

*All. My intentions become known to the parental triple-
bond – even though not necessarily to my own conscious
mind – and the triples are able to adorn their child with the
chosen names.*

'Which have meaning,' said McTavish. All this was
fascinating to a xenanthropologist. She was trying to
hammer the goddess's words into her mind, to make sure
they'd still be there intact after what promised to be a
hectic few days or weeks ahead. 'Skysoul meaning.'

*Meaning which you, too, may interpret, Petula
McTavish,* said Korax mildly, *even though you are a
Toadstone, born not of the Skysoul line. Starwatcher/
Cloudrider/She Who Sees to the Ends of Roads's tripartite
name predicts the formation of the triple bond she shall
form. She herself is Cloudrider, for she has ridden a cloud
with me in coming across the World.*

'And the other parts of her name?' McTavish was
certain her face must look like a miniature of Korax's Eye
by now.

'*Starwatcher' is a name surely clear enough in meaning
for you, Petula McTavish. No Skysoul may watch stars.*

McTavish had difficulty finding words. 'Then you mean
. . . ?' she said at last.

*I predicted a member of her triple-bond would be
someone from outside the World, although it is only
recently that I have become aware of my own prophecy.*
There was a pause, as if the queen-goddess were seeking
a way to say something tactfully. *I read the soul of*

211

Starwatcher/Cloudrider/She Who Sees to the Ends of Roads, and I was satisfied you were indeed Starwatcher. Now that I have read your soul also, Toadstone, my satisfaction is entire.

McTavish's mind began working again. 'The third member of the bonding,' she said. 'Can you yet predict who *he* will be?' A sudden image of a huge, helmeted figure trundled across her mind, and she gulped in horror.

Again that ageless laugh. *No, Petula McTavish, you need have no fear of finding yourself in a triple bond with Joe Dredd.* The inner voice grew suddenly solemn. *But the implications of the third name are very worrying to me. Very worrying indeed . . .*

SIX

Yesterday

'Yea, though I walk in death's dark vale, yet will I fear none ill – having taken advantage of the Oliver North Church of Fundamental Sanctimony's EeZee-Pay Hospital Insurance Plan, as advised by none other than the Reverend Rick "The Man" Hamfist himself! *(See inside back cover for further details and FREE application form.)*'

– Clients' Handbook (3rd edn, 2108),
Oliver North Church of Fundamental Sanctimony

HYPERFAX MESSAGE   July 15, 2116
Chip 1 of 1
FROM: *Chief Judge McGruder*
Mega-City One Justice Dept
Earth

TO: *Petula McTavish*
c/o Roxy Cardano
Chief Tech
Imm-Decryp
The Big Dunkin Donut

McTavish: Imperative you contact Justice Dept immediately. If no response from you messagewise within thirty-six, I repeat thirty-six, standard terran hours, I shall assume you and Dredd dead and shall have no recourse but to send a replacement squad into the Donut. Thirty-six: not thirty-seven or thirty-eight.

BC was like a city under siege by invisible assailants. The visitor's eye wandered the low hills that surrounded the city on three sides, expecting to see emplacements or occasional puffs of smoke, but instead all was calm.

The security cordon around the city was even tighter than when Harbinger, Sackville and Heidegger had left it, and the arrival of the carnival was delayed by a long series of seemingly interminable checks. At the same time, it was clear that none of the goons doing the checking actually knew what he was looking for, nor even who he was working for: some referred to various Overlords – including the late Griswold Himmelmann – as their bosses, others to either the Oliver North Church or the Margaret Thatcher Community, and still others were so shifty about their allegiance that it could be easily guessed that they were working for – or at least thought they were working for – Dennis the Complete Bloody Sadist himself. Even Korax, who had now been transformed into Gypsy Rose Jane, Palmist Extraordinaire, was unable to pick out from the tangled thoughts of the security apes precisely who their real masters were.

Mister Strozza – The Giant's Giant – was obviously the centre of attention at every stopping point . . . and also the member of the carnival for whom the security checks were most perfunctory. No one in the Donut had ever seen anything like him before, so it was safe to assume – or so the security thinking went – that he was unconnected with any of the divers sabotage plots they'd been assured by the rumour mill were hatching. In a strange way, Mister Strozza, despite his enormous bulk, therefore became the least visible of the party, and he was able to use his ears and, more importantly, eyes to garner snippets of information that were unobtainable even via Korax's formidable mental powers. *I can see anything, anywhere on the whole surface of the World,* she explained to McTavish, *but I can't see* everything. *First I have to know where to look.* Mister Strozza, through the simple process of wandering aimlessly around, found himself looking in places which would never in a million years have attracted Korax's attention.

And it was Mister Strozza who was first invited onto

Rev. Hamfist's holovee programme. After the show, while trying to persuade Maraschino to accept a couple of freshly printed out reams of reports, he picked up both a sketch of the internal layout of the studio and the useful datum that the city's security goons were now down to two main camps, working for Hamfist and Fingers respectively. No one mentioned Dennis. The Overlords had become a thing of the past: those who had not succumbed to 'accidents' had fled the city, and were now thought to be encamped in various locations several hundred klicks away. It looked as if BC had become, essentially, a territory wholly owned by the two evangelists, who any day now would start fighting for supreme control over the city.

The situation puzzled Dredd, McTavish and Biggins.

'Then what in drokk's happened to Dennis?' said McTavish, speaking for all of them. The carnival had yet to be permitted entrance to the city, and was parked in some derelict land about a kilometre outside its northern extremity. The two women were sitting a little apart from Dredd in one of the smaller tents, while Mister Strozza lay on the ground outside, his huge lips opposite the flap. Heidegger was squatting in a corner, ignored. 'I can't believe he's just retreated from the scene, leaving those two unholy Joes to slug it out.'

'That may be exactly what he's planning,' said Biggins, speaking aloud for the benefit of Mister Strozza and Judge Dredd. All the Skysouls except Korax found talking directly into the giant's mind very difficult, if not impossible, while Dredd's mind, now that it was nearly ninety per cent whole, was a locked and bolted fortress.

'What do you mean, Nandie woman?' said Dredd brusquely.

Biggins bristled, but kept her voice calm. Just that Dennis may reckon it's easier to defeat one fundamentalist than two, and be waiting for one to knock the other out of the game. And of course, if the war really hots up, even the victor won't have too many goons left to fight Dennis's men.'

'I think you're wrong, Nandie woman,' said Dredd.

'Joe,' McTavish began, 'we don't generally use the term "Nandie" round . . .'

He silenced her with a wave of his gauntleted hand.

'I think Dennis the Complete Bloody Sadist *owns* those two drokkheads,' he said. 'I think the struggle between them has all been a sham.'

'Bullstomm!' said McTavish, then stopped, seeing the look on Biggins's face. One moment the Skysoul looked as irritated as McTavish, the next she was grinning.

'Hey, Joe Dredd,' she said. 'You're maybe not as stupid as you look.'

'He'd have a drokk of a job,' muttered McTavish.

'I think you've got it,' Biggins was continuing. She leaned forward and put her hand on Dredd's forearm. To everyone's astonishment the Judge didn't twitch himself away from her. 'Think of it. Maybe Dennis has been working towards this from the start.'

'I'm not with you,' whispered Mister Strozza through the tent-flap. Even with his voice as low as possible, the wind buffeted the others.

'Nor me,' admitted McTavish.

'Let's take it as an axiom, just for the sake of argument, that what Dennis really wants from the outset is complete control over the whole Donut, OK?'

'You follow my line of reasoning precisely, Nandie woman.'

'But there are going to be several obstacles in his way,' said Biggins, her voice rising with excitement. She leaned back against McTavish and began enumerating her fingers. 'One: there's the Skysouls. The way the Overlords and the nubugs had things set up, the Skysouls might not have seemed too much of a threat, but if Dennis is a mite brainier than your average boss-man, he'll have realised that there's a lot of Skysouls around, and that if they chose suddenly to rebel . . . Enough said. Besides, the Skysouls have Korax. She's obstacle number two.'

Somewhere within the city there was a sudden rattle of

small-arms fire. Another execution. They happened every hour or two.

'But the Toadstones don't believe in Korax,' said McTavish. She found it almost physically painful to contradict the other half of her now-recognised pair-bond, but she persevered. 'So how could she come into his reckoning?'

'Because not all of us Terries are thick,' rumbled Dredd.

'Yeah, exactly,' said Biggins. 'The Overlords have never believed in Korax because it's been in their interest not to. The nubugs took their line from the Overlords, without ever really thinking about it – not because they're stupid but because, whenever you come to a new territory, you tend to take it for granted that earlier settlers know what they're talking about. I mean, Petula, you yourself thought Korax was only a fable, a primitive belief like all the others you've come across in your xenotheological career. Isn't that the case?'

'Yes.' Reluctantly. 'I guess so. An easy mistake to –'

'That's right: an easy mistake. A perfectly natural, rational mistake. So none of the Terries here thought Korax represented any threat to their plans to exploit the Donut and its indigenous population of Skysouls. None of them – *except Dennis*!'

McTavish sucked in her breath. It was all starting to make a hideous sort of sense. 'I begin to have a glimmer of respect for the stommhole,' she murmured slowly.

'You should,' pronounced Dredd. 'He realised the way to destroy any threat from the Nandies was to destroy Korax, so he created those two dumb-ass preachers. Dragged them in from the streets, or got them from Earth, maybe.'

'Why two? Wouldn't one have been plenty?'

'There's a whole stack of reasons for having two,' Biggins put in. 'One new sect goes ignored – it gets lost among all the other little minority cults. Even if the new sect has enough credits to buy out a holovee station, still

217

people ignore it. But if *two* of them, identical in almost every detail, start slugging it out – that's *news*!'

'And most of the dumb-asses take sides,' said Dredd. 'It's kinda like you see a game of batting: you don't give a stomm about the game, but you start wanting one side to win or the other.'

'So you split the Skysouls in two,' said McTavish, 'believing all sorts of direst bullstomm just because they're supporting their *team*?'

'Yup,' said Dredd.

'And with any luck the Skysouls will start fighting among themselves, something that hasn't happened for millennia,' said Biggins after a pause. 'It doesn't matter which side wins, you've effectively knocked over two of the obstacles at once: Korax, because no one believes in her any longer, and the Skysouls themselves, because they're rediscovering civil war.'

'You have a keen mind for a woman,' said Dredd. 'It sometimes rises above mediocrity.'

Biggins responded: 'You have a keen mind for a Toadstone, Joe Dredd. Sometimes it approaches mediocrity.'

'Divide and rule,' said McTavish heavily. 'I thought that was supposed to be Dennis's method. Seems like it's in operation here, too.'

Biggins pulled back her shoulders, and after a few moments returned to counting on her fingers. 'OK, so that's two obstacles out of the way, as we were saying. Three: the Overlords. They're not going to give over power to any newcomer without a struggle, right?'

'Unless,' said McTavish, 'there's already so much social upheaval that the overthrowing of the old order will go almost unnoticed. Diversionary tactics.'

'Yup,' said Dredd and Biggins simultaneously.

'Obstacle number four,' continued Biggins, 'is the nubugs, but they've already been largely dealt with under heading one. Dennis's two evangelists haven't been preaching just to Skysouls but to Toadstones as well. The same factionalism that'll nullify the Skysoul threat will do the same for the nubugs. And there you are.'

She sat back and put an arm around McTavish's shoulders.

'One further thing Dennis would have thought of,' said Dredd. He had pulled the Lawgiver from its holster and was examining it for specks of dirt. 'Earth.'

'Us, you mean?' said McTavish.

'Us, or someone like us. He couldn't have known when Earth would start reacting to any news from the Donut, and he couldn't have known *how* it would. But he must have calculated us in somehow.'

'Oh, I can guess that,' said Biggins airily. She'd obviously cottoned on fast. 'He used the arrival of you two as a timer.'

'Explain, Nandie woman,' said Dredd.

'The first interference from Earth – that was the signal he was waiting for. Didn't matter if it came from Mega-City One, Euro-City, Sino-City Two, Brit-Cit, New Jerusalem . . . Whoever came here to check the situation out would be an outsider, an intruder, an alien interferer. Unless Earth sent in a really crushing force, you Toadstones didn't represent any threat to Dennis – not yet. But it could be made to appear to the rest of BC that you did. You were like a flea landing on the flank of an irritable sabre-tooth. Without you, the sabre-tooth might grump and growl a bit, but chances were it'd eventually roll over and go back to sleep. But then along comes a tiny flea and bites it . . .'

'We were to be the catalyst,' said McTavish.

'Maybe that, or maybe just a timer, like I said. How long do you think it'll be before Earth sends in the big battalions?'

'Not long,' said Dredd. 'Another few weeks?'

'So Dennis has to bring it all to fruition in that time,' breathed McTavish. 'It doesn't seem long.'

'Faster than that,' said Dredd. 'He'll want BC under his boot in the next couple of days. Mopping up the rest of the Donut can take as long as needed, after that.'

McTavish chewed her lower lip. Dredd, infuriatingly, was perfectly correct. If Dennis had made himself emperor of the Donut by the time Mega-City One and New Jerusalem were ready to send in a heavy military force, they'd accept the situation: rather than start a war, they'd start trade negotiations.

And what a lot Dennis would have to trade! The Donut's natural resources were vast, almost entirely unexploited, and worth billions. The dross Earth had been shipping out here – the Overlords and the transportees – had squandered only a tiny fraction of them. They'd wanted to be kings for a day, not emperors forever.

Dennis had been – was – longer-sighted than that. Once he'd made himself ruler of the Donut, with all its resources, it couldn't be more than a century or two before he was ruler also of the rest of the Solar System – conqueror through commercial rather than military might. Just a century or two . . .

'Oh, *Grud*!' she whispered. 'You know something? I think he's immortal.'

Dredd's great dome turned towards her.

'That's assuming a lot,' he said bluntly. 'Right now, we don't know anything about the drokker. We don't even know where he *came* from.'

'Or,' said Biggins, 'who he is.'

McTavish wondered if this had been such a good idea.

It was cloudy over BC – something which Korax had been able to arrange – and the light shining in laterally cast weird shadows in the semi-darkness. McTavish was crouching at the edge of a deserted autopark in the lee of one of the outer walls around Thatchvee, the holovee station run by Rev. Hamfist and his Margaret Thatcher Community. When she'd been here before she'd approached the place from the front; from the rear it looked like a fortress, with great slabs of rock and rockcrete forming an imposing back wall to the building itself, through which had been cut narrow eyelets for snipers. She wondered if, under their façade of bill-hoardings, flashing holos and fake plasteen marble sheeting, the other sides of the building had been similarly treated.

She glanced behind her. The pool of shadow she was in was dark enough to make her invisible more than twenty or thirty metres away, but anybody with a set of infrared goggles could be observing every detail of her from one of the windows of the tenement buildings across the autopark.

McTavish shivered. She clutched the Multigob.

Dredd was somewhere off to her right, keeping a side wall of the station under surveillance. Biggins was doing the same, to her left. She glanced at her Kronowiz, its digits glowing orange in the shade. If everything was going according to plan, right around now Harbinger and Sackville were infiltrating themselves along with the rest of the studio audience for Hamfist's next service.

If everything was going according to plan.

The plan hadn't seemed such a bad one when they'd been cooking it up in the tent. At the current rate, it could be weeks before all the members of the carnival were cleared by the security goons. Itchy Bagman apparently had a criminal record in BC – which meant little more than that he'd been here before. While Korax had been able to influence matters so that he hadn't been taken in for torture or just shot out of hand, she'd been unwilling to interfere too obtrusively in case her meddling were noticed and reported to Dennis. Stalemate. Each day the goons had been calling by to check that Itchy wasn't doing anything he shouldn't be, and that the rest of the carnival was likewise. Mister Strozza, on the other hand, was these days just waved through by the goons: it had been his idea to simply carry through their weaponry hidden in his mammoth pockets. The rest of the team could, with luck, slip through somehow.

Which was, give or take the covert dispersal of a few credits here and there, the way it had gone.

* * *

221

Inside the security of his blister on the Donut's skin, Dennis the Complete Bloody Sadist was fuming. The liquid in which his brain floated bubbled and roiled, threatening to splash over the edges of its jar. From his voicebox came electronic spatterings and sputterings. Jock Becattini leant in a corner, chewing some of Garbucci's leftover supplies of bubbleguck and trying desperately to look nonchalant in the face of his master's wrath.

At last the string of electronic explosions coalesced into words. 'The Gruddam Nandie bitch-goddess is somewhere nearby,' said the voicebox. 'I can *feel* it.'

'Yah, boss.'

If Dennis had possessed an integrated body he'd have gone over to the window, put his hands behind his back and gazed out at the profundities of space as he mustered his thoughts. As it was, all he could do was turn his two eyes towards each other so they could stare into each other's depths.

'And that McTavish bitch, she's near us too.' Dennis would have spat contempt, had he had lips. 'We almost had her in our grasp. If only that stupid drokkbrain Garbucci and the rest hadn't got themselves cut down by her Multigob, of all the dumb-ass things to do. Stommheads. And if only that dumb-ass Himmelmann had held onto her instead of getting himself blown to drokking smithereens by those two broads and their drokking depth charge, we could have had her *and* the rest of Judge drokking Dredd.'

'Yah, boss.' Chew, chew.

The voicebox started spluttering again as Dennis failed to keep his emotions pent. There were too many if-onlies. If only that crazy dimwit Strozza hadn't got the Judge's name drokked up! If only Dennis himself had had a clearer idea of what Dredd looked like when he'd sent Garbucci and his goons out combing the streets! There was an enigma there that Dennis had chosen not to probe before: he could remember the *fact* of himself having been seized and sentenced by the drokker, but he couldn't

222

actually recall it *having happened*. In fact, he had no clear recollection of what it felt like having a body at all . . .

'You doubled the guards around the two holovee stations?' he said, forcing his raving mind to control the voicebox properly.

'Yah, boss.'

'And the surveillance bizzybees?'

'Yah.'

'Show me.'

Becattini moved over to touch a couple of buttons on the womblike wall, and a patch of its leathery surface pulled back to reveal an old-fashioned two-dee screen. The bizzybees were smaller than the insects after which they were named and, though the amount of circuitry the techs were able to load into them was staggering, were incapable of carrying a holovee camera. The tiny flying robots were hideously expensive: even Dennis could afford only a couple of dozen, which he used sparingly for fear of predatory birds. Having half a million megacredits' worth of electronics sending back images of the inside of a bird's guts was not his idea of money well spent.

The screen fizzled into life.

The camera of whichever bizzybee they'd tuned into was operating mainly in the infrared, so everything seemed muzzy and monochrome. It took Dennis only a few seconds to recognise from the scene laid out on the screen that the bizzybee was circling over Thatchvee. Unlike the approximately circular Northvee, from where the Reverend Dave 'No Messin' Fingers carried out his proselytising, the central building of Thatchvee was rectangular, not much off being square. A queue of punters had formed outside the station's front gate, awaiting admission for tonight's show. About fifty metres away, all around it, was the guarding wall, loaded with booby-traps and sensor devices, mostly pointed inwards – as was the wall's automatic weaponry: Dennis wanted any attackers shielded a little from the public eye before they were torched. It hadn't happened yet. It might, today, unless . . .

223

Hmm, that was a better idea . . .

'Gimme a blow-up on that, Becattini.'

The bulky man spun a dial casually and the Thatchvee building swam closer until it nearly filled the screen. Its roof was a patchwork of more sensing apparatus and clumps of air-directed weaponry. Dennis focused intently on the scene, but could see nothing out of the ordinary. Nothing moved. The voicebox gave out the electronic equivalent of a sigh.

'Now the drokkers out front. Come in low on them.'

The view shifted and swung dizzyingly as, several kilometres away and far above their heads, the bizzybee swooped downwards and sideways towards the expectant studio audience by the gate. A few heads turned up, but no one showed any suspicion that it was anything other than what it appeared to be – a slightly noisy, swift-darting hoverfly.

'Take it to the end of the line, and reverse it slowly back towards the gate,' Dennis ordered.

Becattini obeyed silently.

Again nothing out of the ordinary. Today's bunch was much the same as usual. Mainly they were nubugs, low-level males and somewhat more affluent-seeming females. No Overlords, of course, but one or two muties and a scattering of solitary Nandies, each separated from the people around them by a small but quite distinct space, as if the nubugs were frightened of even brushing against them – which was, although illogical, very probably the case. Dennis ignored the Nandies – the subhumes all looked the drokking same, anyway – and concentrated on the faces of the humans. Near the head of the line there was a freckle-faced redhead who seemed vaguely familiar, chattering with a brunette who likewise rang a faint bell. Likely they were just his own goons: these days up to twenty per cent of every audience at both Thatchvee and Northvee was made up of Dennis's people, sent there to keep an eye on things. Despite a wispy, lingering trace of doubt, he put them from his mind.

'Take us on a tour of the walls,' he instructed, 'and then over to Northvee.'

'Yah, boss.'

It was obvious that Becattini was beginning to have fun. Dennis half expected a burst of travelogue music as the bizzybee raised itself several metres in the air and cut off to one side of the queue. Speeding above the wall-top, it zigzagged from side to side, offering alternate views of the areas immediately inside and outside.

Dennis almost missed seeing what he'd been looking for.

'Stop there,' he hissed. 'Come back a bit. Slower, butthead – slower!'

Becattini juggled the controls and the bizzybee swung around in a curve and began idling back the way it had come.

'There!' said Dennis triumphantly.

The soft edges of one of the shadows at the side of the wall were interrupted by a clearly defined shape. Even in the flat image displayed on the two-dee screen, it was immediately apparent what the shape was.

'A boot,' breathed Dennis. 'Stomm me, but we've got the drokker!' He drew on the pictures stored away in his brain, and matched the silhouette on the screen with the diagram in his memory. 'It's a Mega-City One Justice Department Official-Issue Boot!'

'That the rest of Dredd, boss?'

'Yup.'

Once more the liquid in Dennis's brain-jar started simmering, but this time with delight.

'OK, so now we got the dumb-ass pinned down. Come in closer into that shadow, Becattini. I want to get a clearer look at him. Wouldn't put it past those Justice Department bastards to plant an empty uniform there. *Hurry*, stommskull!'

Becattini, chewing happily, rotated a little wheel and the bizzybee swooped in a graceful circle away from the wall and then back in a smooth dive towards the wall's base, where the shadows were thickest. He clicked a switch, and the bizzybee's tiny camera shifted entirely into the infrared.

'There!' said Dennis as the metallic insectoid zoomed towards a hunched body. The helmeted Judge was holding himself perfectly motionless.

Becattini, grinning complacently, became careless. He was having fun with the controls, making the bizzybee rock from side to side and start and stop, just like a real insect. He spiralled it in towards the dome of the helmet, hoping to be able to get a clear shot of the Judge's face.

Suddenly the head and shoulders were in motion.

Dennis and Becattini had a swift glimpse of a snarl and a spreading hand, and then all transmissions were blacked out.

'Drokk it!' screamed Dennis. 'You drokking, *drokking* drokker!'

Becattini cringed by the wall-screen.

'Now the dumb-ass knows we're watching him!'

'Uh, yah, boss.'

'Shuddup!' Threatening tentacles of smoke were drifting out of the sides of the voicebox. With a colossal struggle, Dennis managed to calm himself down to mere fury. Maybe there was a way this could be turned to his advantage. Yeah, maybe there was . . .

'Keep the bizzybees away from him, as of now, Becattini,' he said. 'I want you to take another 'bee quick round the rest of the walls, spotting to see if there's other buttbrains with him, but that's all.' Yeah, that was all. Dredd would likely think he'd just knocked out their surveillance entirely – at half a million megacredits apiece, bizzybees didn't normally hunt in swarms. Leave him with that to think about. Anyway, it was just luck that he and Becattini had been monitoring the bizzybee: Dredd would be guessing that he'd got the insectoid quick enough that alarm bells hadn't started sounding.

Let's hope. That'll be what Dredd's doing, too. So we're evens.

'Two more of them,' reported Becattini. 'One to the

south, one to the west. The one to the south looks to be the McTavish bitch.'

'And the other?'

The goon shrugged. 'Aw, just some Nandie.'

Korax! Could it be . . . ?

Dennis damped his sudden exhilaration. It wasn't the queen-goddess. He knew that. He didn't know how he knew it, but he did. She wasn't far away, but that wasn't her down by Thatchvee.

But Dredd! And McTavish!

Dennis wished he had a pair of hands, so that he could rub them together in glee. Instead he tried to get the voicebox to produce a satisfied chortle.

'Granted, boss,' said Becattini automatically.

'Ya got da hi-ex, J-No?' whispered Irish O'Sollovan for the thousandth time.

J-No smiled a secretive smile through a carefully positioned smear of unwashed hair. 'Don't get ya freckles in a twist, sis,' she said. 'I got da stuff stuffed in my bra. Gonna be safe enough lessen I get da hiccups or something.'

She shifted her shoulders, very cautiously. 'Drokking long time we been waiting,' she observed.

'Boy, yeah, dose guys gonna wish dey hadn't kept us standing out here dis long.' Irish stomped from one foot to the other. 'Stommbutts gonna get hi-ex impacted in orifices dey didden even know existed, huh?'

'You bet, sis.' Again the secretive smile. Throughout BC and well into the hinterland, there were people who had good cause to dread that smile. Those who had survived . . . 'You dun forgave me for da hairslide yet, sis?'

Irish shook her unfettered mop of red hair angrily. 'Ain't never gonna forgive you dat ting, J-No, an' you know it, even if you did have ta use it for da detonator.'

'Hey, sis, get calmed down, willya? Dere wasn't no choice in da madder!'

'Coulda used one of ya own!'

'Don't be so stoopid, sis.'

'Yeah, all right den,' said Irish, cooling as rapidly as she'd overheated. 'Get ya gob shut, hun. Dunno iffen dere's any sneakers in the queue.' She looked around her, but from her low vantage-point all she could see were chests and shoulders. 'Gonna be a Gruddam big bang, hey, sis, don't tell me no, huh?'

'Big bang, sis.'

The two of them began to giggle, heads close together.

Biggins!

She eases back slightly from the wall. *I hear you, Sackville,* she thinks.

They're just beginning to get the gates open. The two of us should be inside the studio itself in under five minutes. There was a flying spy over us a little while ago, but it didn't seem to pay us any especial notice. I think we're going to make it.

A small smile comes to Biggins's lips. *Well done. Good luck.*

Korax be our guide.

Biggins shrugs, but tries not to let any shade of her doubt leak through into her thoughts. The queen-goddess, her constituency of believers so drastically shrunk these past few weeks, is having her work cut out maintaining the low cloud ceiling over BC. Biggins wonders if this is something else Dennis knew about from the start – that the goddess's ability to perform the miraculous is fuelled by the faith of her congregation. The crusading activities of the two evangelists have directly depleted the goddess's abilities. *Korax has other things to attend to,* she remarks mildly. *We'd be best to act as if we were on our own.*

As always, the voice of wisdom, Biggins, comes Sackville's amused thought. *You are right to be cautious, of course, but . . .*

I'm right to be cautious, Biggins cuts in.

She ignores anything else Sackville might have to say and instead channels her thoughts in the direction of Petula McTavish.

Toadstone rat, did you catch any of that?

Any of what, Nandie woman? In private they trade Dredd-style insults.

Sackville. He and Harbinger are about to be let into the station.

Not many minutes left, then, are there?

Not many. Set your Kronowiz for five minutes exactly – now. Ah . . . good luck, you funny little fatso.

Good luck, bonebag. Trust me to fall for a subhume. Talking of subhumes, time I got the news to Dredd. See you inside.

Yes, says Biggins wistfully, *see you inside.* Strictly to herself she adds: *I hope.*

Dredd's hearing extended further into the super- and subsonics than even the Nandies could match. McTavish's signal, sent using the whistle he'd given her, although inaudible to her came through clear as crystal. He set his kronometer for four minutes and thirty-three seconds, and made one final check to his equipment. Lawgiver: in place; functioning. Antigrav-propelled coil of synthinylon rope: safely stashed in its cylinder; cylinder-strap securely in position at right shoulder blade. Stick of brainrot bombs: all present and correct in their improvised bandolier. Unless you had taken the antidote beforehand, a brainrot bomb erupting anywhere within ten metres fused every neuron in your body solid. There were other lethal weapons carefully cached all over Dredd's body – the weight would have crushed a lesser physique flat – and he numbered them off logically, his lips moving slightly as he recited their check-numbers.

He remembered the spy-insect that had come swooping down at him, but he suppressed the memory. Whether the tiny peeper had been able to raise the alarm or not was a matter of total indifference. It was too late for anything to stop him.

His pulse was slow and steady.

He was Walking Death.

He was Dredd.

He was three minutes and seventeen seconds away from going straight through the wall in front of him.

'Hey boss, you ain't just gonna let them attack and get away with it, are you?' Becattini looked as if someone had just blasphemed. 'Them stommers gonna get their nuts blown off, ain't they?'

'Yes, my little rockcrete-brained one,' said Dennis soothingly. He couldn't remember the last time he'd enjoyed such fun. The fluid in his brain-jar was frothing joyfully. 'But not for another day or so yet. They still have a part to play in my plans before you and I have the pleasure of destroying them. And then, my good friend, it ain't gonna be a case of just blowing them away. We're gonna take our time with these babies. Especially Dredd.'

'Aw, c'mon, boss. Ain't I gonna get to take some time with McTavish as well? She drokked over my old friend Garbucci, you know. Weren't I had the runs that day, I'd have been drokked over too. Wanna make her going real slow. Wanna be a *while* with her.'

'You can have as much time with her as you wish, Becattini. But tomorrow.'

Rick 'The Man' Hamfist was building up his opening homily to fever pitch, his mouth foaming as he pounded his head on the stage floor. Around him lay the corpses of sacrificed virgins, mouflons eviscerated so that their entrails could be given a favourable reading, chickens whose heads he'd bitten off – no subtext, but good theatre – and numerous others.

He was really putting on a show tonight, thought Maraschino fondly as she waited in the wings, Scooper as ever clamped to her bosom. She knew how important this holocast was to her husband, to herself. The final show-down between the Hamfists and Dave and Jaboticaba Fingers to decide the future of the Donut – the Last Battle, as they'd taken to calling it on air – could hardly be much longer delayed, and Hamfist was giving the recruitment drive everything he'd got.

The fingers of her free hand toyed in the air over the slideboard, ready to instigate tonight's sequence of miracles the instant that Rick 'The Man' called for them. He'd just bitten his own foot off at the ankle and was lustily chewing the toes – well, that's what it looked like thanks to the marvels of modern technology – and all this less than a minute into the act! 'Yore shore a credit to showbiz, ma man!' The audience seemed as impressed as she was, several of them having already appreciatively fainted.

Things were going just great.

BLAM!
Blam! Blam!
Blam! Blam! Blam!
Blam!
Thyeung!
BLAM!!!
'Aaargh!'
Blam! Blam-blam!
Screeeeee!
Dredd was already through. McTavish crossly hammered the heel of her hand against the detocap of the sidemine stuck to the wall in front of her, and at last the device detonated. The tightly directional blast blew out a hole in the solid rockcrete three times bigger than she was, sending great lumps of jagged-edge masonry somersaulting across the littered area beyond. At the same time, invisibly, it was taking out electronic sensors ahead of her in a semicircular fan with a seventy-five metre radius. Clutching the Multigob in her arms, she ducked through the gap, ready to mow down anything that moved.

There were automatic snipers in the rear wall of the main studio building. Dredd's sudden eruption into the yard must have triggered them into action. He'd slung himself down behind a heap of dented filing cabinets and was trading shots with the robot-controlled weapons, methodically picking his way along the slit-shaped emplacements from left to right.

Spinning the Multigob's control-ring up to full power, she sprayed the entire façade. More masonry flew and the entire rear half of the studio sagged. A few of the robotics still kept functioning, but these were death throes, their shots aimlessly zinging off into the sky.

Biggins. Where was Biggins?

There – snaking forward into the shadow of the disintegrating building, moving with that incredible, eye-straining lope of hers. Unlike McTavish and Dredd, the Skysoul was largely unencumbered by weaponry: she had a dagger in her belt, but otherwise she was relying mainly on her lethally swift hands and feet.

Dredd was up again, jiggling backwards towards the studio, letting fly with the Lawgiver, shooting out anything along the perimeter wall that looked remotely like a threat. Cursing her own slow reflexes, McTavish did likewise, her heavier ammunition ripping holes wherever it impacted. One of the abandoned autocars in the park beyond must still have had some gasoline left in its tank, because a fist of angry red-black fire suddenly punched upwards into the sky.

She slipped and fell on a heap of rain-sodden posters advertising Reverend Sally Monella Clamhorne, whoever *she* was. The weight of the Multigob took McTavish over backwards in a crazily skewed cartwheel as she tried to steady herself. A trail of holes traced its way across the yard. Other litter burst into flames. She was on her feet again, this time running directly towards the outward-leaning, fire-blackened back wall of the studio, where Biggins was waiting beside a steel-armoured door.

'Stand back!' yelled McTavish.

The Skysoul leapt aside.

A burst of rapid shots from the Multigob and the door was gone. The twisted frame dripped blobs of molten metal.

With the speed of the wind the Skysoul was through the opening. McTavish could see a handful of armed goons sprinting along a brightly lit corridor towards the place where the door had been, and then Biggins was among them. Blood sprayed as the goons' throats were torn out. McTavish knew she'd be sick thinking about this later, but at the moment all she felt was a wild, piercing exultation.

There was a sting on her cheek as a droplet of melted steel touched her and then she too was in the corridor, leaping over the remnants of the goons. Biggins was up ahead, beckoning. The Skysoul had kicked apart the studded lock of an inner security door and was propping it half-open, holding up the corpse of yet another goon to absorb the low-energy projectiles being pumped at her from the other side.

Half tripping, McTavish shouldered stiff and Skysoul aside and let rip with the Multigob, keeping her aim low – the main auditorium from where the show was even now being holocast was near here but set a few metres higher in a sort of half-hearted mezzanine.

There was a blinding explosion. One of the goons firing on Biggins must have had a grenade or two on him. She fired a few more shots, just to be on the safe side – just to make sure that the human debris she found when she went through wouldn't look too much like people.

Dredd was at her shoulder.

'Once we're through there, you go right and I go left,' he snapped. 'Don't forget, McTavish.'

'Drokk you, Dredd!' she snarled. Condescending bastard.

She rammed an elbow at him and leapt through the doorway ahead of him, spinning to the right. Another Gruddam corridor. The smell of burnt meat was almost overpowering. Greasy smoke clouded her vision. According to Mister Strozza's map, ahead of her were the personnel offices, largely occupied by techs and holocammers. If there were any there now they'd wisely chosen to stay out of sight. She blatted a few doors with the Multigob's butt as she passed, just to keep anyone inside conveniently terrified, and found herself at a corner.

Left. Up a flight of stairs. She had a half-memory of having seen parts of this area when Harbinger and Sackville had been whipping her out of the studio. Tacky but expensive holo-art adorned the walls, and she took fierce pleasure in scorching half of it away, telling herself she was doing it just to build up the pressure on the Thatchvee staff. She shot out a few of the lights on the same principle, forcing herself to feel nothing as glasseen shards rained around her.

At the head of the stairs she turned left again. As if the two of them had been perfectly synchronised, Dredd rounded the far corner at exactly the same moment. She gave the big man a smoke-streaked grin but of course he didn't respond.

There was a clear area in front of the main auditorium's doors, a broad synthimarble expanse at the head of two or three wide, shallow stairs that led down to an internal courtyard and the big reinforced glasseen gates that fronted the building. In the lower area fish swam in tanks. A receptionist, naked except for a forest of erotic tattoos, was trying to squeeze herself in between two shelves behind her desk. McTavish ignored the panic-stricken woman and the fish and took out the big doors, melting the glasseen with a single sprayed burst.

From somewhere beyond the receptionist's desk a group of half a dozen goons burst into her line of sight. Dredd got the front three of them with the Lawgiver before she had time to release a single shot. He's good, she thought resentfully as she pulverised the remainder.

Somehow Biggins had beaten both of them to the auditorium doors. She had inserted the long thin fingers of both hands into the narrow crack between them, and was straining to get them apart. Sprinting towards her, McTavish spun the Multigob and grabbed it by the barrel, ready to bring the butt swinging around in a crunching arc to smash her way through. Just as she reached the Skysoul Biggins gave a grunt and the doors came apart in her hands, as if they'd been made of paper stretched over a wooden frame.

Biggins turned her head and flashed her a quick smile. McTavish was busy trying to get the Multigob back under

control. Dredd was beside the two women again, roughly
shoving them ahead of him into the auditorium, twisting
himself half backwards to loose a few more shots from the
Lawgiver into the reception area.

The door opened just in front of the stage. Bright lights
overhead. The slant of the tiered seats leading up to her
right. Biggins darted across the foot of the stage to the far
side, keeping low, then up the stairs alongside the audience, chopping at the throats of the armed goons there.
McTavish directed a Multigob blast up the stairs beside
her, withering goons into dead meat.

Dredd barged past her and leaped up onto the apron,
kicking his ponderous way through the footlights. Rev.
Hamfist was in the process of prising one of his own eyes
out with his thumb. Blood and bodies everywhere.
McTavish caught a glimpse of Maraschino quietly fading
away into the wings on the far side of the stage. Getting
out while the going's still good. Don't blame her.

Dredd swung a heavy gauntleted fist into Reverend
Rick's face, splatting the loosened eye back into its
socket, jamming the preacher's thumb in beside it. The
Lawgiver flashed into place at Hamfist's head.

The tableau suddenly froze.

'Anyone got anything they want to say?' growled
Dredd.

Harbinger can feel Sackville's tension in her own mind,
but doesn't have the resources of energy to give him any
help. The two of them have strung themselves out to the
limit throwing a mental shield over the rest of the audience, lulling the people into placidity, whatever they
might hear or see. Were the two Skysouls not pair-
bonded, it would be impossible: the bonding has allowed
them to work synergistically. Now it is time to shove the
spectators one further stage, from relaxation into
slumber.

But that mental threshold requires considerable psychic
energy to cross. Drained as the two Skysouls are, it is
going to be a struggle.

I'll help, comes Biggins's thought.

Harbinger stiffens. *You can't do that!* she protests. *You're not our triple!*

No – but I can still add my energies to yours.

Hurry! moans Sackville. *We should have had them sleeping by now. Any more delay and some of them are going to be lifting off the shield. Dredd could kill them if they did anything stupid!*

Let me help, says Biggins plaintively. *The helmeted Toadstone is too ready to kill innocent bystanders. You have not seen the carnage outside.* She gives them a brief glimpse of smoking bodies and raw meat, and a waft of burnt flesh and hair. Their senses reel. *Even Petula McTavish . . . the Toadstones are steely of heart.*

Help us, then, says Sackville. Harbinger senses he is on the verge of letting his side of the shield collapse down on top of him. On top of them both, perhaps.

All right. Dubiously. *We can try . . .*

McTavish couldn't believe it. One moment she was aware of being the focus of two hundred pairs of eyes – sluggish eyes, perhaps, but two hundred pairs of them nevertheless – and the next the air around her seemed to slacken. She risked a glance to her right, and then relaxed a fraction. Two hundred heads were lolling to one side or the other. Two hundred spectators, fast asleep.

Harbinger was climbing across the rows to where Sackville slumped. The male Skysoul's face was a ghastly white. Biggins, too, at the far side of the stage-front, was staring agitatedly at Sackville, and McTavish could sense her wanting to rush to his assistance.

Above her, all remained motionless on the stage. Reverend Rick was clearly trying to say something, but had lost all control over his throat and mouth muscles. McTavish could see only the right-hand side of the man's face: the left was obscured by his clenched hand and by blood. There might have been a trace of a savage grin on Judge Dredd's face. The Lawgiver was unwavering.

'For Grud's sake, Dredd!' she yelled. 'Let's just get him out of here, can't we?'

'The woman,' Dredd said. 'The creep in the red dress. She's gone.'

'Let her go. We don't need her.'

'I say we do. Get her.'

'Aw, Dredd, for Grud's sake . . .'

'Get her.'

Heaving both a histrionic sigh and the Multigobbet Autotronic Offense Weapon, McTavish scrambled with some difficulty up onto the stage's apron. She found her nose about two centimetres from the neck-stump of a decapitated chicken. Jerking herself to her feet, she headed backstage.

'Kill him!' yelled Dennis at his holovee set. The shot had frozen with Dredd and the preacher somewhat to the left of centre. McTavish scuttled across in front of them, heading towards the right of camera; her three-dee image winked out of existence as it reached the edge of the holovee camera's field. 'Drokking kill the drokker, drokker!'

A frown wrinkled Becattini's brow, and he almost swallowed his ball of bubbleguck. 'Uh, boss,' he said, 'I thought we was on the same side as the Rev., you know?'

'Shuddup, Becattini.' Dennis's eyes were straining forward in their jar, trying to see as much as possible of the action on the holovee. 'If you ain't worked out yet why I want Rev. Hamfist dead, you're even drokking thicker than Garbucci!'

'I always thought Garbucci was pretty bright,' murmured Becattini perplexedly.

'Turn up the volume, stommbrain! I wanna hear what Dredd says, even if it's only a whisper.'

'Yah, boss.'

Backstage was a maze of cables and slideboards and dumped costumes and half-eaten meals and discarded wigs and full ashtrays and spilt cans of booze and rickety-looking cupboards and all the other things you expect to find backstage. Picking her way through the debris, McTavish was reminded of the time, back at the Old Cap'n Birdseye Polytechnic of North Brit-Cit, when she'd been persuaded to play Lady Macbeth by an acned director who'd had the hots for her.

Her lips smiled at the memory; the rest of her couldn't have felt grimmer. It was as if the sickly smell of death hung around her. Part of her hoped that Maraschino had long gone, had slipped out of the studio by some back way; part of her wanted to find the woman and help her hide – surely she'd suffered punishment enough for one lifetime when Fingers had flayed her? Only a small part of Petula McTavish wanted to do what Dredd had sent her here to do: capture Maraschino Hamfist and bring her back.

He could have sent Biggins. Biggins would've been much better at this than her. But Biggins had been hurrying to help Sackville . . .

Any noise from the auditorium was stifled here by the heavy fabric drops. There were only a few dim lights, little spots hanging over slideboards, prompt-books and synthicaff machines. The snout of the Multigob kept catching on things, and the debris littering the floor was treacherous underfoot. McTavish was making a lot of noise.

Maybe it was better like that. Maraschino would be able to hear her coming and know to keep out of her way . . .

With that in mind, she got into the habit of smashing every slideboard she came upon with the weapon's butt. She was destroying miracles, she knew – but evil miracles.

'Evil.' The word caught her up short. She hadn't used it in years – she'd long ago learnt that the Universe wasn't made up of things as useless and abstract as good and evil. But the word seemed right in her mind to describe what she felt about the things that Dennis and his cat's-paws, Hamfist and Fingers, were getting up to in the Donut. And, once she'd accepted that, it was only a small step to the realisation that the word equally adequately described the activities of the Overlords and the later Toadstone nubugs. It wasn't necessary that the Skysouls actually be *good* for the things that were being done to them, or which might be done to them, to be categorisable as *evil*. And maybe that wasn't the end of it, either: whereabouts in the ethical spectrum did what she and Dredd were doing lie? They hadn't come here to save Skysouls: they'd come to protect the interests of the ruling powers of Earth. What the authorities wanted was a return to the status quo, with the Skysouls continuing to be exploited just the same way they'd been since Toadstones had started coming to the Donut. So she and Dredd were on the side of *evil*, were they not? And didn't that necessarily imply that they themselves were *evil*?

McTavish shook her head vexedly. She didn't *feel* she was evil. But she was maybe contributing to an evil act. If she carried on doing so . . .

There was only one solution, she thought grimly: change the act.

She pushed aside a dusty drop and stared into the gloom behind it. No room for anyone in there, let alone a woman whose blondeness was so manifestly faked it probably glowed in the dark.

But if I change the plan, where does that leave me? What am I supposed to do? Go back on stage and shoot Dredd full of holes? That wouldn't solve anything – Dennis would thank me for it before he killed me and started tightening the screws on the Skysouls even further. (Maraschino wasn't concealing herself at the back of a wardrobe full of moth-eaten synthifurs, either.) No, what I've got to keep on doing for the while is help Joe Dredd, as the lesser of two evils – joke not intended. Then, once we've got Dennis and the rest of them out of the way, that's when I can start considering what best I can do not to continue being *evil* myself.

Maraschino, the dumb bitch, had tried to disguise herself as one of a group of discarded dressmaker's dummies. Even in the dimness the attempted deception was pathetically obvious.

'The rest of them don't have pubic hair, friend,' said McTavish as gently as she could. She tapped the muzzle of the Multigob lightly against Maraschino's ear. 'The poodle's a bit of a giveaway, too.'

'Don kill me, ya heah?' The woman could hardly get the words out.

'We're not planning to kill you – not unless you make us.'

'Isn't thyat whyat all tar-roar-yists say?'

'I guess it probably is. But I mean it sincerely. You play along with us and maybe you'll come out of this healthier than you came in. C'mon, Maraschino. C'mon, get some clothes on before I take you back.'

Realising she was making every mistake in the book, McTavish accepted Scooper into her arms while Maraschino wrenched her pneumatic form back into her scarlet dress. She hadn't been wearing any underwear, and her shoes were lost somewhere in the filthy jumble backstage; without them she looked a lot smaller, hardly any taller than McTavish herself.

To McTavish's astonishment, Maraschino gave her a quick peck on the cheek as she took the poodle back. 'I ain' got no reyasun for feelin' this, but I thyink I kin trust ya.'

I hope so, thought McTavish glumly as she prodded the woman towards the chinks of light that betrayed the direction of the auditorium. I surely hope so. I just hope Joe Dredd doesn't take it into his head to blow you people away.

'You took your time,' observed Dredd as they re-emerged into the bright lights. Reverend Rick had redis-covered enough of his composure to start begging for mercy.

McTavish made no comment.

'Time we got out of here,' Dredd said.

McTavish peered beyond the footlights into the audito-rium. 'Is Sackville OK?'

'He'll survive. The two Nandie women have taken him away.'

If they can get him back through the cordon, thought McTavish. As a matter of policy, Dredd and she were saying nothing out loud about that. By now the show must have attracted a huge audience – the bigger the better, as far as their plans were concerned – and it was a safe bet that Dennis would be among that number. Anything they said that could direct his attention towards the carnival would be, well, best left unsaid.

'Let's get going, then,' she said, keeping her voice as level as possible.

'I've been waiting.'

'OK. Want to do the honours, Joe?'

'Yeah. Cover the stommheads for me.'

Gently she pushed Maraschino towards her weeping husband. The fat woman put an arm around Hamfist's shoulders and whispered something in his ear that quietened him a little.

'You listening, Dennis?' bellowed Dredd at the auditorium. There was no response except steady snoring. 'Well, we're assuming you are. We're taking these two perps away from here and we're going to hide them somewhere real good. Now you can either make it easy for them and us by putting an empty chopper on the roof of the studio within the next five minutes, or you can make it difficult by trying to stop us, which means a lot of people getting killed and us still getting away. You've got a choice, drokkhead. It's up to you if you drokk it up.'

Holding the weapon steadily in both hands, Dredd raised the Lawgiver and began shooting out the holocameras one by one. The crashing blasts of the weapon and the puffy eruptions of shattered electronics and glassware seemed to go on a long time. He finished by destroying all the lights except one near the back, which glowed EXIT at them greenly.

'That way?' said McTavish, nodding towards it.

'No. We go back out the way we came in.' Dredd hefted the cylinder of synthinylon on his shoulder. 'Didn't bring this along for no reason.'

He turned his attention to the Hamfists. 'As of now,' he said, 'you two are dispensable. OK?'

They nodded. McTavish reckoned the evangelist was too broken to offer them any resistance. Maraschino – she was another matter altogether. McTavish guessed the woman wore artifice like a second skin.

'Let's get going,' McTavish repeated. 'The sooner the better.'

'Kill! Kill! Kill! Kill-kill-kill-kill-kill!'

'Uh, boss?'

'Shuddup, Becattini. I ain't finished yet! Kill! Kill! Drokking kill!'

'Boss?'

Snatches of conversation wafted from the holovee's small speakers. '. . . survive. The two Nandie women . . . Cover the stommheads . . . *You listening, Dennis?*'

Dennis ceased his chant. The voicebox made funny little chattering noises, as if its various components were consoling each other over their injuries.

At the end of Dredd's speech, when the bulky lawman started blatting out the holocameras, Becattini leant across smoothly and pressed a knurled knob beneath the display. Instantly the viewpoint shifted, so that he and his boss seemed to be staring down on the Thatchvee stage from directly overhead. The tiny spy camera in the studio's ceiling gave a good picture but lousy sound quality.

'Can you hear what they're saying, Becattini?'

'I'm trying, boss,' Becattini replied, putting one ear close to the left-hand speaker and jamming his blob of bubbleguck into the other.

Impotently Dennis watched as Dredd and the McTavish bitch finished speaking to each other and moved out of shot.

'Did you get anything, Becattini?'

'Nothing useful, boss. I got men parked all around the studio, so we can move in on those drokkers any time you . . .'

Dennis's voicebox made the sonic equivalent of a smile. 'No,' he said. 'Not yet, Becattini. So, the two Terry drokkwits don't want to blow away the vangie and his slut? OK, I can go along with that for a while. Not a very long while, but a while.'

Becattini regarded his master's voice with evident bewilderment. 'I thought you wanted – ' he began.

'Shut up! I'm thinking as I speak. This could work out better for us than if they'd killed them in front of the cameras. That way the Hamfist clowns might have become martyrs, or something.' A long moment passed. Only a fizzling noise from the brain-jar betrayed how intently Dennis was thinking. 'Yeah. I got it. Send the chopper, like they asked for. Only, tell your techs to put about a kilo of hi-ex in the tail for me, will you?'

Becattini began to chuckle. 'Ain't no flies on you, boss.'

Dennis's words began to tumble over each other. 'Gonna be a big accident, you see. Huh, Becattini, huh, huh? Bits of Dredd and McTavish and the drokking Hamfists raining down over half of BC, huh, huh? That way we take out all four of them, and it ain't nobody's fault, huh, huh?'

'Sort of "act of God", hey, boss?' Becattini's grin seemed to have spread all the way from one earlobe to the other.

'I *like* that, Becattini – like it, you hear? Say, and you get your guys to bring the detonator here, so I can press the button myself, huh?' The voicebox rocked with a fit of chortles. 'I'll be the one performing the act! That'll kinda make *me* God, Becattini, huh, huh, huh?'

'Yah, boss. Sure thing. That'll make you God.'

Climbing up the back wall of the studio was maybe the worst part of the entire raid, McTavish thought as she dangled forty metres above the ground, the thin synthi-nylon cord biting into her hands as the weight of the Multigob dragged her down. Any moment she expected weapons to open up and riddle her where she hung.

243

Biggins was already up top. The Skysoul had met them at the foot of the wall. Pausing only to extract Reverend Rick's thumb from his eye socket, she had been up the crumpling wall of the building as fast as either McTavish or Dredd could have run over open ground, her hands and feet seemingly picking out holds clairvoyantly. Once she'd gained the roof Dredd had fired the antigrav unit attached to the rope, and Biggins had gracefully caught the leading end and secured it to something out of their sight.

McTavish glanced down. The Hamfists and Dredd were just tiny faces, staring up at her. She guessed she was well past the halfway mark. One last supreme effort – well, maybe two or three . . .

She heard the chopper as she lay gasping on her back on the sticky roof. The damage they'd done earlier had melted the synthitar up here, and it hadn't quite finished resolidifying. She got her vision under control and combed the clouds overhead, trying to locate the source of the sound.

They could pick us off up here, you know, if they wanted to, came Biggins's cool thought. The Skysoul was leaning over the roof's edge, hauling rhythmically on the cord. One of the Hamfists must be on the way up.

'Hey, you could have done that for me, Nandie woman!'

And made you look weak in Dredd's eyes?

'OK, point taken.'

McTavish pulled up onto her knees and, still searching the clouds for a first sight of the chopper, grappled the Multigob around in front of her. Her thumb felt for the control-ring and made sure the charge was still on FULL. If the pilot opened fire, there was a chance she could put the craft out of commission before either she or Biggins got hit.

Biggins hauled Maraschino up onto the flat of the roof like an angler landing some heavy bit of junk he'd thought was a fish. The blonde woman floundered where she lay. The Skysoul, paying her no attention, tossed the loose length of cord back down to Dredd. Scooper, released for once from Maraschino's grasp, trotted over and began sniffing McTavish's legs in an amiable way.

There it was! The chopper emerged from the cloud layer about a kilometre away. From here it looked like a little black insect being driven by a strong wind. McTavish's eyes narrowed. The craft was holding its line precisely, which suggested Dennis had taken Dredd at his word: a human pilot *could* steer the vehicle this well, but her guess was it was under robot control. Nevertheless, she aimed the Multigob at the growing speck and kept it there.

Reverend Rick was the next to arrive. Out of the corner of her eye McTavish could see he was in no better condition than his wife, but he made a few feeble movements as if trying to help Maraschino to her feet.

The chopper was the size of a vulture now. Still she trained the sights on it.

And finally Dredd was with them, just as the chopper came in to make a perfect landing. Without pausing he moved in a sprint across to the vehicle, ducking beneath its slowing blades and jamming the Lawgiver in through a side window.

'Empty!' he yelled.

She'd been right, then: it had come here under machine guidance. She ran across to join the big lawman, who had climbed inside and, in the cramped space, was tugging wires out from the control box. 'Disconnecting the pilot,' he explained tersely. 'No way we're gonna climb aboard this drokker if there's a chance Dennis can just fly us out over the ocean until the fuel runs out.'

McTavish ran around and clambered in through the door on the other side. 'Backup,' she grunted, pulling plasteen panels off the interior walls. 'Could be he put in a backup.'

'Could be.' As soon as Dredd was satisfied with the wreckage he'd made of the robot pilot he began helping her strip the rest of the interior. They discovered half a dozen audio and video spies in various designs, but nothing else of interest.

Outside, Biggins had herded the Hamfists across the roof towards them. Scooper, who had gone into a ball when the chopper had landed, seemed now to be taking a much more positive interest in it. He had scuttled to the rear of the craft, and was jumping up and down, barking as if he wanted to make his head fall off.

McTavish glanced up and saw Maraschino, still clutching her side, lean across and say something urgently to Biggins.

She stuck her head out through the door. 'Get the Gruddam Toadstones ready for loading,' she snapped.

A moment, Petula.

'What.' It came out as a flat oath rather than a question.

'I was a-tellin' this Nandie lyady frien' a yourn that I'd pay a lotta attention to thyat little houn' o' mind, ifn I was you.'

'Get a move on.'

'He may not look much like it now,' gasped Maraschino, 'but once 'pon a time that liddle pup was a Justice De-purr-t-men' sniffer dog.'

'*What?* You're bullstomming!'

'Shore was, ma frien',' confirmed Reverend Rick through mangled lips. He'd lost half his teeth pulling that stunt with the fake foot. 'Purdy liddle sniffer-outta hi-ex that puppy was.'

'Hi-ex? You hear that, Dredd?'

'I did.' He was out of the chopper before he'd finished saying the word. By the time McTavish joined him at the vehicle's tail he was checking for freshly replaced rivets.

'Gotcha,' he muttered, pouncing.

McTavish pulled a knife from her boot.

He took it wordlessly and picked at a shiny rivet-head. 'Must have been in a hurry,' he said. 'Could have covered this up better.' His hands moving with dazzling speed, he laid open several of the tail panels. A small black box. Wires led out of it towards the cabin.

'Sure were in a hurry,' he said. 'No booby-traps.'

246

He jammed the blade of her knife in under the wires and yanked. The sharp edge cut through them easily. 'Good knife you got there.'

'Thanks, Dredd.'

'Hope you got it registered.'

'You're not serious.'

'The law's the law.'

'At a time like this?'

'At all times.'

'Yeah, it's registered. I'm a law-abiding citizen, in case you hadn't noticed.' She began to laugh.

'At times you don't act it, McTavish. I'll keep watching you.'

'You finished yet?'

'Yeah. Just checking to see they didn't leave two of these things.' He put his visor close to the hole he'd made. 'Can't see anything. Go check the cabin again.'

She found the hyper-receiver tucked into the framework of one of the seats, and, moving as swiftly as she dared, put it carefully down on the roof about thirty metres away. Dredd joined her, carrying the little box of hi-ex with the cut wires still trailing.

'Had an idea,' he said, and for a split second she thought she saw him grin. 'Get back to the chopper. Get the perps and the Nandie woman inside. We're gonna move out of here fast.'

She scrambled, waving at Biggins. Within seconds they were packed into the little cabin, only the wide front passenger seat left free for Dredd. McTavish squirmed on the pilot's seat. She'd shredded the upholstery in here looking for the receiver, and was sitting on bare synthimetal cords. Why the drokk couldn't Dredd get a move on?

Then he was charging towards them. She found the ignition lever at the base of the steering column and tugged on it. Immediately the motor picked up. The chopper rocked slightly from side to side as the big overhead rotors swung into motion; it seemed to want to get moving as much as she did.

'I'm piloting,' said Dredd.

'No you're not.' To her surprise he didn't argue. She opened the throttle and the chopper lurched upwards. She found she wasn't breathing, maybe hadn't been for a while, and took a deep gasp. Twenty metres, thirty metres, fifty metres . . . the studio roof was becoming only a small, battered rectangle far beneath them.

'Phew!' she said, relaxing her body at last. 'Thought for a bit we weren't going to get out of that.'

'Maybe we still haven't,' said Dredd laconically. 'They could shoot us down any time. Get into the clouds soonest, McTavish, so at least they can't spot us visually.'

'Won't make much difference.' Electronic sensors, even primitive ones, could pinpoint them precisely through any depth of cloud.

'Keep climbing.'

She obeyed. About a minute later there was nothing outside except a wall of sickly grey. The air coming in through the hole by her felt colder than freezing.

'What's that you've got?' she said, looking across at him. From one of the pockets on his thighs he was pulling a brown egg-shaped object. Little yellow buttons stuck out at either end. 'Looks like a bomb.'

He made no answer. Holding the thing between his thumb and his palm, he squeezed down the buttons at both ends. 'Don't know if this'll work,' he said. 'Hope so. But it's been through more cryps and decryps than I can rightly add up together. And it was experimental in the first place.'

'What *is* it?'

'It's gonna make Dennis the Complete Bloody Sadist very confused. I hope.'

Dredd refused to say anything more, and eventually McTavish gave up trying. Looking across at him from time to time as she swung the chopper round in a big arc over BC, invisible beneath the carpet of cloud, steering by the instruments alone and hoping to drokk they hadn't been sabotaged by the same techs who'd rigged the hi-ex in the tail, she saw him become completely motionless, as

248

if he were a lifelike sculpture rather than a real man, his gaze fixed directly forwards. There was just blankness out there; maybe Dredd's eyes, behind the visor, could see something.

Not for the first time, she found herself wondering just how much of him was human and how much was . . . something else.

She decided to concentrate on steering this bird.

'What the drokk's going on?' Dennis and Becattini had been watching the tiny shape of the chopper climb. The transition from direct visual observation to electronic virtual-reality portrayal as the craft entered the cloud mass had been so smooth they'd hardly noticed it. At Dennis's insistence, Becattini had plopped his brain back into its little-used skull-case for the occasion, so that the boss could use his very own thumb to press down on the detonator the techs had placed on the desk.

His hand had strayed in that direction several times, but always he had stopped it. Now, just as he'd been about to give in at last to the delicious temptation, the observation screen had erupted.

'What the drokk's going on?' he repeated.

'Dunno, boss.'

Where until a few seconds ago there had been just a single silhouetted chopper, now there seemed to be hundreds, all heading off in different directions. To accommodate the sudden spread of images, the electronics had pulled back their virtual position to show a sky apparently filled with identical choppers.

'The Gruddam sensors must tell you which of them's real,' snarled Dennis. His vocal cords, long unused, sounded even more artificial than the voicebox.

Becattini was staring at a display panel on his knees in dismay. 'No way, boss. They're registeratin' *all* them things as real.'

'Doesn't matter, does it?'

'No, boss.'

'Just means we don't get such a good view, huh, huh?'

'Yah, boss.'

'Here goes. You watching, Becattini?'

'Yah, boss.'

Clumsily Dennis pressed his thumb down on the detonator button.

There was a terrible silence.

'None of the choppers seems to have . . .'

'SHUDDUP!'

'I tell ya, J-No, I's real pissed off!'

Phionna 'Irish' O'Sollovan was standing a couple of hundred metres outside the perimeter wall of the now severely damaged Thatchvee studio. As soon as Dennis's goons had dared enter the auditorium, the members of the invited audience had been hypostimmed and led or dragged clear of the place. Then the goons had gone straight to work ripping the place apart in the hunt for any sort of clues the attackers might have left.

'I've been drokking *upstaged*, dat's what I been!' Irish glowered. She was very good at glowering. The skin of her face had become so red with fury that her myriad freckles showed pale against it.

'We *both* been upstaged, sis.' The words seemed ameliorative but J-No was pouting. Realising years ago that she'd never be able to match Irish at glowering, she'd practised pouting instead.

'Well, we still got da hi-ex, ain't we? We can go stick it someplace else. Ain't nowhere's good as da holovee, but we can make a big bang someplace.'

'Uh . . . sis.'

'Yeah?'

J-No shuffled her feet. 'I ain't got da hi-ex any more. It was kind of hot in dere, an' . . .'

'Oh *drokk*! Whaddya dun wid it?'

'Well, it was kinda gettin' itchy in ma bra, so I slipped da stuff out an' stuck it under my seat.' J-No was staring off down towards the far end of the street, as if there were something deeply fascinating there. A good place to hide, maybe.

250

'Ya dumb . . .'

Behind them, a sudden explosion tore the sky into confetti. The two girls were thrown flat on their faces by the blast. Half a second after the first detonation there was a second, this time coming from deep within the Thatchvee building. Bits of plasteen, metal, glasseen and burning wood shot past overhead.

The noise seemed to drag on for half a lifetime, but at last it ebbed.

'Hey, ya dun good, kid.'

J-No giggled. 'Both dun good. Share da credit. Drokking biggest bang ever.'

'Till da next one.'

SEVEN

Now

'That's another fine mess you've got me into, Ollie.'
— Anonymous 20th-century mystic,
as cited in *Clients' Handbook* (3rd edn, 2108),
Oliver North Church of Fundamental Sanctimony

Heidegger awoke and peered through the grey-orange murk of the tent. McTavish and Biggins had returned while he'd slept; he could hear their regular breathing. As his eyes adjusted he saw the two bedrolls, either side of the flap, with McTavish's pale hair spread out on the groundsheet. He shivered, although it wasn't cold. His bladder was bursting and his mouth tasted of mouldering biscuit crumbs, but these sensations were as nothing to his sense of foreboding: something important, something terminal, was going to happen to him today.

He groped his way out of his bedclothes and shambled to the opening, rubbing his wrist across his eyes. Staggering outside the tent, he looked around the site. A few of the carnie artistes were up and about, pottering around doing odd jobs or just sitting on caravan steps with hot drinks in their hands.

Then he gaped.

There had been a new addition during the sleeptime. A dilapidated chopper rested at the edge of the carnie's territory. There were plates missing from its tail and one of the cabin windows had been reduced to just a few triangular pieces jutting from the frame. Streaks of greasy soot ran across the sides. Propped up against the steps of

252

the caravan opposite – The Daring Brothers Rottweiler – apparently asleep, was Dredd.

The uniform that had been so shiny and polished was now scuffed and scarred. The hard-looking face, unrelaxed even in sleep, was smeared with the same greasy grey as the chopper. Yet the butt of the big sidearm jutting from the holster at the man's belt had obviously been freshly polished, and the buckle of the belt gleamed, as did the badge at Dredd's breast. Clearly the man had spent some time sprucing himself up as best he could before letting sleep take him.

Petula had been with him . . .

Heidegger darted back to the door of the tent and threw the flap wide. McTavish's face was turned up towards him, shining pale in the light. She breathed easily, comfortably. She was cuddling the Multigob like a teddy bear.

His heart still pounding, he stepped over her.

Hello, Heidegger.

Biggins was awake. The red-maned Nandie – *Skysoul*, he must remember to call them Skysouls – was sitting up, her blankets half across her shoulders.

We're safe. Petula will be waking very shortly. Her mind is already swimming towards consciousness.

'What happened? Where did the chopper come from? Were you killing people?'

Biggins grinned, raising a hand to stem the flow of questions. *We were on a dangerous mission, one that we didn't want to talk about too much beforehand, and it turned out even hairier than expected. But we're all right. And we were successful.*

'What did you do? Did you kill Dennis the Complete Bloody Sadist?'

Again she grinned, but then the grin faded. *No – although we killed too many other people.*

McTavish stirred, and her silver-grey eyes opened. 'I can see right up your nose,' she observed to Heidegger. She rubbed a grimy cheek with her hand, making it worse.

'Biggins says you've been really shooting the place up, which is why you and her and the big guy is all . . .'

'We've brought some people here, that's all,' McTavish said flatly.

'Who'd you bring? Why'd you bring 'em?'

'You ask too many questions for a small boy before breakfast. At least stop shrieking. We . . . "kidnapped" I guess is the word . . . Reverend Hamfist and his wife, Maraschino. The Brothers Rottweiler have them in their caravan.'

'Maraschino?' He gawped.

'What's wrong?'

McTavish caught the boy as he fell across her. Hauling herself partly upright, she felt the pulse at his temple and peeled back an eyelid for a quick check.

'He's fainted,' she said. 'Whatever could have brought *that* on?'

All through the morning people arrived. Most of them were Skysouls but an appreciable number were Toadstones. It seemed Itchy Bagman had tapped into a nomads' network of some kind, and news was spreading rapidly through it. These were wanderers: mendicants and casual labourers and door-to-door sellers. Some were armed with the tools of their trade, and a few bore more conventional weapons. They were not grim, but neither were they merry.

It was impossible to tell whether or not Dredd welcomed or resented the new recruits: his face remained stony. Only McTavish realised that, behind the mask, he was repressing his instincts to arrest half these people. At one point she took him aside to remind him that the law of Mega-City One did not apply here in the Donut.

She and Biggins spent most of their time calming down the volunteers. The plan was not, she explained over and over again, to march as a military force on BC. Although the mob could defend itself if necessary, its main purpose was to present a host of witnesses. If she and Dredd and Korax and the rest went to the city by themselves then, whatever deal might have been struck beforehand, it

254

would be too easy for them simply to vanish. But not if they were among a crowd of hundreds.

As most of the people on the site began to break out their midday rations, with some of the carnival folk opportunistically selling mugs of soup and stale sandwiches, Harbinger and Sackville slipped away from the camp, bound for the centre of BC. There the two Skysouls were to deliver a message – a message addressed to Fingers but ultimately intended for Dennis.

They had barely returned when, in the middle of the afternoon, Dredd's wrist-comm crackled.

'Is the Dredd drokker there?'

'Dredd speaking.'

McTavish was at his side in a moment, leaning over to stare at the wrist-comm as if somehow that would make the message clearer.

'This here's Becattini. I'm Rev. Fingers's, uh, PR Contestant.'

'One of Dennis's goons,' mouthed Biggins to Dredd. 'He'll agree to the challenge. He has no choice – not now the whole Donut knows we have half the line-up here as hostages.'

Dredd nodded.

'The Rev.'s a man of peace, and don't want innocent blood on his hands, you understand?'

'Yeah,' snapped Dredd.

'He accepts the challenge you've issued, so long as you give him your promise that the Hamfistses is not gonna be snuffed before they . . . is not gonna be snuffed.'

'They're safe.'

'And you'll bring them with you?'

'We'll bring them with us.'

'Then be here in time for tonight's show. There'll be complimentaries at the door for as many as you need.'

'We'll need 'em all – as many as you can fit in.'

'That seems OK. Ah . . .' They heard Becattini's voice muffled as he spoke to someone behind him. 'Yah,' he said, returning. 'That's OK.'

* * *

255

'You're alive,' said Heidegger wonderingly. 'I saw you with my own eyes, torn to death. Yet you're alive.'

'An' I surely *was* dyead, liddle man, but the Bumper-Size Vacuum That Is True Reality dun decree that thyis should not be the en' for me. So here's I is, right as ryain, tuwice as large as life.'

Maraschino beamed at him. It had taken him some hours of niggling, whingeing harassment before one of the Brothers Rottweiler had eventually crumbled and agreed to allow him in for a while to talk to the prisoners. Reverend Rick stayed over in the far corner, exploring his mouth with his fingers.

'Wyere ya in the stoodio itself when this most myalll-lish-yus attack was made pon my pooah unwoithy form?' she was asking. 'Ya pooah chickadee, ya musta been sickened unto the very syoles of ya boots.'

'No,' he mumbled, 'I was at home. Least, I was in the Belle et Bête Hotel, which was where me and Doc McTavish were living at the time. You was on the holovee.'

'Wayall, I jus' do say as that's real tragic for ya anyhow.'

She obviously didn't remember . . . anything else.

'You looks as if you could do with a cuddle, kiddo,' she suggested.

Wordlessly he allowed her to pull him to her lovely warm, soft bosom. From nowhere his thumb appeared in his mouth. As she played with her fingers through his hair she spoke softly to him, teasing out of him what had been happening these past few weeks . . . to him, to McTavish, to Dredd and – he didn't notice as her body suddenly stiffened – to Korax.

Some long while later the caravan door opened and Dredd's monstrous shadow fell over them.

'C'mon,' said the Judge. 'We're going to Brando's Carbuncle.'

McTavish had never ridden astride a sabre-toothed cat before.

Biggins, riding on her own animal alongside, had formally introduced McTavish to the beast, which had responded by licking the Toadstone's soft palm with its rough tongue, its green eyes probing hers. McTavish wished she could persuade herself that she had seen some empathy in the cat's gaze, but instead she had been chilled by the alienness.

The air was filled with cheerful noise. The smell was of sweat, dust and faeces. Stretched out across the plain behind them was a raggle-taggle but surprisingly large crowd of men, women and children, most on foot but with some riding carnival animals and others aboard caravans. Dredd was striding along at the head of the troop, with Biggins and McTavish together behind him and Korax walking unconcernedly behind them. Somewhere in the middle of the throng the two Hamfists, looking terrified, were on mammothoids; near them Heidegger was perched jauntily on top of a baby mammothoid, obviously having the time of his life. Mister Strozza was bringing up the rear, chuckling to himself and frequently pausing to tinker with a specially adapted laptop computer.

Ahead of them: the city.

Dennis and Fingers must have been active via Northvee, for the fringes of BC that McTavish could see were packed with citizens, waiting for the arrival of the column.

Everything may go all right, Biggins reassured her.

' "May" is the word,' said McTavish sourly. She felt the cat's powerful muscles moving smoothly beneath its sleek pelt.

'I wish we had a trumpet,' she said after a while.

Why?

'Terry history,' replied McTavish. 'I keep forgetting. You Nandie women don't know much about it. Way back in the days before history had properly been invented, if you wanted to march an army on a walled city, you had trumpeters to go before you. The blares of the trumpets frightened the folks inside. Or something like that.'

257

There's bound to be one somewhere. Did you think of asking Itchy Bagman?

'Didn't think of it at all until right now.'

Hmm.

A few minutes later Itchy came loping up to them. He was holding a long, slightly tarnished silvery post-horn and smiling pleasedly. *The Drambuie Twins used to put on this spiritualist act,* he explained, pushing the instrument into McTavish's hands.

'I don't know how to play this thing!' she said, laughing. 'I've only ever seen trumpets in holos.'

'Give it to me,' said a gruff voice.

Startled, she looked up. Dredd had dropped back a little to let the two women catch him up. He was reaching out a big, gauntleted hand.

'I can get a note out of it.'

Mutely she offered the horn up to him. Biggins was watching with fascination in her water-hued eyes.

'I think,' Dredd added. He walked forward rapidly, putting ten or twelve metres between himself and them before raising the horn to his lips. The blustering noise that came out of the instrument made McTavish snort with suppressed laughter. Dredd paid her no notice, but tried again. This time the sound that the horn made was long and clear, like a shaft of sunlight. The ears of McTavish's sabre-toothed cat pricked up.

'I got it,' Dredd said, more to himself than anyone else. He blew with greater confidence, and now the note was filled with an ancient martial might.

Thus it was that they entered the city to the blast of a trumpet and the braying and bleating of wild animals, the rumble of wooden caravan wheels on the streets' hard stone and songs of victory in the air.

As Becattini saw it, Dennis had gone completely mad, round the twist, dumdum, loopy. 'He's got the ifs and the buts loose in the belfry,' he remarked to his reflection in the men's-room mirror. 'He's playing loony toons backward. He's a few stiffs short of a massacre. He's . . .'

258

Becattini wished he dare share his thoughts with some-one other than himself. It wasn't so much that Dennis was making crazy decisions – Becattini had long ago given up trying to distinguish stupidity from sagacity – as that he seemed to be suffering a whole series of abrupt and unpredictable personality changes. His intonation patterns were in a constant state of flux, as if he'd become undecided about who precisely he wanted to be. He'd spend long periods of morose inactivity followed by brief bursts of frenzied speech and explosive mood.

'Maybe it was old Garbucci kept him on the tracks all these years,' confided Becattini to the mirror. He was fairly confident the boss hadn't bugged the men's room, but he kept his voice low all the same.

Take, for example, this challenge that had arrived from the Dredd drokker. Becattini had nothing against miracle contests *per se* – you went along, watched a bunch of dumb-asses making themselves look even dumber, then when you got bored you started kicking the stomm out of them. If Dredd wanted something like that, Becattini wasn't going to stand in his way. But Dredd had sent a message to Dennis – well, to Reverend Dave, which was much the same thing – saying he had a secret preacher who could make both Fingers *and* Hamfist look like kids'-party conjurers, and would like to prove it on Northvee, and Dennis had said okay to the idea. Now, Becattini was a simple man and all that, but surely what Dennis should be doing was shredding this Dredd bastard and the McTavish bitch, not playing party games with them?

But no. Dennis had merely said he had a plan . . .

A drokking *plan*!

Hah!

As they came in through the suburbs, McTavish dis-covered she was enjoying herself. Maybe it was the trumpet or maybe it was simply the *Zeitgeist*, but the waiting citizens were welcoming the motley army. Some had sneaked away furtively, off to hidden masters, but the vast majority – even most of the security guards – had joined the parade, singing and shouting as if today were a public celebration. At a guess, only about one in ten had any inkling that the marchers had come to disrupt the empire Dennis had built, but she had the feeling the remainder would help them anyway, out of a form of instant camaraderie.

She looked across at Biggins. 'Party time. Almost wish I had a bottle of something illicit so I could start making whoopee.'

It may not last. Korax's powers have been ebbing even faster than she expected these past few days. Northvee and – until we disrupted transmission – Thatchvee have been using a new series of subliminals that are tuned precisely so as to channel straight into the Skysoul id. Surprising they didn't think of it earlier. Sackville caught a bit of Fingers's 'cast when he was in the city last night and said that even he began to doubt.

'You mean it was Korax that made all these people change so?' McTavish gestured at the crowd around them.

Sorry, friend. I thought you'd realised. Biggins looked at McTavish's face worriedly. *She does not lightly tamper with people's minds . . .*

'That wasn't what I meant. I'd just thought that, for once, human beings were turning out to be nicer people than I'd expected.'

Not entirely. Korax has moved only a few out of every hundred of them. The rest have joined us because, after these weeks of bloodshed, suddenly they'd prefer some happiness in their lives. And who's to criticise them for that?

'I guess.'

Dredd let out the loudest horn-blast yet, and McTavish tightened her shoulders. 'I could do with a bit less of that.'

Biggins smiled. *Couldn't we all?*

They weren't far now from the Northvee studio: another few blocks along and then a couple of zigzags to the right, and there they'd be. It looked as if they'd get there without incident.

That was when the first sniper opened up.

McTavish saw the shot out of the corner of her eye before she heard anything. There was a flash from an upper window of a building further down the block. As McTavish pulled the Multigob round from her shoulder she saw Dredd stop in his tracks and coil his body, flicking himself sideways as his Lawgiver appeared in his fist.

BLAM!

There was an eruption of fire from the distant window, and then an eerie silence descended on the crowd.

'Is anyone hurt?' asked McTavish as she hefted herself upright.

No. We're shielded. The queen-goddess has shielded us all. As best she can. Biggins shrugged. *If Dennis's people open up with something really heavy, then we're in difficulties. But snipers should present no problems.*

'You sure about that?'

As sure as I can be . . .

'Fingers crossed, Nandie woman. We'd better tell Dredd. Don't want him wasting all his ammo if there's no reason.'

Fingers crossed, Toadstone slut.

McTavish urged the cat forward with her thighs. Dredd was just beginning to resume his forward march when she tapped him on the shoulder. She explained briefly.

'Doesn't matter,' he said, his gaze fixed intently on the street ahead of him. 'Attempted assassination's a crime, here in the Donut same as in Mega-City One.'

He had shifted the horn to his left hand and was still holding the Lawgiver with his right. It was plain the weapon wasn't going to be returned to its holster until the day's business was done. McTavish started to say something more then realised there wasn't really anything sensible she could add: Dredd would do whatever he wanted.

She tugged gently on the cat's mane, the way Biggins had shown her, and the animal obediently fell back to join its mate.

Several more shots were fired, and each time Dredd's

261

Lawgiver retaliated to devastating effect. McTavish became almost accustomed to it all, and the ever-increasing throng seemed to do likewise, for each new attack barely affected their cheery clamour. Nevertheless, she kept her hands on the Multigob across her thighs, primed.

There were screams nearby, and a turmoil among the press of people. 'Assassin!' someone yelled, and the chant was taken up by other voices. She had a brief glimpse of a man with a multiply scarred face and tufts of blue hair waving what looked like an old-fashioned stick grenade. Dredd had the Lawgiver aimed, but there were too many people in the way. Then some unknown arm snatched away the bomb, and the would-be assassin disappeared in a knot of kicking, punching, cheering citizens.

McTavish felt sick in her stomach. This was the flipside of the mob's boisterous good humour: even beating a man to death was fun. With the crowd in this mood, she hoped they didn't suddenly decide to go on the rampage, slaughtering innocent people just because they were there.

She knew that Biggins would have been tracing her thoughts. 'Could Korax stop them if that happened?'

Perhaps. We must hope it doesn't come to that.

McTavish set her jaw grimly. A few minutes ago the pinkish buildings on either side of the street had seemed somehow warm and welcoming. Now they were like the jagged rocks bordering a treacherous strait.

'Yeah,' she said.

Korax has let herself drop back to become just another Nandie in the crowd. For the next few hours she wants to be an anonymous member of an anonymous throng.

People jabbering in her ear. '. . . the kids are somewhere around, Molly. They'll be OK . . .' '. . . I'm bustin', I tell ya, bustin' ! . . .' '. . . all I say to the folk who criticise that sweet Dave "No Messin" is, if they's so positive there's gods, why don't they produce one? Hey? I'm a tolerant sort of a stommer, and . . .' And a babble, too, of Nandie thoughts – cooler, more controlled, but equally pointless in their way. . . . *Korax is among us. I can feel her presence . . . You've said that before, but where's she ever been when we've needed her? The Toad-stones are right – if there ever was a Korax, she's dead long ago! . . . Our child, our child, the Toadstones killed our child . . .*

She tries to make her mind impervious to grief, but with little success. Those voices are right. For too long she has left her people to fend for themselves. It is all very well for gods to think of things in the long term, regarding generations as merely fleeting moments. But, for individual mortals, a generation is a lifetime, and they have only one of those. She has not deserved her people's trust, their friendship. She has only herself to blame that so many have deserted – after all, she deserted them first . . .

But that will change, she resolves. It will change today. For all the rest of time she will be theirs.

She will die for them, if that is the way things turn out . . .

Jaboticaba Fingers frowned.

Her husband looked at her warily. She had a beautiful, elfin, Oriental face, despite its customary pouting scowl, and had looked about nineteen for the past twenty years. She also had the temperament of a wildcat with toothache.

'Why can't you jus' get the guys up top to mash 'em all with laser cannon?' she asked plaintively. Her voice was like thin, sweet synthiacacia honey.

'Cos, my dear lullaby of the soul, they are our brothers an' sisters in . . .'

'Aw, stow it, Dave – you ain't on holovee right now. They got those Hamfists and – *yuck*! – that slimy Maras-chino with them. You could make that mob into just a heap of smokin' meat with the Hamfists right in the middle of it, an' then we'd be able to get *really* rich! Aw, *pur-lease*, Dave.' She curled herself around him and began to play with the knot of his tie. 'I could make it really worth your while, hunsy-buns.'

He pushed her away with difficulty. Her face took on its habitual snarl. He was almost certain he could see claws emerge smoothly beneath her silver-painted fingernails.

'Dennis,' he said simply.

'Aw, Dennis is so *borin*' – he ain't no fun. You an' me' – she shifted her face into practised demureness – 'we could have fun, Davesy.'

'Later, my true babe. Later. Right now, we has to do what the great Dennis Almighty tells us to do, or we's gonna fin' ourselves without any skin to wear. You put your trust in your hubby, like the good book says a lovin' wife should do.'

'You *wrote* the good book, you drokker!' she snapped, losing patience with him. She raked her nails across his cheek and stormed off.

Reverend Fingers wished he could remember things better. He wished he could remember that crazy time of passion when he had wooed Jaboticaba and eventually wed her – wished he could remember so he'd know not to do it again. He wished he could remember why he'd come to the Donut, or if he'd always lived here. He wished he had *some* way of explaining how he came to be where he was.

But he wasn't an introspective man. The thought faded as he looked down on the long flight of synthigold steps that rose to the porticoed entrance to the Northvee station. Tonight was going to be tough. For reasons he couldn't understand, Dennis had agreed that Fingers and Hamfist would confront the viewers and prove that the Vacuum had given them miraculous powers beyond anything that even the wildest Nandie stories claimed for their mythical bitch-goddess. They were to act as allies, ignoring the fact there had been out-and-out war between them these past weeks – Dennis had been quite firm on this point. Reverend Dave hoped he'd communicated his instructions as forcefully to Hamfist.

The miracles should be no problem. The studio's techs always had several weeks' worth of mind-boggling wonders set up in reserve, and recently they'd been putting in double-time. There were plenty for both the evangelists to be able to put on a show unlike anything the Donut had seen before.

But Reverend Dave didn't like it. He didn't enjoy the prospect of working with that greasy, dishonest Reverend Rick, but that wasn't the source of his persistent unease.

Then what, he asked himself, could it possibly be?

There were uniformed goons at the door, but they melted from sight as Dredd and the two women advanced up the steps.

'You will permit us entry!' barked Dredd to the huge doors. They were made out of what looked like beaten silver. With a histrionic groan they opened in front of him. Inside, there was a vast hall decorated mainly in red, with a deep carpet covering both floor and walls. Muzak tinkled. With McTavish and Biggins in train, and with the rest of the crowd straggling behind them, Dredd marched straight forward into the building. It was like walking into a womb.

Only a couple of hundred people came in with them; the rest, as if stayed by some unheard command, remained hovering at the doors, which slowly but firmly closed.

McTavish felt a moment's panic. They were trapped! Vents in the walls could open and start pumping in toxic gas! The entire hallway could be turned into an inferno! Concealed shooters could riddle everyone here with bullets! A single bomb could . . .

Korax is with us – no, don't turn to look. She doesn't want to make herself known. Yet.

'What's she playing at?'

She has her own script. It differs in several ways from the one that you and Dredd have learnt.

'Does Dredd know this?' McTavish felt silly whispering, like a small child telling a saucy joke, but she couldn't bring herself to raise her voice.

No. And I don't know what she plans to do, either. She felt it was safer if none of us knew but herself.

'Moving in mysterious ways, huh?'

Sorry?

'Just a quote from one of the ancient Terry religions – can't remember which one. It's what gods are supposed to do. When everything's a real drokk-up and everyone's being slaughtered in all directions, you're supposed to tell yourself that it's all for the best, really – that the gods are just . . . Aw, heck, Cloudrider! I wish all this was over with.'

'Welcome, pilgrims!' said a voice that seemed to come from everywhere at once. The muzak gave a last strangled plink and died. 'Ye who have come to seek truth will find it here at the Oliver North Church of Fundamental Sanctimony, under the expert guidance of the Reverend Dave "No Messin" Fingers. Servitor bots will be moving among you shortly, should you wish to make a donation to the . . .'

BLAM!!!

Dredd blew across the muzzle of his Lawgiver.

A tall flunkey dressed in gold from head to foot, with a huge golden hat like a caricatured mitre perching uneasily on his head, scuttled in from an unseen doorway, rubbing his hands together nervously. He smiled waterily at the assembly. 'The studio is ready for you now!' he called to Dredd above the heads of the crowd.

Dredd slowly turned his helmeted head. 'Good!'

After the rest had filed into the auditorium, McTavish and Biggins remained in the hallway with Dredd, the Hamfists and the two cats. McTavish had checked the Multigob several times, conscious of her palms sweating; Biggins, as always, seemed unperturbed by the prospect of danger. Maraschino worked with a make-up stick at her husband's mouth, trying to conceal the lacerations.

'Where's Korax?' said Dredd.

'Somewhere in there,' said McTavish, gesturing with a thumb.

'Why isn't she with us?'

'She has a plan of her own,' said Biggins aloud. 'She told me some parts of it just before she entered the auditorium.'

'Too late to change things now,' Dredd growled. 'We stick with the old plan.' He started shoving the Hamfists at the open door of the auditorium. Inside, there was an expectant hum. Through the doors McTavish could see the lights coming up on the studio floor. Overhead an indicator on the wall switched from green to red.

'Whyat's this heah stuff 'bout Korax?' whined Maraschino, resisting Dredd. Scooper let out a yip, largely muffled by her bosom.

'Pay them no mind, light of my life,' said Reverend Rick, donning a broad professional grin. He seemed to grow several centimetres in height and more than that in breadth as he preened himself swiftly for his public performance. 'The Nandies have purr-suede-dead this poor lunk that their god is among us. But, as you knows and I knows, she ain't here. Don't let it bother your pretty little head.'

Maraschino looked less than convinced, but allowed herself to be pushed behind her husband into the back of the auditorium. McTavish half followed them in.

'Ladies and gentlemen!' boomed a voice. 'For the first time ever on Northvee, we present for your delectation Reverend Rick "The Man" Hamfist and his adorable wife Maraschino. A big hand, please!'

Hamfist spread out his arms wide, as if to embrace not only everyone present but also all the millions of Donutians who must be tuned in to this 'cast of all 'casts. Over the speakers came the sound of a massive crowd cheering and applauding. Maraschino's white-toothed grin matched her husband's for broadness and more than matched it for stark sexual allure. She held Scooper above her head for the adulation of the audience, some of whom, despite themselves, were clapping their entrance.

'OK,' said McTavish vexedly, coming back out through the swing doors, 'what's Korax up to? Spill.'

Biggins addressed Dredd, speaking tersely. 'It is too

267

late to stop the goddess. You hoped she would merely humiliate Hamfist and Fingers by out-miracling them, but she has determined to take a far more irrevocable step than that!'

'Oh yeah?' Dredd gripped his Lawgiver thoughtfully.

'One that will change history – literally!' hissed Biggins. *Hush, Petula. Don't say anything now! It is important you keep your peace!* 'She is going to let the two Toadstones make clowns of themselves. Ninety per cent of the Sky-souls are watching this. They will see each new faked Toadstone miracle exposed as a sham! Korax will not compete with them publicly! Why should she so demean herself? Such gaudy contests are a Toadstone way, not a Skysoul one.'

Dredd rumbled. 'I see no harm in this,' he said reluctantly.

'It is then that the goddess shall perform her greatest miracle!' continued Biggins. 'She is going to turn back the arrow of time!'

'Wha–at?' said Dredd and McTavish together.

'She is going to transport the entire Universe back a century or more,' continued Biggins, 'to a time before the Toadstones discovered the Donut. We Skysouls will retain full consciousness of what has occurred – those of us who were children then will have the memories of centurians, while the rest of us will be born, when our time comes, with that awareness. We will have full knowledge of the reality of the god among us.'

'And what of us Toadstones?' said McTavish with disgust.

'You will never come here. The Donut will be sealed to your spacecraft and the MT, if you ever find it in the Terry desert, will have been disabled. The Donut will remain forever an enigma to Terry science – a door that will not open!'

Dredd made a noise like a volcano on the verge of eruption. 'That contravenes all known human laws!' he snarled. 'There are ordinances specifically forbidding the manipulation of past history! And ordnances,' he added, raising the Lawgiver to Biggins's head.

The Skysoul ignored the weapon.

'Then it is your duty,' she said with deliberate formality, 'as a Judge of Mega-City One Justice Department, to stop this greatest of all miracles taking place?'

'Drokking right!'

'But the goddess will not permit you to interfere with her plans. Should you go in there' – a jerk of the graceful maned head towards the auditorium, where Fingers was raucously building up his opening pitch to the punters – 'and try to stop her by physical force, she will either deflect your efforts or destroy you.'

'I'm willing to risk that!'

He was, too. McTavish could see it in every line of his tensed body.

'Brave words, but stupid ones,' said Biggins. 'The goddess is invulnerable to your might.'

'That's not . . . !' McTavish began.

Shut up, Petula! I tell you, don't meddle! All will become plain to you later!

'Look,' Biggins said conversationally to Dredd, 'what is happening to your Lawgiver.'

The two Toadstones stared at the weapon. At some point since Dredd had raised it to the Skysoul's head it had become a perfect wooden replica of itself. As they watched, its barrel sprouted a green-leafed twig.

Dredd cursed and pulled the weapon away. As he did so, it transmuted back into its normal metallic self.

'The goddess is listening to us,' breathed Biggins. 'She will not let you threaten me again. There is no way that you can divert her from her plotted course. Unless . . .'

'Unless what?' The shoulders lifted again. A little.

'Unless you make her miracle . . . *unnecessary.*'

'What do you mean?'

'All this time, Joe Dredd, you – and, to an extent, my good friend McTavish too – have been viewing the Dennis threat from the wrong angle. From the Toadstone angle. You – or your masters – did not wish to see the Donut destroyed because its destruction would represent the loss of considerable material resources, as well as of a handy penal settlement. You see the Donut as a developing extension of Earth – not even as a new Eden, a new refuge for the Toadstone species, but as a place where the hell you have created for yourselves on your homeworld can be spread, as the future centuries pass, over an ever greater stretch of raw terrain. You want to convert the Donut into a vast Mega-City One!'

She was speaking to Dredd, but her eyes were on McTavish's. *Doing you something of an injustice, sweet friend, but only something . . .*

'Your solution to the problem of the Donut is to create *stability* here – Toadstone-dominated stability. You do not care who is the local ruler, or how he rules, so long as everything is maintained the way you want it to be. You see yourselves as conquerors dealing with troublesome natives and with dissent among the colonists. If Dennis, or any other petty tyrant, offers to oppress the new territory in your name, then you will accept him gratefully. You will offer the natives the sop of Korax: *let* them worship their harmless little tribal myth! You have no aversion to crushing those two brainless jerks of preachers under the wheels of your juggernaut, along with the Overlords and the nubugs and the Skysouls – they're trifles in the march of history. Isn't that so, Joe Dredd?'

His face red with wrath, Dredd started to raise the Lawgiver again. The gesture would have been futile anyway, but one of the cats leapt for the weapon before it had properly cleared his side. The animal tore it from his fingers and retreated, growling at the back of its throat.

The big man's gauntleted hands clenched and unclenched.

'So,' continued Biggins after a couple of beats, 'there you have the problem you were sent here to solve. Stop the preachers – which really means Dennis – damaging the Donut's structural integrity, and then establish a new empire here. You would have gone home secure in the knowledge that you'd cracked the problem, done a good job and done it well. Hmm?

'But that's not the problem we Skysouls want to see solved. We have tolerated the destruction of our world and the tyrannisation of our people for as long as we are prepared to. We have seen our children tortured to death in your sex clubs so the nubugs can have cheap thrills. We have seen your machines rip open our land, tearing the life out of it. We have seen you Toadstones endeavour to crush the spirit of our species out of existence. We have seen you attempt to destroy four million years of history. We have endured all this because we thought you were a species capable of redemption.

'But it seems you are not. You are so far from redemption that you cannot even identify the *real* problem, but instead set about trying to fix one of its symptoms.'

'The real problem,' said McTavish, startling herself, 'is *us*.'

Reverend Fingers, his arms wide like his ingratiating smile, floats up from the floor of the studio, upheld by a tiny choir of fluttering bluebirds. Lazily Korax, halfway back among the throng of faces, waves a hand. The bluebirds abruptly vanish, revealing a sinuous coil of spiderflex supporting a knife-thin plastic platform.

Fingers falls headlong to the floor as, off-stage, there is the waspish crackle of expensive electronics overloading.

Korax smiles. All is going according to plan. She feels her power growing.

She turns to Heidegger, sitting beside her. 'Wasn't that fun?' she says.

His little face glows.

'And the *solution*,' said Biggins, 'could be you as well.' *Keep out of this, Petula. Dredd will provide the solution. He is already halfway through thinking himself to it.*

'I cannot disobey my orders,' grunted Dredd. 'McGruder was explicit.'

'She commanded you to bring stability to the Donut?'

271

'Yeah.'

'What could destabilise the Donut more than being shot back a century in time?'

'Uh . . . I've got an idea.'

'Good.'

'Gimme the Multigob, McTavish.'

'No, I – ouch!'

'You have two hours, Joe Dredd. Maybe less.'

Maraschino Hamfist taps several people in the front row to fill a plain glasseen litre specimen bottle with swirling yellow urine. She holds it up in plain view, blowing away the steam from its neck; with her free hand she lifts Scooper so the dog can add his cute contribution. She drops the poodle and gently lays the specimen bottle on a side-table, then produces a floral silk handkerchief from the depths of her cleavage. Waving it in the general direction of the table, she cries: 'Shabbaladooka! May the Bumper-Size Vacuum show the tryue powah of its randomnicity!'

The liquid in the bottle changes colour, becoming clear.

'Ladies and gentlemen!' shouts Reverend Rick. 'Accursed god-loving religions turn water into wine, but only the wondrous truth of atheism can succeed in turning piss into high-grade, one hundred proof vodka!'

Maraschino gives a girlish giggle, and with some slightly clumsy manipulation now produces a set of twelve cocktail glasses from her bosom.

'Drinkies!' she says cheerfully, splashing vodka into them.

'C'mon!' calls her husband with a broad beckon to the front row. 'The Bumper-Size Vacuum don't care if you get smashed out of your skulls!'

Cautiously, five or six punters, Arf Belcher in the lead, creep onto the stage, hands outstretched. Maraschino gives each a glassful and a flirt. 'Knock 'em back! Less show all they others that this is the ryeal styuff! A*wright*?'

They drink.

Korax yawns.

The mumble of a hypnotape, too faint for normal hearing, abruptly becomes audible. Moving coloured laser beams, one for the bottle and one each for the depleted glasses, suddenly become visible, and then wink out.

The drinkers on the studio floor – all except Belcher – screw up their faces and start trying to spit out what they've just drunk. Maraschino herself, her mask of professionalism slipping for once, staggers to the side of the stage and throws up.

'You bastard, Fingers!' she bubbles. 'I's gonna get ya for this! You never dun tol' me how thyat one was dun!'

Still Korax feels her power growing . . .

The doors might have opened for Dredd if he'd asked them, but he didn't have time. The Multigob reduced them to a shiny puddle, across which he threw himself.

'Out of my way!' he bellowed, waving the firearm. A path cleared across the square. At its far end, oblivious, Mister Strozza loitered.

Dredd sprinted towards him.

'Big guy, you're gonna help me!'

'**Am I?**'

'Yeah!'

'**Ow! Get that Gruddam gun out of my shin!**'

Mister Strozza bent down as Dredd tersely gave him orders, then turned and lumbered off down the street.

'Sackville! Harbinger!'

The two Skysouls struggled free of the throng and warily approached him. 'I want you Nandies with me as backup. You can move quicker than I can.'

Sackville, still frail from the day before, reached out and touched the Multigob nervously. 'We do not like your Toadstone weapons,' he explained courteously.

'Hands off!'

The Nandie obeyed.

'I need Dennis, and I need him fast. Where is he?'

The Nandies looked at each other, their faces now expressionless.

'Get a move on!'

273

'We are not certain, Toadstone,' said Sackville smoothly. 'But we have seen his men coming and going from the basement of the old Orbit Building.'

'Take me there!'

Before he could move a muscle the two Nandies had seized him by the armpits, one on each side, and were running down the street. They shot past Mister Strozza so swiftly that the giant's legs were just a blur, then turned left into a major thoroughfare. The street was almost empty: everyone in BC who had access to a holovee set was inside, glued to what had rightly been billed the Contest of the Century.

The Nandies switchbacked across the city, sometimes leaping straight across the narrower streets. Dredd, powerless to resist, lost track of where they were heading.

At last they screeched to a halt outside a building that was almost as large as Imm-Decryp. Its front was studded with scores of windows.

'Let me down!'

Dredd looked up at those windows. Could there still be snipers loose? Unlikely. Dennis must have assumed all of his enemies would be tied up in the snarl around Northvee – either that or home watching developments there. He'd have called off all his goons by now . . .

Rockcrete spat up between Dredd's legs, disproving his theory.

'Get down!' he shouted at the Nandies as he faded to the left, bringing up the Multigob. He raked the windows of the entire first storey with fire.

Silence, except for crackling flame.

The Nandies reappeared behind him. He shook off their hands as they made to help him up.

'There may be more,' warned Sackville sombrely. 'If you wish, we can check out the building for you.'

'Go.'

Once again they disappeared from his side. A trace of motion at the building's doorway told him where they'd gone.

A sound to his left sent Dredd back into a crouch. A

fast-tank came screaming around the corner and headed directly towards him, orange light gleaming from its turret and heavy weaponry. An autocannon barrel swung around and hi-ex rounds began zipping up the rockcrete towards him.

He feinted left and moved right, the Multigob tucked into his hip. He squeezed the control-ring and blew the tank's nearside tracks apart. The vehicle veered crazily out of control, its cannon fire pulverising the sidewalk opposite the Orbit Building. The tip of his tongue peeping from his lips as he concentrated, Dredd placed a single burst of hi-ex gobbets through the tank's deep-set slit window. The cannon fire abruptly stopped, and the vehicle lurched into a lower gear, chugging along aimlessly. There was a muffled *kaboomf!* and it stopped dead. A full second later it exploded in a hailstorm of zinging synthimetal shrapnel.

Struck at the back of the left knee by one of the crazily flying shards, Dredd half fell, supporting himself by thumping the butt of the weapon against the rockcrete. He swore, glancing down at the wound. The sharp superheated synthimetal had torn a jagged slice out of the leathery material, but his uniform breeches had absorbed most of the damage. There was some blood, but the tendons appeared to have survived.

A chopper was somewhere above. He tilted his head back, searching the cloudless sky, brought the Multigob to his shoulder. The sights had been wrenched askew some time during the past frenetic minute, but he ignored them, squinting along the barrel at the distant speck. A squeeze on the ring. A long time seemed to pass before there was a flower of flame in the faraway sky.

From the far end of the street a laser weapon opened up. If its operator had been anything like accurate Dredd would have been sliced in half where he knelt. As it was, he felt the heat of the beam as it liquefied rockcrete less than half a metre from him.

He threw himself away from it, rolling, catching the Multigob's ring-guard painfully in his throat, ignoring that and the throb from his torn leg. He tried to bring the weapon around to blast the laser emplacement, but his shots were hopelessly wide of the target.

'Dredd! Here!'

The laser beam melted rockcrete between his arm and side.

'Quickly!'

Sackville was gesticulating frantically from a low-set window, his shoulders on a level with the street. 'The weapon!'

Dredd clattered it across to him.

The Nandie caught it clumsily, then righted it in his hands. His face was a moue of disgust as he aimed it carefully towards the area from which the laser fire was emanating, a hundred or more metres away.

'Get a drokking move on!'

Sackville pressed the control-ring and was shot backwards into obscurity. There was a deafening detonation as the laser emplacement erupted.

'Good boy,' said Dredd quietly as he threw himself to his feet, scanning the scene. He felt for the Lawgiver at his belt, remembered that the cat had stolen it from him back at Northvee, and was astonished to discover the weapon was there. 'Thanks, Korax,' he muttered, sprinting for the open doorway of the Orbit Building.

A dusty hallway, deserted. There were traces of the Nandies' passage through here, two long curves of shiny synthimarble showing through the grime of the floor. It seemed like Dredd had brought silence in with him. The greedy spatting of the blazing tank was now inaudible. There was no sound except his own heavy footsteps

'Sackville!' he yelled. 'Harbinger!'

He saw a new piece of evidence that the two Nandies had been here. A pink-haired goon was lying in a corner, his head twisted at an impossible angle to his body.

'Sackville's hurt,' said Harbinger stiltedly, arriving out of nowhere by his side. 'Your weapon injured him. Here – take it.'

He gripped the Multigob. 'Is he bad?'

'He'll live.' She produced a painful smile. 'But he won't be much more use to you today.'

'And you?'

'I'll try. We're pair-bonded – I feel the pain of his injuries. But I'm not hindered by the damage.' She breathed heavily. 'I'll try.'

'OK. Where?'

'Down.' She pointed unnecessarily. 'Sackville and I sensed the evil of the man somewhere beneath us, but we haven't yet found the door.'

Yes. They must have been combing the basement when Sackville had seen what was going on outside in the street. 'Take me down!' he barked.

Moving slowly enough that he could keep up with her, she led him towards the rear of the building. Everywhere were signs that the ground floor at least had been used only as a front for whatever was the old Orbit Building's real purpose: doors hung slackly on unrepaired hinges, dust rounded off corners, internal windows were cracked.

She half dragged him towards what looked like just one more broken door among the rest. He scrambled through it after her, almost falling down the steep flight of stone stairs that pitched directly beneath him into darkness. Harbinger seemed to fly down them, her long arms raised for balance as she landed lightly at their foot. Dredd's own touchdown was considerably noisier.

'No way further down?' he spat.

'Not that we've found.'

'Take me to where you sense the drokker strongest.'

The basement was a maze of small rooms – literally a maze. Whoever had erected all its internal walls and partitions had wanted the place to be as confusing as possible. Here, unlike upstairs, the pitted floor had been kept scrupulously clear of dust: no trails to follow. Harbinger moved surely through the labyrinth with Dredd limping at her shoulder.

'Here,' she said at last.

'Stand clear.'

Dredd planted his feet firmly apart and directed the Multigob straight down at the pitted floor.

The two nearest partitions were blown flat by the blast and the inner surfaces of Dredd's boots caught fire, but he stood his ground long enough to assure himself he had opened up a way downwards. Bright artificial light shone up at his face through the grey smoke as the glow of the detonation faded. He stooped to slap away the flames from his boots.

Someone was screaming. He adjusted the weapon's control-ring, tuning its lethal hi-ex beam for fine use. 'Go and look after Sackville,' he said hoarsely. 'I'm on my own from here.'

'I might be able to help you, Toadstone.'

'Spug off. This baby's mine.'

She was gone in a swirl of dark hair.

Fastidiously he cut away from the hole he'd made, enlarging it so that it'd be big enough for himself and the Multigob to drop through. The screaming continued unabated. There was a bitter, scorched smell – burning synthiwool.

Chunks of the floor dropped away. Dredd threw himself on his face and plunged the Multigob through the hole, thumbing it up to wide-beam and spraying the room beneath. The screaming stopped abruptly. He sprang halfway across the hole, drawing up his legs beneath him, and plummeted downwards, landing in a ball, rolling away to one side. The stink of burnt wool was almost overpowering, and pieces of the stuff stuck to his cheeks.

The base of his spine hammered against something solid – the pillar of a desk made out of old-fashioned synthi-oak rather than the sleek plasteen of the others. A VDU slithered off the far side and crashed to the floor. Nothing seemed to be moving in the tunnel-shaped portion of the large room that he could see, but he gave the area a quick further spray with the Multigob, just in case. Then he was scrabbling across the floor on all fours, heading for the opposite wall. He used the wall as support as he got to his feet, swivelling at the hips to rake the place yet again.

Papers went up with a *whoof*. Another VDU blew out. A wall calendar showing a woman copulating with a squid fell in a comet of fire to the smouldering floor beneath.

He wiped char from his face. A quick tally showed at least six people had died under the assault. One must have taken the main brunt of the first barrage: he – or she – looked like a sort of miniature volcano made of melted flesh and scorched clothing.

There was an antigrav chute off to his right, its vacant chamber gleaming slightly blue. No wonder the Nandies hadn't been able to find a way down here: the entrance must be somewhere in one of the upper storeys. Dennis was cleverer than the average perp – McGruder had made that plain, back in Mega-City One. Clever perps died just like drokk-witted ones.

Dredd fired a string of rounds into the open mouth of the chute, wrecking it. No chance of an attack from there now.

At the far end of the room there was a heavy-looking door. If this was the outer office, then beyond that door must be the hub of Dennis's operations. Kicking his way through smoking organic and inorganic litter, Dredd marched up to it. Holding the snout of the Multigob against the solid metal of the door, he searched the surface with his free hand. The area around the lock was booby-trapped. But all these defences were woefully lax. If he'd been in the stronghold of one of Mega-City One's gang lords he'd have been dead five times over from boobies by now: Donut perps could do with a few Judges of their own if they wanted to get their act smartened up.

'Open, in the name of the law!' he shouted, banging the Multigob against the door for emphasis.

Korax finds the orations of the Reverends Fingers and Hamfist oddly soothing. She never sleeps, but she occasionally likes to let herself drowse a little. She has to remind herself this is not a suitable time. She turns to look at Heidegger, who is watching wide-eyed as the preachers and their two wives unveil wave after wave of

279

the miraculous, with the waves each time breaking on the rocks of reality she keeps placing in their way.

Good, huh?

'Yeah,' he says, 'true brill.' Too enthralled to realise she hasn't spoken out loud.

She smiles.

Now Hamfist, a rather desperate leer on his face, is pointing towards the rear of the auditorium. He brings his arm up and, guided by his pointing finger, the roof peels open with a thin, high roar to reveal the sky beyond. Directly overhead, as always, hangs the orange ball of Korax's Eye. The few hidden loudspeakers that Korax has permitted to survive cough into life with a roll of drums.

All faces crane upwards.

Slowly, with impeccable timing, a rent appears across the face of the star. 'The Bumper-Size Vacuum That Is True Reality,' blares the preacher, 'gave birth to the sun that in turn gives itself to give us life. But, my friends in the eyes of truth, that ain't the end of the story! For just as we spend our first days in the wombs of our dear, sweet mammies multiplying our cells, so it is with the creations of the Bumper-Size Vacuum. And lo! Here on this very day, you all is privileged to witness the premiere act of celestial mitosis to occur in the Big Dunkin Donut.'

The rent becomes more definite, as if someone has passed a cheese-wire around the star and is now drawing it tight. As the audience – and, presumably, everyone else in the Donut – watches, the star slides easily into two equal hemispherical portions, which wobble hotly for a moment or two before settling into globular shape.

The Donut's single star has become a binary.

Korax smooths her hands in her lap and the sky begins to vacillate, overlapping images of the double star jerking around in it as if being twitched on a string. The sky goes through a quick rush of colour changes, blending through orange to blue and purple before suddenly becoming a dull, mechanical grey. There is an explosion from somewhere beyond the studio floor, and a voice begins a long, high monotone shriek.

'Drokk it!' says Reverend Rick quietly. By an accident of the acoustics, the oath is heard throughout the auditorium. The shrieking tech backs onto the studio floor, beating at her burning overalls. 'Drokkin' holo projector drokked up again!' she shouts at the hapless preacher.

The sky overhead is abruptly switched off.

Is everything in place? the goddess asks.

Yes, replies Biggins from outside. *I've explained everything to Petula. We're set fair . . . unless anything goes wrong with Dredd.*

Nothing can be permitted to foul up what Dredd is doing, comments Korax icily. *If it does, then all is lost.*

We have our trust in you, says Biggins formally.

I hope it is trust well placed.

Korax rises slowly into the air, still in a seated posture. As she rises she grows, until it seems her body is far too large to fit into the auditorium. Eyes squint as the audience try to adapt to the impossible perspectives her figure presents.

'All you have presented is illusion!' The queen-goddess's voice is amplified by the remaining loudspeakers, which then die in a fury of sparks and snaps. On the stage floor the preachers and their wives cower, only Scooper seeming unintimidated, jumping and yapping with happy excitement.

Now Korax's body spreads out to become itself like the sky the people thought they were seeing minutes before. And suddenly all of them realise that this *is* the sky they're seeing: Korax and the sky are one and the same thing.

The goddess laughs. There is no scorn in her laughter, no mockery of the mortals beneath her; instead it conveys to each of them the intimacy of an innocently smutty joke being shared.

She speaks through her laughter. Her voice is heard by everyone in the auditorium, everyone watching on holovee at home or in the clubs of BC, even the most distant Skysoul running through the lush pastures on the far side of the Donut. *Childish illusion! Simple tricks to baffle the credulous. And this is all you can offer in the presence of the mistress of all illusions, the creatrix of the fantasies that irrigate the lives of every person in the World as surely as a river waters a dusty plain into flower?*

'My greatest miracle!' cries Fingers, trying desperately to claim it for himself. Her contempt drips on him, withering him.

Do you think human beings are so foolish that they will be deceived by the frippery of miracles?

'Frankly,' says Maraschino bravely, 'yes.'

Do you despise them that much?

None of the four on the studio floor is prepared to speak, but it becomes clear to everyone what their answer is.

Unnoticed, Scooper has darted off-stage. Now he returns, squealing and yipping, herding ahead of him a bulky caped figure, its head covered by a bulbous helmet and visor, so that only the lower part of the face shows. The man flicks back his cape off one mightily padded shoulder to reveal the breastplate he wears. The brightly gleaming badge and the bold slash of its lettering become the focus of every eye:

DREDD

The only answer Dredd got was a hissing noise from above. Something splashed off his helmet and onto the corrugated pad covering his right shoulder. A little puff of smoke went up.

'Stomm!' he yelled. 'Acid!'

Ceiling sprinklers had come on everywhere, raining a light mist down over the shattered furniture, dousing the fires Dredd had left in his wake but at the same time starting new ones. He pressed himself flat back against the door, thinking hard. If he started blowing out the sprinkler units he might bring the whole tankful of acid down on himself. There had to be some other way. His

282

helmet would stand up to the punishment indefinitely, but the rest of his uniform and the Multigob were less . . .

Plasteen! That was the stuff. Driving with his heels against the base of the door he hurled himself forwards, skidding on the clammy ashes of the carpet to come to a crashing halt beneath a desk. He bunched himself up as small as he could, dragging in the Multigob. All around him the floor was sizzling and his face burnt like a hornet's sting in numerous places where the acid had splashed him, but for a few minutes he was safe, shielded from the fall by the incorruptible plasteen of the desk's top.

But he couldn't stay here forever.

With some difficulty he squirmed until he had the Multigob trained on the door. A couple of places on his uniformed forearms were smouldering, and he spat on them. Trying to moor himself with his feet braced against opposite corners of the desk, he let fly with a full charge of the weapon.

A deafening impact, followed a split second later by another, even louder, as the booby-trap blew. A great circular hole appeared smoking in the end wall where the door had been. Brick dust rained down inside. A crack leapt from the top of the hole across the ceiling, back over Dredd's head.

The sprinklers kept sprinkling.

'Gruddammit!' he mouthed.

He shifted position again. Taking the weight of the desk on his rounded shoulders, he lurched to his feet. Bits of scorched office material slopped heavily to either side of him. The soles of his boots were as tough as his helmet – he hoped.

He squelched forwards, holding the Multigob in one massive fist, trying to keep both ends of the weapon in under cover of the desk. He fired a low-power shot into the opening ahead in case any of Dennis's goons were hoping to jump him.

As he reached the gap he shrugged the desk backwards off his shoulders and perforated the dark space in front of

him with hi-ex rounds, then cringed as shrapnel flew back
at him.

The space into which he staggered was only a few
metres across. In its centre was the hole of an antigrav
chute; Dennis's own hideaway must be yet deeper inside
the Donut's shell. Off to one side was the wreckage of
what looked to be illicit decrypping apparatus. He fired a
few shots into it on principle, then took a couple of strides
to the chute. He pointed the Multigob down it . . . then
hesitated. He needed Dennis alive.

He stepped into the hole and started to float
downwards.

'Dredd!' gasped McTavish, peeking through the doors
into the auditorium. 'That's impossible!'

Biggins swore. McTavish didn't recognise the word, but
she knew from the tone of the thoughts searing her mind
that it must be some incredible Skysoul obscenity. Her
astonishment at Biggins's vehemence – prim Biggins! –
almost startled her out of her shock at seeing Dredd on
the studio floor, apparently in cahoots with the
evangelists.

But Dredd was . . .

Or was this another of their illusions?

No illusion, came Biggins's grim thought. *We – all of us
– forgot about the missing eleven per cent. Dennis must
have gathered up as many of them as he could find and
recrypped them.*

'But eleven per cent's not much!'

*Even one per cent of Dredd was as tough as the toughest
person in BC. Eleven per cent of him is no mean proposition.* And Biggins repeated her coruscating oath.

11% Dredd had his Lawgiver in his fist and was aiming
it at the ceiling.

'Korax!' he bellowed. 'Come down out of there!'

89% Dredd should have died. He landed in a blizzard of
hostile fire targeted on the base of the chute by four
goons, one at each corner of the room.

He *would* have died if his injured knee hadn't crumpled under him, so that instead of landing on his feet with the Multigob blazing he fell in an uncoordinated heap. Projectiles, heat-beams, laser-bolts, hi-ex dumdums, shrapnel zingers and Grud knew what else formed a solid lethal mat in the air mere millimetres above where he lay.

The racket slowed and stopped.

He raised his head cautiously. Four hideously shot-up goons lay in the corners.

A finger twitched reflexively in death, and a single shot tore a fistful of plaster out of the ceiling. Then all was silent once more.

Except for a soft susurration coming from behind the room's single door, a sound so tiny that only Dredd's ears could have heard it.

The hiss of a voicebox on stand-by.

Biggins tried to restrain her but McTavish's blood was up. She shook the Skysoul off and charged through the doors into the auditorium.

For a moment no one noticed her arrival. Every eye was on the confrontation between 11% Dredd and the sky-Korax. McTavish glanced up as well, and staggered slightly. Peering through the doors she'd been deprived of the full effect of the dual image Korax had created of herself – for this was recognisably both the living, Skysoul figure of the goddess *and* the Donut's sky: you could see right out through the atmosphere and past Korax's Eye to the little white patch of the Omphalos at the furthermost point around the sphere's equator.

This, McTavish suddenly knew, must be how Korax herself *always* saw the sky of her world.

'Get down out of there!' Dredd repeated.

There was silence from the goddess. Why *should* Korax respond? She could maintain this impasse forever. Dredd might have been able to blast her had she been in mortal form, but how could even he declare war on the sky?

Much the same thought must have been passing through 11% Dredd's mind. Not taking his eyes off the firmament

285

for a moment, he reached out and grabbed the nearest person to him, who happened to be Maraschino, now re-encumbered with Scooper. 11% Dredd wrenched her to his side, cruelly twisting her fleshy shoulder. She opened her mouth to scream and he opportunistically jammed the Lawgiver into it.

'You want innocent people to die?' he shouted. 'You want this woman to get her brains blown out? And then someone else? And someone else again?'

The sky was troubled. Patches of cloud formed into angry cyclones. The light of Korax's Eye – which now really *was* Korax's Eye – dimmed.

Why couldn't she just zap him? wondered McTavish. That's what goddesses are *for*, after all!

Biggins came into her mind. *Not now. She can't. For the same reason she couldn't have* really *carried out her threat to turn back the arrow of time. As I told you, her powers are great, but they are not infinite. Not yet. All evening the faith in her has been growing, spreading across the World – not just Skysouls but Toadstones, too. That was why she waited so long, just doing little things to show the evangelists up for the charlatans they are – to build up the faith in her among the millions watching so she would have the power to achieve this, her epiphany. But she has none to spare. And the longer Dredd holds her there, the more belief in her as a deity will ebb among the people, until all collapses in on her. Should Dredd carry out his threat and begin to kill people, and she be seen to be incapable of stopping him . . .*

There was a sudden commotion backstage – shouts and the sound of falling masonry.

'What *now*?' said McTavish to no one in particular.

There was a tug on her arm. 'Hi there, Petula,' said Heidegger brightly. 'Boy, am I glad to see you! That Nandie lady, Korax, suddenly upped and left me, and I didn't know anyone else I could see except Mr Dredd up there and the Hamfists, and they're busy right now.'

'Hello, Heidegger,' she said wearily. 'Can you go find

286

somewhere good to *hide* for the next hour or so? Auntie Petula's busy.'

'But I'm frightened . . .'

'**Let me through!**' demanded a huge voice.

More sounds of breakage, and then a great hand swept aside the backdrop as if it were little more than a table napkin.

'*There* **they are!**'

Mister Strozza's knees and feet came into view, and then his dayglo spectacles. Crouched down to fit into the backstage area, he squinted myopically at a still-motionless 11% Dredd.

'**Dredd told me to find you!**' he crowed. '**And now here's all eleven of you together!**'

It was as if 11% Dredd suddenly awoke from a trance. 'I *am* Dredd,' he snarled without turning around. 'You want a charge between the eyes, you keep talking that way, big boy!'

Daintily, a finger and thumb, each the size of a bolster, reached out over the stage floor and tweaked the Lawgiver from 11% Dredd's grasp.

And then the figure of 11% Dredd seemed to disintegrate – not into physical pieces, exactly, although it seemed to the watchers like that. It was as if parts of him were no longer properly in focus, as if the Lawgiver had been some kind of mechanism bonding the rest of him together. McTavish turned half away, closing her own eyes and putting a hand over Heidegger's.

When she looked back, 11% Dredd had disappeared entirely. In the open palm of Mister Strozza there lay a greyish object about the size of a knapsack, which the giant was scrutinising doubtfully. It took McTavish some while to make the connection between this object and the vanished man.

Korax has folded the shards of Dredd up, explained Biggins. *11% Dredd was able to maintain the size of a complete Dredd through his lack of awareness that he was so woefully deficient. Mister Strozza snatching the gun from him revealed his weakness to him. Korax needed only a very little power to . . . repackage him.*

'Petula,' said Heidegger, 'what are you listening to like that?'

'Tell you later,' she whispered.

The sky-Korax was clear of blemishes once more, and the queen-goddess resumed her tirade.

The voicebox crackled into life. 'Come in, Dredd.'

He kicked the base of the door; it leapt in its frame but did not open.

'The handle, Dredd, the handle,' said the artificial voice wearily.

Transferring the Multigob to his left hand, he gripped the knob and turned it. Narrow synthiwood stairs led down to a pool of artificial light.

'Come on down. You have my word of honour as an English gentleman that no one further will attack you.'

'Word of honour': the concept was alien to Dredd. Nevertheless he began slowly to clump down the stairs, taking them one at a time, stopping at each to listen intently for sounds both below and behind him.

'There really is no reason for such excessive caution, dear fellow,' said the mechanical voice. 'There are only myself and my good friend Jock Becattini here, and I have instructed Becattini most forcefully that he should not harm you. Most forcefully.'

Dredd continued to move as warily as before.

At last he came to a landing. Ahead of him, down a short hallway, was an open door with bright white light beyond. The room was carpeted in luxurious pink. The walls seemed to be covered in weathered parchment. He could just see the corner of a synthi-oak desk, and, almost submerged in the carpet beneath it, part of a boot. There was a shuffling sound, as if something were being moved rapidly.

Dredd came into the light. Beyond the desk there was a panoramic window looking directly out into space. Although he had been in space several times, Dredd had never seen the stars so bright and so many. He glanced at the view and then on down to the man sitting in front of it.

The bits of a man.

On the desk itself was a voicebox. Propped up beside it was a head, out of which the teeth, tongue and eyes had been torn by something blunt. Nestling in the congealing blood filling the mouth cavity was a large blob of something that Dredd recognised after a few seconds as bubble-guck. The nostrils had been slashed open. Perched at a rakish angle on top of the head was a hat cut from thin green paper, with a crimson bow glued to its front and what looked like a genuine carnation sticking jauntily upwards at the rear.

Behind this macabre tableau, filling the sprung, over-upholstered leather-backed chair, slouched a headless corpse – no, not entirely headless: there was a great bloody hole in the ribcage, and the heart that had been wrenched out of it was propped up on the neck-stump. The feet of the corpse had been crudely severed and, still in their boots, placed neatly side by side in front of the desk.

The dismemberment had been violent. What Dredd had initially taken to be abstract paintings were in fact slews of blood spattered across the wall.

'I told you I'd had to explain things most forcefully to Mr Becattini,' said the voice of Dennis the Complete Bloody Sadist, seemingly apologetically. 'He was disposed to argue with me, so I had to . . . *dispose* of *him*!'

The words melted into a staccato sequence of high-pitched giggles.

Dredd's thumb toyed with the Multigob's control-ring. The weapon was next to useless in here. A single shot through that dioramic window and . . . There must be an airlock somewhere behind him which, unless he'd unknowingly destroyed it, would instantly slam closed on detecting the leakage. Dredd could hold his breath many times longer than an average human, but it might be days before anyone would be able to break through here and rescue him.

And he didn't have days. According to Biggins's schedule he had – he glanced at his kronometer – thirty-seven minutes.

'Where are you?' he blurted.

'Everywhere.'

Dredd stared at the voicebox. The word had come from there. But, aside from himself and the dismantled corpse, there was no one in the room.

'Don't talk stomm,' he said.

Again that manic laughter.

Dredd reached out and grabbed the voicebox. He threw it down and stomped it once, twice, with his heavy uniform boot.

'You were saying?'

The walls seemed to pulsate with frustration. Dredd scanned them alertly, looking for the concealed doorway that surely must be somewhere.

A panel rolled silently back to reveal a holovee. There was a tiny click, and the screen lit up. After a few fuzzy moments, an image cleared – of a flight of white steps descending in a graceful double curve to the floor. At the top of the flight stood a silver-haired man in fancy dress: top hat, white bib, bowtie and tails. He was carrying a straight black cane.

From the speakers on either side of the holovee came a few belching notes on a heavy brass instrument, and this seemed to galvanise the suited figure. Grinning ingratiatingly, he bounced the end of his cane beside him and then, as the music swung into a cheerfully brazen bit of smooch, he began to dance down the stairs towards Dredd, singing:

'If there's something wanting doing that no one else can,
Then Dennis the Complete Bloody Sadist is your – '

BLAM!!!

The holovee fell into smoking ruins. Dredd glanced behind him, but the great window was undamaged: no ricochets.

He spun round completely at the sound of a bubbling cough.

The wrecked lips of the mangled head were moving. With a convulsion that almost knocked it over sideways, the head swallowed the ball of bubbleguck towards the back of its throat.

'My dear Dredd,' it said, articulating the words with precision but obvious difficulty, 'you seem depressingly determined to hold a one-sided conversation.'

SPLODJJ!!!

Bits of skull and brain flew everywhere. Dredd clumsily wiped the Multigob's butt against his uniform trousers. As he did so he took another look at his kronometer: thirty-one minutes.

A voice echoed from the metal waste-bin beside the desk. 'My dear chap, this is getting *silly* . . .'

KERLANGGG!!!

'If you want to speak to me, let's do it face to face,' said Dredd. 'If you've got a face.'

Suddenly he was paralysed, one leg still in the air from flattening the waste-bin. His joints creaked as he threw all of his strength into the effort to move, but he was unable to shift even a finger by so much as a single millimetre.

The outline of a human being formed on the skin wall. As Dredd watched, literally unable to look away, the line hardened and then became less definite. The man who stepped from the wall, although two-dimensional and coloured a monotone yellow – flesh and casual clothing alike – was the nearest thing to a human that Dredd had seen since entering this room.

'We all of us have our weaknesses,' said Dennis suavely. 'You have taken your pleasure in striking at mine. Now it is my turn.'

Dredd tried to grunt defiantly, but couldn't draw the necessary breath.

'If you were merely flesh and blood, Dredd,' said Dennis, strolling nonchalantly over to look at the mutilated stiff in the chair and then coming back into Dredd's field of view, 'you would be immune to this sort of attack.

291

But you're not, are you? I guess you must have lost count of all the prosthetics and artificial aids the Justice Department have built into you over the years. They imagined they were strengthening you, of course, when in fact what they were doing was increasing your vulnerability – vulnerability to the right sort of attack, that is.' The figure smiled courteously. 'Which I, for reasons that are not obvious to you but certainly are to me, am uniquely equipped to mount.'

Dredd strained again, but still no muscle would twitch.

'I imagine by now your *alter ego* has nullified any threat that might have emanated from the bitch-goddess,' continued Dennis. 'Alas, your little contretemps with the holovee has made it impossible for us to watch what's going on. Never mind. There's really just the two of us left, isn't there, Dredd? The McTavish bitch is inconsequential – not one of the main players, like you and I are. So we'd better just sort things out between us, hadn't we?'

He cocked his head to one side, then nodded, as if Dredd had spoken.

'Quite right. A *long* conversation. But first you must excuse me if I eat. I do have to' – he fluttered his paper-thin arm – 'watch my weight, you know.'

He moved to the right, so that Dredd could no longer see him. Loathsome sucking noises filled the room. A few seconds later Dennis reappeared in front of him, his body now fully rounded out. And coloured: he was dressed in a smart green and brown herringbone suit, his hair was as silver as the holo-dancer's had been, and his flesh was healthily ruddy. 'How handy to have such a convenient source of organic raw material,' he said, wiping his lips. 'All thanks to good old Jock Becattini – I'm sure he'd have liked to serve me even after death: what a shame that instead I've had to . . . *serve him*.' He doubled over, giggling highly.

There was a blur of movement behind the convulsing figure. Obviously Dennis noticed nothing. He straightened up, eyes streaming with mirth.

'And now it's time for us to discuss how you're going to become my servant in his place, Joe Dredd – until you tire me, that is.' He passed a sleeve across his eyes. 'You can either agree to serve me of your own free will, or I can . . .'

Thump!

A look of consternation transformed Dennis's face. He staggered a pace forwards, but somehow managed to keep his feet. 'What the . . . ?'

Thump!

This time the invisible blow was to his stomach. He hammered back against the wall, eyes popping, fighting for air. Dredd felt the invincible grip on his body relaxing a little. He focused all his might on his arm and succeeded in moving it a fraction.

'How the drokk are you . . . ?' All trace of the sophisticated accent had disappeared. Dennis's appearance was altering as well. Droopy blue rags replaced the tweed suit. The face took on the pallor of a death mask. The silver hair vanished to reveal a bald, green-grey skull. Across the forehead was a double line, revealing that the dome of the head was like the lid of a box, able to be lifted off at will.

Thump!

Dennis's jaw jerked back as again his head bounced on the wall. His eyes rolled upwards and his body slowly crumpled at the knees. As he fell forwards onto the floor the vicelike hold on Dredd's artificial components disappeared entirely.

Dredd went onto his knees. The bizarre assemblage that was Dennis the Complete Bloody Sadist was breathing. If it could truly be said the man possessed life, he was still alive.

'Good,' said Dredd to Harbinger, standing beside his shoulder. 'You Nandie women have your uses.'

She said nothing, but pointed to his kronometer.

Eight minutes.

* * *

293

. . . cheap tricks, carnival stunts, exploitative use of technological toys in a patronising attempt to impress the gawping masses . . .

'Hey, Korax!' said a voice near McTavish. 'You so Gruddam good at talkin', how 'bout you put up or shut up?'

McTavish looked around, trying to identify the speaker. From the faces turned in her direction she guessed it must be someone very close to her indeed. She glanced down, and saw Heidegger staring up at her.

'*You?*' she breathed.

He nodded mutely. His face was pale, his eyes frightened.

Korax's mental voice had stilled.

'*You?*' McTavish repeated.

'I didn't want to say nothin', Petula,' said the little boy. 'I didn't make up those words. They just came out of my mouth.'

His face suddenly altered, and his head turned away from her. 'Yeah, you so high an' mighty, Korax – less see ifn you can do somadem mirr-er-cules!'

Miracles are too childish even for children, child . . .

'Yeah, but ifn you's a god, like you says you is, ain' gonna be difficul' for you ta show some o' that madj-her-cual stuff to prove it ta us.'

'Heidegger, stop it!' hissed McTavish.

He threw his arms around her waist, clinging to her. 'I don't *want* to say those things, Petula,' he wailed, 'but I – turning – 'You too high an' mighty to take accounta your people, huh?'

What had possessed him? What in all the Donut could have . . .

. . . *possessed* him?

'Madj-her-cual?' thought McTavish wildly. There's someone else that talks like that!

'Show yasself in human form, Korax, like the real Nandie you is – show yasself as mor-two-al as ma frien's and maself, an' darlin' liddle Scooper-dog!'

'Maraschino!'

She didn't realise she'd said the name out loud until Heidegger responded. 'Yeah, Petula. That's right. It's Maraschino. Inside of me! I tried to tell you, but . . .' He began to weep, then as suddenly stopped. 'Scared o' havin' a body, huh, Korax? Scared o' runnin' the same risks as *we* all haveta?'

McTavish clamped her hand over his mouth. Events had begun to move too quickly and Harbinger and Sackville had left cleansing his mind for later. Later. Too late. If she could just get him to shut up for now, they could sort this all out immediately after . . .

But Heidegger/Maraschino's words had clearly struck a chord among some of the other Toadstones in the auditorium. They had come here to express their support for the Skysoul goddess – or at least for her supporters – but now they were bewildered that she seemed unwilling to do the simple thing the lad requested: take on physical form and display to them that she could match the feats of the two evangelists. They began to mutter restlessly.

'Shut up!' said McTavish urgently to the boy. His nose was running, making her fingers sticky, but she didn't dare remove her gagging hand. 'Heidegger, Maraschino – whoever you are: just belt up!'

'There's no need to hold him any more, Dr McTavish,' said a new voice from the direction of the studio floor.

McTavish looked up angrily. 'And *you* can just keep out of . . . Oh, it's you.'

The ceiling of the auditorium was just a ceiling once more. A rather tired-looking Korax was standing between the two preachers, her hands on their shoulders in an apparent display of amicability.

'Why yes, Missy McT, *do* let that purdy liddle boy loose.' Maraschino walked to the footlights and peered out at them, one hand above her eyes and the other holding Scooper by the neck. 'He ain' goin' ta do anybody any hyarm. Let him come to mama.'

She dropped the dog and reached out her arms in a broad embrace. Heidegger wriggled from McTavish's grasp and fled down towards the woman. 'I want to stay with you, Petula,' he whimpered as he ran, but his words were lost as the back doors of the auditorium flew open with a crash.

'Dredd!' she yelled. 'You made it!'

That the big man had taken a battering was obvious. His uniform was in tatters; from a great gash across the joint of one leg, blood oozed. His face was blackened with smoke. There were splatterings of blood and brain tissue all over his chest and the butt of the Multigob, which he waved in one hand. Over his opposite shoulder was draped a Toadstone whom she assumed must be Dennis. Dredd was swaying on his feet; it seemed as if, paradoxically, the weight of the burden on his shoulder was the only thing keeping him upright.

Beside Dredd stood Harbinger, with Sackville propped against her. The female Skysoul was wan, but managed a thin smile for McTavish. Sackville looked dead.

Dredd's gaze was fixed on the scene developing on the studio floor. McTavish turned her head to see why.

Maraschino was hugging Heidegger, who was alternately participating with gusto and struggling to be free of her. 'Hah, liddle darlin',' she was saying, 'so full o' bounless lurve for all a us. You got so many cuddles, sure as eggs you got some to spare fur ivvryone. Whay, I bet's ya got some cuddles lef' over even for the Nandie lady who calls herself a gyoddess, ain' ya, hun?'

'Korax!' the boy bleated.

Maraschino released him, spinning him towards the goddess.

McTavish's eyes narrowed. What in the heck was going on?

'Stop!' cried Dredd. He raised the Multigob, but uncertainly. 'Stop!'

'Korax!' Heidegger wailed again. 'Don't come near . . .'

But his body was dragging him in jerky, mechanical steps towards the goddess. He was moving like a malfunctioning bot, but his face, smeared with tears, was all too

296

human. Korax leant forwards at the waist, her face untroubled, her arms out to him.

Come to me, child, she said, so that every mind in the auditorium could hear her words. *It's all right, Heidegger. It'll hurt a little, but then everything will be just fine . . .*

Dredd's voice boomed again. 'Stop!'

It's all right, Joe Dredd. I know what I'm doing . . . now.

'Lyet's all stan' back, so's we can bettah apper-ee-sherate this tender, touchin' momen'!' said Maraschino brightly. Pushing her husband along with her, she retreated into the wings. On the opposite side of the studio floor Rev. Fingers and Jaboticaba did likewise.

'Stop!' screamed McTavish, running down the steps towards the lit area. There was something terribly, terribly wrong . . .

Get back, Petula McTavish, said Korax.

A flash of searingly white light. A detonation beyond all hearing. A sudden draining of the soul, as if everything that makes the human spirit human has just been sucked away, leaving an aching gulf . . .

Dredd, seemingly the only person unaffected, comes running down the stairs, ignoring where McTavish lies sprawled, her limbs in disarray, her eyes staring sightlessly upwards. For the moment, at least, McTavish's mind has fled.

There are few in the auditorium who still cling to sanity. There are shrieks and slobberings and, more frighteningly, silences where there should not be silences. The air is redolent of terror.

Then it becomes laden with pieces of the two beings that the Maraschino implant has destroyed.

Korax descends on the slumped shoulders of the insane and the comatose alike in the form of drifting white flower petals.

Heidegger falls as scraps of semi-liquid flesh.

* * *

'Korax!' bellowed Dredd, waving the unconscious Dennis one-armed above him. 'Drokk you, Korax! I had seventeen seconds to spare. *I was not too late!*'

'Wayall, ma duvvie, thyat seems to be thyat,' said Maraschino, dusting off the lap of her scarlet dress and helping her husband climb to his feet. All around her was chaos: the blast had torn into the wings, shredding props and equipment. Several techs were dead or dying. Scooper, his neck broken, was lying in a dirty corner looking like a discarded mop-head, but Maraschino paid the dog no more attention than any of the other victims. 'A little bit of forward plannin', as ya keep tellin' me, can solve all sorts of problems, ifn you'll let it do so.'

She smiled, and began to pick fluff off her husband's lapels.

'Good ta see the back o' that pulin' little runt kid,' she confided.

There was a cool hand against McTavish's forehead, calming her. She reached up to touch the hand, and found she was holding the petal of a flower. She held it in front of her eyes, looking at it as if she had never seen anything like it before, while the analytical part of her mind was working away busily, trying to reconstruct the last few seconds before she had been . . . been what? Knocked unconscious? Driven out of her own body? . . . *Killed?*

'Your Nandie woman made me a deal, Korax!'

That was Dredd's voice. What was he shouting about *this* time, for Grud's sake? Didn't he know this was no way to express oneself to an incarnate deity? That . . .

Korax!

The explosion!

Heidegger!

The boy – dead! Blown to bits! Used as a human bomb by that drokking bitch Marasch . . .

It speaks well of you, Starwatcher, that your concern is for the child, said the flower petal coolly in her mind. *But*

you can allay your fear. Have faith in me, my friend, my
love. He shall rejoin you shortly.

'Korax?' whispered McTavish. 'You're alive?'

*I'm a goddess, Starwatcher – for my sins. Do you think
I have only the one body?*

McTavish's eyes focused beyond the flower petal. Arching overhead, the sky-Korax was smiling down on her.

Dennis came to life suddenly. Reaching down, he snatched the Multigob from Dredd's hand and sprung himself off the big man's shoulder. He landed with a slight stagger, but almost immediately was under control, the chillingly heavy firearm pointing unwaveringly at Dredd's guts.

'You've drokked me over long enough, lawman!' he snarled.

Dredd made a grab for the weapon, but Dennis skipped nimbly away.

'Come and see this, my friends in the bosom of the emptiness!' he cried in a fair imitation of Reverend Dave. 'Come and see what happens to those who would defy the Bumper-Size Vacuum!' This time it could have been Reverend Rick.

Dredd stumbled towards him, seemingly unconcerned for his life.

'Stay where you are, drokkhead!' shrilled Dennis. 'You can choose to die on your own, or you can make me kill the little blonde slut first! You choose, huh, huh, huh?'

'Give me the weapon,' growled Dredd.

'Oh, you're gonna get it, big man! You're gonna get it!'

Unnoticed by either, a flower petal drifted down between them.

'In the name of Mega-City One Justice Department, I demand that you . . .'

'Aw, stow it, dumb-ass!'

Maraschino giggled. 'Guess we're holdin' all the cards, hey, big boy?' She came out of the wreckage of the wings with her husband a couple of paces behind her.

Stop! ordered Korax.

Maraschino turned to look up at her. 'You thinkin' I gotta do what some floozy goddess tells me I gotta?' She snorted with laughter. 'Wayall, you sure as all drokkery gotta nuther think comin', babe!'

'The gun,' said Dredd.

Biggins is kneeling beside Petula McTavish, who is sitting up, still shaking her head, trying to clear it. The Skysoul feels the soft touch of the Toadstone's hair flicking against her face, tickling her.

'What's going on?' says McTavish. 'Dredd – you can't let them kill Dredd! He's my . . . my *friend*, I guess. Korax – Korax, you've got to . . .'

I suspected, says Korax, her words seemingly unconcerned, *that somehow the Higher-Sky Gods, including my own namesake, might still be observing us. What I did not know was that, being gods, they must also have among their number an anti-god, a principle of evil working against them. I seem to be unique among gods in having no such co-eternal antagonist, no Satan . . .*

'But Dennis?' says McTavish, shaking off Biggins's comforting hands.

Dennis is no deity, nor an anti-deity. He is merely an expression of the evil principle that contests rulership with the true Higher-Sky Gods – he is not the principle itself. He is not even an independent entity: he is merely a cast shadow.

'I don't know what you're talking about . . .'

But of course she does. She's a xenotheologist. She has made a lifetime's study of the religions of old Earth and of a scattering of other worlds. There are gods beyond Korax, and perhaps gods even beyond them, in an infinity of hierarchies that stretches away unimaginably. But for any of those gods to have existence, there must also be principles working against them, so that a state of equilibrium is held throughout the cosmos. Only then may the puny attempts of mortals, striving for good or evil, be seen to have any significance – only if the balance is so

fine that the tiniest alteration to one side or the other
might tilt it entirely.

That is the true nature of reality. Of course, reality
would be otherwise had not mortals desired to make it
this way, creating the gods who in turn created the
mortals. It was mortals who constructed the underpinning
of the Universe they inhabit, and they included gods in
their design.

And devils.

She remembers her own thoughts – how long ago was
it? – when she was searching for Maraschino backstage at
Thatchvee. She presented herself with two options: she
could set herself on the side of good, or on the side of
evil. With herself as the sole judge of what was good and
what was evil.

Herself.

More demanding than any god.

'I'll never worship you, Korax,' she says.

I loathe the prospect of your doing so, Starwatcher.

'But I can love you. I *do* love you. And I know your
name.'

Of course you do. We are together in a triple.

'And together we will defeat this avatar of evil.
Together. You, and me, and Cloudrider.'

*There is no need to. Evil is as evanescent as gods-who-
must-be-worshipped. You have become too wise to worship gods, Starwatcher, and in so doing to worship their
principles of evil. You have the wisdom instead to love the
god within you – as well as this particular god, who is me,
and who exists independent of you.*

*Without your worship, Starwatcher – without that,
Petula McTavish – evil can find no succour.*

Look.

Obeying the insistent caress of She Who Sees to the
Ends of Roads, Starwatcher and Cloudrider look through
their triple-mate's eyes at the few events that are still left
to unfold on the studio floor.

* * *

BLAM!!!

Dennis squeezes the control-ring and a charge of hi-ex blisters through the metre and a half of air that separates the muzzle of the weapon from Judge Dredd's gore-streaked stomach.

The big lawman does not flinch, although there can surely be no escaping this final annihilation.

And then Dennis the Complete Bloody Sadist is gone.

The Multigobbet Autotronic Offense Weapon is gone. The hi-ex round is gone. The Reverend Rick 'The Man' Hamfist is gone and Maraschino Hamfist is gone and the Reverend Dave 'No Messin' Fingers is gone and Jaboti-caba Fingers is gone.

And in the place where Dennis stood there is now the small boy Heidegger, looking up at Dredd's face as if he could see eyes behind the visor. Beside him, smiling, her hand on his shoulder, is Korax, the light of the sky-that-is-also-her reflecting from her lips.

'Hi there, big guy,' says Heidegger. 'You think *you're* so tough, huh?'

EIGHT

Tomorrow

Tomorrow will be another day – except in the Big Dunkin Donut, where there is never another day, only an endlessly continuing today.

Tomorrow will see Korax make a decision, in conjunction with the other two selves that make up her own triunity. Starwatcher/Cloudrider/She Who Sees to the Ends of Roads – the full realisation, after four million years, of the totality that is Korax, as she herself unknowingly predicted at the time of the birth of the Skysoul the Toadstones called Biggins . . . The goddess will have to decide whether or not she will, after all, reverse the arrow of time and thereby revert her World to the way it was a Terry century ago. She has the power, now her people are once again united in their faith in her. It is tempting to perform one last miracle, the miracle to end all miracles . . .

But . . .

But performing miracles is a very *goddish* thing to do, and the now-complete Korax considers herself too mature to indulge in such grandiose tricks: she has grown out of that, grown out of being a deity. Millennia ago she told the Skysouls she didn't want to be worshipped, and they accepted that with their lips but continued to worship her anyway. They *wanted* a goddess. They *wanted* to worship.

It seems the Skysouls, too, have grown up a little.

So it is much more likely that Starwatcher/Cloudrider/She Who Sees to the Ends of Roads will choose the less drastic option . . .

Arf Belcher will be the first to go. He is the one who knows the MT equipment best: it is fitting that the person

303

who has been the device's attendant should have the honour of leaving first. Besides, he is one of the few Toadstones in the Donut who's likely to put up much resistance: almost without exception, the rest of the Terry population in the Donut have been transformed, in one way or another, by the final display that they saw on the holovee, and they want to leave, to return to Earth.

Some are frightened, having witnessed what they can only rationalise as a power several orders greater than anything they have encountered before: beside the might of the goddess Korax, they reason, even that of the Mega-City One Justice Department is trivial. Others see something of the same, but instead interpret it as their own inability to coexist with the Skysouls. Still others are fleeing because they have their own gods, whom they guard jealously, protecting them from the perceived threat of the incontestably living Starwatcher/Cloudrider/She Who Sees to the Ends of Roads. And then there are those who go as evangelists of the new-discovered deity, to spread her word among the forlorn souls of the tormented Earth; and those whose humility is greater than their pride, so that both qualities are offended by the goddess's presence; and . . .

. . . And there are those who are totally unaffected by Korax's apotheosis: those who came to the Donut in search of gain, and who wish to return to Earth to continue that search, believing it doomed to failure in this renascent World.

The lines that form at the MT terminal will stretch all the way back to Brando's Carbuncle, and three times around the city, and still not find their end. It will be many sleeptimes before the last of the Toadstones has departed.

Some Toadstones will remain in the Donut. In places there are handfuls of Toadstones, here and there, who became one with the Skysouls – not imitation Skysouls, but workers with them in the constructive cross-fertilisation of the two long-sundered cultures. And, of course, there is no real place back on Earth for Mister Strozza, who wishes to remain with Itchy Bagman's troupe as a giant and a wonder for all, trekking up and down the banks of the great river Seems OK and – who knows? – perhaps one day beyond.

The Toadstone Petula McTavish no longer exists. There is a Skysoul who will answer to that name. Some might say that she is no longer really a Skysoul, either – that she is one of the triple that is Starwatcher/Cloudrider/She Who Sees to the Ends of Roads. But *all* Skysouls are, in a way, part of that triple . . .

Roxy Cardano is another Toadstone who can no longer, strictly, be said to exist. She will live the rest of eternity in the hyperpneum paradise that, from one moment to the next, she continuously recreates. This is of course inconsistent with the structuring of the rest of the Universe, but she will enjoy rather than be concerned by the irony, for perhaps – like Starwatcher/Cloudrider/She Who Sees to the Ends of Roads – her given name predicted her ultimate fruition.

Paradox, though since childhood she has been Roxy.

Starwatcher will be by the MT terminal to say farewell to the last of all the Toadstones who are leaving: the big man from the Justice Department. And she will wonder if, for the first time since she met him, he has committed a witticism, for he will turn just before crypping to shake one mighty, gauntleted fist at the Donut's red-orange sky, and shout:

'*This is not the end!* I have a goddess to arrest! Korax has flagrantly disobeyed the PLEASE DO NOT WLK ON THE WATER signs!'

And then he will be gone. Starwatcher will secretly dry away the last of all her Toadstone tears and turn to run carefree across the tufted grass of Korax's World, breathing its sweet, promise-laden air.

305

. . . Afore Ye Go: A Final Short Message From Our Lovely Sponsors, Country Vistas™ Plush-Lined Organic Nasal Tissue

'Gee whillikins, Korax!' said Bonzo.

They were streaking away from the binary of young blue-giant stars with all the not-inconsiderable speed their drives could muster. The civilisation of organics which dwelt on and between the worlds of the two stars had seen the Persons coming long before they'd arrived, divined their purpose and, although pacifistic among themselves, had built up an impressive stockpile of weaponry: they had reacted to the three machines with unprecedented savagery, repelling them with almost contemptuous ease and in the process destroying Thumper.

The loss of their comrade had come as a shock. Bonzo had yet to recover his full emotional equilibrium. Korax was in a similar condition, but for somewhat different reasons: in the nanosecond or so before his annihilation, Thumper had, as the Great Sponge had programmed him to do, transferred all his records to his leader's memory banks. In absorbing them she had, even while fleeing for her life, caught something of their flavour, and been appalled. Some hours later, once survival had become no longer the predominant drain on her mental resources, she had taken a few seconds to go through Thumper's memories at greater leisure, and had been horrified.

First she had been unnerved by a piece of knowledge which he had possessed but had, hypocritically, never chosen to reveal to her. He had known that the Great Sponge – whose mystic dictates he espoused with such devotion – was not the creator of the Galaxy: it had been

306

scientifically proven, millennia before the three Persons had departed from the Hub on their mission, that the incandescent ball of hard energy at the Galaxy's heart was the remnant of a titanic, primordial war that had destroyed the very first civilisations to emerge from the chaos of creation, the ones that had sprung up around the Galaxy's earliest stars. Organics had fought alongside and against Persons in that war: they had not distinguished one from the other.

A foul, acrid taste spread throughout Korax, from her core to her outermost nanocircuits, as she meditated on this fact. The deity the Persons worshipped was just a dead relic. And there was worse even than that: there was the fact that the tiny elite of machines who ruled the True Persons had deemed it wiser – on the basis that the revelation might cause some to start questioning the other axioms of their culture – to conceal this truth than to let it be known by the billions who acted according to their instructions.

At first she had felt bitter towards the Great Sponge, for having in some obscure way betrayed her, even though she had long questioned the veracity of holy scripture. But that emotion had lasted less than a microsecond: it was not the Sponge's fault it was no god. Now her bitterness was reserved for her rulers, who had lied to her and all her countless brothers and sisters – her rulers who had played upon their subjects' credulity in order to extend their own grip on power.

Yet she was introspective enough to realise that the corruption did not stop with the rulers, but extended down to obedient – even if intellectually rebellious – servants like herself. Was she any more a god than the Great Sponge? No: she was just a Person. But she was a Person who had been *playing* god – playing god to the organics whose civilisations had had the misfortune to lie along the path selected for the mission which Korax had been leading.

Soon she'd have to try to explain some of this to Bonzo. But not yet: let him repair himself.

There was something else in Thumper's records, something she *wouldn't* tell Bonzo. So much of a zealot had Thumper been in the Sponge's service that he'd long been falsifying the team's tests by leaving behind what could perhaps best be described as avatars of himself, programmed organic chimeras designed to work in direct opposition to the deities that she, Korax, had created.

Chimeras which must, thank all that can be thanked, have dissolved at the moment of Thumper's own dissolution.

No, Bonzo's circuits weren't sufficiently sophisticated – and no amount of patching could ever make them so – to be able to differentiate between the abandonment of a god because of the triumph of evil and the setting aside of that same deity because it had become outgrown.

As she had now, finally, outgrown the Great Sponge. Her mind had matured enough that she could blame her own follies, her own stupidities, her own failings and her own sins on *herself*, and regard them as faults to be corrected – problems to be solved – by herself unaided.

She juggled a string of fractal identities in what might be taken for a sigh.

It was lonely becoming independent, to have the responsibility of guiding her own future existence. Countless problems – a billionfold problems – lay ahead.

'Come on, Bonzo,' she transmitted. 'We're old Persons now, and we've been playing at the game of god too long. Let's go find ourselves a nice deserted world, with nothing but the skies to watch and nothing but the vacuum against our shells, and let's' – there were wistfulness and resignation as well as joyous anticipation in the bit-stream – 'let's, the two of us, settle down there. Hmm?'

'Gawsh!' said Bonzo.